➤   ➤   ➤

About the Author

An award-winning novelist and reporter, Bill Granger was raised in a working-class neighborhood on the South Side of Chicago. He began his extraordinary career in 1963 when, while still in college, he joined the staff of United Press International. He later worked for the *Chicago Tribune*, writing about crime, cops, and politics, and covering such events as the race riots of the late 1960's and the 1968 Democratic Convention. In 1969 he joined the staff of the *Chicago Sun-Times*, where he won an Associated Press award for his story of a participant in the My Lai Massacre. He also wrote a series of stories on Northern Ireland for *Newsday*—and unwittingly added to a wealth of information and experiences that would form the foundations of future spy thrillers and mystery novels. By 1978 Bill Granger had contributed articles to *Time, The New Republic*, and other magazines; and become a daily columnist, television critic, and teacher of journalism at Columbia College in Chicago.

He began his literary career in 1978 with *The November Man*, the book that became an international sensation and introduced the cool American spy who later gave rise to a whole series. His second novel, *Public Murders*, a Chicago police procedural, won the Edgar Award from the Mystery Writers of America in 1981.

In all, Bill Granger has published seven "November Man" novels, four "Chicago" police mysteries, two nonfiction books written with his wife, and three novels. In 1980 he began weekly columns in the *Chicago Tribune* on everyday life (he was voted best Illinois columnist by UPI) which were collected in the book *Chicago Pieces*. His books have been translated into ten languages.

Bill Granger lives in Chicago with his wife and son when he is not traveling to distant climes, researching his stories.

Warner books by Bill Granger

Hemingway's Notebook
*Newspaper Murders** (writing as Joe Gash)
*Public Murders**
There Are No Spies

*forthcoming

BILL GRANGER

THE November Man

WARNER BOOKS

A Warner Communications Company

For Lori,
who shared the adventures

Things are seldom what they seem.
—W. S. Gilbert

WARNER BOOKS EDITION

Copyright © 1979 by Bill Granger
All rights reserved.

This Warner Books Edition is published by arrangement
with the author.

Cover art by Bohdan Osyczka
Cover design by Rolf Erikson

Warner Books, Inc.
666 Fifth Avenue
New York, N.Y. 10103

 A Warner Communications Company

Printed in the United States of America

First Warner Books Printing: November, 1986

10 9 8 7 6 5 4 3

AUTHOR'S NOTE

While reading this book, one should keep these facts in mind:

Despite the general public belief, the Central Intelligence Agency is not the only intelligence-gathering operation conducted by the United States.

Fiction and nonfiction works have made popularly known the former section names attributed to British Intelligence—MI5 and MI6. Because of organizational changes in recent years and a penchant for maintaining secrecy even at mundane levels, British Intelligence has changed its nomenclature.

The Irish Republican Army guerrilla activity in Ulster province of Ireland is funded both by individuals and unofficial channels of foreign governments.

The Soviet Union maintains spy networks in most Western countries and, wherever possible, such spies operate under cover of diplomatic immunity granted them by their status as employees of their respective embassies in those foreign countries.

Though a routine ferry service connects Liverpool and Dublin, there is as yet no rival Hovercraft service operating on the Irish Sea.

NEW YORK CITY

The larger man, whose white body resembled a slug, took a step forward and ripped his glove lace-side up across the forehead of his black opponent. Blood exploded from the sudden cut on the black man's head and sprayed red on the slug's body and on the canvas floor of the ring. Yet the darker, smaller man seemed oblivious of blood or pain as he stepped forward himself, between the lumbering swings, grinning with the pleasure of a man controlling a machine in perfect use. The slug's second swing banged harmlessly against the black man's shoulder. Now the smaller man was inside and he tattooed a series of jabs into the expanse of that mottled trunk. The slug stumbled against the ropes, his head snapped back, and sweat sprayed both their faces. The white body heaved hopelessly, floundering in the net of the thick ring ropes. The smaller man moved forward precisely then, jabbing surgically. He hit the punching bag of a body seven more times even though the blood from the cut blurred his vision.

"So much for the great white hope again."

Devereaux let his program drop to the floor.

It was not a signal, although it might have been, because everything about the meeting had been couched in similar melodrama and romance. A signal or not, Hanley chose that moment to begin talking even while the fight was belled to a merciful conclusion.

"I really thought he had a chance," Hanley began. "Well." Pause. "We're worried about Hastings."

Devereaux—and, indeed, everyone in R Section—was aware of Hanley's annoying habit of uttering non sequiturs. Few realized, though, that Hanley had acquired the habit deliberately as an accoutrement of the profession he had entered thirty years before. It was Hanley's belief that non sequiturs confused and misled potential eavesdroppers, made it convenient to insert appropriate code words and other verbal signals in everyday speech, and, finally, improved the attention of the listener.

Devereaux merely thought Hanley was an asshole.

In the ring, the white man was protesting the decision. Around Hanley and Devereaux, in the smoky, flat atmosphere, figures were hurling programs toward the square of light in front of them.

"Hastings?" Devereaux looked at Hanley.

The latter seemed momentarily lost in a private reverie. Finally, he resumed: "You know what Hastings is. Strictly a Second Man in a not-terribly-important posting. He hasn't had anything for six months and now he wants thirty thousand dollars. Won't explain and won't reply to our cables except to hint that he has devastating stuff. 'Devastating.' The very word he used. National security involved, he claims, international ramifications, that sort of thing. He's continued on payroll and we meet his expenses, but frankly, we haven't the faintest hint of what he's talking about."

Hanley folded his program neatly and put it in his vest pocket. Devereaux wondered if Hanley had a hope chest of old programs.

"So now you're going to rein him in," said Devereaux.

"Kill that turkey motherfucker," screamed a black man sitting next to Hanley. In the ring, the two fighters who had waltzed for most of the eleven rounds were now vigorously engaged in a postfight charade. Separated by managers and trainers and the referee, they lunged at each other, hurling promises and insults.

"Not necessarily," said Hanley. Pause. "He was a good man."

Devereaux stared at his own flat fingers. He was not going to point out that Hanley's faint praise was inconsistent with what he had said moments before. Devereaux hated Hanley the way people in the field always hated the clerks back in R Section.

"Get that nigger outta there," cried a white man two rows back.

"Who you callin' a nigger?"

Devereaux looked around. Anxious blue-uniformed security men came rushing down the aisles, and received a barrage of paper cups for their pains. "Christ," he said. "Why didn't you plan for us to meet on the stage of the Met? We could've been extras."

"Sarcasm," identified Hanley.

The black man next to him had vaulted over the back of his seat and was swinging at a white fan.

Hanley continued in the same flat, slightly too precise tone of voice: "Well, it took some doing but we now have the money and the clearance. You're to take the money to him and find out what is going on."

"I'm not a headhunter," Devereaux replied.

Their voices were unnaturally quiet in the chaotic din around them.

Hanley smiled unpleasantly and spread his hands in a gesture of sincerity. "This is not a contract. We merely want you to evaluate our friend and his information and to remind him of certain aspects of . . . discipline . . . and to find out what Samuel is getting for his money from that funny little Englishman."

Samuel was the current jargon name for the U.S. Hanley was always up on the jargon.

Devereaux suddenly turned away. He despised them all and all the cute espionage talk that filtered down from R Section. It came from all those dreary clerks spending their dreary lives in Mitty-like imitation of what they thought was the reality of the operation. In fact, their reality came from television and the movies and the latest spy fictions they read on their lunch hour in the marble cafeteria downstairs. Devereaux's reality did not have names or comfort or jargon, and it did not have time for Hanley's potent sense of melodrama.

"I'm going to get a drink," Devereaux said finally and got up. He started to edge along the row to the aisle.

Hanley flushed: "I'm not through, goddammit."

His voice pierced the din because it was so unexpected and so angry. The crowd around them suddenly fell quiet. Devereaux paused and turned back to Hanley. Hanley gaped around him and was instantly aware of the attention.

Devereaux smiled: "Don't be such a tired bitch. Buy us a drink."

Hanley gaped on, now at Devereaux. The black man snickered behind him, and Hanley's face turned red.

Devereaux leered, "Coming?"

"I'm coming," said Hanley meekly, and he rose and followed Devereaux down the row.

"Fags," said the man behind the empty seats. "Fuckin' fairies." The bell continued to sound in the prize ring.

Hanley ordered rye.

A midtown New York bar at ten P.M. Ill-lit, too small, pretentiously priced, it projected a kind of relentless insomnia, just like the city. Devereaux and Hanley sat at the curve at the window end. The street was shut out with red curtains; red flocked wallpaper tarted up the interior with a sort of comfortable insincerity. The bartender plunked down the drinks in large rounded glasses.

"I always order rye in New York," explained Hanley. He made a face as he sipped at the drink. "That's a good habit, you know—order the local drink. Makes you fit in. Rye here. Bourbon in the South—"

"Scotch in Scotland," said Devereaux. He sipped his vodka and felt tired. Hanley, who grew up in Nebraska, had gained his indelible impression of the habits and mores of New Yorkers from the countless B movies that had ground their way through his local movie house in the thirties.

"Speaking of Scotland." Hanley sipped again like a man just trying to get through a drink. "Did you know that's Hastings' base now?"

"I haven't seen him for years. Since Athens."

Hanley frowned. "I'm aware of that. You don't keep up."

"Why doesn't the Section send around a newsletter?" Devereaux was sick of talking to Hanley and sick at the thought of what the job was going to turn out to be. He had liked Hastings once.

"Despite your sarcasm," Hanley began, "I'm aware of what you think. You know you could have done better if you had kept up." Like me, implied Hanley.

"What's the job?" It was maddening.

"You leave tomorrow to see Hastings. It has to be made clear to him that he won't get the money until we have a solid idea—an idea that will satisfy you—of what his information entails."

"Thirty thousand dollars is hardly exit money," said Devereaux. The cold vodka was numbing his tongue pleasantly.

"There's more," said Hanley, sipping dutifully at the rye.

Devereaux waited and let the coldness of the drink warm him.

"I didn't get the chance to tell you everything."

Pause.

"Hastings wants thirty thousand now." Pause again. Devereaux sat still and stared at the ice bobbing in his drink. "For the first part of whatever he has. And a hundred thousand dollars deposited in a Swiss bank in nine days for the second part."

Devereaux had had enough. "I'm not playing, Hanley. Until you give me some idea of what the hell this is all about."

Hanley spread his hands in the same familiar and insincere gesture of openness.

"I've told you. We simply have no idea of why he's being so secretive. We've talked to our London people— my God, they should certainly be on top of things. Hastings has never played this sort of game. Frankly, he's never had much to be secretive about. Some of the people at Britdesk in the Section think most of his stuff has been clipped out of the *Economist* or *Telegraph*—"

Which it probably was, Devereaux thought.

Hanley realized, with something like horror, that he had finished his drink without finishing his conversation. "I suppose you want another," he began. Devereaux nodded to the bartender. They did not speak until they were served. In a booth at the other end of the bar, a large, heavy man placed his hand on the thigh of a drunk young woman. He was not asked to remove it. Hanley stared at them.

"Hastings has been our informal link, as it were, with Brit Intell. He retired from them two years ago, you know."

Brit Intell. For God's sake, thought Devereaux.

"Well, as you may know, there's damned little the Section is interested in getting from the blokes." He used the old military expression of contempt for the English. "Still. He was worth his allowance, just to have all bases covered. Never gave us very much but . . . well . . . Hastings was justifiable. Then, six months ago, he stopped giving. Just . . . stopped . . . giving."

Above the bar, the television set flickered on. There was no sound. The screen filled with the images of the slug and the black man. The fight was being repeated. Devereaux felt strangely disoriented. The edge of his tongue stung with cold vodka.

"Was he dead?" asked Hanley rhetorically. "No, old Hastings was very much alive. We sent a Third Man over a month ago to talk with him. No, he couldn't tell us what was up. Hastings said he was putting pieces together. He said he'd let us know. The Third Man said he looked like a cat who'd swallowed a bird."

Hanley now folded his hands and looked confidentially at Devereaux, rather like an employment counselor about to explain a company's pension plan. "As you know, the Section operates rather loosely compared with the Langley company."

Devereaux winced at the phrase—Langley meant the Central Intelligence Agency headquartered off the Beltway in that sleepy Virginia suburb.

"Because we are a much smaller operation—and because our charter is so much more limited—we have developed a rather loose field program and our operators are permitted a rather wide latitude in information-gathering. Still, Hastings has sorely vexed us with his silence—"

"As I have."

"As you have," agreed Hanley. "I can tell you there were some on the committee who wanted to pull the plug on him."

"In what way?"

"Perhaps reveal his . . . ah . . . role in our organization to someone in Brit Intell—"

"That would be stupid," said Devereaux.

Hanley smiled. "Right. That's what the Chief said. That's what I said. Stupid and self-defeating, I said. Look at the matter logically, I put it to the committee: There are several possibilities. One, Hastings is stringing us along and merely wants the money and has nothing at all. Two: Hastings has information of genuine worth and is entertaining bids for it from our side, from the Langley company, and others. Three, Hastings has the information and genuinely does not want to blow it—"

"—by telling your second-rate couriers about it—"

"We sent a Third Man," complained Hanley defensively.

"Four," said Devereaux. "Hastings has made the hit of his life. He's going to milk it for every last drop. And then he's going away."

"Four," agreed Hanley. "So good that it can make the Section. I don't need to tell you we've had our problems with the committee."

"No, you don't need to tell me," said Devereaux. He considered it. "Hastings. He must be fifty-five years old now."

"Fifty-four," said Hanley.

"Does he have a network?"

"Not much of one. Nothing too important. A couple of school chums involved in Brit Intell's domestic operation in Belfast, keeping an eye on the Boys." Such were members of the Irish Republican Army called. "But that's not really of much interest to us."

"No," said Devereaux.

"That's what's got us stumped," said Hanley. "I mean, where the hell did Hastings put his hands on something really important?"

"His British probes?"

"But you know what British Intelligence is. I mean, what could they know that we don't know?"

Devereaux nodded. On the television screen, the slug was against the ropes again, again being hammered in slow motion by the smaller man. "So it might be important for a change, what old Hastings has found."

"Every bit of information is important," Hanley said with blithe inconsistency. Devereaux's attitude seemed always to threaten Hanley and the structure of the world in which he found comfort.

"Nonsense," said Devereaux. "You don't believe that. Even you don't believe that. Almost none of it is important. And the important stuff we usually get by accident. That Soviet fighter plane last year. Flown into our waiting hands and those of the Japanese because Yuri What's-his-name was pissed off at his wife in the Soviet paradise. Don't make it all seem more than it is."

Hanley was angry again. He had had quite enough. He reached into his vest and said, "This is all you need."

He had pulled out the fight program.

"Am I supposed to give him that? Do you think he'll believe it's thirty thousand dollars? Or a Swiss account book?"

"Damn." Hanley flushed. He shoved the program back into his coat and then reached into the vest and came out with a brown envelope. He placed the envelope on the bar, between the two glasses. Then he pulled a little notebook from a second pocket and put it in front of Devereaux. "Sign, please, there," he said.

Dĕvereaux made his scrawl.

"Thirty one-thousand-dollar bills. An account with the State Bank of Zurich containing one hundred thousand dollars in his name. Just in case he has both parts. It's your judgment, Devereaux, remember. That's a lot of money—"

"Why not fly him back here?"

"Our Third Man suggested it to him. He wouldn't buy."

"Doesn't he trust us?"

Hanley shrugged. "We've always played him fair—"

"Except for recruiting him in the first place," said Devereaux. "Remember? I was there." A long time ago. On an island in the Aegean. The last time Devereaux had seen Hastings, the happiness had drained out of that puffy face, the eyes were both mocking and betrayed.

"If that's all," said Hanley. His voice was coming from a distance.

Devereaux smiled again. Hanley was irresistible. "One more thing as long as you're here."

Hanley glanced at him.

"My American Express card," Devereaux said quietly. "I picked up my mail this weekend and there was a notice threatening cancellation. I thought you had taken care of it."

"I'm sure we did."

"Don't give me that 'sure' shit. Just call up the goddam AmEx tomorrow and get the fucking thing straightened out. They said they hadn't received a payment in four months—"

"You submitted your bills—"

"Fuck my bills," said Devereaux, just as quietly. "You think those cowboys in the CIA worry about their credit cards getting canceled?"

"The error is probably on the part of American Express—"

"I don't care who's part it's on. Just fix it." Devereaux was actually enjoying himself, because Hanley prided himself on the efficiency of the Section, particularly the intricate paymaster system which he had created. Comparisons with the CIA's lavish budget bothered Hanley as well. All of which put Devereaux in a better mood.

"The Langley people have their problems, too," said Hanley. Then he saw Devereaux's smile and refused to play anymore.

They finished their drinks, staring along with the bartender at the silent television screen.

"Oh, yes," said Hanley at last. "If it's one or two. Well. Let us know right away."

"One or two?"

Hanley nodded. "Scenarios. That he's stringing us or becoming an independent contractor."

Devereaux was suddenly very tired and drained. He did not want to talk with this vile little man anymore. If it were possibilities one or two, in Devereaux's judgment, it meant the end of Hastings.

"You pay," Devereaux said. He got up then and went out the door without another word.

2

EDINBURGH

November rain, full of ice and bleakness, dashed against the black and gray stones of the old city. Scottish noon: no one had seen the sun for days. Ugly clouds convened above the spires, permitting only varying shades of dull, gray light. Outside, the rain stung faces red and soaked into heavy tweeds and numbed the bones of shoppers bent against the wind whistling down Princes Street.

"Terrible, terrible."

Hastings muttered like a priest's housekeeper as he bustled around the room, picking up pieces of clothing and straightening the cover on the creaky couch. The air in the room was close with leftover odors of gin, Scotch, and cigarettes. A sudden puff of wind flung a hail of raindrops against the window.

"Damn it all." Hastings felt suddenly depressed by his morning-after activity and sat down fatly on the couch. He fumbled as he lit a Player's.

The smoke did not satisfy him.

He sighed and ran his hand through his thinning brown-tinted hair. Then he expelled a big puff of smoke and sighed again. The chill in the room crept up on him. The place was always damp and musty and always cold.

Not like the islands. Something softened his eyes at that moment, as though he saw the past clearly in the pattern of brown smoke. He had grown accustomed to the heat then. Too much so.

He dashed out the cigarette, ending the mood. After

all, the cable had arrived that morning and it was no dream. Money due today.

Money due today. The money. The exit money.

The excesses of his life were obvious in lines on his too-red face and the swell of his paunch. But what excesses, really, dearie? Drank too much? Who wouldn't with the loneliness of it all. And now this climate—why, duck, half the city is drunk from morning till night in winter. One always needed a little money, just to mitigate the pain. Hanley had once wired from R Section: How do you manage to spend so much money in such a miserable poor country? Hanley's idea of repartee.

The wind knocked at the window again like an insistent visitor.

Well, there wasn't anything funny about it, my darlings. It was a miserable and poor country and one needed money just to retain one's sanity. Just to stay drunk when the night comes at three in the afternoon. The men were stuffy, righteous, close, even pompous in their smug tams and tweeds; the places of pleasure were opened only grudgingly; one felt as though one were a child again living here—only the childhood consisted of a single, eternal Sunday afternoon.

For a moment, a tear appeared in the corner of Hastings' eye as he thought of that poor child of himself, trapped in tweeds and knickers, staring out the window at the rain on the immense lawn, tiptoeing through the adult house of shadows and too many rooms. Poor darling boy.

He shivered. He rose and went to the gas ring and turned it on. The blue flames hissed evenly and he held his hands over them.

Well, ducks, weep not for Hastings but for yourselves. The money was coming today and Hastings must be up and about his father's business. His uncle's business, in any event.

He giggled.

God bless America and all its money and endless need

for intrigue and a chance to meddle in others' business. Yes, bless them all.

He began to hum the old war song as he went to the grim, oak wardrobe by the door. He selected a shabby green Harris tweed jacket and shrugged it over his round, sad little fat-man shoulders. Then the mackintosh. No wonder all this heavy, foul-weather stuff bore Scottish names.

He closed the door carefully, inserting the bit of match box just so between the jamb and door. Then he turned and hurried down the musty hall, down the worn stairs to the street. As he opened the outer door, the wind slapped his face in greeting; he joined the other pedestrians in homage to the force of it and bent his uncovered head as he hurried along the narrow mews. Nearly one P.M.

Hastings had the gift to see himself clearly, even when he presented a ludicrous sight. Now he thought of the white rabbit in Alice and managed an odd, twisted smile. Hurry, hurry, old darling. No time to waste. . . .

He finally emerged onto the broad, windy expanse of Princes Street. On the other side, away from the row of fashionable stores, lay the long gully that carried railway lines out of Edinburgh Station. Above the lines loomed the rocky menace of Edinburgh Castle, carved into the lip of the hill. The rain turned to hail.

"Oh, Christ," Hastings prayed loudly as the hail began to pelt him. "Give us a rest."

For a moment, it was too much for him. He took refuge in the doorway of a tailor shop. Not a cab or omnibus in sight, only the thin miserable line of private cars sloshing through the eternal downpour. Clouds boiled up from the west like new stock. What a miserable country.

He waited in the entranceway for the sudden, furious onslaught to ease. He felt damp already, and cold.

The meet had been decided weeks before. When he had talked with that boy they sent—a Third Man. Not his type at all, ducks—a little too macho, with a ferret face.

He recalled with satisfaction that warmed him how he punctured Ferretface's tough-guy act. It had been quite easy. And then Ferretface had listened to Hastings' instructions.

Your humble servant, Hastings, had selected the buffet in Edinburgh Central Station. Miserable little buffet not a hundred feet from the gate to the afternoon express to Glasgow. Just in case.

Hastings was aware they might not trust him anymore.

He plunged into the street again and half ran down the sidewalk, staying close to the shop buildings. Across the magnificent and gloomy expanse of the famous thoroughfare, the wind built volume that whirled capriciously behind him and prodded Hastings along like a crusher with his nightstick. Move along there, yer bloody queen. . . .

The brooding gothic columns of the Walter Scott memorial loomed up and then away and Hastings hurried on until he was down at the entrance of the station, breathing hard, his face flushed, his mackintosh soaked. His breath came in foggy jerks.

He wanted to rush into the cover of the station.

Caution, old luv, he told himself. He stood in the entry and waited for his shivering to cease. One o'clock and all's well. The train for Glasgow sits steaming at the far gate. Ticket. There it is. Leaves in ten minutes. Just enough time to judge the situation and make a run for it if he had to.

He strolled to the window of the buffet in the main concourse of the station and peered inside.

Typical British Rail. All bright plasticky colors already fading. Stacks of stale sandwich rounds. A fat woman in a heavy coat with two small, red-cheeked children sat slopping their tea at one table. An old man with a copy of *The Scotsman* sat near the window, judiciously muttering over the headlines. Two British Rail conductors sat at a third table, leaning over the tits-and-bums page of *The Sun*.

And Devereaux.

Hastings caught his breath, felt heavy in his arms.

Rather too much, luv, isn't it? I mean, sending a Ninth Man from Section? Don't they trust dear, dear Hastings? The thought overwhelmed him. He slowly continued his inventory of the buffet and then let his eyes rest again on Devereaux, who sat in a smoking wet raincoat, cupping a mug of milky tea in his broad, flat-fingered hands.

Still the same. Same gray-and-black hair. Same crosshatched face that was neither handsome nor ugly. Devereaux's features all showed age in an oddly appealing way; probably he had not been as attractive as a young man, but, with age, had accumulated character. Same marble-gray eyes and wintry face. Even when they were in Athens a long time ago. Aren't you cold, luv, with a face like that? Then he would smile—Devereaux had liked Hastings—and Hastings had begun to feel comfortable with him. Strictly platonic, old darling, not my type at all.

Six minutes to the Glasgow train.

Hastings fingered the little cardboard ticket in his pocket. The Section would never kill him in a British Rail buffet. No, no. Wouldn't do at all. Indeed, they would prefer not to kill him in these blessed isles at all, since R Section did not exist.

Five minutes.

Lost your nerve, old darling?

Hastings made his decision then.

He pushed open the door of the buffet and strode in with what he fancied a hearty manner. He shambled to the food counter and ordered a cup of white and carried the plastic mug to the plastic table where Devereaux sat.

The previous occupants of the table had left a half-eaten ham sandwich. Hastings sat down and covered it with a paper napkin. "*Requiescat in pace.*"

Devereaux did not speak. The trip had been a brutal one. The plane had landed late at Heathrow just after dawn and the northern airports were all socked in. He had driven five hours north to make the meeting.

"You look older," said Hastings at last. "But well."

"I am."

"Well, jolly to see you and all that. Been years." Hastings affected a bishop's manner. "How long?"

They both knew how long.

"Ten years."

"My, ten years in service to my American cousins," Hastings said. The milk-and-tea was warm and a little bitter. "Time flies so when one is so thoroughly enjoying oneself—"

Two minutes to the Glasgow train. Dash. Upset the table, throw the tea in his face, through the door, the gates, the train just pulling out.

Steady now, old luv.

"You're quite important now, I should say," Hastings said. "I really didn't expect you at all. I mean, from the ridiculous to the sublime—first that little ferret and now you. Nothing in moderation?"

Devereaux watched him.

"Wretched stuff," Hastings complained suddenly. He flung down the cup. "Disgrace when the bloody British can't make a decent cuppa." He glanced up. Devereaux had not moved. "Of course," he continued. "One can't expect civilization from the Scots."

All was still. The woman with the apple-cheeked children had left.

Hastings dispensed with the bishop. "You've got the money?"

"What have you got?"

"Ah," said Hastings. "Ah." He decided. He eased back on the plastic chair and, releasing the Glasgow ticket, pulled his hand from his coat.

"Ah, what I have," he said.

"I am prepared to evaluate it," said Devereaux quietly.

"To give it value." Hastings "ahed" once more. "So that's why they sent you along. Of course. Certainly.

Makes a good deal of sense. Field evaluation." It was all going to work out satisfactorily.

"They are puzzled by your silence," Devereaux said carefully. "They want to be filled in."

"And filled in they shall be, luv," said Hastings heartily. "Filled and refilled and filled again until they have had their fill."

"Do you have both . . . both parts?"

"Do you have all the money, luv? That's more to the point, ain't it?"

Devereaux said, "We're prepared."

Hastings winked. "You wouldn't fool an old man, would you?"

Devereaux looked at him closely, at the mottled face, and felt something like pity. "You wouldn't fool us now, would you?"

Said mildly, without hint of malice. Which made it frightening.

"No, no, never dream of it," the older man cried. "Not at all. This is the goods, my dear, as you might say. This is the McCoy, the Derby Day."

Devereaux tried a cautious smile. Merely as an exploration. "The last one, eh, Hastings?"

Hastings glanced up.

Devereaux tuned the smile two degrees upward. "We're prepared for that. Don't worry. Even agents have to retire."

"Ah, well, then." Something like relief. Forgetting his previous comment, the Englishman slurped down the remains of the milky tea. "I'm free then. A free man."

"Soon," said Devereaux.

"As you say, Dev. Well, to business then, me darlin'. You must get a room and get out of those clothes. Bloody climate here. Not like the islands, eh, Dev?"

Devereaux did not respond.

"I'd let you stay in my digs but you wouldn't care for it, luv. It's not you." He laughed. "All me." Patted his belly. "And then some. Simply no room at the inn, old duck." Becoming the avuncular country cleric. "Station hotel upstairs is as good as any and better than most. Very convenient. Been in this filthy city before?"

"I suppose." Devereaux knew airports, not cities.

"Well, you clean up and soak in a hot bath and I'll meet you at six o'clock sharp right across the way at the Crescent and Lion. Splendid pub. One of the few decent pleasures left in this Calvinistic, moralistic, tight-fisted hole—where was I? Six P.M. I'll lay it out for you and then we can arrange to talk with a couple of my . . . my colleagues." He was lapsing into a stage-Irish dialect. "Me boyos."

"A total fill-in."

"Well, let me put it this way," said Hastings. Improbably, he winked again. "It will be worth it all to both of us."

"We expect that."

"Or what?" asked Hastings playfully.

Now Devereaux smiled. Not by degrees. "Did you think I came here to kill you?"

He coughed. "Thought crossed my mind at one point, luv."

"No." Devereaux rose. "It's not that simple, Hastings. You should know that."

The gaiety forced up by fear and the restless weeks of waiting was suddenly drained out of the Englishman's face. He felt tired. Felt like an old man.

"I know that," he said.

There was only time for two double whiskies before the midafternoon pub closings. Hastings had reluctantly drained the last of his warm Johnnie Walker and then hurried outside into the bitter chill again, up the Royal Mile to Edinburgh Castle. Hastings' walk resembled nothing so much as a baby's first tentative steps on uneven ground.

He was meeting Sheffield at three.

They had been schoolboys and then friends and now

they were business agents, dealing in information. As far as Hastings knew, Sheffield was the only man in British Intelligence who knew Hastings' real masters.

The wild morning storm from the Atlantic had blown away across the Firth of Forth outside Edinburgh, dancing on into the icy, roiling mass of the North Sea. A gentle rain, as welcome as sunshine, fell on the city.

Hastings huffed up the hilly street. He was cold again, the whisky in him perfidiously chilling. Without looking, he passed warm shops of tailors and curio sellers and tobacconists; shops decorated with tartans and shops that promised to trace your clan lines for two quid.

Sheffield was supposed to wait for him at the edge of the broad square that fronted the grim, gray stone gates of the castle. Below the square was the expanse of the New City, stretching to the Firth.

The square was empty. Fog rolled in the light wind crawling across the bricks.

Sheffield appeared quite suddenly from the doorway of an office building. Hastings was startled; he felt a pain in his chest.

"You startled me," he complained. His voice carried annoyance; sweat formed at his thin hairline. Sheffield was the younger man and Hastings held a sort of dominance over him in their friendship. They had been at Cambridge together; Hastings had been quite brilliant and there had developed a trace of deference in the younger man's manner which had never left him. It was as though Hastings might, reasonably, insist Sheffield fetch his boots from the cobbler or go on an errand to the Rose pub in Rose Crescent.

Sheffield was a thin man, shy and pinched in face and manner. But at the moment there was something like amusement in the simple brown eyes as he regarded Hastings.

"Sorry, Hastings," Sheffield said. His eyes carefully swept the empty square as they talked.

"I should say," huffed the older man, who was feeling

very foolish indeed today. First Devereaux and now Sheffield. Hang on, old luv.

"We have the documents," Sheffield said in the manner of royalty.

"And I have our American friend."

"And the money?"

"As good as gotten," the older man replied. "Let's have them then, Sheff."

"My dear fellow," Sheffield began. "I rather think it might be protocol if you handed over the agreed sum first—"

"I ain't got the bloody swag yet," Hastings cried, changing the accent to Australian. There were so damned many obstacles and now this bleeding pouf bastard—

"Dear me," said Sheffield. He glanced down the Royal Mile to the center of the Old City.

"Don't be a bloody fool, Sheff," he said. "He has the money but he's not going to turn over a bloody farthing unless he's convinced, and I need those papers to convince him."

"Well, let's both go to meet him, then, darling," said Sheffield.

"No, we're not both bloody meeting him, darling," Hastings snapped. He made an effort to choke off his anger. "Ye don't start changin' yer bleedin' rules midway in the match—" Unaccountably, the rougher Australian accent had settled in. "Everything is as we agreed, me bucko, and as we agreed it'll stay."

Sheffield altered his tone as well: " 'Me bucko' me all you want, old darling, but I have rather a stake in all this. It's my neck on Her Majesty's block. I'm the one who took the risks—"

"And I'm the one what showed you what the risks were worth, you bleedin' poufter!"

Hastings suddenly pressed his fat body against the younger man and both disappeared into the shadows of the doorway. Sheffield found his arms pinned by the door and wall and his life's breath being choked out of him by Hastings' big hands. *Amazing,* he thought dreamily as he began to die. *Really quite extraordinary that old Hastings could move so quickly. . . . Never would believe—*

Sheffield would have died, if Hastings had not ceased. The breath came back in burning jerks into his lungs and he could not speak. He coughed and gobbled more of the cold, damp air into his mouth.

"Now, my luv," said Hastings softly.

"I had only meant—" Sheffield tried to begin.

"I know, I know," Hastings said in a soothing, motherly voice. "Don't blame you, Sheff. But I have promises to keep and miles to go before I sleep. You understand."

"Yes. Yes, of course," said Sheffield, joyous that his life was returned and the other had forgiven him. He almost felt like crying.

"Now the papers, dear Sheff," said Hastings in the same croon.

"Of course," said Sheffield. He almost gurgled as he removed the photostats from inside his shirt. They had been taped to his chest.

Hastings did not glance at them but stuffed them quickly into his mackintosh.

"I know you'll do right by me," Sheffield said.

"Ain't I always, Sheff? Of course I will. Trust your old pal, luv. There's no need to worry. It's all complete now, all the parts—"

Sheffield nearly missed the slip.

"What other parts?"

"Never mind."

Sheffield was silent.

"Don't trouble yourself," Hastings said gravely.

Sheffield touched his neck. He knew there would be bruises. Without another word, the fat man turned away and began to toddle down the Royal Mile, back to the center of the old part of the city. Sheffield stood in the shadow of the office block for a few more moments until Hastings was lost in the fog beneath the hill.

Sheffield promised to kill him.

The tiredness had felled him. First a shower, and the hot, slashing water soothed the ache out of his arms and back; then a giddy wave of nausea was replaced by this utter sense of exhaustion. Devereaux did not even pull back the covers but fell asleep, naked, across the bed.

It seemed only a moment later when the telephone rang.

The ring repeated several times before Devereaux could even comprehend the sound. He did not know where he was. The room was black but a sliver of light came from the bath. Hotel room. He always awoke the same, never sure of himself or of where he was. He picked up the receiver and a heavily burred voice said, "Five o'clock, surr."

It did not mean anything.

He fell back on the bed, only wanting sleep; but the voice had started his thoughts up again and he would not sleep. Suddenly, he pushed his forty-three-year-old body upwards and staggered again into the ornate, old-fashioned bathroom where the tub had clawed legs. He splashed icy water on his face and shivered. Then he looked at the gray, drawn face in the mirror.

On the basin was a small packet marked aspirins. Except they were not aspirins and Devereaux never had a headache. Swallowing two of the white pills, he went back into his room and began to pull fresh clothes from the leather two-suiter on the bed.

By 5:55 P.M., he was marching across the road from the station hotel into the dark streets to the Crescent and Lion pub. Night had brought an end to the rain. There was only a sweeping sense of cold blowing down the old streets. Devereaux's face had lost its pallor; his eyes glittered almost unnaturally.

He had a rhythm to walking on a job. He moved

methodically, his eyes sweeping the street in front of him: Doorway, post, street, car, bus, doorway, window—

He stalked into the pub.

After work. A gentle murmur and hard drinking. Brownish whisky in plain glasses and large British pints of Tartan Ale and Guinness and Bass Ale. Glasses sparkled in the subdued light as they sat on the shelves above the bar top. The pub was not a fancy pub; there was no saloon side in the English style. Devereaux ordered a double Johnnie Walker and took the drink to a table that hugged a wall next to the front window.

Scotch in Scotland, he thought and smiled to himself. He sipped the brown, liquid warmth. Better. Much better. He looked out the window at the cold as though it was a stranger. The pleasant, burred voices around him soothed him.

By seven o'clock it was clear that Hastings was not coming.

The warmth had left Devereaux. He sat contemplating his third double whisky and reviewed the options.

One, Hastings had nothing and it had all been a bluff as Hanley suspected.

Swirling the whisky in its stemmed glass, he watched as it rose and fell against the bubbled sides like waves.

Nonsense. Out of the question. Hastings was not mad enough to believe the Section would pay him those extraordinary sums without seeing his information. A bad scenario.

Around him, the hard-drinking crowd had settled in at the bar, pushing against the ten o'clock closing time in Presbyterian Scotland. Those with homes or supper waiting had already left.

Two. Hastings had been delayed by the sort of freak accident that even spy flesh is heir to. He'd fallen down, had a heart attack, was struck by a bus. In that case, it was merely a matter of waiting to be recontacted.

He sipped at the whisky.

Three. Hastings had been killed.

Who would kill Hastings?

A lover. An enemy. A friend. Someone who knew what he had. And who knew it was worth a life. At least a life.

Devereaux drained the whisky and set the glass back down on the scarred black oak table. The pills and whiskies were producing an odd effect: Devereaux's body was slowly falling asleep though his mind was awake and outside the body—watching it and commenting on it.

What did Hastings have that he was sure was worth exit money? And which he knew we wanted?

And why deal with R Section?

That had puzzled Devereaux most from the moment Hanley had given him the assignment. After all, Hastings had been recruited by the Section and he was the Section's man—but if it was a matter of getting exit money and retiring, he could have dealt with the company as well. The CIA was more generous than R, and the CIA could have guaranteed his safety. Even from us.

Go back to the beginning of option three.

Hastings is dead. Someone killed him.

The killer eliminated him for one of two reasons: To get his information or to stop him from giving it to us.

Devereaux tried to remember Hastings as he had seen him six hours before.

He felt sure Hastings was dead.

"Ah, y'll be havin' to get it yourself, you know."

Devereaux looked up.

The man wore an ordinary rumpled business suit of heavy wool that looked as though it was usually damp. His white shirt-collar was a trifle dirty and the shocking red tie was knotted so fiercely at the thick throat that it resembled a noose.

"I beg your pardon?"

"Whisky, lad. Yer be havin' to get it yourself. At the bar." The face was middle-aged Irish and so was the accent. The man smiled.

Devereaux did not. "I know," he said and turned back to his thoughts. He was not finished with Hastings.

"Now, I intended no offense—"

Devereaux nodded slightly, politely. But the Irish businessman seemed not to care.

He leaned over confidentially from his table—all connected by the same bench that ran along the wall—and said, "Yer an American."

Devereaux looked at him.

"I'm Irish," he said unnecessarily. "From Belfast." As though the name of the city would invoke a reaction. "Poor old bleedin' Belfast." He saluted the city with his own whisky glass. "On business here. Edinburgh is a lovely city, don't you think?"

He was irresistible.

"Lovely," said Devereaux. He got up and went to the bar to order another. He intended not to return to the table. He would wait for Hastings a while longer.

But the Irish businessman pursued him to the bar as well.

"Me," he began as though there had been no interruption. "I like the Scots, you know. Not like some. We're all Celtic people. I'm Catholic, though, you see." Saying it, he lowered his voice as though it were still against the law to be a Catholic in lowland Scotland.

"But they're an honest enough people and who can we blame for our troubles now, I want to ask you," he went on. The whisky came and the Irishman placed a five-pound Irish banknote on the bar.

"I canna take yer Republic note," the bartender said gently. He was a red-bearded giant with a flat, pleasant face.

For a moment, the blue-eyed Irishman bristled. Then he let it go. "Ah, well, it's all the same, isn't it now? The Sassenach won't take yer Scottish money down there but they expect us to all take theirs at their bloody convenience." He tried out a smile of Celtic comradeship but the barkeep was having none of it. When the businessman finally produced an English fiver, the barkeep snatched it away with a grumble and made change.

With a stage wink, the Irishman turned to Devereaux and nodded at the bartender's back. "And den some of them are like that stiff-backed Prod with no sense of humor atall and you wanta join the IRA yerself."

Devereaux allowed a smile. Thought was impossible before the onslaught of Irish charm. He surrendered with a shrug and the Irishman looked as though he had won a battle.

"Yer health, sur," he said and drained half the whisky at a swallow. After the Irish habit, he had mixed tepid water with the alcohol.

"What about the money?"

The Irishman looked startled.

"What money?"

"The Scottish and Irish money. I don't understand—"

"Oh." The Irishman looked relieved. Devereaux picked up on it. Something out of place. "Oh, that. Well, y'see, the Republic prints its money and the Bank of Scotland prints its money and the Bank of England prints its money. Y'follow, now? This is a Scottish note here. But it's all the same bloody money because the Republic is tied to the English pound and the Scottish pound the same. If the English pound is worth so much, then the Irish pound is worth the same. Y'follow now? Same money. If yer go into dear Dublin and yer an Englishman, ya hand over an English pound and they give you change nice as can be. Anywhere there. Me mother's people ran a pub there, always takin' English notes. They treat it the same as if it was Irish pounds. But if yer take yer Irish money into London and yer in a pub somewhere and you put down the note on the bar, well, they'd as soon spit at you, the Sassenach bloody bastards. That's the English for yer. A bloody rude people."

He swallowed more whisky and it liberated his speech.

"Same with the Scottish pounds. Take them south of

the river Tweed and yer English look at ye like yer
trying to pass a bloody yen or somethin'. But English
pounds is all welcome in Scotland. Yer see what I'm
sayin,' sir? Here the English treat us both like we have
the bloody pox but then how do we treat each other?
Like brothers, sir? None of it. Look at that ginger-
bearded fella behind the bar!"

He slammed down his glass for emphasis and waved to
the red-haired man for another round.

"And I tell ya, it's the same with we Irish. We treat
each other like enemies. Poor bleedin' Ireland." He
paused. "And look at this poor country as well. They'll
get their North Sea oil in a few years and they'll ship it
all down south to London and be lucky to see a bob on
every pound of profit. Mark me. No one ever bested the
English in a deal or a war."

"Save us," said Devereaux.

"Ah? Oh, aye. Save the United States of America.
God bless 'er."

Devereaux listened on while his mind tracked Hastings.
His body tried to nudge him toward sleep but his mind
pursued the fat Englishman. He glanced at his watch
and was surprised to see the black Omega dial blur
momentarily. No more whisky. He got up to disentangle
himself from the Irishman's one-sided conversation. It
was not easy. Devereaux was forced to nod and smile
and poke the Irishman's conversation with a question,
hoping it would permit him the chance to depart; but
O'Neill held on like a wrestler, his monologue pinning
Devereaux down. The Irishman had offered his name at
one point but Devereaux did not introduce himself.

Finally, Devereaux bought his round and begged fare-
well and broke the web of words. At last, he managed to
plunge again into the icy darkness of the Scottish capital.

The streets were nearly empty already.

He tried to play his game again: Doorway, post, street,
passing cars. But the drinks and tiredness seemed to overwhelm his concentration. He hurried across the wet street

to the station entrance and down to the cab line. He felt careless, but unable to do anything about it, for he had to know about Hastings.

He ducked into the tall black car and gave an address to the driver. The stately Austin pulled quickly away from the curb and plunged into the traffic on Princes Street. In the darkness, the battlements of Edinburgh Castle were lit with eerie light; fog began sifting in from the highlands beyond the city.

Devereaux felt ill. He wondered if it was from the whisky and pills or from thinking about Hastings. He had helped trick Hastings into service for R Section: He'd never felt guilty about it, because Hastings was a greedy man. Until now. Maybe that's why his stomach churned.

A four-story building, dour and dark.

He paid the cab and went up the steps to the entry. Beyond the outer door he could see worn carpeting on stairs leading up to an ill-lit landing.

He pushed the door. It was locked. He was puzzled by it for a moment before he inserted a thin, strong wire into the lock and twisted the tumbler. He entered the hall.

There was no sound except for his heartbeat, which he thought was thunderous.

Mr. Percy. Second floor rear.

Percy. Why did he choose that? His mother's maiden name? A friend? A lover? An enemy?

The stairs creaked under Devereaux's weight.

He wondered if he should be afraid. He knew his body was tense but he knew it in a disassociated way. That was the pills acting on the whisky. He thought if there was danger finally at the top of the stairs, his mind would react too slowly.

He managed the landing.

A naked bulb of low wattage burned faintly from a fixture in the ceiling. Electrical cords—painted over scores of time—ran along the wainscoting.

He had no weapon except for the garroting wire wound

in the copper bracelet on his left wrist. The bracelet was the type sold as a cure for arthritis. The thin wire inside it had killed three men—quietly and quickly. The technique was quite simple: Behind the victim, over his head, turn your body and throw your shoulder into his back and then bend over, lifting the victim's body as it dangles on the wire around his neck. Usually, death is instantaneous; in any event, the victim cannot cry out. Very neat, Hanley had said; R Section was pleased with it for its simplicity and effectiveness. And cost. The wire was indestructible and cost—Hanley had been especially proud of this—seven cents to produce.

The door to Mr. Percy's room was ajar.

The hallway was dark; vague, dank odors of mold and heat permeated it.

Devereaux stood at the top of the stairs and waited. He tried to listen for a sound that wasn't there. He waited two minutes for the silence to end.

He walked across the hall then and cursed the creaking of the wooden floor under the flowered carpet. He pushed open the door of Percy-Hastings' room.

He nearly stepped into the blood.

It was everywhere.

He walked around the soaking pool by the door and looked down at Hastings.

The fat older man looked like a broken doll. His face was puffed up by death, his eyes protruded comically. His swollen tongue lolled out of his mouth.

As Devereaux stood and looked at him, the first wave of nausea rose in him and then fell back. He stood perfectly still while his eyes catalogued the room:

Hastings had been stabbed. The wounds were all over his naked body. He was sprawled face up but his legs were drawn up and his hip rested on its side on the floor in a grotesque fetal position. His penis lay on the blood-soaked couch.

Devereaux squatted down, holding his raincoat off the floor so that it would not be stained.

He touched Hastings' neck. There was a deep cut running from ear to ear. A thin cut, cruelly made. It had killed him, Devereaux decided. And it had not been made by a knife. Hastings had been garroted.

Hastings' body smelled. There was excrement on the floor, mixed in the blood, released at the moment of death.

The room was torn up; papers were scattered on the floor; books were heaped in a corner. Everything Hastings owned had been violated, searched, torn apart, destroyed.

Devereaux stood up and took a last look at the agent and turned and retraced his steps to the door. He backed into the black hall and went to the stairs. For a moment, he stood and listened.

He thought he heard a door closing quietly.

His heart thumped; there was the beginning of a dull pain in his shoulders, spreading and warming across his upper back.

He started down the stairs.

Outside, on the empty street, the houses were all in darkness. Old-fashioned street lamps barely stabbed at the fog shrouding the buildings. Devereaux moved to the middle of the street and began to walk toward Princes Street. His mind had now surrendered to the exhaustion of his body; he felt drunk, and he knew that if they were waiting to kill him, he would die. He gave up and surrendered to any death waiting for him.

It took nearly an hour to get back to his hotel. The lift to his room seemed to take an hour as well. He pushed his legs down the corridor to his room. Opened the door. He was vaguely aware the match was still in place. He shut the door, heard the lock click.

Then the sickness rose up in him.

Going to the bathroom, he turned the light on and vomited into the toilet. When he was not sick anymore, he put his finger in his mouth and gagged and vomited again, a yellowish liquid.

Carefully, he pulled off his clothing and placed the pieces on the toilet seat. Then he climbed into the tub and turned on the ancient shower. He let the cold water run across his body until he felt it, until he began to shiver. Finally, he toweled himself, went into the darkened bedroom, and fell into the bed, pulling the covers up to his chin. He lay and shivered for a long time until his body warmth regenerated him.

Hastings' face in life appeared in the darkness. They were on that island again. Hastings' eyes stared at him; he had betrayed Hastings, turned him into a double agent, a spy for a friendly power.

Finally, Devereaux's brain could not stand it; a dizzyness seized his consciousness; he fell asleep without realizing it, because the night was full of bad dreams.

3

WASHINGTON

R Section had been formed after the Bay of Pigs fiasco in 1961.

President John F. Kennedy was furious at what he considered treacherous incompetency on the part of the Central Intelligence Agency in planning the invasion of Cuba. His fury finally found outlet among a group of former Senate colleagues who were also unhappy with the growing dominance of intelligence by the CIA.

"What's the point in having an intelligence agency that can neither gather intelligence nor undertake successful covert operations?" the young President had complained at the first no-notes meeting. The three other men who attended were: Senator John VerDer Cook of New York, Senator Thomas McGuire of Massachusetts, and retired Navy Admiral John Stapleton. All were close friends and all had expressed similar distrust of the CIA's ability to function while it continued to receive undue public attention.

"I think this country needs a good five-cent intelligence operation, one that gathers intelligence and doesn't plan wars in banana republics," Stapleton said at the meeting. (The conversations were later recorded by Stapleton in a diary. The diary turned up, somewhat mysteriously, at R Section headquarters shortly after Stapleton's death in 1971.)

At first, Kennedy suggested revamping the CIA and breaking it into two operations—one for gathering intelligence and a second for planning and executing covert and overt overseas operations.

Stapletón had argued then—and at subsequent meetings —that any attempt to break up the CIA would be disastrous to the young President.

VerDer Cook agreed, adding ominously, "Mr. President, they are very powerful people. They have really . . ." He hesitated for a moment as he tried to find the words to explain the agency's power. "They have the secret power that Hoover at the FBI seems to have publicly."

Kennedy appeared puzzled. For most of his political life, he had revered Hoover and had accepted the myth and substance of his power.

VerDer Cook stumbled on in explanation: "Mr. President. You are aware that Hoover keeps dossiers on . . . on us. On members of Congress. Undoubtedly, you've seen them."

Kennedy did not bother to deny it. He stared at the young New York senator.

"Sir, those dossiers are child's play compared to the reality of information at the CIA."

"Like the information they had before Bay of Pigs?" snapped the President.

"Sir," VerDer Cook continued doggedly, "I want to give you an example, which you may feel is farfetched. I would have too at one time. It was given to me by a man—now dead, as a matter of fact—whom I considered absolutely reliable and truthful in every way. I cannot tell you his name even now."

They waited. They were sitting in the ornamental Oval Office of the White House. The President leaned back in his maple rocker and gave VerDer Cook his full attention.

"Remember when the House of Representatives was attacked in 1954? By the Puerto Rican gunmen who had gained access to the visitors' gallery?"

The question was rhetorical. They all remembered the frightening incident.

"My source was at the Puerto Rican desk at the Agency at that time."

Kennedy leaned forward in his rocker, his hands folded across his stomach.

VerDer Cook looked down at the rug. "Mr. President, they knew."

"Knew?"

"They knew. They knew who was going to mount the attack, when it was going to be mounted, how they would get into the gallery—everything, Mr. President."

Even Stapleton was impressed. "And they told no one?" he asked.

"That decision was made by the CIA Council, sir."

McGuire interjected: "Not the top man, Jack. The Council. The old hands inside. It was never referred to the top—"

"Why, for God's sake?" asked John F. Kennedy.

VerDer Cook smiled but it was not in amusement. "To lobby, Mr. President, for expanded funds in the next Congress. To increase surveillance of Puerto Rican terrorist activities and to increase the size of their Caribbean operations—"

"They seemed to have had enough funds—" the President said dryly.

"The money, Mr. President, would be used for other things. The Council inside the Agency reasoned that overt acts against this country would only increase the need for CIA—"

"Crude empire-building," snapped the President.

"Extremely effective empire-building, Jack," said McGuire quietly. "The most sophisticated plans are not as important as the crudest plans that are successful. The Council—and the membership in it—is really like a club within a club and keeps changing as some members grow old, retire, die—the Council is really the master of the CIA."

Again, Kennedy said, "Well, they weren't so damned smart about Cuba."

"No," agreed McGuire.

VerDer Cook said, "And that's what's puzzling, sir."

There was a little silence.

"You mean," Kennedy began slowly. "You mean they might have sandbagged me?"

"It's a possibility," McGuire said.

Kennedy said, "Those men . . . On my order . . ."

Stapleton broke through the building tension: "Jack, what these men are telling you is that you have to end-run the CIA to control it. You can't fight them, and you don't have to join them. Put the fear of God and the United States back into them—"

"How?"

Stapleton smiled savagely: "Create another agency, to keep them honest."

Kennedy had not liked the idea but eventually he became convinced of the monolith of power inside the CIA and of the inability of any one man—even an extraordinary President—to control it. And that was where the first suggestion of what became R Section started. VerDer Cook and Stapleton put it down in an "Eyes Only" single-copy memo to the President.

R Section (though it was only called "the alternative agency" in that memo) would be funded out of appropriations buried in research and development within an unlikely department—like the Department of Agriculture (which eventually did become the front for R Section's funding).

Though an official secret, the agency in fact would be known to the President, obviously to the Secretary of Agriculture, and to the Senate and House committees on intelligence. And, just as naturally, it would be known to the CIA—which was part of its purpose in being. The agency would, indeed, gather information from foreign countries on their agricultural outputs and needs, but there would be other intelligence activities as well. (In fact, R Section successfully predicted the Soviet grain shortages in the early 1970s, but its report was buried in red tape—which eventually led to the infamous grain robbery by the Soviets of U.S. surpluses.)

As Stapleton put it in the memo, the new agency would be the watchdog of the watchdog, the litmus test against which to place CIA findings and evaluate their worth. In effect, the alternative agency would be a freewheeling attempt to compete with the CIA in the matter of general information-gathering—thus spurring the CIA to reveal its treasury of secrets to its own government—before the next Puerto Rican gunmen invaded the chambers of the Congress or before the next Bay of Pigs invasion was planned.

The plan was swiftly and almost secretly approved, and passed routinely through Congress in 1962. For once, the CIA was caught with its clout down; the new agency was in operation before the CIA could mount effective internal opposition to it. Like all things, the establishment of the new agency insured its eternal life in the future budgetary recommendations of Congress.

More than a decade later, in secret deliberations, another Senate committee would attempt to determine if the CIA had permitted the assassination of John F. Kennedy in deadly retribution for his act of independence from "the company."

The CIA—which gradually became known as the company and then the Langley company or Langley firm—tried three times to kill off the alternative agency. The first attempt came in 1964, when it blitzed the accidental president, Lyndon B. Johnson, with a cornucopia of information on Communist activities in Southeast Asia and suggested that it take over the intelligence-gathering function of R Section—which had acknowledged Communist activities in the same area but recommended a hands-off attitude on the part of the U.S.

Johnson had been undecided and, in keeping with his senatorial background, kept looking for a way toward compromise of the opposing recommendations. The reports from the two agencies puzzled him: CIA warned the North Vietnamese were about to take over South Vietnam, that Laos was on the verge of totally falling into a Communist dictatorship, and that mild Cambodia was also endangered. The report from R Section downplayed dangers at the moment in Cambodia and Laos and said that U.S. involvement in Vietnam was not justified by the level of guerrilla activity there.

Johnson finally chose to follow the CIA reports when the agencies could not be reconciled.

R Section went into decline and was kept alive for two years only by funding pushed through by a handful of powerful senators—including VerDer Cook—who still did not trust the CIA and the growing American involvement in Southeast Asia.

In 1966, Johnson privately rebuked the CIA for its inflammatory reports and personally breathed new life into R Section. A young R Section agent named Devereaux, working in Vietnam at the time, filed a long coded cable report accurately predicting the 1968 Tet offensive some four months before that event. Unfortunately, the President of the United States simply did not believe it, and Johnson's generals in Vietnam had downplayed the report's accuracy.

In 1969, the CIA again approached a President—this time, Richard M. Nixon—and sought to have him terminate the stubborn life of R Section. Nixon, on the advice of Henry Kissinger, then his National Security Council advisor, decided not to act.

(There is some fragmentary evidence now that certain members of that administration considered giving R Section a domestic-intelligence function but that the plan was not pursued.)

A third attempt to kill R Section was made in 1972 when the CIA informed the President, through the usual courier, that they had information of the extraordinary facts behind the simple burglary that June in the Watergate building complex.

With traditional stubbornness and anger, Nixon ignored

the company's veiled blackmail attempt. He is reported to have said, "If those goddamned spooks think they can blackmail the President of the United States, I'll show those goddamned sonsofbitches just what the power of the President means."

Eighteen months later, Nixon resigned. The company made no attempt to influence Gerald Ford, Nixon's unelected successor. They assumed—correctly—that Ford would be a mere interregnery. But the eventual Democratic president who succeeded Ford appalled the Council inside the CIA: Jimmy Carter had served in the Navy under the late Admiral John Stapleton, who had become the first head of R Section and might properly be called its father.

Carter, however, turned out to be the CIA's first ally in an attempt to kill R Section: Carter privately told senators concerned with maintaining R that he did not believe in multiple intelligence-gathering agencies and would like to see R die a quiet death. But the Senate—made feisty by Watergate—was in no mood to blindly follow the recommendations of a President. The life of R Section—maintained by slender, strong supports—seemed assured.

Why R Section?

Like most designations, it came as an afterthought.

In the original appropriation setting up the agency in the 1963 fiscal budget (submitted in 1961), the cloudy description of the "research and development" section of the Department of Agriculture was listed in Agricultude's budget in paragraph 789, subparagraph R.

So it would always be.

4

EDINBURGH

Devereaux awoke shortly after nine, his face to the window. Gray mist outside obscured the world. He knew someone was sitting by the door.

He lay, his eyes open, breathing regularly. He thought of Hastings naked, dead. Saw himself.

He could roll off the side of the bed. He rejected that. He couldn't see whoever was at the door. He had no weapon at hand. He decided there was nothing to do. He didn't move as he spoke: "I don't suppose you're the maid?"

There was a low chuckle. He heard the familiar snap of a gun clicked off safety.

"No, I'd not be being the maid, atall."

"I'm going to turn over," said Devereaux. "I'm tired of this view."

"Ah, very slowly then, lad. Believe me when I say it." Devereaux believed.

Rolling on his back, the covers bunching up behind him, he faced the man. And the barrel of a .45 caliber automatic that was pointed in his general direction.

"Did I leave my money at the bar?" Devereaux asked.

"Naw," laughed O'Neill, still wearing the same dirty-collared white shirt and tightly knotted red tie. "No, lad, ya didn't atall. Quite generous, though; did I thank ya for that last whisky? It was a pleasure to talk with you. I mean that quite sincerely, sur."

"I'm sure you do," said Devereaux.

They stared at each other silently. Slowly, the stage

Irishman receded into the depths of that dark, mottled Irish face. Now there was no smile, no frown. The voice lowered and a nasty edge came into it.

"Where's the bloody money, Yank?"

"Money?"

"Me ten thousand Yank dollars! Hastings' ten thousand! Be quick now. Up and about and give me that roll or you'll be the deadest Yank in Scotland this mornin'."

The voice had turned hard. The kidding, soft Irish lilt of last night had been swallowed up somewhere in the barrel of the .45 automatic.

"You want both shares—Hastings' and yours?"

"And what's poor bloody Hastings gonna do with his now?"

O'Neill knew Hastings was dead, then.

Devereaux smiled and slowly extended his naked legs from beneath the covers over the side of the bed. He stood up slowly.

The gunman did not speak but kept the gun barrel pointed at Devereaux's bare belly.

Devereaux bent and pushed the upper mattress aside and revealed a brown envelope. He reached for it.

For a moment, as he knew would happen, the gunman's eyes glanced at the envelope. It was tricky. They were about three feet apart, which was just enough room. Devereaux held his breath as he moved.

His left foot struck O'Neill full on the face, breaking his nose with a crunch of bone; blood welled out of both nostrils. His toe caught O'Neill's eye. At the same moment, Devereaux's right foot clattered the gun aside, though O'Neill pulled the trigger reflexively and sent a wild bullet into the plaster ceiling.

Bruce Lee would be proud, Devereaux thought as his body hit the floor. He never managed the act with grace, even in training. He was only effective.

In a second, he had rolled to his feet and kicked O'Neill —still sitting in the chair—hard in the lower abdomen. O'Neill vomited on the spot and continued to fall forward in the chair. Devereaux pulled O'Neill out of the chair by his hair and kicked him in the left kidney, sending him sprawling to the floor.

Picking up the brutish gun, Devereaux waited for O'Neill to stop being sick on the rug.

Devereaux was out of breath. "Not bad for an old man," he said aloud.

O'Neill moaned again and vomited at the sight of his own blood.

"Yer broke me fuckin' nose," he said in a muffled voice.

Devereaux smiled.

"Me fuckin' face is caved in," O'Neill said.

"You ought to see yourself," Devereaux agreed.

O'Neill staggered to the bathroom, blood on his white shirt and jacket. He managed to stop the bleeding in a few minutes by placing a cold, wet towel on his mangled face. Then he sat on the edge of the bed, holding the towel.

"Why'd ya do that, you bloody murderin' bastard?" O'Neill said. The voice was self-pitying.

Devereaux sat in the chair O'Neill had vacated. He had pulled on his tan trousers. He held the .45.

Devereaux waited.

"Yer gonna kill me," said O'Neill. "Kill me just like ya killed that poor old pouf."

"Who did I kill?"

"Hastings. Hastings, ya bloody-minded man, ya."

Devereaux decided he did not need the gun. He emptied the clip and threw it on the floor, but placed the gun on the table.

"Tell me about Hastings," Devereaux said quietly.

"Ya know about him, ya bloody bastard," whimpered O'Neill. "I saw ya kill him."

"Tell me about Hastings," Devereaux said again.

"I followed ya from the pub. Ya went to his room. When ya came out, I went up meself and saw him. Ya cut his privates off—God rest his soul, the poor old bastard."

"What are you to Hastings?"

The same voice, quiet and even, delivering the words with menace.

"Ya know all about me—"

"Who are you?"

"O'Neill, I tole ya last night—"

"Who are you?"

"Don't keep askin' me the same bloody question—"

"Who are you?"

"I'm a commercial traveler. Out of Belfast—"

"What are you to Hastings?"

The pain, the dull voice, frightened O'Neill. It was maddening, it was like hell. O'Neill felt sick again at the smell of his own vomit on the rug. He wanted to get up, to flee, but he knew his legs would not work. The Yank sat still on the chair with bare feet and bare chest and stared at him. Without pity or a sign of humanity in him.

"I knew . . . Hastings . . . fer years and years—"

He looked at Devereaux's face.

"Y'see, I dealt with him when he was workin' fer the English, y'see."

O'Neill blushed. Sweat beaded on his forehead again.

"Y'might say I trade in a little information from time to time."

Devereaux waited.

"Well, y'see, after he retired, I just kept on tradin' with him. Nothing very serious atall. I'm a commercial traveler."

O'Neill could not gauge the other man's face anymore: A winter face with no mercy.

He suddenly dashed into truth the way a swimmer runs into a cold mountain lake: "I had something for Hastings. It was better than anything I had before. And he was goin' to give it to the Yanks and he was goin' ta get me ten thousand dollars fer it."

Devereaux got up and opened the drawer of the dresser. He took out a dark blue shirt and put it on. Slowly, he buttoned the front as he waited for O'Neill to go on.

"I went to the Crescent and Lion last night to find that English whore. I figures you and him made a deal without O'Neill, is what I thought—"

"How did you know about the meet—"

"He tole me, didn't he? How the hell d'ya think I knew about it, man?"

"And you knew it was me."

"And weren't you the only bloody Yank in the place? My God, O'Neill is not a bloody fool."

"And why did I kill Hastings?"

O'Neill shivered. "How the hell should I know that?"

"Why did I kill Hastings?"

O'Neill considered it. "Ya didn't need him and ya didn't need t' pay him the money—"

"Did he know everything you knew?"

"Of course he—"

"So I didn't need you—"

O'Neill fell silent.

"Or need you now."

O'Neill moaned like a lost soul. "I don't want the money—"

"I would not need you now, now that I know—"

"Oh, Mother of God—"

Devereaux buttoned his cuffs while he watched O'Neill. He felt angry, with himself and with the Irishman. First, he had been foolish enough not to set the deadlock last night. And before that, he had permitted an idiot like O'Neill to follow him. He had been drunk and careless and he deserved O'Neill this morning. And O'Neill deserved his fear now because he had wanted to kill Devereaux and might have.

"Get some towels out of the bathroom and clean this mess up," he said.

"What?"

"Clean this mess up. We've got a lot to talk about this morning. I'm going to order tea."

O'Neill looked at him. "Tea? Now what would you be after meanin'?"

Devereaux went to the telephone on the nightstand. "You came here for your ten thousand dollars this morning."

O'Neill nodded.

"Perhaps you'll get it. After we talk. And I find out the worth of what you have and what you were willing to tell Hastings. Find out what was good enough to get Hastings killed."

O'Neill felt reprieved. "Well, now," he said. His face was flushed and streaked with dried blood. He felt pain over the mask of his features. None of that mattered. He tried out a jaunty voice, the voice of a man of the world: "Well, you're a man to talk with, I can see, sur."

The talk proved considerably more painful than O'Neill expected.

Devereaux probed like a dentist without a care for pain. He drilled around O'Neill's information and then went deep into the past until he struck the nerve. What had been his relationship with Hastings? (R Section had scant knowledge of Hastings' informal network of contacts.) Why had O'Neill agreed to run for British Intelligence in the first place; was it when Hastings was still with them? Why had he stayed with Hastings after his retirement? Was O'Neill still feeding the Brits?

O'Neill sat like a schoolboy in a chair by the misty window and looked down at the railway lines streaming out of Edinburgh. He wished for home.

O'Neill was a traveling salesman for a major British shoe manufacturer that had extensive factories and offices in Northern Ireland and in the Republic to the south. Because he was Catholic, his upward progress in the English-owned firm had been slow—especially in the Belfast offices—and he could reasonably aspire to no greater job than he now held and had held for the past fifteen years.

Which had fed a spark of bitterness in him against the Prods and the English who ruled Northern Ireland. And which, for O'Neill as others, had found outlet finally in the civil rights demonstrations begun in 1969 with Bernadette Devlin.

O'Neill had merely been a spectator at first in the civil rights movement (as it was then called). He attended a few of the peaceful rallies but did not take part in the protest marches in Londonderry and Belfast which so excited the Protestant minority. The tactics used by the civil rights people were borrowed from the black civil rights movement of the 1960s in America. Like that black movement, it finally fell victim to despair. Doubting the efficacy of peaceful protest to win rights, it turned to violence.

Then—as the provisional Irish Republican Army gradually replaced the civil-rightists as the rallying point for the unrest in the Catholic majority in the North—O'Neill felt himself stirred to something like patriotism. Or as much patriotism as a man with a family of nine children could afford.

O'Neill's uncles from Mayo had fought in the "troubles" against the English in the teens and twenties. That fact dwelt heavily inside the little salesman.

That was the most difficult part to explain to the American who sat across from him and did not speak. "Love of one's country—" O'Neill had begun at one point, but the gray eyes that stared at him did not seem to comprehend the words, let alone the motive.

"You don't know what it is to be an Irishman and a Catholic in the North," O'Neill had said finally.

"Nor what it is to be black in America or a Jew in Russia or a stateless Palestinian," Devereaux had added. And O'Neill had shrugged because there were some things beyond explaining.

O'Neill had volunteered his services to the IRA shortly

after the British moved to illegally intern thousands of suspected IRA sympathizers in August, 1971. O'Neill himself had been arrested and held briefly and then released without apology. The incident had angered and humiliated him.

None of this greatly interested Devereaux, but he probed carefully at the edges of the life story with the methodical interrogation rhythm he had used debriefing Russian defectors.

The IRA had decided to use O'Neill as a courier because of the large territory he covered for the shoe firm in both the Republic to the south and to western Scotland. He was trusted and considered an ideal man to move sums of money from the South to the North (much American money was being laundered through southern Irish banks) and to move certain "packages" from the Belfast "factory" to Scottish postal addresses where they would be sent to targets in England.

All of which had led to O'Neill's "problem"—as he put it.

One bright August morning in 1972, two CID men from Scotland Yard seized O'Neill as he debarked from the British Rail ferry at Stranraer in Scotland. He was carrying fourteen letter bombs in his luggage, all addressed to various London banking officials and all to be mailed from a box in Glasgow central station.

O'Neill hesitated as he told this part of the story. But the probing never let up; gently, insistently, Devereaux pried it out of him.

First they took him to Manchester, and then moved him to a jail in Birmingham for reasons he never fathomed. And they beat him. With rubber truncheons. All afternoon. All night. He was forced to stand for hours. They took all his clothing and made him stand naked. They beat his kidneys until burning urine dribbled down his naked leg. They would leave him for a time and then they would return and beat him again.

In the morning—the second morning—they told him

he would probably spend the rest of his life in Her Majesty's prisons.

In the afternoon, he received his first visit from Hastings. They had kept O'Neill—naked and shivering—in a cell without windows. He had wrapped his stinking body in a rough blanket. That is the way Hastings first saw him. The light from the corridor beyond the cell blinded O'Neill. He did not know if it was day or night.

Hastings was civilized and O'Neill wept when the man offered him tea and biscuits.

They sat in O'Neill's cell and talked for a long time. About Northern Ireland and the IRA and the problems of being the Catholic majority in the North ruled by a Protestant minority.

Hastings was so sympathetic.

Said he was a Catholic as well and that his family had been persecuted in the days of the first Elizabeth when it was a capital crime to hear Mass or hide a priest. Yes, Hastings sympathized entirely.

Although, this business with letter bombs. Well, old darling, this was really shameful. Didn't he think so?

Hastings went away that afternoon and, as promised, O'Neill was given his clothing back and transferred to a cell with a window that allowed O'Neill to tell it was night.

They didn't beat him anymore.

On the third morning, Hastings returned and they had breakfast together. At that point, O'Neill had turned to the Englishman almost as a friend and asked him to get word to his wife at least about his situation. Hastings said he would.

And again, Hastings expressed sympathy for O'Neill's plight. But added that O'Neill had gotten his quite commendable sense of Irish patriotism all mixed up with service to these criminals now operating under the disgraced banner of the IRA. "I mean, the "troubles" of the twenties were one thing, but this. Come on, ducks, it isn't patriotic to go blowing off the hands of mail clerks, is it?"

Another day passed. No sounds from beyond the cell. O'Neill sat alone. Hastings' words worked on him. O'Neill prayed to God and promised to atone for his sins.

The next morning, they got down to business. It was quite simple, really. Hastings explained it gently: O'Neill would now work for British Intelligence.

"Now, now, old luv, don't become agitated. There's really nothing for it. On the one hand, we have these letter bombs and a certain sentence of at least thirty years in Wormwood Scrubs or some other perfectly awful hole and hardly a chance of ever seeing kith and kin again— and that means those nine lovely children, darling—or, really a quite safe and painless service for Her Majesty's government which would put a couple of extra quid in the old pay packet—certainly could use that, I'll be bound, ducks—and a chance to save poor, dear Belfast from the ravages of both the IRA and all those soldiers. I mean, it's hardly a contest, is it?"

Devereaux rose and went to the window to stare at the castle in the fog while O'Neill told his story of becoming an informer for the English. Devereaux could hear something like a sob in the Irishman's voice. He did not look at O'Neill again until he was through.

In the end, commercial traveler O'Neill resumed his journeys and turned up at home quite recovered from the rubber-truncheon beatings—except for the pain of urinating—and no one was the wiser. And just as routinely, the *Daily Mirror* told a splashy story about a mail clerk in Glasgow who discovered a cache of letter bombs in a London-bound bag and heroically flung the lot of them in the Clyde river.

"So, you see, sur, they had me and turned me into an informer," O'Neill said at last. "I'm not proud of it. I will wear it to me grave. But what was I to do, sur?"

Devereaux had cleaned the vomit from the rug himself, compulsively smoothed the bedclothes, and examined the bullet hole in the plaster ceiling, while he listened. But he did not know what to say to the sad little Irishman with nine kids caught up in a game he could not play well.

He prodded O'Neill with another question, and O'Neill —almost gladly—went on: Hastings had fiddled O'Neill's papers in British Intelligence before he retired and O'Neill the informer had become an unperson in London. But not to Hastings, who still held those papers over O'Neill. Hastings and O'Neill transferred their total allegiance to the new masters in Washington and O'Neill still felt the chains around him.

"So you looked in his room—"

"After you. After you—after he died. I saw his body—"

"After?"

"I couldn't kill a man—"

"Only by letter. Only by bomb," said Devereaux.

O'Neill turned his eyes down. "I'm a coward then as well as a traitor."

"Yes," said Devereaux. His voice was too hard, too without pity.

"O my God," O'Neill began, and stopped.

"You looked around the room, didn't you?" said Devereaux gently.

"Yes," whispered O'Neill.

"For the papers about you," he said.

"Yes."

"Stepped around the body?"

"Yes."

"And you didn't find them."

O'Neill looked up. "You have them—"

Devereaux shook his head. "No one has them, I'll bet. I doubt very much that dossier still exists."

"Do you now, sur?"

"It seems unlikely Hastings would keep it around, and it would be doubly dangerous—for him—if it were discovered. No, I think our departed brother undoubtedly destroyed the fact of O'Neill's existence when he retired from Intelligence."

"Do you now, sur?" Skepticism mixed with something like hope in his voice. A gentleness began to spread over the flat, broken Irish face.

Devereaux went to the window and looked out at the sun trying to burn through the fog. "Which brings us now to our business, O'Neill."

But O'Neill saw himself free now. "If it's the same to you, and I appreciate your kindness, sur, I'd as soon be quit of the business if you think old Hastings has really gotten rid of that dossier—"

"No," said Devereaux. "You're quit of it when I release you. Sit down."

O'Neill hesitated and then sat down again. The gloom replaced whatever hope had infected his features a moment before.

Devereaux thought the moment was right. He opened the brown envelope and took out ten one-thousand-dollar bills. He placed them on the sill of the window by O'Neill's chair.

"Mother of God," said O'Neill reverently.

"Indeed," said Devereaux.

O'Neill simply stared and calculated. The money represented three years' pay.

Finally: "Well, sur. That's impressive, sur, it certainly is." Somehow, the chains seemed lighter. "Impressive but not as impressive as what I have to tell you, lad. Not half as much." How lightly they could be worn. "Me, the O'Neill himself, has more than enough information— and you've not heard the like of it—"

Devereaux watched him. He was not prepared to be surprised—he had heard the like of many things. He was surprised at his own feeling of fascinated revulsion at the look in O'Neill's blue eyes as the Irishman watched the money laying on the sill.

"Well," he began. "The Byes." Byes meaning boys, and the Boys meaning the provisional IRA. "The Byes are puttin' together a plan. Didja never hear of Lord Slough?"

Devereaux nodded. He had heard.

O'Neill ignored the nod: "The cousin of the Queen, he is. And the richest man in England."

Devereaux tensed.

"Y'heard of him, all right," said O'Neill. "The bloody world drinks his beer or drives his motorcars or reads his bloody papers or—" O'Neill's eloquence left him; it was too unfair that this one Englishman should own the whole world when O'Neill had scarcely a piece of it.

"And—" said Devereaux. But he knew what O'Neill would say.

"Well, sur, the 'and' is that the Byes are gonna get him. Get the bloody great English Lord Slough, the cousin of the Queen of England—"

"Kidnap—" said Devereaux.

O'Neill's eyes glittered with greed and mirth: "Oh, no, sur, not at all. Not at all. They're gonna make him dance. They're gonna get him fer good. They'll make him dance with their guns, and when they're through, Lord Slough will dance no more." His voice carried an edge of patriotic glee—"Dance him, sur; they're gonna kill the bloody man."

Devereaux still stared, but O'Neill did not see him. His voice continued to rise:

"How's that for ten thousand bloody dollars' worth of information? How's that, me lad? How's that bloody suit you, that the Byes are going inter England itself and kill the richest man in the land and a member of the royal bloody family!"

Devereaux did not arrive at Blake House until shortly after eight P.M., when the hum and bustle of west London's traffic had finally settled down for the November night.

There had been matters to settle in Edinburgh and questions to puzzle out.

First, there was the matter of O'Neill's information, which never went far beyond the bare outlines.

O'Neill had explained that he was not an insider. The talk of the coming assassination had been garnered in bits and pieces from a half-dozen sources. No one, he said, knew the exact membership of the gang who would effect the assassination, though a "Cap'n Donovan" was supposed to be involved.

Lord Slough would be killed sometime before Boxing Day, the day after Christmas. That was for certain. Devereaux had probed at this date but O'Neill was adamant. That was the word in every quarter but nothing more specific.

Why? Where?

Finally, O'Neill's confidence in his own information and its importance sagged under the weight of Devereaux's questions. There were too many things the Irishman didn't know.

Too many things for it to be a lie.

The questioning had continued without interruption into the pale Scottish afternoon: Who else was part of Hastings' information network? As Devereaux expected, O'Neill knew little. It had been a stab. Hastings had always submitted four names—code names—all with routine retainers and expenses, all paid for their scraps of information. But did they really exist or had Hastings fiddled with the facts again and created a bogus network to pad out his own salary?

Were some of the names real?

And why did the Boys want to kill the richest man in England? What would it accomplish? What did any of the chaotic acts of mad bombing of innocent people in Dublin and Belfast and London accomplish?

At last, O'Neill was allowed to leave, with a single thousand-dollar bill, and four more torn in less than half. They would be mated, Devereaux said, when O'Neill had the answer to his questions. O'Neill would be contacted by someone from the Section in Belfast.

By two P.M., Devereaux felt drained and confused. O'Neill was a greedy fool and his information—while valuable to an extent—was not worth Hastings' proposed $100,000 exit money. Hastings was an experienced hand —what had he gathered beyond what O'Neill knew? And why was O'Neill an important part of the total information that died with Hastings?

Devereaux tried to sort through his thoughts as he packed and left a five-pound note on the bed for the chambermaid who would inherit a monumental cleaning task. He checked out and had a drink in the hotel bar because the pubs were all closed for the afternoon.

In the bar, Devereaux noticed a copy of the *Daily Mirror* with the screaming headline that North Sea oil would make Britain a sheikdom. It read: *Suddenly, We're Very Sheik!*

Sitting at the bar, he sipped his vodka as if it were medicine. It was too warm and the bartender gave ice grudgingly. Scotland was a country of cold rooms and warm drinks.

Devereaux finally realized he did not want this job and that had led to his confusion. His present laziness was induced by his hatred of the assignment: He wanted to clean it up quickly, to believe that Hastings had flim-flammed the Section, that O'Neill's vague information could be simply passed on to British Intelligence and forgotten.

But Hastings was dead.

His killer—very professionally—had garroted him. And then arranged his body to make it look like a fag killing. Hastings was a notorious homosexual and, Devereaux suspected, well known even in Edinburgh for his sexual preferences. Thus the severed penis.

Why kill him for nothing? Had the IRA done it?

Devereaux ordered a second vodka. The bartender did not add ice. Devereaux requested ice. The bartender placed the plastic ice bucket on the bar in front of him. Devereaux reached for a handful of cubes and let them fall into his glass with a splash. The bartender shuddered at such visible waste. Americans!

The IRA would not have killed Hastings that way. And certainly not to suppress something that even O'Neill knew about. Devereaux could not believe that British Intelligence was not onto such a simple plan. On the other hand, they might not be—but it was still not that important. Except to Lord Slough.

Parts.

Devereaux knew he had been keeping that word out of his thoughts so that he might not include it this evening when he talked to Hanley and disposed of the assignment. But there it was.

Parts.

Hanley had mentioned parts. Parts of information. So much for one part and so much for another. He had given Devereaux the money for both parts.

Hastings had mentioned parts.

There was more to this than the planned assassination of Lord Slough. But Slough must have been a key to understanding the rest of the information.

At last, resigned to the truth he had tried to hide from in his own thoughts, Devereaux took a taxi to the airport.

There were the usual delays at both ends, which was why he did not arrive at the safe house and the R Section London quarters until midway through the English November evening.

Blake House was off Hyde Park in what had been the edge of an earlier, quainter London city. The house was the end one in an attached housing block that wound down off the Marylebone Road. All the houses had been built in 1801, and William Blake, briefly, had lived there in later life, conferring his name upon one house.

After insistently ringing the bell for several minutes, Devereaux was finally admitted. A surly housekeeper with an unpleasant midwestern accent let him into a bare foyer, where he was told to wait. He stood in the overstuffed warmth and waifed while, he knew, someone watched him.

After another ten minutes, the door opened and he

was taken silently into a second room and provided with a chair. He was asked to wait again. This time, he sat for a half hour until suddenly the door burst open and a cheerful young man with red hair and—yes, by God—freckles strode in to greet him.

"Sir, this is a real honor, sir," the younger man said in an accent that sounded insincere because of its apparent sincerity.

Devereaux was unused to handshaking but he let the young man do it.

"Sorry to keep you waiting, sir. Martha had to find me, you know. Slipped down to the park for a walk and then to the pub for an . . . evening drink. Like this kind of weather. This is my first winter in London and I want to savor it all. . . ." He went on like that for some minutes as he led Devereaux into the library and poured him a liberal Scotch on the rocks. Devereaux noticed the young man was also liberal with his own drink—without the ice.

His name was Green. Not fancy Greene with an E, he bubbled on, just plain Columbus, Ohio, Green, and so he was Devereaux, something of a legend to the younger men, predicted the Tet offensive, a real Asia hand, a bit out of your element here, what brings you to London? No, we never received a message from Hanley—

On and on.

Devereaux found Green's rattling on did not distract him as he sat in the leather wing chair and mentally composed his message to the Section. It would be difficult to explain to Hanley, especially in code. He decided it would be a very long message. Glancing at his watch, he saw it tick toward 9:15 P.M., 4:15 P.M. in Washington. He would have to catch Hanley before he left for the day. Devereaux asked for the coded transmitter.

"Oh, sir," said plain Green brightly. "We don't have one now. Have one of the new double scramblers—scrambles your voice going out twice through two voice baffles and then reverses the process at the other end. Much easier than coding and those tedious signals—"

"What do you do when you want to commit something to paper—"

"Oh, sir," laŭghed Green, a member of the nonwriting generation. "Rarely, rarely. And then we use the machine at the embassy, on Grosvenŏr Square."

Devereaux was annoyed with Green's faint trace of English accent. Or perhaps with Green.

"The embassy's handy—" Green continued.

For you, thought Devereaux—and for the CIA, which undoubtedly read every message transmitted there.

"Right this way, sir," said Green. He led him to a small, obviously, soundproof room where a simple telephone rested conspiciously on a box with many dials.

Devereaux did not like it but there was no choice. It was already November 14—little more than a month until Boxing Day.

Surprisingly, the long-distance connection with Hanley came off smoothly. Allowing for the distance the voices had to travel and the echo that always occurred—and allowing for the disagreeably tinny voice alteration done by the baffles—it was satisfactory.

For five minutes, Devereaux filled Hanley in quietly, step by step, from the meeting with Hastings in the buffet through the first meeting with O'Neill and the discovery of Hastings' body in his room. At least Hanley knew how to listen and absorb information. Devereaux could imagine Hanley sitting at the cold steel desk in the unnaturally cold office (the temperature never rose above sixty degrees on Hanley's special order) tucked in a dead-end corridor in the Department of Agriculture building. He would not be taking notes but listening with his eyes closed and his free hand drumming quietly on the glass top of the steel desk. Hanley remembered everything and was not loath to tell you so.

Finally, Devereaux did not speak anymore. He waited and pressed the receiver to his ear and listened to the pop and crackle of the cable buried beneath the cold North Atlantic.

"What are your recommendations," Hanley asked at last.

"My first recommendation is that I return. I have no expertise here. My assignment was contact with Hastings. That's completed."

"Hardly satisfactorily," said Hanley. Whatever sarcasm he hoped to transmit in his tone did not communicate itself. Except that Devereaux knew the sound of Hanley's normal voice.

"My second recommendation is that Hastings' death implies his information has already been compromised. By the IRA? Possibly. But certainly by someone. And I suggest we turn what we know over to British Intelligence."

Hanley waited. He knew Devereaux's computer of logic was undergoing a systems search.

"British Intelligence," Devereaux continued, as though talking to himself.

"They may have known that he was our agent now and killed him. They may have known parts of Hastings' information—parts we do not know—and sought to get the rest from him. The IRA or British Intelligence— those are the two possibilities I can think of now. The death was obviously a professional job despite the clumsy attempt to make it seem a homosexual killing—"

Devereaux paused. Saw Hastings' mutilated body again. Wiped away the image of blood and death.

"What about the Russians—"

"What about them? This seems purely an internal British matter and I suggest we keep it that way. I suggest we turn over our information to British Intelligence to show that we're good boys, and then we quietly keep a tab on O'Neill and share information with CIA—in case they have any interest in Irish terrorists these days."

There was silence. Hanley broke it.

"That seems unacceptable."

"The Section is thin enough without getting involved in the Irish situation," said Devereaux. "Ireland is England's problem, not ours. I see no interest in the situation from our end."

"Lord Slough is an important man—"

"So are half the Italian politicians shot or kidnapped daily by the Red Brigade. So was that Egyptian journalist assassinated by the Palestinians on Cyprus. But—"

"I admit that the irrational actions of terrorists is a fact of life," Hanley said. "And I admit that it would seem we have little interest in the events in Northern Ireland. But I keep thinking about Hastings. Why the secrecy? Why did he think he could flummox us out of a hundred and thirty thousand dollars? O'Neill's information is not worth it."

Hanley had put his finger on the same piece of the puzzle that disturbed Devereaux.

Hanley went on: "We have been trying for years— with little success—to establish our own rapprochement with British Intelligence, separate from the Langley firm. This might be an opportunity, if we could present them with a fuller picture. Perhaps they know of the plot on Lord Slough's life, perhaps not; but if we could give them the who, what, where, when, why, and how of it— well, perhaps we would have a wedge with them. Which would give us a wedge back home—"

"The CIA owns British Intelligence—"

"There are signs of strain in their relationship of late. And with the North Sea oil business, Britain is not as weak as she looks today. In ten years, she will be a major oil-exporting country. They know that over there. And we're just beginning to realize what that means."

"Perhaps we don't have time," said Devereaux. He did not want this assignment. He wanted a winter night on the mountain in Virginia, sitting in the dark front room, the fireplace making ghosts for him to stare at for hours. He wanted warmth. "O'Neill said the Boys will act between November fifteenth and Boxing Day, December twenty-sixth. It's the fourteenth."

"I will have to talk to the Chief about this."

Devereaux said, "And what if Lord Slough is shot in the meantime?"

"That would be a great loss," Hanley said in a voice that did not express sympathy.

"Yes," Devereaux said.

"This may take a little time. The Chief was in San Francisco this morning. He's due back later this evening. It may not be until midnight—"

"Five A.M., here," said Devereaux.

"Yes. Sorry. Did you have a good trip?"

"Awful."

"Sorry." Politely. "Well, I think we must have twelve hours at least. I'll get through tomorrow morning. Let's say seven A.M. here and noon there. You may sleep late."

There was no way of not delaying, Devereaux knew. Still, he was restless and he wanted to be out of this country and this sordid business with the Boys and their fucking Lord Slough. He hated the victim in that moment. Plain Green was right. This was not his milieu. He was too far afield. Since Asia had closed down to the extent of becoming a series of China-watching or Cambodia-watching listening posts, Devereaux had felt cut adrift. Asia had been his world and he had traveled in it with the familiarity of a realtor in a small town. He knew the properties. It had been his real country, his people, his smells. He had been alive then in the red-sun mornings and the hut-level villages living precariously for a thousand years in a valley or on the side of a hill. . . .

Something like homesickness threatened to overwhelm him. But where was his home? Letting his face fall slack and his eyes dull, he replaced the telephone receiver. Asia faded like a watercolor painting left in the rain.

Enough.

Getting up, Devereaux stretched and walked out of the room. Plain Green had a fresh drink in his hand when Devereaux returned to the library. There were not enough books to cover the shelves. Devereaux noticed the boy's hands were not steady. He placed that information somewhere in his memory bank.

"Well, everything all right then?"

"Yes," said Devereaux. "I'll be back in tomorrow. At noon. For another message. Thanks for the drink."

"Oh, any time. You're welcome to stay——" Devereaux's single leather bag had been brought into the library.

"No, thanks. I'm a little restless. I prefer a hotel tonight. Thanks anyway."

Green nodded, smiled idiotically. Who was he? Why had they chosen such an unprofessional youth to be a station keeper? And in London?

Devereaux checked in at the Inn on the Park and showered and shaved and still felt restless. Finally he went down to the lounge and permitted an underdressed waitress to offer him a vodka martini with ice. It was after eleven and the pubs were closed, but the hotel bar was still all hearty good-fellowship in the clubby, insincere—and yet warm—way of the English when they meet as strangers. Devereaux sat at a ridiculously small table and sipped a cold drink. They catered to Americans here. He looked around at the fake English-pub furnishing, designed no doubt by a California consulting firm and made in plastic Japan. Just the thing to make Yanks feel at home. After a second drink, the murmur of voices faded and allowed him a sort of reverie. He let his guard down. He began to think about Asia again—

"Mr. Devereaux? I'm sorry. But aren't you Professor Devereaux?"

For a moment, he thought his silent travelogue had taken on a soundtrack. It could have belonged to that time when he *was* Professor Devereaux and Asia was a new present to him.

He had, of course, noticed her when she came into the lounge, but she had drifted out of his field of vision. Now the question, uttered softly with a shy confidence, brought her back to him. He turned off the lights of Asia and looked at her. Still, he could not remember her except from the moment before.

"Yes? I'm sorry——"

"My God," she laughed, shaking her head and letting her brown hair beat softly around her pale, oval, open face. She laughed as though she had rehearsed it, which was all right. "I don't expect you to remember me but it's—it's just such a coincidence that I had to say hello after all these years."

He tried out a smile and decided it would not do, so he tuned it up several degrees. That was better—she was responding. Her own smile did not need fine tuning. It was just right. He encouraged her to speak with a little professorial nod of his head that he thought he had forgotten.

"You wouldn't remember me. It was fifteen years ago at least. You were teaching a course in Chinese history at Columbia and you had just come back from the Peace Corps—Asia—and you were so . . . enthusiastic. And, well, I kept asking you about the experience, I was just eighteen and you were——"

She hesitated. Was what?

So she was part of the travelogue in his mind, he thought. No one had mentioned the Peace Corps to him since—since then, he supposed. That was his last full year of a kind of idealism; although, as these things happen, it did not go away all at once. Like a once-prized ceramic cup, whatever had been inside him merely got chipped a little more each year, and one day it was cracked so badly it was thrown away because no one cared anymore.

"Elizabeth?" She said her name the way a television game show contestant might offer a guess.

"Of course," he lied. "Elizabeth. My God,"—he did not attempt to laugh but managed a smile—"fifteen years later and we're here."

She looked delighted and the delight seemed genuine

enough to be out of place in the atmosphere of the plastic pub.

"So what did I do?" she went on. "Joined the Peace Corps and they sent me to Addis Ababa for two years—which is not Asia. Not what you said it would be." She smiled. "You were so enthusiastic. But you know something? You were right. It was the best thing I ever did for myself."

The Peace Corps. Those old ideals that had seemed so fresh and sophisticated to him. Before Vietnam and Watergate. He called up the Peace Corps in the theater of his mind and saw himself, the younger Devereaux, squatting in the rain, new Asia hand, extending himself for the poor and wretched in black pajamas. But the Peace Corps, unlike the rest of the travelogue, did not move him. He had edited out that segment for too long.

"What are you doing in London?" he asked politely.

"Working," she said. She seemed to guard her answer.

"Oh," he said.

"You?"

"Working," he said in the same tones.

She smiled, blushed. He wondered why embarrassment was a charming trait in women and a foolish one in men.

"There's no secret about it," she said. "It's just that I hate to bore anyone." She paused, but he said nothing, "I'm actually here for a month working with my people. You've heard of Free The Prisoners?"

"Is that something like Amnesty International?"

"Not the same thing," she said. She seemed to have a private energy source barely hidden behind her blue eyes. He could feel the pleasurable tension in her. "Amnesty does marvelous work—bringing these things to the attention of the world. Free The Prisoners is more of an activist group."

She hesitated. He noticed but pretended not to.

"I mean, there are just tens of thousands—more than a million in total that we are aware of—men and women languishing in rotten jails all over the world, their crime being dissent or political differences. We don't lobby for their release. We do something about it." She said the last flatly and it carried an edge of menace.

"Such as," he said. Still politely.

She was the eager student who stayed after class to talk about world problems and was half in love with the professor. Who joined the Peace Corps. Who protested the war in the streets. Who never grew old. Who never chipped the cup.

She went on: "You'd think of England—the font of democratic ideals—"

The professor in him corrected: Ancient Athens. He did not say it.

"It's been six years since internment and they still have prisoners who have never been tried or even formally charged—"

He frowned. Ireland again. He did not want to get into this or discuss August, 1971, when British soldiers had gone from house to house and arrested hundreds of suspected IRA sympathizers in Belfast and Londonderry. The British had locked the men on boats in Belfast's harbor and kept them incommunicado, without charge, while they tortured them. He knew about it as a professional in the world of information; knew about it the way someone knows about his field but does not concern himself with every part of it.

He noticed her hands. She gestured like a man.

"You must know about the efforts to free those men—"

Protests. Rallies. He had put them out of his mind a long time ago. He was bored by it all, by rhetoric and empty passion.

"Our people are in negotiation right now with the justice ministry and the Northern Ireland office to do just that. To get the remaining interred freed. And—I can tell you. We are making real progress. Not the kind you hold press conferences about but real progress. The hell with publicity anyway."

Did she believe that? He saw a clerk in the justice ministry, polite, offering tea, listening, making notes, nodding his head. Sympathetic to all they said, like Hastings to O'Neill. Did she believe it meant anything to the British government now?

But she was so intense. There was something a bit frightening about her intensity, which he found attractive. He suddenly wished she would stop talking and just sit with him in the darkness looking at the old travelogue about Asia and about being young.

He did not remember her, but she remembered him. It was almost enough, almost a perfect imitation of friendship. As close as Devereaux had gotten in years.

"I'm happy to see a friend, Elizabeth," he said at last, pronouncing her name formally.

"And what are you doing?" she demanded gaily.

"On my way through. To home. From Thailand," he lied. "Doing stories for Central Press Service."

"Oh, God," she said and did not laugh now. "It is good to see you." The warmth of her words would have alarmed Devereaux in New York. But there was so little warmth in England, so little comfort. "I mean, you were the reason I got into all this, do you know that? You're . . . you were my beginning—"

She impulsively grabbed his hand. And held it.

"I was so vapid, so drifting. I can't believe myself then."

He was glad she held his hand.

"For a long time after Kennedy was killed, I felt it was all uphill—but there were so many just like us who never gave up—"

Not us. My cup is cracked; I've thrown it away.

"All those kids in Chicago—"

He felt uncomfortable. He wanted Elizabeth to hold his hand and to share her warmth and energy. And yet he felt the little corners of coldness in himself react against her, against what she said. He would have liked to tell her what he felt about "those kids" in Chicago in 1968 and 1969 and their rhetoric and their minor rebellion which masked their own private fears. Tell her about the faces in Asia then, while caviar radicalism reigned in Chicago. About blacks and hillbilly whites he saw, gaunt and tired and just as frightened, but without the wealth or leisure to understand that it was not their war either—

"Well, I just never gave up, you know? That's why I'm here now. Look at me—past thirty and still a radical, still a bomb-thrower." She laughed at herself.

"Good," he said. Maybe that was wrong. Her smile faded. He found it difficult to small-talk anymore. With anyone. He had forgotten the little bridges of words that did not lead anywhere.

"I didn't know you were with the media—"

He hated that word.

"When you left Columbia to take a government job, I remember I wanted to thank you. After I came back I was in New York, but you were gone. I couldn't believe it—you were a great teacher. Central Press?"

Never heard of it, I'll bet, said Devereaux to himself.

"Tell me, what do you do? What did you do? For the government?"

Did. Do. Became a listener, Elizabeth. A professional betrayer of secrets of others. A friend, an enemy. A spy, Elizabeth. I killed nine men and arranged the deaths of others, but that was strictly professional. Betrayed a fat Englishman on a Greek island. Professionally. He was killed, though, much later.

He blinked then and warned the self-pity away; he told the coldness in him to stay in its dark corner. He would not give in to these things, even if he was tired and alone.

"Dull things," he said at last. He thought his voice sounded a little stagy. "But an opportunity came from the State Department to study Cambodian culture and I took it. When the war came along—I found myself stringing for a few magazines and then I fell into this Central Press Service. There's not much to say—I've been dabbling for a long time, treating everything like a hobby, and then one day I looked up and found myself a forty-three-year-old dabbler—"

No, that was not what he should have said; but she didn't seem to hear him.

"And you still love Asia so much," she said. She invested the remark with such enthusiasm that he could not hide it in himself; he let her see, by a gesture, by the color of his eyes, that it was true: He did still love the East of the world.

"I wish I had something like that," she said. He looked up, surprised by her tone; the remark, so banal, sounded true.

Or was he only imagining it for the sake of his own self-pity?

"Staying here?" He hated fake-casual the way he asked it.

She pretended not to notice. "Not here." She smiled. "Too grand for our organization—we have a bank of rooms at the Shelbourne Arms. It's a decent enough place. I suppose you're staying here—"

"It was the first place—" He realized that he was apologizing. She smiled.

"Would you like a drink?"

"No," she said. "I'm too tired." Her signal to leave? But she did not leave, did not release his hand. Another signal. He was flattered by her attention. He realized again he was not handling it very well. So he did not say anything further.

She looked at him.

Speak. "Elizabeth, I would like to say all the right things," he said. "But it's impossible because I don't seem to have the gift for small talk anymore. Or seduction." He tried a smile at the last.

The smile seemed to give a lie to the rest of his face, to the cold eyes and the flinty features. For a moment, the smile said he was no longer so certain.

He had been very sure of himself at Columbia. In a way, it had made him oddly off-putting. The world is too bound up in its own uncertainty to very much like a winner, Elizabeth thought, returning his smile, making it truer.

Pulling his hand away, he removed three single-pound notes from the pocket of the brown corduroy coat; he was a little surprised to see that the money barely covered the price of the drinks.

They didn't speak, of course; no one does at such moments. She rose; her pale face, lit by the low yellow lamps in the place, was warm and soft, and he thought: Thank God she's older; at least the years took their toll on her as well. Thank God for the spidery lines at the corners of her blue eyes.

The sex was not particularly satisfying but neither of them had really expected it to be. The ghosts of old relationships—with others—intruded on their lovemaking and each was generous at the wrong moments and too little selfish.

They fell away at last and lay side by side on the unsoft hotel bed, staring at the ceiling. Devereaux really could not remember Elizabeth as she had been—there had been so many of them—those students—full of Kennedy fervor and a kind of idealism not yet tainted by smugness. And there was himself, the way he had been—so singularly interested in himself.

They lay together and thought separate thoughts.

"It really is absurd," Elizabeth said.

Outside, the darkness buffeted the windows of their room. They could not hear traffic or church bells or the sounds of cabs or anything that might have placed them in London instead of a million other places. Yet the slight, familiar wail of the wind forced around the skyscraper was comforting, too, because all hotel rooms are alike and familiarity can be home.

"Yes," he said. After a very long time. "It would have been easier not to have known each other." He turned and looked at her. "Although then, you would not have agreed to sleep with me." He felt somewhat eased by saying that.

"I would have preferred not to be so grateful," Elizabeth said.

She really was quite beautiful, Devereaux thought. He kissed the first lines of age on her neck; her skin was cool, pale, fine and smooth, like marble in the shade on a hot day.

He kissed her then; but Elizabeth gently pushed him down and turned and kissed his chest; she kissed his nipples, surprisingly pink and vulnerable beneath the matted gray hair. She kissed his navel and licked it.

Yes, he thought. He put his hands in her hair and tried to touch her face. He felt her lips; he felt the inside of her mouth.

She continued until she heard him moan, softly, almost with a trancelike reverence for the act.

He lifted her face; her eyes were shining, greedy and dark.

He pulled her atop him and fitted himself into her, gently feeling the softness of her breasts; she closed her eyes and moved on him, her mouth on his.

What did she remember now?

He pushed up—once, twice, again and again—into her, hard, almost without tenderness.

It was not expert at all; it was all moaning and thrashing.

But all traces of the past had been swept out and they made love like strangers. Which suited them and gave them comfort.

5

BELFAST

The slight, mean figure hurried quickly up the Crumlin Road while a light rain coated the broken street. He swung himself along harshly, angrily, pushing his bad leg forward and lunging with his good one. He was a little man with harsh, sunken cheeks like God's wrath and high cheekbones full of righteousness. His restless black eyes went from doorway to post to the occasional passing car. He was not looking for a friend. His eyes carried a message of contempt and watchfulness. For who in bloody London would not like to have Faolin himself in Her Majesty's stinkhole prison?

He walked past the house and then turned, swinging around on his lame leg, and walked past it again. Slowly, unobtrusively, he stopped and looked around.

A wretched boy with a green woolen scarf stood in the middle of the street and looked at him. The scarf was wet with the rain. Behind the boy, on a crumbling brick factory wall, was the whitewashed message: *Up the IRA.*

It had been painted a long time ago, perhaps before the boy was born.

"So what've ya seen, lad?"

"I seen nothin'," the boy said in a heart-rending squeak.

"Ya know a soldier, boyo?"

"I know a fuggin' soldier," he said and spat on the wet road.

"Ah, good lad," said Faolin. He pulled a gleaming

coin from his pocket. "Ten bob. Here's ten bob to watch for 'em." He held the coin out. "And whaddaya do when ya see a soldier?" He almost sang it. He understood the boy and the boy him.

"Bang the dustbin lid," the boy said promptly.

"Ah," Faolin laughed. For a moment, the perpetual contempt in his eyes was softened by something he saw in the child. He sailed the fifty-pence piece high into the air and admired the boy as he caught it on the fly.

"You'll be here when I come out?" Faolin asked.

"Oh, aye," said the boy.

And, with a final glance around him, Faolin disappeared into the doorway.

Three others were already in the bare room when Faolin walked in. The odor of foul cigarettes clouded the room—it was a front sitting room with doilies and pictures of the Blessed Virgin on the mantel. Faolin frowned at the three men in greeting and going to the table, threw his cloth cap down on it. He pulled the front of the heavy tweed coat from his frail body and they clearly saw the .45 automatic stuck in the thick, black trousers belt.

"Captain Donovan?"

There were no formalities in meetings chaired by Faolin. Or grace. He leaned his tone on the word "Captain," making it full of a heavy irony. He was addressing a thick-shouldered, sea-brown man with a sailing cap perched on the back of his head. Donovan stood up like a child in recitation class.

"They've moved it back again, Faolin," he said.

"Again?"

"Trouble with the trials on the bloody thing. One of the engines fouled. They've moved it back to December first—"

"A wonder they don't wait for spring—"

"Indeed," said Donovan. "A force-ten wind and it's no go fer her."

"Ah, well, we can expect the great Lord Slough will

have a personal word with the Almighty about holdin'
the wind down fer the crossin'," said a third man. He
had smiling eyes and a calm manner, as though the
bluffness of Donovan and the sarcasm of Faolin called
for a steady middle hand. His name was Tatty.

"Indeed, Tatty," said Faolin, who was almost defer-
ential in manner to the mild, quizzical man in his battered
old cap. Tatty's perpetual Gallagher cigarette hung from
his lip.

"Will yer be on her?" asked the fourth man. His name
was Parnell and he wore a regular shirt over the blue
trousers of a Liverpool policeman.

"Oh, aye," said Donovan. "I've had the trainin', y'see.
I'm quite indispensable t'her." He said it proudly.

"Oh, aye," said Faolin. "But y're more need to us."

Donovan grinned. But Faolin moved on. "Tatty, y'll
apprise our friends in Liverpool of it, then?"

"Oh, aye. They probably know by now anyway," said
Tatty. "It'll be in the papers, I wouldn't be surprised."

"P'raps not. It is somewhat an issue and they'll want
to throw us off by keepin' the date secret for as long as
possible—"

"Not secret enough not to get mention of the first
hovercraft service in the Irish Sea—"

Parnell nodded. "He's right, is Tatty. They'll want
England's eyes all on her as she crosses—"

"The eyes of the world if we do it right," said Faolin.

"The world," repeated Donovan dreamily. He could
not conceive it.

Faolin let them talk on about the details of the plan.
Details were not important to him a month before the
event. Faolin would cut through the details at the proper
time. He thought of them as children, like the boys of
the old days who had worn trench coats and dark hats
in imitation of American gangsters.

The plan was his, really; and it was perfectly matched
in his mind's eye.

He had come to the chiefs of the IRA provos with a plan they were willing to accept.

The IRA was in desperate trouble after nearly a decade of civil war and urban-guerrilla actions in Northern Ireland. The bombings in England had not cowed the English and had not made them weary of their dirty little war. Likewise, the bombings in the South had not stirred the Irish public to support—rather the opposite. The greatest mistake of all had been the bombing in the center of Dublin which had killed nearly two dozen poor shoppers.

Faolin had argued persuasively that such bombings did not finally terrorize but rather enervated people and made them accept the horror of random death with the fatalism of people who must live with it every day. The way the Londoners were in the Second War, he had said: Each day that passed made them stronger, more resistant to the Nazi terror from the sky. The same thing appeared to have happened to the Americans in their war in Vietnam, he said.

The hearts and minds of the Irish must be rallied again to the Cause by a bold and stunning action which would both finance the future—and direct the attention of the ordinary people toward their true enemies.

The council had listened gravely—spellbound—to this glittering, twisted man as he laid the plan out to them.

No more bombings, he had said. Not just to end the horror, but to lull the British into thinking the IRA was giving up.

They had been reluctant to agree—until they had heard the second part of the plan.

Lord Slough, Faolin had said, the first cousin of Queen Elizabeth the Second. He would inaugurate the first hovercraft service uniting England and Ireland in the fall (the original date had been October first).

The council members had nodded. They knew this. Everyone in Britain knew it. Lord Slough had commissioned a new model of the jet-powered boat that rode above the waves and was already in operation in the English Channel between Dover and Calais. The new hovercraft would be a larger, faster, stronger vessel, capable of handling rougher seas than the early models and capable of making the tedious eight-hour crossing between Liverpool and Dublin in forty-five minutes.

In a long article in the *Sunday Times,* Lord Slough—identified by the papers as the richest man in Britain and one of the richest in the non-Arab world—said the rejuvenation of the Dublin-Liverpool run would be the first step in linking Britain and then Europe by these superhovercraft. In two years, he said, he would operate private hovercraft lines between London and Edinburgh, London and Glasgow, Belfast and Liverpool, and Belfast and Dublin. Pledges of cooperation and support from the governments of the Republic of Ireland and from Great Britain had already been offered.

They had all read it by the time Faolin met with them; Faolin had made sure of that. And made sure at the meeting that they all became heartily sick of Lord Slough and his wealth and power; of his oil interests in the North Sea and the firm he controlled which was at that moment drilling test holes in the murky Atlantic depths off Galway Bay on Ireland's impoverished and beautiful west coast. Faolin recounted Lord Slough's holdings in the biggest motorcar firm in Britain and of the factory in Northern Ireland where Irish workers—at below-scale pay—assembled the machines. What Lord Slough did not own outright, said Faolin, he could buy, including all the right politicians in the Irish Dáil and in the English House of Commons. It was common knowledge, said Faolin, and the council members had nodded their heads sagely.

Faolin built up Lord Slough in that meeting, and as he did so, he built up their resentment of him. Finally, almost eloquently, he had said;

"I said to you that our enemy is not the ordinary man and that is why y'must stop yer bombing. Is our enemy

a mail clerk who opens a parcel for Lord Slough and
has his hands blown off fer the trouble? Is it that woman
and her child blown to kingdom come on Royal Avenue
the other day because some fool decides to blow down
the doors of the *Belfast Telegraph*? No, they are not; not
any of them; not English or Irish or what. Our enemy
is Lord Slough, but we let him alone. He starves Irishmen
in his factories, accumulatin' greedy wealth with the
tears of orphans whose daddies have died in his Welsh
mines. Our enemy is Slough as privilege and power and
unaccountable wealth is our enemy."

They had been silent. Folding their hands like students
on the first day of class, they had listened.

"And what of our great political leaders? Of the Prime
Minister of England who ruthlessly sends his soldiers to
kill our wives and children in the streets of our broken
old city? Or the Taoiseach of the Republic—a republic
in name alone—who cynically sells out to the British
at every opportunity and who betrays us and our com-
rades when told to do so by Whitehall? I don't need
to tell ya who our enemies really are—but I do so because you have been blinded by their wealth and power.
Y've doffed yer caps like Clare farmers t'them. Y've de-
ferred to them because they are yer betters—"

Oh, they had resented that. They had become angry.
And Faolin had played on their anger.

"Yer children," he hissed. "Children who play at revo-
lution and war and then run away when yer old one
comes t'get ya."

"What's yer plan, Faolin?" one finally asked angrily.
"What's yer bleedin' plan?"

Faolin had turned on his bad leg, turned and fixed his
questioner with a dark, withering eye. "Me plan, boyo, is
to drive our enemies into the sea."

Was he mad? They had stared at him and watched a
smile slowly spread on that face which was not made
to smile.

As his final argument, he read a piece from the *Irish Times* concerning the hovercraft aloud to them.

" 'The cost of the scheme, while not announced, is thought to be a hundred million pounds. However, it is only the first step in a network of hovercraft services to be operated by Lord Slough's Anglo-Irish Lines linking major cities on both islands. Lord Slough said he had the full confidence and cooperation of the British government.

" 'The Taoiseach (of Ireland) said that Lord Slough's scheme would provide two hundred fifty new jobs in the country, and that it was estimated that eight million pounds annually would be pumped into the economy. He praised what he called "the foresight and courage" of Lord Slough.

" 'It is expected that the Prime Ministers of both countries will accompany Lord Slough and his party on the inaugural run of the first superhovercraft, which Lord Slough said would be named for his daughter, Brianna.' "

Faolin let the clipping fall on the floor. He stared at the nine men before him.

"It is expected," he said. "It is expected that Lord Slough and the Prime Ministers of England and Ireland will accompany him on this inaugural journey. It is expected."

And he had given them the plan. Faolin and his men would seize the craft at Liverpool harbor and take it out into the middle of the Irish Sea with its precious cargo. And there they would broadcast to the world that the lives of Slough and the politicians—and whoever else accompanied him, perhaps even a member of the royal family—would be spared on two conditions—the payment of a ransom of one hundred million pounds and the release from Long Kesh and the other internment camps of all IRA prisoners.

The men of the council were stunned at first. They believed in the old ways of war—believed in bombs and sniping at soldiers and shooting informers down on dark streets; believed in terror. Faolin had been prepared for their intransigence: He talked all morning and into the afternoon and he beat down their conservatism. They realized that the IRA had fallen on bad days; they had no money and little support; the conduit of funds from America was drying up, although still strong by standards placed against funds from other places. The Palestinians had withdrawn their financial support. Worse, a peace movement had grown up spontaneously among a group of Catholic mothers who professed themselves sick of the killing in the North. Everything that Faolin said was true —a bold action was needed to recover the initiative in this war of attrition that the British were winning. Yet what he said was so radical—

The argument had raged in the council itself at that and subsequent meetings. But finally, they decided that Faolin's plan was the bold move they needed; with the money, they could carry on the war indefinitely; with the hostages, they could redirect their energies against the men of wealth and power and win again the sympathies of the ordinary Irish worker, who was among the poorest-paid in Western Europe. Faolin was right, they agreed at last.

Only the money seemed to stagger the council—one hundred million pounds. Who would pay such a sum?

"That's not our concern, is it?" asked Faolin then. "D'ya not think that Lord Slough himself—the great provider of Irish jobs—would not think his royal personage worth one hundred million?" And they had agreed.

From that first meeting in August, Faolin had gone forward, carefully constructing his net to catch Lord Slough and the rulers of Britain and Ireland. Two men had been critical: Donovan, who worked for Slough's Anglo-Irish Lines as an engineer and was being trained to tend the machinery on the new superhovercraft; and Tatty, the quiet leader of the potent IRA operation in Liverpool. Liverpool—where the kidnapping would be effected—was a great seafaring city on the English west coast that contained so many Irish that it was often called "the largest city in Ireland."

Donovan had not impressed Faolin; he was a slow but loyal man. Tatty, however, had become something of a confidant to a man who had rejected confidants all his life. Tatty and Faolin pieced together the details of the operation. It was not terribly complex:

The *Brianna* would carry a full cargo on her first journey. In that cargo would be five hundred pounds of gelignite, which could be set off by radio transmitter.

Faolin would carry the transmitter aboard the *Brianna*. Once out into the Irish Sea, the craft would be hijacked. The demand would be made and the threat that the boat would be destroyed—along with all the important people aboard her—unless the demand was met. The money would be paid the IRA in Northern Ireland and the men of Portlaoish would be freed.

The *Brianna* would be taken then to Dublin. This was the best part of all. The Irish government would provide an airplane for the hijackers, to take them to Libya—Faolin said he had arranged that already—and they would keep their hostages aboard the *Brianna* until the plane took off. The transmitter which could set the gelignite off was good to a range of fifty miles.

"Libya," said Tatty. "Why there?"

"Because they'll have us," said Faolin.

"Ah, it's a far place. I believe we sailed there once, many years ago—"

"Far enough," said Faolin.

"Oh, aye," said Tatty. "But it'll be hard to leave—"

"Only for a time, Tatty," said Faolin. "We could go back—"

"No, there's no returning," said Tatty. "You'll fool yerself if you think that, lad. You'll be an exile then fer yer life."

Faolin had been silent then. In only one respect had he been less than candid with Tatty.

On the getaway.

There would be no plane. There would be no Libya. There would be no exile. These hardened terrorists—even Tatty—were like children when it came to facing what Faolin saw as the unmistakable reality of the moment and the times. Did the IRA think the Irish would just go on to war with the English as before? They would never win—unless the English, in monumental rage at a heinous, irrational act—went berserk. Then Ireland would rally to itself and throw them finally from their shores.

You always had to give children hope, though, to tell them that morning would always follow night, that death was sleep.

Faolin was not a child.

He realized that the money was not enough; that the release of the prisoners was not enough. What was needed was a final, severing act of war from which the IRA could not retreat and which would turn the Irish from children into men.

Faolin would depress the button on his transmitter at the final moment.

And Lord Slough and the Prime Ministers and the entourage from the royal family—all of them, including Faolin and Tatty and Donovan—would be blown to kingdom come.

Elizabeth was in the shower when Devereaux awoke, and he lay in bed, waiting for her. She came out still naked, her head wrapped in one of the white towels that luxury hotels oversupply to mitigate the loneliness of the rooms. She looked at him and shared the smile of the morning after love.

Devereaux forgot to smile in return until hers began to fade.

"Is something wrong?" Elizabeth asked as she went to the edge of the bed. She stood and looked down at him. He looked up at her, up at the gently swelling breasts, at the curls of brownish hair between her legs. He touched her. She did not move. He explored.

"Elizabeth," he said.

She stood and let him touch her.

"I wonder if it will be another fifteen years," she said at last.

"No. Not that long again." He wondered if he meant it. She closed her eyes. He felt her moistness. He pulled her down gently on the bed, next to him. He kissed her on the neck, slowly.

"Where do you live? I want to see you," Elizabeth said as though there was hunger.

Devereaux smelled her hair, damp and like flowers. "Fifty miles west of the District of Columbia," he began. "You come to Front Royal. It's just a town, nothing special, except for the mountains. It's at the start of Skyline Drive along the Blue Ridge mountains. Have you ever been in Virginia?"

"Not beyond the suburbs," she said. "You live there?"

Devereaux kissed her insistently. "On a mountain top. The complete hermit."

"Can I come to your mountain?" she asked lightly, kissing him in return.

He took her then. Like a cold man reaching for the flame.

First they exchanged the code words and then the identification numbers of the telephone and then Hanley spoke:

"This is a delicate matter, Devereaux. I don't have to tell you that." But he did. "We have decided to play a lone hand at the moment."

Devereaux waited. He did not feel as he had felt twelve hours before. He had been warmed.

"As we told you—" Why the pompous tone? Was the Chief in the same room with Hanley? "We have never established a dialogue with British Intelligence on the same footing as the Langley firm. This is a chance for us to do that and to give the Brits information they could not get from CIA."

"Could not?"

There was a pause. What was Hanley saying?

"We want you to proceed to Belfast immediately and determine the details of the IRA plan. Get on this man O'Neill and his friends. If we are to make a present of our information to Brit Intell, it must be worth enough to convince them they can cooperate with us fully in other spheres. As you have said, we are not interested in the internal problems of Britain at the moment and we are most certainly not interested in the Irish Republican Army. But this is a chance to help Brit Intell and squeeze in line next to Langley at the English trough."

Elegantly put, thought Devereaux.

"I raise the same objection I did yesterday," said Devereaux. For the record. "We don't know when the IRA plans to assassinate Lord Slough—in fact, we are not totally convinced that they will—and every minute we delay in this matter, it hangs heavier that the assassination will come off—"

"We considered that," said Hanley. "We made discreet inquiries overnight and determined that Lord Slough is, at the moment, safely enjoying the pleasures of life in Detroit, Michigan. Where he is in negotiation with a major American company to distribute his autos in the U.S. He leaves in two days for an oil conference in Quebec City. That is to last two days as well, and then he flies home to his castle in County Clare. The danger starts then—"

"Where's the conference in Quebec City?"

"At the Chateau Frontenac. He and his Saudi Arabian partners in the North Sea drillings and the new ones off the Irish coast—"

"This is hopeless," said Devereaux. "I know nothing about him—"

Hanley went on unperturbed. "A coded cable follows. You'll receive it in Belfast in a few hours. You'll be in Belfast, then—"

"A logical place," said Devereaux. "But not in code, please. I'm an agent of Central Press Service. Plain English backgrounder will suffice."

"Good point," Hanley muttered.

Devereaux smiled.

"So, in summary, you go to Belfast, find out the why and wherefore of the assassination of Lord Slough—and we present it to Brit Intell—"

"In Christmas wrapping," said Devereaux.

"Sarcasm," identified Hanley.

"And if Slough is hit in Detroit or Quebec despite his apparent safety there?"

There was a pause in Washington.

"Then it will all be wasted," said Hanley.

"And so will Slough," said Devereaux. "But, thy will be done."

"Yes," said Hanley.

"There are two other matters—"

"Can't they wait for—"

"No, dammit. One, what about the American Express card? Has it been taken care of?"

"Yes, damn you. I didn't forget. Is that all?"

"Two, I want to give you a name." He paused. "Two names. One is Free The Prisoners. Cap F, cap T, cap P. Sort of like an Amnesty International. Working in London now. Headquarters in Bern. Can you check it out?"

"Yes," said Hanley. There were times when he did not question Devereaux too closely. For all his problems with him, Hanley respected Devereaux's instincts and, rather than obscure those instincts with words requiring explanation, let Devereaux run free until he had tracked down whatever aroused his curiosity.

"Second name," said Hanley.

Devereaux only hesitated for a moment while he remembered the long, caressing curve of her full body and the smooth innocence of her back. No one would have noticed the hesitation unless they knew Devereaux.

"Campbell," he said, "Elizabeth." And broke the connection. For a moment, he listened to the silence, and then he got up and walked out of the tight little room.

Two hours later, he was looking down at the rubble-strewn mass of Belfast still decorated with brave church spires. The plane banked sharply at three thousand feet and whined down to the landing strip.

Devereaux unbuckled his belt as the plane taxied to the terminal building. A misting rain fell, as usual.

Seven miles away, at that moment, a limping man came up to a little boy in the Crumlin Road. He touched the child and asked him what he had seen.

"Nothin', sur," said the boy.

He slipped a second coin into the childish hand.

"I woulda banged the dustbin if I had," the boy said.

6

QUEBEC CITY

William Henry Christopher Devon, Lord Slough, ninth Earl of Slough in a line back to the time of George III, first cousin of the Hanoverian Queen Elizabeth of England, marched into the stately lobby of the Chateau Frontenac in Quebec City with the conspicuous anonymity that all great men crave and seldom achieve.

He was, by good chance, exactly a day early for the conference with the Saudi Arabian oil ministers. He had not planned the unexpected schedule change but he had accepted it because it would allow time with Deirdre, and time for himself. Like all men who own the world and run it, Lord Slough had little time for himself. Not that every pleasure was denied; only postponed.

The conference in Detroit with the American automobile executives had gone smoothly. In fact, Lord Slough discovered there was no need to spend a single day—a single hour—more in the company of the fawning aristocrats of the American motor industry. He despised them secretly for their cowardice in the face of mere titled royalty—though he also enjoyed it. Amusement and contempt rested comfortably in Lord Slough's ample store of emotions.

The Chateau Frontenac, scene of the historic wartime conference between Winston Churchill and Franklin Roosevelt, commanded a promontory over the wide and turbulent Saint Lawrence river that flowed past the ancient city of Quebec. From its spires, which poked into the broad and gloomy Canadian sky, one could look down on the snow-covered Plains of Abraham in the lower town, where the French had lost Canada to the English for good. And just as well, thought Lord Slough, who disliked the French.

The English lord had not chosen the site of the meeting with the Saudis. They had. Canada was picked because of its proximity to Washington, where the Saudis were meeting with the President shortly after the meeting with Lord Slough. Then, too, the Canadian government—itself torn in loyalty between oil needs and its perpetual dominance by the United States—had recently proposed a new tilt in foreign policy, favoring the Arab states over the Israelis. New friends—even oil friends—were encouraged by the quiet Saudis. Lord Slough had not objected, though Canada in November presented no welcome face.

Everything had been arranged for him, of course.

Deirdre Monahan, his daughter's tutor, had been summoned first, while he still wrangled in Detroit with the auto magnates. One of the best of his private air fleet had whisked her from the Slough home in County Clare, Ireland, to Quebec in seven hours. Dierdre was afraid to fly; only Lord Slough's command could have brought her.

Brianna, still at school in Lausanne, would not join him until they all met at home, later in the week. Which would leave Deirdre with nothing to do. Except comfort his Lordship.

Slough waited at the elevator for a moment, aware that every glance was directed at him. He was discreetly dressed, evenly tanned; his hands were large and his ginger mustache bristled. He bore himself well, though past fifty; he had been one of His Majesty's colonels in the last war and he had never gotten out of the habits of the military.

People stared at him and he expected it. Wealth and

power imparted their own luminescence. A fact those who were born with both seem indifferent to.

"I'm sorry for the delay, my lord," said Jeffries, his secretary. Behind Slough was Harmon, the bodyguard he had personally recruited out of the Royal Marines five years previously. Harmon did not speak; or, if he did, he did not speak in the presence of the body he guarded day and night.

Lord Slough did not answer. Jeffries was a competent secretary. The incompetence of a hotel or the perfidiousness of a lift did not fall into his sphere; nor did the petty annoyances of life upset Lord Slough. He had infinite patience. Which is why, he supposed at times, he got everything he wanted.

The elevator arrived, the door opened. He stepped on confidently, trailed by Jeffries and Harmon. Harmon barred the way to further passengers. The clerk, a French-Canadian, spoke to the operator in French. Without a word, the operator slammed the doors and the elevator ascended to the top floor, where Lord Slough's suite awaited. And where Deirdre awaited as well.

At the suite, he walked directly into his bedroom. Jeffries followed with a clutch of cables that had caught up with Slough since his sudden departure from Detroit.

Slough started to shed his clothes and said, "Begin."

Jeffries sat down at a table in the room and began to read the messages. Dictating his responses, Slough stepped, naked, into the shower. Jeffries rose, went to the bathroom door, and continued to read and take notes while Lord Slough soaped himself behind the shower door and dictated. The scene was ludicrous. But the ways of a man with a thousand enterprises demanding a thousand personal touches were suited to himself and not to common behavior. If there was to be time for himself ever, it had to be snatched away from other things.

And there would be time for Deirdre this evening, he had decided.

* * *

Belfast had been a lovely city, Devereaux recalled, trying to superimpose the image from years ago on the patched and broken hulk he now saw. Tough and charming, cold and open; a small town as all Irish cities were but with the steely edge of the English and Scots about her, too. Something important always seemed about to happen there. And it had, finally.

The driver pulled up at the Belfast Continental, a grandly named gleaming tower of anonymous rooms and an air of sadness. The hotel was in a bad way, they had apologized at the London booking office, but it was the best in Belfast. They had looked curiously at him. American to Belfast. Then they saw his press credentials. Just another reporter, dragging up the horror of Northern Ireland for readers apparently never sated by the spectacle of bloody fratricide.

He checked in. The immense lobby was nearly empty. An aging bellboy with a bulbous nose and an air of artificial gaiety led him to his room on an upper floor. The room was standard American motel, down to the mass-produced modern painting on the wall above the television set.

Devereaux, who hated puzzles because they were so rarely solved satisfactorily, was in the midst of one. Hanley had ordered him to Belfast to find out what the Boys intended. Information was never that easy to obtain; it was always incomplete—half the truth and half a lie and never satisfying. Jobs like this one gnawed at him, put him on edge.

He sat down in a chair and looked out the window at the brave steeples of the city; beyond lay the wide harbor where once great warships were launched.

Early evening crept across the city below.

He sighed and stood up and reached for a clean shirt. It was time to find O'Neill.

There was no telephone.

The cab deposited Devereaux down the road—as he

had ordered—from the depressing block of council houses. The houses made of red brick and attached to each other by common walls, shared the same architecture; the same stoop fronts; the same flat doors; the same sad, narrow windows. Devereaux walked along the sidewalk, skirting the rubble on the edge of the pavement.

Number 19.

He knocked at the door. After a moment, it opened. A woman peered out into the darkness. A child clung to her skirt, another was held loosely in one arm.

There were sounds from within, more children talking above the noise of a television set. The block was full of such noises; it was dark beyond the little squares of light from the windows; the street lamps appeared broken.

"Mr. O'Neill," he said. "I'm Doherty. From the firm."

"Mr. O'Neill," she repeated stupidly, as though he were a stranger instead of her husband.

Devereaux waited.

"He's not in," she said.

"It's very important—"

"He wasn't to be at the job, was it?" she asked, suddenly suspicious.

"Oh, no, ma'am. This is special. I'm with the American branch, Mr. O'Neill is—"

"Because if he was to be at the job. Mother of Mercy, he's not here," she said. She appeared confused.

"Where is he?"

"Down t' Flanagan's," she said.

"Flanagan's?"

"A public house. 'Tis his dart evening. He's with the local's team, y'know."

"It's very important. Where is Flanagan's?"

"Ah, he's tole me not to be botherin' him on his dart night."

"Very important," Devereaux mumbled.

"Ach, sure, but it won't be you he'll go after," she said.

"It concerns money. Owed him."

Money. She pushed away the child at her skirt, sending

the dirty-faced urchin reeling against the wall of the hall-way that led into the squalor beyond.

"I can take the money—" she said.

"I have to see—"

"It's me money," she said. "I'm t'take it, he said."

"I can't do that, Mrs. O'Neill," Devereaux said.

She stared at him and then shrugged. The child she held laughed. "Down the end of this road and then right. Y'll see it." She had nothing more to say. She slammed the door on him.

Devereaux turned and started down the dark road. I should write a recruiting brochure on the glamor of espionage, he thought.

Flanagan's was in an old stone-front building. The smell of stale beer and stale cigarettes coming from the pub lingered in the street outside. The night was surpris-ingly gentle. There was no wind and only a light, misting rain, like summer.

On the sidewalk, two men in cloth caps and dark old suit jackets stood drunkenly against a fence. The fence enclosed a vacant lot. As Devereaux passed them, he heard the sound of urination; they were pissing into the lot.

When Devereaux entered the public house, everyone turned to look at him. He saw O'Neill at the dart board; saw O'Neill grow pale.

Going to the bar, he ordered a pint of Smithwick's Ale. He sipped at the bitter amber when it came.

And waited for O'Neill.

O'Neill approached him, saying, "So it's you, is it? I thought they'd be after sendin' someone else."

"We both did."

"Well, sir, I'm just back is the short of it. I've nothing to tell you—"

"Still have those torn bills?"

"Oh, aye."

"When will y—"

"Sur, I'd rather y'not come to me local. Let me talk with you some other—"

"I told your wife I was with your company. That I had money for you—"

"Ah, yer daft," O'Neill said. "That bitch'll be after me now for it—"

"Y'didn't tell her about the thousand—"

"Ah, God of Heaven, shut yer gob, man, y'll be tellin' half of Belfast—" O'Neill rolled his eyes in exasperation. Ever the clown.

"All right," said Devereaux.

"After it closes t'night. At yer hotel."

"All right."

"In the bar there. I could do with a drink." In fact, O'Neill appeared a little drunk already.

"Belfast Continental."

"Ah. Grand. Grand. I'll be there."

"Don't fail," said Devereaux.

"I won't. Y'people are at me night and day. I tole the one this mornin' that came t'the house—"

"Who?"

"The other American was after comin' to me house."

"Who was he?"

"Me very words. I says, 'Who the bloody hell are ya?' He's with R Section, he says, whatever the hell that is—"

O'Neill only knew Hastings had been with something called the Section.

"Who was he?"

"How the bloody hell do I know? Me darts. I gotta go to me game."

Devereaux held his arm.

"Who was he?"

"Ah, wait on it. I'll tell ya. He tole me his name—"

"What was it?"

"Irish name."

"What?"

"I fergit now. I tole him I didn't bloody know what he was talkin' about—"

"What was his name?"

"C'mon, yer up," yelled one of the dart players, glaring at Devereaux.

"I'll be comin', in a moment. I have to deal with this here gentleman—"

"Who? What was his name?"

"Ah. I remember."

He waited.

"Devereaux. Devereaux he says his name was."

He was frightened now.

He felt the chill of it. Perspiration plucked at the back of his shirt.

As he stepped out of the pub, he looked up and down the street. The mist shrouded silent Belfast. Halos formed around the streetlamps.

"Devereaux," O'Neill had said.

He heard his own steps on the sidewalk. The noise of the public house faded. Utter quiet. He stepped into the biackness of a side street where vandals had blown out the lights of the street lamps.

In the distance, Devereaux could see the tower of the Belfast Continental hotel, looming above the downtown district.

Gloomy, starless night, made gentle with rain.

Doorway, post, parked car. Doorway—

He did not want to think. He wanted to walk, to be alert to every sound, every movement.

Another American knew about O'Neill. And Devereaux. And the Section. Had made a joke about it.

Absurdly, he wanted to be safe.

He had accepted the dangers and the anonymous fact of death long ago; accepted it now. But it frightened him, always, when it was near, when it seemed to breathe on his face.

Bang. A flash before him.

The rattle of a dustbin. A cat leaped across the sidewalk, growled, scurried into darkness. The dustbin rattled against the fence.

He had no weapons.

An auto growled into a turn, flashed onto the side street. Its lamp-eyes silhouetted Devereaux, bore down on him, and then flashed away as the car rolled by. He heard the roar of it.

And, in that moment, did not hear the footstep behind.

Jerked back.

Felt the wire around his neck, suddenly cutting deep.

7

BELFAST

He did not so much wake as struggle upward until he broke the waterline. He could breathe. That was the first thing he was aware of. He lay in the darkness, struggling for breath, and found it.

The second thing was the pain. Searing his throat with each breath. He had not expected pain after death. Not expected anything.

He opened his eyes. Thought he had opened them but saw nothing. He was aware of another presence close to him. If only he could open his eyes, he would be willing to stand the pain. The pain in the darkness frightened him; the sound of his breathing body did not comfort him.

He could not see. New nightmares, phantoms over him. Was this his biblical hell? He was suddenly cast down, a child sitting with Great Aunt Melvina in the ornate old church, Latin mumbled from the altar.

No.

Sometimes, when he dreamed, he would dream that he awoke and then, frightened by the dream, would try to awake really; he would awake again and not be awake, still held in the nightmare.

He opened his eyes.

The room was not dark. There was a lamp on the wall, lit. Television set. Curtain. Window. Hell is a motel room, he thought and tried to turn his head. But there was too much pain.

"Yes."

Not his voice.

"Your room."

His room. In the hotel he could not reach. He had been on the street. A pub. O'Neill. And then—what then?

"I can't see you." It hurt to speak. "I can't turn my head."

"No wonder. It is extremely good fortune to you that you have a head."

The voice moved away from his blind side, around the end of the bed. Then he saw its owner: A short, thick man with black, flat hair and a flat forehead and clear, childlike eyes behind glasses. And a smile.

Denisov.

"Hello, Devereaux," said the Russian. "I get a chair and sit down and have a yarn with you." He pulled the rickety plastic chair from the rickety plastic desk-table and put it by the side of the bed.

"Denisov." The named caused him pain.

"Yes, me," said the Russian. His English was nearly flawless in tone, but he was betrayed at times by odd words thrown into the middle of elaborate sentences.

Devereaux did not feel wary, as he should. He could not be on guard. He remembered the blackness on the street, remembered how foolish he felt as he knew he was about to die.

"Are we in hell?"

"Of course not. There is no hell, therefore I cannot be in it," said Denisov. "I think Descartes said that."

"Or Woody Allen."

Denisov frowned. "Very awful to see your neck."

"Thank you."

"It is my appreciation."

Devereaux waited for the Soviet agent to speak. He was thirsty.

"Do you know what occurred?" Denisov finally asked. He had taken off his fashionable rimless eyeglasses and was wiping the lenses on his tie.

"I was killed."

"No, not hardly. In a second more, you would be killed, but not hardly. I was there. You owe me a life, now. Like the Buddhists."

"You've got it backwards. You saved my life, you must now take care of me."

Denisov frowned. "That does not sound equitable."

"Exactly the reason it has been abandoned."

The Russian placed the glasses back on his face. They illuminated his already saintly eyes.

Devereaux waited still.

"Do you want to know who killed you?"

"Yes."

"Do you think it was me?"

"Perhaps."

"I can rest you, if I killed you, you would have died."

"Perhaps."

"Perhaps, perhaps. Is this the way you have learned to say nothing?" Denisov smiled. "It would be better to be quiet then."

"Perhaps," said Devereaux.

Denisov would not be put out of his good humor. "A man named Blatchford. Do you know him?"

"The one who garroted me?"

"Yes. Almost."

"Who was he?"

"Blatchford. I said this. He was at the Royal Avenue Hotel for today. He was in the airplane before you came to Belfast. He came from Edinburgh."

"I don't know him."

"Oh. An American in Belfast is almost made dead by another American in Belfast. A coincidence."

"We're a feisty people."

"Feisty? Never mind. I can understand the meaning. But this is not a coincidence."

"Perhaps not."

"Denisov has saved your life."

Devereaux waited.

"They were in an automobile. A Fiat. Made in Italy. Also, now, made in the Soviet Union. You leave the saloon—" Denisov preferred American terms when speaking English. "They go ahead of you. Drop off Blatchford. They circle the block, come up again as you pass Blatchford and blind you with the lamps. Then Blatchford moves to kill you."

"And where was Denisov?"

Denisov smiled. He looked like Saint Francis of Assisi, as conceived by an Eastern religious painter. "Where was the cat? Bam, the garbage can, and the cat jumps out. Stupid Denisov banged into the can. Thank goodness there was a cat, or you would have seen me."

"Goodness?"

"A saying in English."

"I didn't want you to revert on me."

"You would like a drink?"

"Water."

"Water of life."

"Water, not whisky."

Denisov shrugged and got up. He came back from the bathroom with a glass of water. Devereaux sipped it slowly. It numbed his throat but the pain lurked beneath the surface.

"Who is Blatchford?" he said at last.

Denisov smiled and shrugged.

"Don't shrug."

"I was following you—"

"You were following Blatchford. You knew when his plane arrived."

"Perhaps both of you."

"You have a problem. Professional paranoia. You're going to have to learn to trust someone."

"You?" asked Denisov.

"Trust me."

Denisov smiled. "Trust me, Devereaux. I saved your life."

"Why?"

"Because I like you."

"You didn't like me in Saigon."

Denisov did not stop smiling. "Saigon was different. There were different reasons in Saigon. We could not be friends there. We can be friends now."

"Détente."

"Exactly. We have the same interest in this, believe me."

He began again, as though he were the interrogator: "Who is Blatchford?"

Denisov said, "An American. I thought you knew him."

"What happened?"

"He was behind you in a shot in the dark. I saw his hands. He was going to garrote you. I was not prepared for that, if I must tell you. There was nothing to do."

"So you did nothing."

"No. I mean. Another choice. There was no other choice. So I eliminated him."

"How?"

"Professional secret."

It was maddening. But Devereaux pursued it. "Who was Blatchford?"

"An American."

"Why are you here?"

"To help you."

"Really? Who was Blatchford?"

Denisov got up and went to the window. He looked out. "It is raining," he said.

"It is always raining," said Devereaux. He waited. Denisov seemed to reflect on the rain beyond the window.

"I thought I knew who he was," he said at last.

Devereaux waited.

"In his wallet, he carries a card from the Department of Agriculture of the United States. Do you know what the card says on it?"

Devereaux said, "Devereaux."

Denisov looked shocked. "You *did* know him."

"A lucky guess."

"No—"

"And what else?"

"Oh, things to carry in a pocketbook. A picture of a woman and a children."

"Not 'a' children."

"I'm sorry. And an American Express card, also with your name on it—"

Paid up, I'll bet, thought Devereaux.

"And a great deal of money."

"Feel free to keep it, there's more where that came from."

"I shall," said Denisov solemnly.

"Buy yourself a good meal."

They fell then into a listless silence, each warily imagining what the other would say, would want.

"Denisov. why are you here?"

"On holiday."

"I see. It's going to be like that."

Denisov frowned. "No, not like that. I will start again. I am here to observe."

"What?"

"The strange behavior of the American people."

"You could have done that better in Columbus, Ohio, for example. Or Peoria."

"I would like to go to Peoria, Illinois. I have heard about it."

Devereaux tried to sit up, but felt dizzy. Somewhere, beyond the window, a boat called through the mist.

"Why are you here?" asked Denisov.

"Agricultural survey. To see if you can grow tomatoes and bombs in the same garden."

"We have to trust each other."

"No we don't."

"Our position is delicate."

"Not our position, white man."

"I don't understand."

"Neither do I." And he didn't. Did not understand Denisov or Blatchford or the attempt on his life. Was Blatchford sent by Hanley to eliminate him? Who knew he was here? Except everyone?

"I will begin. Blatchford was not what he seemed."

"You mean he was not me? I realized that immediately."

Denisov frowned. "I am trying to be serious."

"Be serious."

"Blatchford was with your government. Why does your government wish to kill you?"

"I don't know. Maybe I voted wrong in the last election." Devereaux suddenly felt giddy with life. He was alive, he was not dead. Denisov was there. An old enemy. Almost as good as a friend. He tried to sit up again and made it. He smiled to himself.

"Joke," said Denisov. "Don't tell a joke. Be serious."

"I am." He thought a moment. "Let me see the American Express card."

Denisov got up and went to the desk. He came back with the card.

The card bore Devereaux's name. And the right expiration date. He said, "Get my wallet. In the coat, there."

Denisov brought it.

His card. The same. The same account number.

"It wasn't Hanley's fault," he said.

"What?"

"Nothing. The card is the same as mine—"

"That is not impossible."

"Nothing is. Can I see the rest of Blatchford's wallet?"

Denisov put the contents on the coverlet of the bed. Devereaux picked them up.

The card from the Department of Agriculture.

A press accreditation from Central Press Service, made out to Devereaux. But the picture was another man, a younger man, with sandy hair and light features. The dead Blatchford.

He picked up the other cards.

Visa card. Made out to Devereaux. He knew it would be the same as his.

The carbon receipt of an airline ticket. Edinburgh to Belfast.

And the pictures.

A woman and a child standing in front of a suburban home. A Weber grill smoking in the corner of the picture. Sunlight. The child—a boy—grins into the sunlight.

He stared at the picture.

Denisov stared at him. "What do you see, Devereaux?"

He did not answer.

The woman was Elizabeth.

At that precise moment, in Hamburg, a young man with light red hair named Michael Pendurst stood in the doorway of a hotel he occupied while a man with a cigarette tried to light it against the wind.

Michael Pendurst offered him a match.

"*Danke*," the man said.

"*Bitte*," said Michael Pendurst.

The man lit the cigarette, puffed at it, and threw it down. Then he looked at the mild-faced young Pendurst. "The next job is in Liverpool, in a week's time."

"*Gut*," Pendurst said. "I need the money." His voice, though deep enough, had a curious childlike quality to it. His accent was German, sprayed with American expressions.

"There'll be enough for this one. Twenty-five big ones."

Even Michael Pendurst was impressed. "Who is it?"

The other man opened the paper and pointed at the photograph.

"And where will he be?"

"It's in the story. The marked paragraph. Good luck."

"I don't need luck."

"Whatever," said the American. And he stepped in the dark street.

8

QUEBEC CITY

In the beginning of their relationship, it had seemed to Deirdre that Lord Slough was much too shy; after all, Deirdre Monahan was not without passion, and though she was ignorant of all the techniques of lovemaking, desire could overcome those mechanical obstacles.

But perhaps it was not a matter of shyness, Deirdre had come to decide. Perhaps it was hesitancy to proceed further—Deirdre understood now that Slough wanted to proceed further than Deirdre had ever intended. And Slough might have felt he would lose her if he revealed himself too soon.

What a foolish man, she thought. It was nearly morning and the city of Quebec still slept, beyond the ornate windows of the Chateau Frontenac.

They had slept and played; then slept again; and then played his games. Now, dawn waited to crackle harshly across the half-frozen river beyond the windows. The lower city, bunched against the cliffs that divided it from the upper city, was empty and serene. Deirdre could see these things from the window where she stood, naked but not cold. And not afraid of him.

She had been sleeping when he called her again.

He now sat on the overstuffed chair at the other side of the room. He had asked her for coffee and for her nakedness. Both were little presents. If he had the sexual appetite of an adolescent, she thought, he also had a child's gift for delight in small favors.

Going to the service bar, she poured the coffee from the silver coffeemaker provided by the hotel.

Deirdre had been frightened a little when he began to play games with her; it seemed unnatural; it seemed a little evil. Finally, she had decided it was all of that and that she desired him the more for it. Was she herself evil or unnatural?

She smiled. There was no secret too vile for the heart of a good girl, a good Catholic girl who went to Mass and wept at the Stations of the Cross and delighted in the ecstasy of sin.

She had small, round breasts and large, brown nipples and sometimes Slough would ask her to stand before him so that he could admire her. He would touch her then, touch her breasts, her vagina, reach into her womb, as though counting his pleasures.

Deirdre Monahan was thirty-one years old and looked younger even; her eyes were green and soft; she was born in the village of Innisbally, below the heights of the burren hills. Her mother was pious and her father was a drunk and her brother had gone away to live in America; Deirdre knew she was just an ordinary woman desired by a man.

Not that he loved her. In her wisdom, she even understood that he was fond of her.

He had come to her the first time at night, when Brianna was fourteen and she was twenty-five. He had come to her in her rooms at Clare House and made love so naturally that it seemed they must have made love before, at least in dreams.

He opened his silk dressing gown as she put down the coffee on the side table. Kneeling naked before him, she took his large penis into her mouth.

She loved him. She would not say that to him because it would have made him sad—to think she loved him.

He had been dressed for an hour: Black turtleneck

shirt, black trousers, dark leather jacket. He wore a black beret. He sat by the door.

He looked again at the weapon in his black-gloved hand. Again, he removed the magazine from the pistol grip and reinserted it with a sharp click. Everything was going well.

Uzi, the name given to this ugly thing that appeared to be some sort of pistol. It was a small machine gun, made by the Israelis. Nine-millimeter, small recoil, very reliable. The barrel was contained so that its upward climb when firing—a common problem in all automatic weapons—was greatly reduced.

He knew the French criminal investigation division used it—it was also being made by a Belgian firm and distributed in France. He trusted the weapon as he trusted few things: forty-round magazine, SMG set to fire automatically. It was deadly at two hundred yards; devastating in a closed room.

In a hotel room.

He glanced at his watch and got up from the chair by the door. Eight A.M. Within the next fifteen minutes, the bellboy would bring up the morning papers to Lord Slough's suite.

The bellboy would die. That bothered him. The boy did not deserve to die. He had nothing to do with what had to be done. But there was no way not to involve him.

Toolin shrugged. Perhaps he would die as well. It didn't matter.

He entered the old, ornate corridor. He went to the elevator. The pistol—machine gun was under the leather jacket. He pressed the "up" button.

8:01.

The bell sounded. The doors clicked open.

My God, he thought, it was close.

The boy was on the elevator already.

"Up, sir," he said. Politely. He had red cheeks and red

hair and bright, clever eyes. Toolin felt pity. Walked on the elevator and turned away from the boy so as not to see him.

The boy glanced at the headlines on the front page of the *New York Times* he carried in his hand. He hummed to himself.

Click, click, click—the elevator glided up past the floors. The numbers flashed on the control panel.

Toolin held his hands folded together across the front of his jacket.

The bell rang, the elevator doors flashed open. The top floor.

Toolin felt sweat on his palms beneath the gloves. It had been quite simple, really; Lord Slough had dismissed the bodyguard for the night. His room was to the right, not part of the suite. Jeffries' room was next to that. Lord Slough had wanted privacy for his tête-à-tête with the Irish bitch.

They had not expected it to be so easy. They were prepared to kill him in the dining room, but this was much better. Only the boy would be in the way.

The boy waited for him to step out. Politely.

Toolin nodded and went down the corridor. He heard the boy walk across the carpet to the door.

Knock.

"Your papers, sir," he said.

Toolin reached for the machine pistol.

The voice on the other side of the door was muffled.

The boy said, "Very good, sir." He placed the papers on the carpet of the hall next to the door. He turned back to the elevator bank. The door had closed. He pressed the "down" button.

Damn.

Toolin suddenly did not know what to do. He decided to walk the length of the hall, away from Lord Slough's door and the boy waiting for the elevator. He walked slowly. He felt the weight of the Uzi inside his leather coat.

Ping. The door of the elevator opened.

He turned back. Saw the the boy enter the elevator and turn at the last moment and look at him. The boy smiled. Toolin smiled in return.

Quietly. Back along the hall on the thick carpet. Now he stood opposite the door.

He unbuttoned his coat carefully. He took the machine gun from his coat, felt the folded stock, touched the bottom of the forty-round magazine wedged into the pistol grip chamber.

He held it straight out from his body, pointed to the door.

Moments of silence.

Toolin did not know what to do. When would they get the papers? Would the bodyguard come? How much time was there?

8:09 A.M.

Steps behind the door.

He heard his breath. It was too loud.

The click of the lock.

The door opened.

He saw her for a moment. She was bending to pick up the morning newspapers when she became aware of him. She looked up. She appeared amused. He never saw her eyes.

She was naked.

Because she was bent over, the bullets—which should have struck her in the belly—smashed into her face. She did not utter a sound.

Her body exploded back into the apartment. Her face was only blood and bone.

He ran forward, over her already-dead body, now sinking to the floor. Blood spattered his trouser cuffs.

Four steps in the little hall. He ran it.

Lord Slough turned at the window. The sputter of the machine gun had reached his consciousness only a moment before. Adrenalin pumped into his blood.

The bullets burst out, smashing to the line of windows. Glass shattered. Lord Slough fell.

Toolin turned now, the gun still firing, bullets ripping into the plaster walls, smashing the television set. The picture tube exploded with a savage pop.

Behind him.

Turning, firing. Harmon, in the hall, fired three times. The bullets surged heavily into Toolin. He could not stop the trigger. The machine gun bucked in his hand, spraying up and down, splitting Harmon's face. He saw Harmon fall back, onto the dead, naked woman.

Toolin lurched forward, the magazine—incredibly—spent of its forty rounds. He fell onto the carpet. Smelled his own blood. Felt the damp warmth of the carpet against his face. Nuzzling his cheek.

The redness filled his eyes.

At least the boy did not have to die.

There was that.

At least—

9

BELFAST

Devereaux awoke thinking of Elizabeth at the end of his sleep. He had seen her in his dream and it had startled him and he had awakened. For a moment—as always—he did not know where he was. He lay still until he remembered. A gray light broke through the square of window beyond his bed. It made the dark room look sinister in the pale, dusty shadows. Yesterday, he had been with her, felt her warmth next to him. Now there was nothing but the gray light and the cold. And pain.

He struggled up and felt dizzy. He had slept in his clothing. He felt tired and dirty. The pain in his throat made it difficult to swallow.

He fumbled to the bathroom, turned on the shower. The balm of water. He pulled his clothes off and climbed into the shower and stood still and let his mind sort out the confusion.

Elizabeth. In a picture.

Apparently, Denisov had left after Devereaux fell asleep; he could not remember.

The dining room of the hotel was immense and dismal, reflecting the nature of the hotel. It was also nearly empty. Commercial travelers, forced by mere industry to ignore war, sat at their tables alone, digesting their bits of food and bits of news from the *Belfast Telegraph*.

And Denisov, sitting alone. He would have to sort it out with him.

"Good morning," said Denisov. "Your neck looks terrible."

He gestured with his fork to the empty seat. Devereaux sat down and looked at Denisov's plate: scrambled eggs and a tomato that had been squashed and grilled and some fatty bacon.

He realized he was hungry. Since he had been a child, he had not taken pleasure in food; it had only been fuel, added as an afterthought, taken for social reasons or when his body demanded it. He had not eaten since Edinburgh, more than a day before. The lack of food had not made him faint.

The thick waitress took his order and went away. Devereaux looked at the Soviet agent. Saintly eyes looked back.

"You put my envelope back in the same place," Devereaux said finally. Actually, he had not checked the brown envelope.

"Yes. I am careful. You should be careful as well, Devereaux. All that American money. Why did you tear those dollars in half?"

"Not in half. Slightly larger. So I can still cash them."

"Who holds the other parts of them?"

"Who is Blatchford?"

Denisov smiled, speared a fat piece of bacon and placed it in his mouth. He chewed slowly. "I do not understand why I am responsible for your life if I save it."

"Because that's the way it is."

"It bothered me all night."

"You have the conscience of a child."

Pause. Chew. "Yes. It is useful. I think I understand what you say."

"Who is Blatchford?"

"Was, my friend."

Devereaux waited. The tea came and then the plate of food. He poured milk into the tea. It tasted nearly sweet. It warmed him. Curiously, the presence of Denisov warmed him as well. He understood the Soviet agent without understanding any part of him. They had been in Asia together. Not together. A friend; an enemy; it didn't matter.

"I want you to trust me."

"And I want your respect, so I cannot trust you."

"I don't understand that, Devereaux."

"If I trust you, you will not respect me."

"All right."

They ate silently.

"Why are you here, Devereaux?"

"You know."

"Perhaps."

"Is that your way of saying nothing?"

Denisov smiled. "Why are we both here? We belong in Asia. In another time."

Two Asia hands. Adrift in the West; the cold, unmerciful West.

"Why are you here?"

"To help you."

"Thank you."

"I'm entirely serious. You should be serious, too."

"I cannot take you seriously when you say things like that."

"I will put my cards on the floor," said Denisov. "Blatchford was an agent. Of your government."

"Good. Keep on."

"We think we know who he was but we do not understand fully."

Devereaux waited.

"He was CIA."

He stared at the face of the Russian. It was not just the eyes but the shading of the skin and the broad, peasant's face. Perhaps he was Saint Peter and not Saint Francis of Assisi.

"Well, what do you think now?"

"Nothing. I can't think."

"What do you think of the young woman?"

"What woman?"

"The one you took to your room in London. And you made love to, I would say."

"Were you the one under the bed?"

"Joke," he said, just as Hanley would say it. "Tell me jokes. Do you think that woman finds you so beautiful she says, 'I must have this man'?" Now Denisov smiled. "You are become vain."

"You *have* become vain."

"Sorry. But you are. It makes me smile, Devereaux."

"I can see that. Anything to provide amusement."

"What if I told you that woman was here."

"Where?"

"Here."

"In the hotel?"

"No, in Belfast. Another place."

"Do you ever sleep, Denisov? Or are there more than just you?"

He shrugged. "Just me. No, you know I do not sleep. Ever. Always watching."

"It must be tedious."

"What?"

"Your professional voyeurism. Not to mention the paranoia."

"You're not interested in the young woman?"

"Very interested." He poured another cup of tea and dashed in the milk. "Very interested in you, Denisov. For your interest in me."

"Wait. Too many. Interest in me because I am interested—oh. I understand."

"I don't."

"You said that last night."

"I know. It's still true."

"This is not a game, Devereaux."

"Of course it is."

They were quiet again. The waitress came and asked if they wanted anything more and they said no. Devereaux took the bill absently and scrawled his name and room number on it. Denisov watched him. In an odd way,

Devereaux only felt able to speak with Denisov. He could go for weeks alone, in the mountains, without speaking, without hearing another voice, without turning on the radio or TV, without going down to Front Royal for supplies. Or he could sit silently for hours and listen, absorb information, without commenting. But Denisov seemed always to probe another place within him, the place where words waited to be said. He had to speak to Denisov; in that way, the Russian seemed stronger than he.

"Why did you come to Ireland?"

"For the climate."

"Please, Devereaux—"

"No, no goddam please. Listen, you sonofabitch, you know I was being set up. That that prick you killed was going to kill me. You know about my fucking and how many times a day I shit. Well, listen, I want you to tell me why you know everything and then maybe we can talk."

All said quietly, with an edge of hissing menace, the language tough and from the streets. It had all been covered over by the years, by the veneer of education, of age, of distance from that kid who had been in the streets of the city and carried a knife in his boot and first killed someone by carving him with a straight razor.

Denisov stared, appeared shocked. And then he smiled. The calm smile embraced even the ugly face Devereaux made and his words.

"All right, my friend. It is good for you to become with emotions at last. It shows me that you are concerned."

"Where my life is concerned, I am concerned."

"Come. I don't want to sit here. Let us take a walk. We can walk into the city. You should buy a turtle shirt so that your throat does not look ugly."

"Fuck you." But said quietly again, in the old voice. Why had he spoken to Denisov like that? The voice had been pulled out of him by the Russian.

The two men rose and left the immense dining room. Through the lobby, desolate in early morning. Into the foggy street. Devereaux wore only a sport coat of brown corduroy. They walked to the heart of the city. Around them, shop girls click-clacked in their heels along the sidewalks, bundled against the weather. There was an air of ersatz commerce to the city, as though the bombs and the deaths did not exist, as though only business were real.

"It was a peaceful city," said Denisov sadly. He had his arms folded behind him. He looked slightly professorial in his drab brown raincoat. He was bareheaded. His eyeglasses became damp and the wet in the fog touched his red cheeks and made it appear there were tears on them.

Devereaux walked with him. The city did not terrify in bleak morning; perhaps that was how they stood it, stood the years of bombing and war and rubber bullets and barbed wire and soldiers on the street. The people of the city waited for morning. For a little peace.

"I will ask you some things but only to explain. I am trying to make you trust me."

The fog chilled them. But it was warmer than in Edinburgh.

"Do you know who finances the IRA now?" Denisov asked.

"No."

"Good. An answer at least. I am not sure I believe you but at least it is an answer."

They turned down Royal Avenue, away from the center, toward the docks.

"We know it is the CIA. Your CIA."

They walked along. Past the immense offices of the *Belfast Telegraph*.

"You are not surprised?" said Denisov.

"You're not through."

"No, I am not through. You're right. The CIA channels the legitimate funds—from the Irish in your country

—through Dublin banks and then adds its own. We are not even certain that the IRA know this."

"How do you know this?"

"A little mouse told me."

"A little bird."

"Are you sure? Sorry. A little bird."

"You're crazy, Denisov. You've told me nothing. I'm going back to my hotel."

"I am insulted. I have told you the truth. A great truth. To make you trust me."

"If the CIA funds the Boys and you know this, I cannot find a plausible reason for your telling me. If the CIA funds the Boys, I cannot find a plausible reason for them to do it. Your information, then, cannot be true."

"Do you like opera?"

"No."

"I love English opera. The Gilbert and Sullivan. Do you know the *Pinafore?* No? You are too badly educated, Devereaux. They have a song in this. It sings:

> "Things are seldom what they seem;
> Skim milk masquerades as cream;
> Highlows pass as patent leathers;
> Jackdaws strut in peacock feathers—"

Devereaux was amused by the startled looks of several passersby. Denisov smiled. "You see?"

"No."

"You look to something and you say, 'I don't understand.' So it does not happen."

"Talking to you is like trying to draw a perfect circle."

"I am being direct, Devereaux," said Denisov, just as mildly as before. "I do not understand why the CIA funds the Republican Army. Until now, I do not care. But now I must help you and you will not let me."

"Who is Blatchford?"

"I have told you. CIA. A very bad man."

"We're all bad men."

"He killed your friend, Hastings. Does that make him bad?"

"Hastings was not my friend."

"Blatchford had a picture of this woman you sleep with. There." He gestured to the hotel across the street. "Do you know she is there now?"

"Now I do."

"Yes, because I tell you. That is Blatchford's hotel. That is her hotel. Blatchford had her picture with him. He tries to kill you. All these things happen to you, to Blatchford. I see this. The woman meets you and makes you love her. Blatchford eliminates Hastings and then eliminates you. You go to Edinburgh to meet Hastings. Everything I have told you is true." Denisov stepped ahead of Devereaux and turned to face him. His eyeglasses were misted so that the clear, blue eyes swam behind them. His hair was plastered wet with the mist.

"Why are you here, Devereaux? You must tell me this."

"Tell you so that you will not have to kill me."

Denisov took off his glasses and looked at the American. "Yes. So I will not have to kill you."

He yearned to speak to Denisov. The words, buried in him, yearned to be articulated.

"I don't know. That's the truth."

"That is not the truth, Devereaux."

"Perhaps."

Denisov wiped the glasses on the sleeve of his brown raincoat. "Then we cannot be friends."

"No."

"I am sorry."

"Now you will kill me?"

Denisov shrugged. "I do not know. I am sorry we cannot be friends."

"Yes."

The two men stood a moment longer, forming an island in the stream of pedestrian traffic along Royal Avenue.

And then the island broke up and the pieces of it flowed into the stream, away from each other.

Tatty was waiting in the back of the public house when Faolin strode in. Faolin appeared angry, his thin face twisted even more with some grievance. He had a copy of the *Telegraph* rolled under his arm. He saw Tatty and went to the back table and sat down.

Tatty sipped at his Guinness and looked at the younger man.

"Y've seen it, then," said Tatty.

"Oh, aye. I've bloody seen it," said Faolin in a furious whisper. "IRA is it? Some bloody fool walks into Lord Slough's room and tries t'kill him and nearly ruins a half a year's plan?"

"Who says it's the Boys?"

"Here. The bloody English say it."

Tatty did not look at the paper. He peered at Faolin as one might peer at a monkey in the zoo; or as a monkey might peer at the people watching him.

"What fool ordered this?"

"None that I'm aware of—"

"Then you're not bloody aware—"

"Watch it, lad," said Tatty. Mildly.

"I want t'know the bloody fool responsible. This cuts it, finally—"

"It cuts nothin', Faolin."

The younger man glared.

"'Tis almost Providential."

"How the bloody hell is that?"

"D'ye think that our plot would have remained so bloody secret? Right t'the moment? This is Ireland, boyo, bloody full of fools and gossips and informers. So now if there is any suspicion that the Boys are gonna get Lord Slough, the suspicious ones suddenly have their fact t'gnaw at like dogs. And, like dogs, t'look no further—"

Faolin stared at Tatty and then understood. His anger could not leave him so easily, but he managed silence.

"Ach. Yer see? It's the best thing that could have occurred. Lord Slough has been shot at and not hurt, the Boys have been blamed and all's well—"

"But who ordered it?"

"Who can say? Perhaps he was on his own or had a grievance against the Great Man. Who cares now, Faolin? 'Tis done. And our plan is still in place. Stronger than ever."

"He'll get another bodyguard—"

"Oh, aye. P'raps two of them. Does it matter, lad?"

Faolin shook his head. "I don't like the unexpected—"

"Woosh, lad. Y'talk foolishness. The unexpected has aided us in this. And thrown the gossips off the track. Let someone say, 'The Boys are after Lord Slough,' and they'll say, 'Yer great bloody fool, they already tried t'kill him in Canada. Now what are ya sayin'? That they'll do it again?'"

But Faolin could not feel assured. He sat with Tatty and watched the black Guinness slowly descend the pint glass and he drummed his fingers on the table until it was time for them to leave.

The unexpected frightened him. Even if Tatty thought it was welcome news.

10

SHANNON

There were three things that needed to be done; each was linked to the other like three parts of the same event.

Devereaux was back in his room; he glanced around and everything was as it should have been—the laundry had been returned, the bed made, new towels in the bath.

He opened his leather two-suiter that sat on the dresser and felt along the lining for the compartment. It opened without a sound and he removed the black .357 Magnum revolver and held it up to the light.

The game was starting again: He looked at the person in the mirror—a man with a gun and a gray face and merciless eyes—and watched him like a stranger.

There were six bullets in six chambers.

He had refused to use automatic pistols since the time a .45 jammed on him at an awkward moment in Amsterdam. Actually, he did not like any sort of pistol. Or the death he always brought.

He slid the pistol onto his belt, attached by a small metal clip protruding at the side of it.

He wondered how Denisov had managed to kill Blatchford. Pistol? Knife? His hands. Probably his hands; it had to be quick and sure.

The bullets in the chambers had flattened heads which made them somewhat inaccurate beyond forty yards. But in the close game Devereaux played, they would be sufficient. They would tear at the flesh like dumb, blinded animals.

Three things to be done before he called Hanley again.

He slipped on his brown corduroy jacket and left the room; in a minute he stood in the hotel cocktail lounge. It was empty and a fat woman stood behind the bar.

"I was supposed to meet a man here last night—" Devereaux began.

The words had a cathartic effect on the woman's speech; she began to babble: "About what time, sir? I was on late 'cause Red Boylan was ill. You'd be talkin' to Red Boylan any other day, but he got somethin' last night. I think it was the fish—don't touch the fish, I tol' him, but Boylan is fond after fish, it's almost unnatural and—"

No. No. No one came in. No man who looked like O'Neill. No one after eleven P.M. Business was so slow that—

Devereaux extricated himself from the monologue and crossed the lobby again to the street.

O'Neill had not come to the hotel; perhaps because he did not expect Devereaux to return to it either.

His instincts were in charge now; he hailed a cab and slid inside, giving the address of the hotel on Royal Avenue. The second part of the matter involved Elizabeth.

When he asked for her at the desk, the clerk looked carefully in box 602 for the key and then said she was not in. Devereaux nodded and went back across the lobby to the hotel bar while the clerk watched him. He ordered a vodka drink but did not sip it; when the clerk turned, he went to the elevator and took it to the sixth floor.

All Devereaux's movements now were contained and economical. Walking down the dark, old-fashioned corridor, he counted the numbers on the doors. Her room. He stood still and listened. The silence was as heavy as the damp, cold air; nothing was as quiet as a hotel corridor in afternoon. He removed a piece of thick wire from the copper bracelet on his wrist and inserted it into the lock. In a moment, the door sprung open as though it were surprised. Without a sound.

The bed had been made. He closed the door behind him.

Her suitcase was on the desk. He went to it. Opened it. Empty. Felt along the seam. Felt nothing. He took a pocketknife from his coat and flicked it open. Felt the bottom of the suitcase and slit the lining neatly with the edge of the knife. There was a compartment. He stared at it for a moment. Empty. He closed the suitcase lid.

He went to her bed and picked up the top mattress and slid it off the box springs. Her passport was wedged between the top and bottom mattresses. He picked it up and flipped it open. Elizabeth stared at him. There was a stamp on the first page. Ethiopia, 1971; Taiwan, 1972; Republic of Korea, 1972; United Kingdom, 1973. He looked through all the pages. Every year marked by stamps of countries. He placed the passport in the pocket of the drab raincoat.

He lifted the box spring and felt along the bottom of it. Nothing.

He opened the drawers of the night stand: a *Guide to Belfast and the North of Ireland;* Gideon Society Bible; nothing.

He went to the closet and opened the door. His body moved in a kind of fury, without sound—even without breath. He felt along the top shelf. Scattered the dust with his fingers. Nothing.

He examined her coat. Felt in the pockets and along the lining of the coat. Touched something. He opened the knife again and tore the seam wide, like a surgeon. He removed ten one-hundred-dollar bills which had been folded into the seam at the bottom of the coat. He put them in his pocket.

Two pairs of shoes on the floor of the closet. He picked them up and took the heels off—prying them off with the knife. Solid heels. Nothing. He threw them back on the closet floor.

He examined the buttons of the coat. Solid. He flicked the knife shut and put it in his pocket.

He went into the bathroom.

Lipstick. Hand cream. Shampoo in a plastic container. He smelled the shampoo. Smelled her. He poured the shampoo into the sink and looked again at the bottle. Nothing.

He opened the jar of hand cream and slowly scooped it all out. Nothing.

He threw the jar into the wastebasket.

He opened the medicine cabinet. A little purse. He opened it and dumped everything onto the counter next to the wash bowl.

A green plastic case, oval-shaped. He opened it. A rubber diaphragm inside. He took it out and examined it and placed it back in the plastic case.

A tube of anti-sperm vaginal gel. He squeezed out the tube slowly. He put it down.

There were four tampon sticks. He opened the wrapper of each and examined both sides of the wrapper for writing. He tore the cotton sticks apart.

Nothing.

He took the lipstick tube and opened it. Her color. But he did not think about her; he did not see her in these things. He was a morgue attendant, cataloguing the artifacts of the dead.

Taking a piece of toilet paper, he pulled the lipstick out of the tube. Then he ground it slowly. Nothing. He threw it into the toilet. He looked inside the tube. Nothing.

He went to the shower curtain and examined it, felt along the seam at the bottom.

Nothing.

He went back into the gloom of the bedroom and felt behind the dresser mirror. He moved the dresser out and examined the backing. He pried off a loose piece of trim. Nothing.

Going to the television set, he opened the back. The dust lay evenly and thickly over the tubes and circuits.

Nothing.

Finally, he stood at the window and looked into the gloom of the darkened bedroom. His face was impassive, clerklike: He looked slowly over the room, imagining little squares superimposed on his vision of the room as though the room were a photograph. He examined each square before going on to the next. He had neglected nothing.

He sat down in the chair by the window, took out his pistol, and put it on the desk next to the chair. He sat, waiting, in the darkness.

The door opened slowly. She felt along the wall for the light switch before stepping into the room.

Afraid of the dark.

She found the switch. He heard its ugly click. Two lamps blazed on, the one at the bed and the one on the desk. She was half turned away from the room as she entered and pushed the door closed behind her. He had an instant to look at her again.

She was beautiful. He had, in two days, forgotten how tall Elizabeth was, how her body carried her fullness. Her legs were full and oddly graceful. He remembered. He looked at her. But nothing showed on his face; the things he felt were hidden.

Just an instant. And then she turned into the room. Saw him but only saw in that moment a human presence. She was frightened; her face went pale. When she knew it was him, she started to speak but then she saw the room.

"What?" It was all she could say.

She saw the pistol on the desk. He had not moved to touch it. He sat still.

"What?"

She leaned against the door, afraid to step into the chaos of the room. She saw her closet door opened. Saw the mattress on the floor, tangled in bedsheets. Saw the drawers of her dresser opened, her clothes heaped on the floor.

Devereaux let the shock take her. She shivered. She stared at him. He noticed that her hands were clenched.

Her dark hair was not attractive now—it was wet, pasted to her forehead. Her lipstick had faded. She stood still and looked at him and then suddenly went to the dresser as though she had to run across a narrow bridge to reach it. She looked at her strewn clothing. She picked up her underthings from the floor where he had thrown them. She put them back into a drawer and shut it.

"You bastard," she said. The shock was past; rage gained. He waited.

She turned and went into the bathroom. There was no sound. After a moment, she came back into the bedroom. Her arms were folded now across the gentle swell of her belly as though she were sick. Her tailored suit was wet.

She could barely speak. Her eyes searched his features. "Why?"

He got up. "Sit down here." He pointed to the straight-backed wooden chair.

She stood still and stared at him.

He took her arm quickly and twisted it; she half bent over; she did not cry out. He forced her to the chair and let her arm go. Going to the desk, he turned out the glaring light, leaving only a single soft stab of light from the night stand beside the bed. He went to the wall by the door and turned. He had left his pistol on the desk, nearer to her than to himself. He wondered if she would reach for it. Her back was to him.

He began: "Who are you?"

"You bastard," she replied.

"Who are you?"

She was silent.

He waited. He looked at her wet brown hair. He remembered the smell of it. He looked at her shoulders. She sat still, her arms across her breasts. He thought of the pleasure she had shared with him.

"Who are you?" Again.

She turned in the chair then and looked at him. Her eyes were dry, hard, angry. "What do you want?"

"I want to know who you are."

"Elizabeth Campbell."

"Who are you?" He said it again, in the same maddening voice. His voice was flat, without edge, without menace. He might have been a recording or a machine.

She repeated her name. "I'm coordinator of investigations for Free The Prisoners, an international—"

"Why are you in Belfast?"

"I came here with the detachment—we're going to Long Kesh. Why are you here? You were going home."

He waited.

She tugged at an earring—a gold circle—and pulled it off. Then the other. She held them in her hands and then put them on the desk. She waited.

"Who is Blatchford?"

Movement. Slight. Her eye. "Who?"

He did not repeat the name.

"I don't know what you're talking about—" But she knew it was too late for that lie. She had given it away.

He placed the picture on the desk next to her. It was a photograph of a younger Elizabeth and a little boy. He watched her while he did this.

She looked at the picture and then at him.

"Where did you get this? How did you get this from me?" Her voice was suddenly tired.

"Who is the child?"

"You bastard," she said. "How did you steal this?"

"Who is Blatchford?"

"I don't know what you're talking about."

"Tell me about you—"

"How did you get this picture? You filth. You slime."

"Tell me about Blatchford. And this child."

"I won't tell you anything." But she had, already.

Now it was time. Going to the desk, he picked up the pistol and held it loosely in his hand.

"Elizabeth," he said. She had to understand that everything he said was true. That everything he would now threaten would happen. She had to understand that; that was the difficult part.

"Elizabeth. I want you to tell me about the people you work for. To tell the truth. If you tell me the truth, it will be better. Not all right—but better. I am in the business of information, not vengeance. Do you understand me?"

She stared at him. She shivered; she was cold.

"Blatchford tried to kill me last night, but he's dead. I have Blatchford's wallet. He had a number of items in it, including identity cards in my name. I was set up. By someone. By your people."

She touched her throat. She kept staring at him.

"Blatchford had this picture of you and the child. Do you understand what I'm saying? Two nights ago, I was sitting in the bar of a London hotel. Suddenly, I met you after fifteen years. You came to me. You went to bed with me. I loved that, Elizabeth."

For a moment his voice lost its flatness.

"I want you to understand that part too. You're a beautiful woman. But I did not understand it then and I don't now. Why did we meet? And make love? And now why are you in Belfast? And why is your picture in the wallet of a man who tried to kill me? Do you understand what I'm saying? Elizabeth? Say you understand it."

She spoke slowly: "I don't understand."

He shook his head. He said everything again. He said he wanted information, not vengeance. He said Blatchford had tried to kill him. He said Blatchford was dead. He told about the photograph again. He talked about her, about making love to her. He said these things slowly, carefully, as if he were a teacher going over the alphabet with a slow child.

"Do you understand now?"

She nodded.

"Say it then."

"I understand."

He brought up the gun in his hand. He held it on the level of her eyes. "Now, Elizabeth, think before you speak now. It's very important. Look at me, please. This is a .357 Magnum revolver. Each bullet has been altered by the addition of a heavy charge and a flattened nose. At the distance of six feet, a bullet would tear your face apart. We are closer, much closer. I am going to kill you, Elizabeth."

He paused.

She stared at the muzzle of the black gun.

"Or I will not kill you. I told you I wanted information, not vengeance. I want the truth. I want you to tell me everything. If you tell me, I will let you live. I will give you a day to leave Belfast. I promise that and I won't lie to you. But if you do not tell me the truth, I will kill you. I have no choice if I'm going to survive. And I'm going to, Elizabeth."

"You won't kill me."

He looked at her sadly. "This is not a game now. I have killed nine people. I don't enjoy killing or torture; I didn't enjoy tearing your room apart; I don't enjoy this, any of it. But I have to know. You intruded on me; you came into my game. The game's ended. Do you understand?"

She nodded.

She stared at the dull, black pistol.

He waited. The silence tore at both of them. A demon had seized his body and voice; it was as though he could stand outside himself and watch. He wondered if someday the demon would take his body and never return it.

"I would betray—"

He said softly, "Betrayal is nothing. Life is worth that, Elizabeth. Your life."

He waited a moment and then spoke: "Who are you, Elizabeth?" To say her name softened the question.

She began slowly, in another voice, holding her body. Her voice was dead and empty.

"Two years ago," she began. Paused. "I met a man. In Washington. I went to work for him."

He watched her. Her eyes looked lost. "He was with. With. The R Section."

The demon held Devereaux's body perfectly still.

"His name was Hanley. Is Hanley."

He thought to breathe, but holding his breath seemed more natural. He wondered if he could stand still for hours, for days? He knew he could.

"You know Hanley. You know all this now." She said it flatly.

"Tell me, Elizabeth." Was the demon losing control?

"He said—you'll kill me now." She seemed distracted, about to weep again. "He said he needed information about you. It was my second assignment. I was to go to New York to meet you. To find out who you were selling out to—"

Suddenly, beyond the dark window, in the darkness of Belfast, there was a sound like an explosion from a far way off. The window of the room rattled slightly as though a train had passed or a puff of air had struck it.

"You were suspected—are suspected—of being a double agent. It was my assignment to find you. To . . . make love to you. To—" She could not speak for a moment. She finally took the water and drank the glassful at a gulp. "Hanley said because I had known you. And then, when you were not in New York, I was sent to London to wait for you."

"And do what?"

"To find out about you. To become . . . your friend." She did not look at the black pistol.

"You work for R Section."

"Yes," she said.

"For how long?"

"Eighteen months."

"Who recruited you?"

"Hanley."

"Describe him."

She described a man.

"Where is the Section?"

She told him.

"What is your status?"

"I'm a field man."

"Why am I here?"

"I don't know."

He looked at her. She looked again at the pistol.

"Why am I here?"

"I don't know. That wasn't part of my assignment."
She did not continue.

"Who is Blatchford?"

"He's with the Section as well."

"I never met him."

"I know. Hanley knows."

"Why did Blatchford try to kill me?"

"I don't believe that. It wasn't part of the assignment."
He let it go. "Why did he have your picture?"

"I don't know."

"Did he take it?"

"Yes. He must have. I don't know."

"Why?"

"I don't know."

"How could he have taken it?"

"In my room. In London. Before you came. I didn't
know it was missing. I never look at it. I carry it."

"How could he have taken it?"

She felt drained, tired, sick.

"How?"

"When we . . . When Blatchford and I were together.
I don't know."

The demon was gone now. His hand shook. But he
still held the pistol, pointed at the floor.

"Why did Blatchford try to kill me?"

She shook her head. "You killed him—"

It was not necessary to bring in Denisov now. He
nodded.

"God." She shivered. "I didn't know. You killed him."

He felt an absurd need suddenly to justify himself. To this tired woman with matted brown hair and rain streaked on her cheeks.

He stood in the light.

"Look," he said.

She recoiled from the ugly weal across his throat.

"He did that?"

"Yes. And he killed another man before he tried to kill me."

"No." She shook her head.

"Elizabeth. Who is the child?"

She seemed confused. And then she looked at the picture. "Do you have to know everything? Do you have to dirty everything I feel—"

"Who is the child?"

"David. My son."

"Where is he?"

"Dead."

There really was nothing more to ask her. He wanted to touch her, to pity her, to tell her. What? What comfort could he give her?

Hanley had sent them. Elizabeth and Blatchford. To spy on him and to murder him.

And why had Denisov become his guardian angel?

Devereaux stared at Elizabeth. *You warmed me. You reminded me of my other life. You touched me.*

Slowly, he put the pistol on his belt and drew his jacket over it. She saw this but she did not move. She sat holding herself, trying not to shiver.

"Do you know a man named O'Neill?"

He had no need for the pistol now. Or the threat.

She shook her head.

He believed that.

"Now." He looked at her. "Begin. Tell me about R Section and why they sent you to spy on me."

Slowly, wearily, she started at the beginning.

The silver sliver in the sky broke through the galleons

of clouds sailing off the west coast. The sliver fell in the afternoon sky, catching the rare November sun on its wings, turning and dipping, it fell again, toward the large field below.

At that moment, Brianna Devon stood at the window in an immense lounge at Shannon Airport and watched the sky. She could not see the plane yet.

She wore fashionably tight French jeans, their cuffs stuffed into long, sleek brown boots. Her hair was an auburn red, cut short and severe. Her face, which was quite pretty, was clouded with worry. Her dark eyes searched the field before her but she could not see anything.

She was annoyed by the presence of the man next to her. He had been sent down from Galway City's *gardai*. He was a tall, ungainly man with neatly plastered black hair and a lantern jaw and large, cowlike eyes. He had dressed in plainclothes that could not have been more conspicuous if he had worn his uniform. He looked like nothing so much as the universal policeman in plainclothes for the first time.

He'd told her that Chief Inspector Cashel was going to visit them in the morning at Clare House. It was all so horrible, made more horrible by the police. All Brianna wanted was her father and Deirdre. She thought of Deirdre, who had been more like a sister than a tutor to her. Thought of her little laughing face. Deirdre.

"They'll be comin' along shortly, now, miss," said the *garda* from Galway City. "I've just got the signal. Yer father's landed."

And she had not even seen it. She ached for him. Her father was distant, and frightening even, but, somehow, she had found love in him. An offhand love that suited her.

She saw him at the end of the immense corridor. They had taken him through a special door, away from the customs area and the gaudy tax-free shop where weary hours were spent waiting for planes by buying bottles of Irish whisky and bolts of Irish cloth.

She did not wave. They did not wave or shout to each other—that wasn't their way. Like the horse. On her fifteenth birthday, she had awakened and dressed and gone down to breakfast, but he had not been there. Rushing from the house, she ran down along the stony road to the stables and there it was—a big brown stallion with boltish eyes. Farrell—old Farrell—was standing there holding the rein for her. Her father was not at the stable. He had gone away, but that was all right; she understood it was not indifference in him but an embarrassment at showing love.

Coming toward her now, he looked so tired, so sad. His hand was bandaged. When they were close enough, he beckoned for her to come to him and hug him.

"Hello, Brianna," he said softly.

The Rolls purred effortlessly up into the burren hills of Clare, along the coast road around Galway Bay. Winter in the west country: The hills were empty ridges of stone, treeless, fenced with stone fences of a thousand families who had finally fled the inhospitable land in the face of English landlords and Irish famines.

Brianna and Lord Slough did not speak. The bleak scenery comforted them. They had known it all their lives, from the time when Slough bought the crumbling castle and restored it and defiantly decided to live in it— an English lord in the midst of the impoverished Irish west.

The black car flashed through the little town of Innisbally, wipers silently driving the tears of rain from the windscreen. A drunk stumbled in the street on his way to the pub; he paused and let the immense car splash past him. His face was stupidly amazed. And then gone. Brianna barely saw it. She sat back in the comfort of the cushions, in the silent world of wood paneling that smelled of oil on the leather, and warmth.

Lord Slough looked out the window, at last. Deirdre's face was still before him. Still in the shape of the bleak land. She said the Irish laughed because God cried enough for them. She told a story about the burren families and of how they had stood on the point of Galway Bay and watched the ships pass on their way to America, and of the tears of those left behind.

He imagined her now, in the reflected window glass of the car, as she had been. On that last night and last morning, up until the moment she had gone to the door. He saw her as the fresh-faced teacher who had first come to Clare House after Margaret had died. He saw her alive because he would not look at her broken face in the Chateau Frontenac. He had refused because he had seen enough bodies in the war—bodies of friends—and he could never think of those friends again as they had been in life; they were always only bodies, bits of bone and flesh, mangled for eternity by death. He had not wanted to remember Deirdre like that. So he had refused to look at her.

He sighed.

Feeling the presence of Brianna next to him, he thought he should do something. Tell her something.

At last, he reached and touched her hand and held it. It was all he could think of.

Enough. She pressed next to him. When she was a baby, she'd had milky breath. He thought he smelled it now, the same innocent breath.

"Home, Brianna," he said at last. The word included the car and the plain hills. It was all he could think of.

She knew he meant to comfort her.

11

BELFAST

Inspector Cashel of the Special Branch, Dublin, piled his heavy bag into the black Ford Anglia. He could have taken a police auto, but the black Ford—the first car he had ever owned—was his not-so-secret joy. Cashel, who would go on and on about the mechanical wonders of the sturdy little car, did not realize that he and the vehicle were an object of fun in his division. And if he had known, he would not have seen the humor of it.

A surprisingly tender kiss from his wife, a little wave, and then he was gone, plunging into the streets of empty Dublin.

He turned down Baggot Street, past St. Stephen's Green and the Shelbourne Hotel and the mile of colorful old homes and just as colorful public houses. At the bridge over the little trickle of water that eventually becomes the broad Shannon River, he turned again, following the road to Limerick. The highways of Ireland have no name or number designations—they are merely roads which guide at intervals with white stakes pointing toward cities. It was a system considered confusing by tourists and comfortable by people like Cashel.

The windshield wipers clicked at the rain and the little heater warmed Cashel. His broad face reddened, making his black mustache seem blacker, blue eyes more blue. He thought of taking a pipe but decided to defer the pleasure of the first bowlful until he broke his journey in mid-morning.

In a little while, he was in the country.

He would be at Clare House before noon, he thought.

Denisov stood in the dark doorway of St. Anne's Church. He had been waiting for an hour.

He glanced again at his watch and saw the time; he waited for the bells to tremble the hour in the belfry above him. They finally did, two minutes late by his reckoning.

From where he stood, he could look down the hilly O'Donnell Road to Flanagan's public house, still blazing lights past closing time. Denisov had tried mightily to understand the pub-closing laws of England, Ireland, and Scotland and the exceptions to them and the history of them, and he still could not. He had waited in the church door an hour too long.

The rain had been falling since afternoon when Denisov had begun his search for O'Neill. He knew about O'Neill, of course, and Hastings and the connection in Edinburgh with Devereaux; but he did not understand the content of Devereaux's mission or the extent of Hastings' information. There were moments—now, waiting in the doorway, feeling cold and almost ill—when he did not understand his own reason for being there.

He yearned for the warmth of Asia to warm his cold bones. He yearned for games he could understand.

He felt in the pocket of his raincoat for the little Beretta. Old-fashioned weapon, light, not terribly accurate. So they told him. But he didn't care. He never intended to use it.

Finally, Flanagan's began to close in the slow and reluctant way of bars all over the world. He watched the patrons stagger out of the pub, stand on the steps and talk in the rain, and then scatter to their separate streets. He was amused to see one carrying on a conversation while he leaned against the fence around the vacant lot and urinated. The lights of the pub were extinguished, one by one, and, at last, he saw the figure of O'Neill trudging up the hill to St. Anne Road.

He did not like contact; he was basically a gatherer of information, and contact always made him feel a little uneasy.

O'Neill began singing, inexplicably, in the darkness of Belfast and in the rain falling straight down. Denisov heard snatches of lyrics carried on the wind as O'Neill came nearer:

> ". . . It's not the leavin' of Liverpool,
> That's grievvvvvvvin' me,
> But the love I'll leavvvvvve behind. . . ."

Denisov smiled and then stepped from the shadow of the doorway.

"You sing well."

O'Neill was startled but not frightened; he turned to the stranger and smiled. "C'mon inter the light like an honest man," he cried and waved vaguely towards the darkened street.

Denisov complied.

O'Neill's face was red and bloated and rain-streaked; his collar was damp and a red tie was knotted at his throat.

"Who're ya?"

"My name is Denisov."

"What kinda bloody name is it, then?"

"Russian."

"Yer a fuggin' Russian then?"

"I am," said Denisov.

O'Neill seemed to absorb this information slowly but with equanimity. "Well, let's go inter the city and find a jar."

"A jar—"

"A bloody jar of Guinness—"

"Stout—"

"Porter—"

Denisov shrugged. "The pubs are closed—"

"But not the hotels. Not the bloody hotel bars, not by a sight. And me, the O'Neill himself, has got the quid fer it and he'll buy even a fuggin' Communist a drink on it."

"That's very nice," said Denisov.

They walked along St. Anne Road together; Denisov had been there before. They strolled past the place where Blatchford had died and Devereaux had nearly been killed. It looked like every other spot on the pavement.

O'Neill began to sing "The Leaving of Liverpool" again. He sang it through in a steady, off-key voice and Denisov did not interrupt him. The feeble lights of the center of the city beckoned ahead. Magically, the rain ceased too.

"Ah, it's a bloody climate, man. I don't know how ya can stand it," O'Neill said at last, wiping rain from his broad, mottled forehead. His face was so bloated that Denisov thought it looked about to burst.

"It is less violent than the Soviet Union," said Denisov.

"Aye. I've heard about Russian winters," said O'Neill in sudden comradeship. He slapped Denisov painfully on the back. "Yer don't look like a Russian," he said.

Denisov shrugged. It was probably meant as a compliment.

They found a bar at last. They sat with the late crowd, sipping at Guinness. O'Neill—warm, dry, and with drink —said, "I'm a commercial traveler—what's yer line?"

"Similiar," said Denisov. He sipped manfully at the thick, sweet black beer.

At the second round, Denisov began slowly. "You know a man named Devereaux."

"What? Oh, aye. I met him once. He came to the house one mornin'. Yesterday? The day before? I fergets."

Denisov realized at once that O'Neill did not know Devereaux by his real name—that, in fact, the dead Blatchford had been Devereaux to O'Neill. He tried again.

"There's another fellow," he started.

O'Neill looked at him with a dawning suspicion.

"One you met in Scotland. An American."

"He didn't say his name was Devereaux. There might be two, I suppose—"

"Mr. O'Neill. I want to be honest to you. I am a representative of my government—"

"I thought you said you was a commercial traveler, too."

"In a sense, I am," said Denisov. "But I am buying, not selling. And I have the money to prove it."

He opened his wallet and showed a thick ream of pound notes. O'Neill stared at them in a glazed way. Denisov carefully left the wallet on the table.

"So." O'Neill swallowed. "What is it ye be after buyin' then?"

"Information," said Denisov carefully.

"And yer come to me?"

"I want to know what you told Devereaux. Rather, the man in Edinburgh."

"There were two men in Edinburgh," said O'Neill, his eyes hooding themselves in a gesture of shrewdness.

"Yes. I know. The other man was Hastings. He's dead."

"And Devereaux killed him. The second Devereaux. The one in Edinburgh."

Denisov weighed that and decided there was no reason to tell the truth. He shrugged in confirmation.

"He's a cold bastard," said O'Neill. "He broke me bloody nose. And he cheated me on me money—"

"How much did he give you?"

O'Neill glanced down at the wallet. "Five thousand American dollars—"

"There is one thousand in pounds in that wallet," said Denisov. "I want to know what you told the man in Edinburgh."

"Why should I tell ye fer less what he tol' me fer more?"

Denisov shrugged. "It is second-used."

"Yer mean it's old information?"

"Precise."

They waited. Finally, Denisov reached for the wallet.

"Now, now, not so fast," said O'Neill.

"Yes?" asked Denisov. He held his hand over the wallet.

"It's not as though I'm not bein' loyal," said O'Neill to himself out loud. "Me loyalty was forced from me t'begin with. But I'm not a Communist. I've never been."

"You don't have to be."

"Yer people ain't about to try to take over Ulster, are ye?"

"Of course not." Denisov smiled to himself: *We wish Northern Ireland on the English forever.*

"Well, then."

The bulging wallet seemed to beckon voluptuously.

"Well, then," O'Neill repeated.

Denisov looked at him mildly. He took his hand away from the wallet.

"Ah, it doesn't matter anyway now, does it?"

O'Neill reached for the wallet and opened it and looked at the pound notes inside.

"A thousand yer said?"

"A thousand," said Denisov.

"All right. It's a bargain, then." He spat on his hand like a farmer and shook Denisov's hand. Discreetly, Denisov wiped his palm on the raincoat. The wallet had already disappeared into O'Neill's clothing.

O'Neill began and told as much as he knew about the plot against Lord Slough. The information seemed to disappoint the Russian, so he tried to elaborate on it, but there was little. O'Neill had spent the past two days on a roaring drunk and he had not gathered more information; and, when he had heard about the assassination attempt on Lord Slough that afternoon, he had assumed he would never see the mates of those torn thousand-dollar bills. With a fatalistic nonchalance, he had spent the night drinking to his bad fortune. And now here was a Russian, wanting the same information.

Denisov could not believe it. Why would Devereaux have come to Ireland? For this? And why had the CIA plotted against his life—for the sake of protecting an assassination attempt three thousand miles away? It was craziness.

Further, how would he justify the paying of one thousand pounds for such worthless information? They had been brutal about expenses on the last assignment and Denisov feared they suspected, correctly, that Denisov was secretly putting expense money into his own Swiss account. Would they believe he gave this foolish Irishman a thousand pounds for information so scant—and so old —that it would not have justified any payment at all? He wondered if he should kill O'Neill for the money.

"There's nothing more?"

"More? More, ye bloody man? I've given ye a bargain —five thousand pounds they paid me—" O'Neill, believing for a moment his own hyperbole, was indignant.

"Devereaux would not come here for that—"

"Oh, aye. He seemed disappointed too—but yer see, that's not me fault. There were other parts and Hastings had put it all together. Hastings understood everything and that's why he wanted me to meet him in Edinburgh. I was just one of the parts he was sellin' the Americans."

"Did Devereaux—did the American in Edinburgh— have the other parts of information?"

"How the bloody hell should I know that?" O'Neill took a deep gulp of Guinness.

"For my thousand pounds I would think you know," said Denisov. He was annoyed both with O'Neill and with the thick black beer. And he was already worried about his expense report.

"Well, as a matter of fact, I do know that he seemed t'question me like he didn't know much more than I told you. He seemed bloody sad in the puss like you are now. It's only money, man; c'mon, I'll buy you a jar of whisky—"

"No." He waved his hand. But O'Neill pressed him

and he finally let the Irishman buy him a large glass of Irish whisky—with his own money.

"T'yer health, sur," said O'Neill, and he took a large swallow.

Denisov drank silently. Gloomily.

"It's funny about it all, though," said O'Neill at last. His mood had become quiet. "I tell yer what I know and yer sad in the puss. I tell the fella in Edinburgh, whoever the hell he is, and he's down in the mouth. But when I tol' the other fella—Devereaux, the one what come t'me house in the mornin'—I tol' him just what I had tol' his partner in Edinburgh—why, he seemed almost bloody cheerful!"

Denisov looked up: Blatchford had seemed cheerful.

"It was bloody strange, yer ask me. I was hardly half awake and me nose was painin' me from where the fella in Edinburgh had broke it on me—and so I'm not in a good humor yer might say, and this fella starts on me, askin' the same bloody things the other one did. Well, when I tol' him what I knew—why, I thought he'd bloody laugh he looked so bloody happy! Like a bloody child on Christmas Day! Well, there's no accountin', is there?"

Denisov nodded.

O'Neill took another sip of whisky. "It was just as if he knew all about what I was tellin' him but was just happy that was all there was. If yer understand me, sur?"

Denisov nodded.

He thought he was beginning to understand.

Devereaux had not left her until he had it all. He picked through her life carefully from the time she had been in the Peace Corps (that had been true), and into her marriage to a government lawyer and her divorce and the death of her son. That had been difficult but he had pulled that out as well. Then into her struggle for jobs in the circles of government in Washington. Up to the day she met the man called Hanley.

She described R Section. Wearily, she went over the

same ground again and again. She got up once and went to the window and looked out at the ring of hills around the old city; she talked dreamily of her past life—of her child, of her husband—and crisply of the life of R Section and the cover with Free The Prisoners.

What did Hanley drink?

She would shrug and say she did not remember.

He would come back to it again, circling back, edging the conversation: What did Hanley drink?

Scotch, she thought. He didn't seem to like to drink.

Elizabeth had been given the codes and tested on them. She had studied at one of the four schools in the East in which R had set up special sections for their agents in training. Her instructor had been a Sixth Man named Petersen.

Devereaux didn't know him.

She had been to R Section once, walked through the offices. Agents rarely appeared at the section—it was a rule established by Stapleton when he had been the chief of R. He did not want clerks to know agents or the other way around.

Devereaux was convinced finally that Elizabeth told him the truth. Or her part of the truth.

But he could not believe that Hanley had set up a ghost organization in R Section to spy on the spies. It was too bizarre; there had been only one serious defection from R in nearly fifteen years—when Dobson had defected while serving as field agent in Cambodia. That had been nearly seven years before.

Still . . . the facts: An agent named Blatchford had attempted to kill him; Blatchford had identification that seemed authentic; now Elizabeth confessed she worked for Hanley as well. But Denisov had said Blatchford was a CIA agent. Did the CIA, then, have a ghost R Section? Perfect down to the details of Hanley's drinking habits? And why?

Finally, he could not shake Elizabeth's story, so he left her; Devereaux was confused and tired and felt disoriented by the knowledge that there existed a ghost Section, even a "ghost Devereaux"—whom Denisov had killed.

Devereaux walked slowly back to the hotel, along the wet pavement, dimly aware of shapes of buildings and hills through the mists swirling down upon the city. He was surprised to discover he felt a sliver of pain because of Elizabeth's betrayal—betrayal of his bed and his little bit of love and their common pasts. When he identified the reason for his pain, he dismissed it; it was no more than another of the inexplicable aches he carried.

For a long while after Devereaux left, Elizabeth sat still on the single wooden chair in her room and looked at the photograph on the desk; he had left it in her purse and she had removed it. She stared at the picture of the child and at her younger self; she tried to catalogue her feelings but could not.

She could have told Devereaux about why she joined R Section—or what she had believed to be R Section. But she did not; she understood that Devereaux was not interested in her emotions or in her vague feelings of needing some sort of occupation to fill up the empty corners of her life and sweep out all that had been in the past.

Including the little boy and the happier time.

She was not so pale then, she noticed; her face was fuller and smiling. She would have judged her younger self even unfashionably plump, as though her contentment then had settled itself in her body and made it ripe and blooming. Like a flower.

The little boy stared at her from the photograph; she might be a stranger. Would he have known her now? Would he have said "Mother"? Of course not. It was maudlin to think about death and after death. There was no little boy anymore; he was a memory imperfectly captured by an old photograph, a photograph kept by a lonely young woman to provide wounds when needed.

Was she so masochistic, then? Of course not. But she needed the pain of remembering all that had happened.

After a long time, Elizabeth rose and began to take her clothes off. She let the wet clothes fall in a pile at her feet. Then she trudged like a sleepwalker into the bathroom and took all the things he had torn apart and dumped them in the waste can under the sink. Turning on the shower, she waited until the steam of the hot water filled the room and then she stepped into the tub, hoping the water would restore her.

When she got out, she did not feel better or worse.

She wrapped the towel around her.

She had wrapped the towel around her body in that anonymous room in London and gone to him, lying on the bed, had stood by him and let him caress her until it was time for them to make love to each other; he had opened her legs and touched the lips of her sex and she had closed her eyes at the touch, gentle touch; she had waited and let him touch her until they knew they must hold each other.

She opened her eyes now and shook her head and went into the bedroom; nothing of the nightmare present had changed, not even its reminders. There was the pile of dirty clothes on the floor where she had dropped them and the photograph of the little boy and her opened dresser drawers, all her clothes and possessions violated and abandoned. She went to the bed and wanted to lay down and sleep; but she could not sleep, she knew, and the room was closing in on her, forcing the past and present together, and the jumble of thoughts pushed against her as physically painful as a wound.

She cleaned the room suddenly and compulsively, whirling through the work, making the bed, putting clothes away, like a housewife suddenly caught unawares by unexpected company. When she finished, she began to cry.

On the other side of the city, in the blackness, there was an explosion.

It wasn't any good; she was going to drive herself mad.

Elizabeth got up finally and pulled on a dress and her coat and left the room. She made sure all the lights were on.

She rode down to the lobby in an empty elevator.

When the doors opened to the lobby, she heard distant noises in the streets beyond the hotel: The cry of ambulances and the curious relentless ringing of the police cars. Someone had died, someone had been hurt, there had been another bomb; it was the usual symphony of Belfast at night.

Elizabeth went into the hotel bar and ordered a double whisky with ice and drank it while the bartender watched her, disapproving.

She finished it and ordered a second; she wanted to feel the whisky inside her.

At first, Elizabeth did not even notice the man next to her until he spoke. He was an American with a flat voice.

He was pretty, she decided as she sipped her whisky. He had blond hair and small, almost delicate hands. He was the sort of man some strong women keep as pets, the sort who would be weak and wasteful but too charming to get rid of.

The second whisky had no warmth; it only eased the pains. She ordered a third and realized she was going to be drunk and that was what she had wanted.

The man next to her was speaking to her and the Irish bartender stared at her.

It didn't matter. She finished the third double and, feeling unsteady, signed her room number on the tab and left a careful tip. She realized she always left a tip, even when they didn't like her or were rude to her or gave poor service; she was afraid not to tip.

The American beside her spoke again.

What was he saying? The voice was plastic, smooth, without seams. When Devereaux spoke, it was flat and harsh, like winter.

He suggested they make love?

She looked at him; no, she wanted to be warm and there was no warmth in the young, blue eyes, so sure of themselves. She felt old with him.

"Go 'way," Elizabeth said, surprised by the slur in her voice: Though the thoughts still raced through her mind like a speeded-up film, they were becoming dimmer. It didn't hurt now.

She climbed off the stool awkwardly and went back to the lobby. She fumbled for her key and then walked slowly across the lobby—slowly and carefully, pretending not to be drunk—and waited at the elevator door.

She did not notice the American had left the bar as well.

She did not see him go to the stairs.

When the elevator came at last, she entered the cubicle and pushed her floor number; the doors closed uncertainly and the elevator began its slow ascent. It creaked as it moved, cables and wheels straining as though the elevator had not been used for a long time.

At last, the doors reopened and she stepped into the dim-lit corridor.

There was a pop, like the explosion of a light bulb.

Then she felt pain from the spray of wood. The bullet had thudded into the balustrade at the stairs behind her.

She thought of Devereaux: Had he returned to kill her? He had promised twenty-four hours. It was so unfair—

The young blond man stepped out of the shadows. She saw the pistol, the pale blue eyes that were too young.

Some instinct forced her back into the elevator, and the doors hissed shut again just as the second bullet struck them. At the level of her face.

Frantically, she pushed the "L" button. Slowly and reluctantly, the elevator grumbled to the main floor.

She stared at the doors with wide, frightened eyes; her naturally pale face had turned ashen. Yet, a part of her was calm—who had come to kill her? Why?

She knew he was running down the steps that surrounded the elevator shaft, running to meet her in the lobby. To kill her.

The doors groaned open at the lobby; the night concierge, at the desk across the floor from the elevator, looked up, startled.

The blond man emerged from the staircase. She could not see the gun. He smiled to her. "Come here, Elizabeth," he said.

Slowly, she walked across the lobby toward the desk. "I want a telephone," she began. The young clerk pushed a telephone towards her. "You can use this, miss, or the telephone booth in—"

"This will be fine," she said. She turned away from him as she dialed—was zero the number for operator in Britain?

It was. She heard the tired voice at the other end of the line.

"Please. I'm in the Royal Avenue Hotel and there's a bomb in the lobby. Please notify the police." She said it calmly and reasonably. Then she put down the telephone and turned back to face the blond man across the lobby floor. She smiled to him, returning his pasted-on smile.

He did not understand; he glanced nervously around him.

She waited, staring at him.

And then he saw the first policemen at the door, pushing into the hotel. The night clerk ran to the door in greeting. And so did Elizabeth. The blond man ran up the stairs as unobtrusively as he could.

Elizabeth hurried past the policemen into the street. "There's a blond-haired man in there, up the stairs. He told me he hid a bomb in the hotel. He has a gun," she cried.

The startled police ran for the stairs. There was confusion on the street. No one looked at her. The bartender came out of the lobby bar and stared at the policemen.

And Elizabeth ran.

Down the wet, glistening street. She ran until she felt the stitch in her side traveling up into her back. She kept running until she had no more breath.

Her heels clicked on the pavement. There were no cars, only the ringing bells of the police wagons coming from far away.

A church bell banged the hour of one, solemnly.

Devereaux had not come to kill her.

They had sent someone else.

The Section wanted to kill her. As they wanted to kill Devereaux. The Section was mad; the world was mad; she was going to die.

She stood at the last intersection on Royal Avenue by the ornate city hall and shivered; there was a mist over the city but a kind of calm with it. No rain, no more wind.

She felt utterly alone.

The city waited for her, bleakly; the stupid stones stared at her. She touched the lining of her coat for the money. The lining was ripped; the money was gone. She did not even have her purse. Only the key to her room.

She couldn't go back. Would they catch him? Would they kill him?

There was no place to run to.

He was responsible; Devereaux was responsible; he had stripped her past from her; he had killed her.

She remembered the photograph she'd left on the dresser. She yearned for it.

The Section wanted to kill her and kill Devereaux.

Devereaux heard her knock; heard her voice at the door.

He was not asleep. He had been sitting in the chair by the window, dressed, staring at the mist from the hills. There was a long open cable on his lap. It confirmed that Elizabeth worked for the CIA and that Free The Prisoners was a CIA front. And it asked, in Hanley's faintly sarcastic way, what all this had to do with the matter at hand? Now that R Section was too late to uncover the plot against Lord Slough? Or did he ever read the newspapers? All the last had been archly worded, in a kind of jargon code. The cable and the paper had been waiting for him when he returned to the hotel.

Devereaux had read about the assassination attempt on the life of Lord Slough and about the murder of the Irish tutor and of Lord Slough's English bodyguard. He had read about a man named Toolin. And he had been sitting, wondering about why someone would try to kill him to prevent him learning about an isolated event taking place three thousand miles away.

He had not resolved the question when he heard her knock. Getting out of the chair, Devereaux took his gun from the dresser and went to the door. He heard her voice. He waited.

"Dev," she said again. "They tried to kill me."

He let the catch on the door fall; he pulled off the deadlock and twisted the door handle. The door opened inward slowly, of itself and of Elizabeth's weight against it. She rushed into the room. He stood against the wall with the gun and looked at her.

He pushed the door shut again with his foot and rolled back the deadlock. "Take your coat off and stand away from it."

She turned to stare at him. She took her coat off and threw it on the floor and backed away.

"Turn around."

She turned to the window.

He went to the coat, felt it, dropped it. He went to her. He held the gun to her head as he felt along her body. He touched her legs, her breasts, without a feeling of really touching. She stood still and let him search her. Finally, he was through. He walked to the other side of the room.

"They sent someone to kill me after you left."

He stood and watched her. She did not turn around.

"A man with blond hair. He had a gun. And a silencer,

I suppose. He fired but it hit the elevator door and I went back inside and I went down. I called the police and said there was a bomb and then I ran. They tried to kill me. It was your fault. They tried to kill you. I ran here."

He just stared at her.

"My God, they're going to kill us," she said.

Putting the gun in his overcoat, he took it to the closet and hung it up. Slowly, he took off his corduroy jacket, draping it over the back of a chair.

She turned around at last and leaned on the window ledge.

He sat down in a chair without speaking. Then he looked at her. She looked frightened and brave, he thought. But looks lie; eyes lie; words lie. Even bodies do not tell the truth, or affection or lovemaking. Was she lying? Did it matter?

He got up and went to her.

He took her hand. He looked at her.

Does it matter?

"I don't want to die, Dev," Elizabeth said.

Devereaux held her then. Felt her tremble. Felt her yielding softness. Felt a little of her fear and all of his own; of his own loneliness and confusion. His thoughts were in anarchy; he did not understand. He could not keep track of the lie or counterlie anymore; he could not tell what had happened or would happen.

Only what was. Now.

What could he tell her? What words would be balm?

He stood, finally, just holding her in the half-darkness of his room, while the mists from the mountains came down into the city and obscured the steeples of the churches beyond his window.

12

LONDON

They slept together finally, not as lovers—they did not make love—but as tired animals, huddling for warmth against the cold. Holding each other in sleep, the rhythm of their breathing became as twins, waiting for the world beyond in a womb of sleep and dreams. Elizabeth cried out once and Devereaux heard her. He cupped his body around hers, belly to back, arm over arm. He felt her naked body and it was part of his own; she felt him, smelled him, let his arms encircle her shoulders, and fell asleep in a kind of dream of awakeness. She had cried out not when the man shot at her but when David died.

Morning broke, full of wintry forboding. A new, more cruel wind seemed to come down from the ring of watching hills.

Devereaux awoke first, waited.

Heard her breath. He kept his eyes opened, smelled her hair. When she awoke, finally, and stirred and felt him next to her, she did not speak. He had to say the first thing.

They lay, cupped, and waited.

He would not speak.

He knew there were words in him but he could not say them. He wanted them to be spoken, wanted to give her what she wanted to hear.

"Devereaux," she said at last. The cloudy light flooded the room and made all the colors only shades of black and white. She did not move but was still in his encircling arms. She looked at his wrists.

"Devereaux," she said again. "Are we going to die?"

"No, Elizabeth," he said, as if he were telling a child there is no death and that morning always follows darkness.

"Dev," she said. "I didn't know I could be afraid. I wasn't afraid of anything anymore. And then that man with the gun. I was afraid of you, too. Last night."

Don't be afraid. I wouldn't have killed you. It didn't happen. He said none of those lies.

"Dev." Pause. She could not see him, only feel his body next to her. "I didn't care. The first night. When I met you. I didn't care about. About this—about going to bed with you. It was just . . . just the job."

Don't speak. Don't speak.

She seemed to understand. She was quiet. He held her tighter. Then he kissed her. Once. Tenderly. Behind her ear. He kissed her once again, on her neck. Then he was quiet, too, lying still in the bed, watching nothing. Waiting and listening until it would be all right.

You can't wait for that, he thought; it's never all right. The cold doesn't end. The darkness has no morning on the other side.

She felt him pulling back from her, turning in the bed; felt her body falling toward him on the sheet. She closed her eyes; felt him kiss her on the eyelid, then on her breast. Softly and then clumsily, in want. He kissed her belly.

He covered her with his body.

She reached for him, took her hands between his legs, felt him ease into her.

Soft and groping, no longer afraid of the darkness.

He warmed her at last.

His Lordship was not prepared at that moment to speak with the Chief Inspector but asked pardon for his delay. It was a matter of a call to Quebec City and the oil ministers who had excused him from their meeting. Could he, Jeffries, be of service in the meantime?

And so Cashel found himself in the immense library of Clare House, talking with a still-shaken but supremely confident Jeffries. They discussed the murders, and Cashel thought he understood exactly what had happened.

But he could not understand why.

Cashel had been served claret; it was just before noon. Jeffries sipped at tea. Cashel stood at the window and looked down the long lawn from Clare House which ran to the barren edge of the hills descending in gradual slopes to the Galway road five hundred feet below. Beyond lay the bay.

"Fer what purpose?" Cashel asked quietly.

"I beg your pardon?"

"Oh." He turned. "I was talkin' to meself. Fer what purpose would Toolin go t'a strange country and wait t'kill his Lairdship?"

"I'm sure I cannot comprehend his motives," said Jeffries.

"Nor I," said Cashel.

The phantom of a thought flashed across his mind. "Mr. Jeffries, would ye be kind enough to give me some idea of what public gatherin's his Lairdship is going to be undertaking in the next few weeks?"

"Why? If I may ask, Chief Inspector?" The tone was precise, a studied London non-accent like that favored by television people.

Cashel smiled. "I don't know, Mr. Jeffries. I can't make sense yet out of what has happened, so perhaps I can make sense out of what will come to be."

Jeffries smiled. "I don't understand?"

"Neither do I, my lad," said Cashel. "Perhaps there was a reason for Toolin to go after Lord Slough in Canada, rather than here. Was he trying to prevent something? I don't know and I'll tell ya, I'm at sea. I've gone round with Toolin's old woman in Dublin till I'm blue in me face and I haven't a clue."

Cashel's smile and confession seemed to warm the cold demeanor of the private secretary. Getting up, Jeffries went to a Queen Anne table and picked up an appointment book.

"Tomorrow is Saturday and the funeral for poor Deirdre Monahan, of course. With her people down in Innisbally. His Lordship will not attend the wake but will be at the funeral mass tomorrow morning. And at the grave. Incidentally, the graveyard is along the Galway road, north of the village."

Cashel nodded and wrote it down.

"As for poor Harmon. Well, he was English and had no family. His Lordship has made arrangements for him—"

Jeffries glanced again at the appointment book.

"Very little Sunday. No public meetings, if that's what you're interested in. He'll be here at Clare House all day. On Monday, he flies to London for a meeting with directors of Great Western Oil. That's a private conference, at Devon House, Lord Slough's headquarters there—"

Cashel noted it.

"Tuesday is quite full." Jeffries glanced at Cashel. "And quite public. A meeting with his editors at the *Scottish Daily News* in the morning in Edinburgh. And then the Royal Cancer Society benefit—"

"A concert, is is then?" asked Cashel.

Jeffries grinned. "Hardly. A benefit match arranged by Slough Newspapers Limited at Ibrox Park in Glasgow."

"Match?"

"Between the Celtics and Rangers."

"Oh, Lord help us," said Cashel. He knew—everyone in the English-speaking soccer world knew—that a football match between the two Glasgow teams in Glasgow was an occasion for riot, drunkeness, and general anarchy.

Jeffries went on: "Wednesday, December first, is most important—launch of the *Brianna* at Liverpool with the Taoiseach and British Prime Minister in attendance."

"The Taoiseach?" Cashel was impressed; it was a rare occasion when the Prime Minister of Eire—the Taoiseach —went to England for any man.

"This is a launch is it?"

"More like an inaugural flight," smiled Jeffries.

"Ah, an aeroplane—"

"No," said Jeffries. "The *Brianna*—named after his Lordship's daughter, of course—is a hovercraft, the first to go in service on the Irish Sea. Certainly you've read about it."

Cashel shook his head.

"His Lordship's new ferry service on the Devon Line— hovercraft between Liverpool and Dublin in forty-five minutes. It's called a flight because the ship literally flies on jets of air above the water. The jets push it out of the water and along the surface, reducing friction and allowing for great speed. They have hovercraft in service on the English Channel."

"I see." Cashel nodded. "And when is this inaugural flight then?"

"On December first. It was pushed back."

"I see."

Jeffries looked up. He liked the slow, rather stupid detective for some reason.

He smiled. "Would you like to be a passenger? I could arrange it?"

"Ah, no, sir, I wouldn't. I don't care fer flyin' if you must know. Never have. I like me feet on the ground."

"Well, it's not flying exactly—"

"Ah, thank you kindly in any case, Mr. Jeffries. But I don't think I will."

Jeffries nodded.

"But would you be so kind—you stopped at a meeting with the Prime Minister. Would you be kind enough to go along?"

Jeffries continued.

Cashel listened and made notes, thinking about the hovercraft. He had never seen one; he had no curiosity to see one. But if Toolin wanted to kill Lord Slough, why did he go to America to do it? Why not take a pop at him at Liverpool with all the mucks about, launching his great new ship?

Absently, Cashel felt in his pocket for his pipe and just as absently filled it. He lit it as Jeffries finished.

"Ah, it's a puzzle isn't it, Mr. Jefferies?"

"What, Chief Inspector?"

"How poor old Toolin found his way t'America with him being on the dole fer a year and got himself a shiny new gun in Quebec City t'knock off his Lordship—beggin' yer pardon. Why, Mr. Jeffries? Why would he go all that way? T'kill a man who is here and will be here?"

Jeffries watched him smoke his pipe. He did not comment.

"It don't make sense."

Jeffries nodded.

They sat then in silence, sipping tea and claret, and waited for Lord Slough's leisure.

The thing shuddered into life, whining and then howling until the cold dawn stillness was shattered into a million irretrievable pieces of echo. Shaking and screaming like a beast in rage.

The man they called Captain Donovan, though he was not a captain, stood on the apron which led gently down into the Mersey. Forty feet away from him, the beast shook and roared. Donovan wore special ear protectors because of the sound.

The immense hovercraft finally lifted itself off its dry pod and struggled into the water. But she was no more at home there; the waves beat back from her giant fans as though terrified; the giant propellers on her stacks created a gale across the enclosed deck which splashed into the water behind, leaving a trough of depression. Then it began to move more quickly, bellowing with rage, plunging into the white-capped foam of the gray, sickly Irish Sea.

Donovan smiled. His heart almost felt light. He loved the beast, loved the ungainly beauty of it that was no ship's beauty or no airplane's beauty but the beauty of monumental rage. It was Donovan's rage, too; he bellowed with the craft as it tore into the sea and turned back the waves from its bow.

She turned sharply beyond the harbor wall and headed back toward the apron. Thump, thump, thump over the breasts of the waves, shaking and screaming in the wind —louder than the wind, and that made Donovan cheer her. Oh beauty, he thought. Oh beauty.

It was the second week of trials.

There had been problems with the steering mechanism at first, but Donovan—as engineer—had finally found the trouble in a pair of loose bolts along the shaft.

They had taken her out every day and every night, into every sea there was. She had even bucked the force-ten winds two days before. The waves had crashed into the breakwater of the harbor at heights of ten feet, but the *Brianna,* with its newer design, had cut into them and ridden above them, smoothing them down to manageable size so that the forward speed could be maintained.

And what speed.

He watched her now, cutting into the empty harbor faster than a motorboat, her great fan propellers chopping at the air.

She would be ready December first.

In a Liverpool warehouse, there were two cases of gelignite, waiting to be cargoed aboard the *Brianna.*

Everything was perfect, including the craft.

No, beauty, no, we won't hurt ye. We'll collect our ransom and we'll take ye t'Dublin and we'll be gone. I'll miss ye, beauty, but we won't hurt ye.

He crooned to the craft bearing down on him and on the apron. He had never felt such love before, for any ship he had sailed or for any man or any woman; the others laughed at her, hated her, hated her cowlike clumsiness. Captain George. He said it wasn't a proper ship. Bloody English bastard. Not a proper ship. She was more.

Almost anticlimactically, the craft lifted itself on the apron and settled down on its bottom like a lady adjusting her skirt. The whining of the engines cooled down; the wind suddenly shrieked louder.

She would be ready. In time. That was nearly certain. Donovan pulled off his ear protectors and listened to the wind and the whisper of the craft's dying howl. She stopped shaking. Donovan started across the apron to her.

They would all be ready. In time.

Green stood at the window and watched the first snow fall on the narrow street beyond the window of Blake House. He had no idea that the snow was coming too early for London's climate. He only knew it sparked a remembrance within him.

He had loved the snow when he was a boy in Ohio. But that snow had been very different from the polite English snow now falling slowly and picturesquely on the slanted roofs of the London houses: This snow was like the snow in paperweights, which seemed to fall almost with majesty. The Ohio snows were life-killing, blinding, gouging snows, shivering down the streets, coming in the blackness of night, blowing across two thousand miles of flatland before they struck. And yet, the savagery of it had thrilled him when he was a child.

Green turned from the window as the housekeeper entered the library.

"It's the Section," she announced. She was an unpleasant woman with an unpleasant face and a bad odor; Green nodded and went past her, out of the book-lined room, into the soundproof room where the double scrambler sat in a black box.

He picked up the telephone. The voice from Washington came through the double scrambler, faintly at first.

"I can't hear you," Green said.

"Is this better?"

"Yes, thanks."

"Damned thing." Hanley's annoyed voice came over clearly.

Green nodded and was quiet. Idly, he wondered if it was time yet to have a drink. He had become very careful about that recently. He wouldn't drink before noon. Then he would go out of the house, to the club. Quietly. Away from that old woman who undoubtedly spied on him as he spied on her. It was all routine, all for the reports that were sent back to the Section every month.

"We haven't heard from our man in Ulster."

Green said, "Nothing at this end."

"Damn him."

"Yes, sir."

"I want a call as soon as he makes contact."

"Yes, sir."

"Not a word?"

"Is he supposed to contact me? The house?"

"I don't know. We didn't make that clear. He hasn't contacted anyone. He had requested information, we sent it by open cable. We know he received it. Or someone received it. I don't want to call that hotel. On an open line. Why doesn't he make contact?"

Green stared at the black box before him. "Perhaps there's been difficulty."

"Yes," said Hanley. "Perhaps. But everything's botched now with—" Pause. "Well, Green. Dammit. I want immediate contact from you when he makes—" Another pause. Green smiled. He knew that Hanley did not want to say "contact" a second time. Finally: "When he makes contact." Green continued to grin. What a fool Hanley was.

Replacing the receiver finally, Green sat for a while, staring at the telephone and the black box. He conjured up the image of Devereaux in his mind, and wondered what Hanley meant by "botched."

When he left the room, he closed the door and then automatically gave it a tug, to make certain it locked.

The old grandfather clock in the hall began its song for noon: First the sixteen notes of the Westminister chimes and then a pause and the faintest of clicks and then the first bell struck and the second and the third . . .

Green stood in the middle of the hall, transfixed by the sound. At last, the notes were all struck and the clock resumed its slow, even tick-tock.

Noon.

The dark wood of the hall surrounded him, seemed to oppress him. The housekeeper would be in the back kitchen. There would be the stupidity of lunch again, the awkward conversation. . . .

He went to get his coat from the hall tree.

It was time.

13

CLARE

"In the name of the Father, and of the Son, and of the Holy Ghost. Amen."

Faolin made the sign of the cross with the others who were packed into the tiny church.

An old woman began to cry, sobbing softly. She buried her face in her hands. Her hands were wrapped with the beads of a black rosary. Her head was covered with a black scarf.

Faolin looked at her. She would be Deirdre Monahan's aunt, the last person left in that little family. He had learned who they all were.

"I will go to the altar of God." The priest held his hands apart and lights of the candles caught the shine in the satiny material of the black chasuble. The golden cross imprinted on the back of the loose garment glittered in the low, intense light of the candles.

"To God, the joy of my youth. Give judgment to me, O God, and decide my cause against an unjust and unholy people. From unjust and deceitful men, deliver me."

Faolin stared at Lord Slough. The Englishman sat stiffly in the pew behind the coffin. His daughter sat next to him. They sat looking straight ahead, strangers to the service and to the surroundings.

"For you, O God, are my strength." The old priest pronounced the English words as distinctly and solemnly as he had pronounced the Latin words in the old form of the Mass. He spoke as though he were pleading the psalm for himself. "Why have You forsaken me? And why do I go about in sadness, while the enemy afflicts me?"

Deirdre had not lived in the village for ten years, and her relatives were mostly dead, buried in the rocky spit of land up the road where her own remains would be buried in a little while. But most of the village of Innisbally had come to the church anyway, to stare at the spectacle of the English lord who lived in the old mansion in the burren hills.

That was why Faolin had come. He had told no one. They would say it was foolish, a risk. Perhaps. But he had to see this man he hated enough to kill.

Faolin held his cloth cap in hand. His eyes glittered in the candlelight. A statue of the Sacred Heart of Jesus looked down on him. His coat was unbuttoned and open but he did not care. He did not wear a gun. These were not the enemy; only the English lord, who would die another day on the Irish Sea.

Faolin had come to Innisbally the day before, "passing through," he'd said at MacDermott's public house—on his way to see his aunt down in Limerick. A walking trip from Derry. What news of Derry, then? They had stood him a jar and then another, and even the young, toothless *garda* had bought him a whisky. The *garda* wasn't a bad sort, just a country boy who had gone into the national police because he didn't have the skill for the fields.

"Is it work ye're doin' in Derry, then?" the *garda* asked. The lad had never been beyond Galway City some twenty-six miles up the road.

Shaking his head, Faolin mumbled something about the dole and not findin' work and perhaps emigratin' to America—

They could all understand that. The village, which had had nearly five hundred families before the great famine and the subsequent waves of emigration, now had fewer than seventy-five people, most of them old. The children grew up and moved away. There was nothing in Innisbally, even by the standards of a poor country.

Faolin had gotten drunk with them; he could not remember the last time he had gotten drunk. They had warmed him with their openness and their generous hands —though they had so little—and they had made him angry, too. They had talked about Lord Slough who was coming down for the funeral Mass, a grand gesture, and then how his Lordship had taken on all the expense, even to the sandwiches and tea after, because old Mrs. Tone, Deirdre's aunt, didn't have a bob to her name. . . . Their gratitude made him angry but he had checked it, he thought, nearly to the last.

So he had fallen asleep drunk on the publican's sofa and now, groggy with drink, he had agreed to go to the funeral mass to see the English lord.

A sight to see, they had said. And Durkin had urged him to stay the morning and have a jar before he went on his way.

The bell rang and the priest raised the bread.

"This is My Body."

Faolin instinctively bowed his head as he had done as a child and struck his breast lightly. Then he looked up again and surveyed the faces in the church; finally, he met a pair of eyes staring at him from across the church.

He returned the gaze.

A middle-aged man in a dark coat with a black mustache and clear blue eyes.

"This is My Blood," the priest began. He raised the chalice. The bell rang again.

Faolin took his eyes away from the face and lowered them and struck his breast. When he looked up, the face had turned away and was staring at another part of the church.

The other man was not from the tiny village, Faolin decided.

He looked so sure, so certain that it was his right to stare at people.

A policeman, Faolin thought.

Devereaux had finally decided to act. He knew actions were foolish, but he could not wait any longer.

The afternoon after Elizabeth had come to him, he'd made up his mind. After love and after a kind of trust that comes with nakedness and lovemaking; he had felt her shiver and felt a little of her fear and finally had believed she was afraid of death.

They had stayed in the hotel room all that day, until late afternoon. They had not eaten, only slept and made love. Devereaux knew that was foolish, too; that he must decide about Hanley and R Section and about this double game against him, and now against Elizabeth. He must decide about Denisov and the blond-haired man.

And about Elizabeth.

The computer of his brain broke down; logical sequences did not seem to work; there were too many random facts and conclusions that did not seem to have any connection.

He lay in bed with her beside him. He stared out the window and let his instincts begin to reprogram the computer.

After a long time, he thought it was working again.

He thought he began to understand. Not all the parts. But there was a sort of logic to it if he excluded certain things that did not make any sense. There were always random threads in any assignment, parts that did not make sense. Parts that did not relate in the long run to the problem at hand.

When he thought she was awake, he began: "I want you to go to London."

"My passport—"

"We'll go back to the hotel. Before it's dark. I want you to go to London tonight. To a house. A safe house. Then I want you to—"

"There's no safe house," she began.

"Yes."

"R Section wants to kill me. *And* you—"

He looked at the dying light beyond the window. "No. Not the Section. Not Hanley."

He felt her shiver next to him. He had already decided about Elizabeth.

"I thought of everything you told me," he said. Devereaux was not comfortable with explanations. He did not like to explain the process of his thoughts. When he reported to Hanley at the end of assignments, he only told him what had happened, not why he had chosen to act. But Elizabeth was frightened. He felt it and wanted to make her understand.

"It doesn't work," he said. "It doesn't make sense. There is no logic to a double section operated by one man. Therefore, there is no double section. There is a real R Section and then there is *your* ghost R Section. *Your* Hanley is a ghost Hanley; the office you saw was another office. I don't understand it, how they did it, but I think I begin to understand why. And why you were sent here to spy on me. And why Blatchford was sent to kill me. It didn't have anything to do with this mission."

"I don't understand—"

"Neither do I," he said. "Why wait until now? Why wait to strike in the middle of a mission that is not very important? Unless it is important and I don't know it yet. Or unless I am so close to the truth of it that they are afraid. There are parts and parts of it I don't understand. But you didn't work for Hanley. Elizabeth. Or R Section. You worked for someone else. Something else that intends to destroy the Section."

"The Soviets—" she said and bit it off.

"Yes. Perhaps. I don't know." Denisov would smile at that. Equivocation. *Perhaps—what does perhaps mean, Devereaux?* Why was Denisov here?

"Then who wants to kill me?" she said. "And you."

"Perhaps they're different people," he said. "Perhaps

they are on different sides, have different missions. Perhaps you've failed—you have failed, you told me, they may know that. Maybe they had your room bugged—even though I couldn't find anything. I don't know. But in London I know a safe house and I want you to go there tonight—"

"But if the blond man is at the hotel?" she asked.

"Yes. He may be there. He may be here. Outside the door. But he has to be dealt with."

"I want to get away. Let's get away."

"No," he said. "We'll deal with him first. And then with the other parts of the problem. The parts I don't understand."

"Are you sure?"

He looked at her. "Of what?"

"About Hanley? About the Section? Is it safe?"

"Yes," he said. "I'm sure."

"Oh, Dev," she said. "I'm not sure."

"I'm sure," he said again. He wondered if he lied well. He never wondered that before; he always assumed that he did.

They dressed quietly, apart from each other. When it was time to go, he took the pistol from the closet and checked it and unsnapped the safety and held it in his hand.

"Open the door," he said.

As she pulled it open, he stepped to the door. Right and left. The shadows of the other doors. The end of the hall. He stepped into the hall, feeling exposed. He waited. She stepped into the hall behind him.

No one.

They walked to the elevator; the halls were empty; Devereaux swept his eye up and down the corridor but saw nothing, heard nothing.

When they reached the street, it was nearly dusk and the city looked mean. Faces were bent in the wind. They took a cab to her hotel in the thin traffic and it was dark when they arrived.

As planned, Elizabeth got out first and walked quickly across the sidewalk into the lobby and went to the elevator.

Devereaux waited at the front door.

Elizabeth entered the elevator and doors closed on her. She was to take it to the fifth floor, one floor below her own room.

Devereaux saw the blond man emerge from the bar and go to the elevator after her. Maybe he had been waiting too long in the bar; he was a little slow.

Devereaux walked into the lobby, to the elevator, and stood behind the blond man, waiting for the cage to return.

The man smelled of cologne and whisky. His suit had an American cut.

The doors opened and both men entered. The blond man pushed six.

Devereaux moved to the other side of the small cage.

"Floor?" the other man asked, staring at him.

"Oh. Sorry." Devereaux pushed the button marked eight. The lift began its ascent.

Careless. Devereaux feared he was getting sloppy.

The doors whooshed open at six and the other man stepped off, slowly, cautiously. The doors closed behind him.

Devereaux quickly pushed seven and got off at the next floor. Moving to the stairs at the end of the hall, he waited a moment. Nothing. He took his gun off his belt as he pushed open the door to the stairs.

The stairwell was dark below.

Had a light gone out?

Devereaux held the pistol in front of him in the darkness.

His step did not make a sound.

On the landing below, the blond man was waiting, in

the darkness. But he did not see Devereaux until it was too late.

The single shot from his gun whumped through the silencer and exploded its bullet harmlessly on the plaster wall behind Devereaux.

Devereaux's pistol did not have a silencer.

The explosion rang in their ears. The bullet flattened as it hit the blond man's groin and exploded through the fabric and flesh, shattering the bones below. Blood spurted out and stained the lower half of his body as he fell. For a moment, he did not make a sound; shock was protecting him from the unendurable pain.

The man stared at Devereaux and his pistol clattered harmlessly down the steps.

Devereaux put his own pistol into his belt and went to the landing.

The dying man looked at him. "Please help me," he said slowly, almost dreamily.

Devereaux reached into the dying man's coat pocket. He took out a case for glasses and a small, thin wallet.

Devereaux looked at him. "Who sent you?"

"Please—"

"Who are you?"

The man stared at him.

Devereaux pushed him over and felt in his trousers. There was blood. And money. And a room key. And something written on a scrap of paper: ETRAYSDVER-DANTYGER

Devereaux stared at the room key.

"Please help—" Suddenly, the voice was drowned in blood. The man shuddered.

Devereaux got up. Ten men now. Ten. He looked at the blood and the body in the darkness. He would have to be very quick. He ran down the stairs to the fifth floor and pushed open the door. Elizabeth stood at the elevator, waiting. She turned and saw him and then saw the blood-stains on the edges of his cuffs.

"Go to your room. Get everything. In five minutes, and go to the lobby and check out. Quickly. I'll meet you in the lobby. Quickly—"

"The man, the blond man, I—"

"Shut up, Elizabeth," he said. He looked as though he were in pain. "Do it. Now. Hurry, there's no time—"

He ran back to the door of the stairs and down again, to the fourth floor. The blond-haired man had stayed in room 487.

Devereaux removed the pistol from his belt again as he opened the door. But there was nothing. No one. A room like his own, like all rooms of men who spend their lives traveling. He noticed the simple suitcase on the desk.

Putting his gun away, he took the little knife from his pocket and slashed at the lining of the suitcase. There was nothing. Going through the clothes he found the man's passport and stared at the picture for a moment. It was not a good likeness.

Devereaux felt the paper. The passport was real; it had been used. Mr. Johannsen. A salesman for an American aircraft company.

Came to Belfast to sell airplanes.

The exit money was in the hollow of a black leather shoe in the closet. Devereaux took it and counted two thousand dollars in hundred-dollar bills. He put the wad into the pocket of his brown corduroy coat.

Johannsen. He had a name at least.

Devereaux worked furiously. Who had heard the shot? Who would go to the stairs and see the body? Would anyone stir himself from his own life and own routine to call the police?

Elizabeth was waiting at the desk. Devereaux waved off the bellhop, grabbed her bag and hurried outside. Opening the door of the black cab, he shoved her inside ahead of him.

The city was dark; its slums were hidden by night and rain; Friday night. They passed a fish-and-chips store with a long line of people waiting in the rain. Get your pay packet and down to the fish-and-chips and maybe a pint of beer at home, sitting in front of the telly, getting numb in warmth of it, erasing the day and the week from mind. . . .

Devereaux told Elizabeth how to get to Blake House and what to say when she got there. He told her they would watch her and make her wait. He revealed the code word for access to the safe house, the word that betrayed the house if she were to betray him.

"The blond man?" she asked as they neared the airport.

Devereaux looked at the driver. He shook his head.

They did not speak again until they stood at the departure gate. Outside, on the wet runway, the last plane of the evening waited to take its load of people from this dismal, dark land of bombs and madness into something like the sanity and safety of England. It was the day's last direct plane to Heathrow airport.

"Did you kill him?"

"Yes," he said.

"He would have killed you."

Devereaux looked at Elizabeth. Her face was anxious, tired. The game had become too great for her. Her eyes were wide.

Distracted, he looked out on the rainy runway. "It doesn't matter," he said. "He would have died anyway. I'm sorry I didn't get to talk to him. To find out what was going on."

She wanted comfort. "This is so bad," she said at last.

"It always is," he said.

Elizabeth wanted to kiss him. No, to touch him; to have him touch her. But it was not the same now, in the bright airport, waiting for the gate to open, surrounded by weary travelers in dark clothes who were going back to England.

Elizabeth realized Devereaux only wanted her to go now. She even understood it. He was acting now, moving, going from point A to B to C without consciousness; he did not know it was raining or that it was nearly eight o'clock or that his trouser cuffs were stained dark with spots of rain and spots of blood.

Elizabeth realized all that. And it frightened her.

14

WASHINGTON

Hanley was still there when the call came.

Four o'clock on a languid November afternoon. The trees still held colorful leaves, pasted wet against the branches; there was a light breeze that seemed springlike. The city had already assumed that ghostly atmosphere it usually donned on Friday afternoons in winter.

Hanley was sure that everyone in Washington took off on Friday afternoons, spending the day in little restaurants with French names; or in dim bars; or in hotel rooms with secretaries who were not reluctant; or on the narrow, clogged highways leading across the river into the Virginia suburbs where townhouses leaned against each other like colorful toy blocks. Senators and congressmen were gone now, flown home on the morning planes, to woo votes or accept memorials or raise money or to work deals; Washington was a weekday outpost.

But Hanley was there, in the cool little office in the Department of Agriculture building. The thermostat was turned down to sixty degrees, which made Hanley comfortable.

At noon, Hanley had gone as usual to the little bar on Fourteenth Street where he had taken his usual lunch: a salad, a very large cheeseburger with a slice of raw onion, and a dry martini straight up.

He returned to his office shortly after one, but Devereaux's call did not come through till around four Washington time, nine there.

"Yes?"

Hanley waited for the connection. It wasn't very good and the voice seemed to fade at first from the other end. But it didn't matter: He knew the voice. In a strange way, he was glad to hear it finally. He waited and listened.

"Thirty. Repeat. Thirty." Devereaux spoke slowly.

Suddenly, Hanley tensed. He leaned over the receiver to be more private though there was no one else in the room. "Red sky."

The words were an extra code, one they had worked out themselves at Hanley's insistence. It was not recorded anywhere, except in their memories. Thirty was "the end," an old telegraph signal used by newspapermen to sign off their stories; "Red sky" had been Hanley's contribution to the code—"Red sky at morning, sailors take warning."

Hanley picked up his pen and began to write: Devereaux slowly repeated a telephone number but in such a way as to make the numbers meaningless to anyone listening in; there were six extraneous numbers in the sequence and each real number had a ghost number attached to it, arranged to be recited in a backwards sequence.

It was the most dire of signals. Devereaux had never sent it before.

What had happened?

Replacing the receiver without a word, Hanley got up from his desk and locked it and locked the gray file cabinet behind the desk. He pulled on his raincoat and left the office.

"You're leaving early, Mr. Hanley," Miss Dickens said, more in surprise than admonishment.

He looked at her sharply. "What do you mean?"

"I mean just . . . that you're leaving early."

"Yes," he said. He had never liked her and had never made a secret of it. She was too proprietary for his taste. But he realized too that she adored him; he couldn't help it.

There would be no taxis, of course. Every available vehicle was in full flight from the capital, funneling into the inadequate bridges across the Potomac.

Hanley left by the Fourteenth Street exit of the Agriculture building. Across the greenery, he could see the Washington Monument, surrounded by a determined, out-of-season gaggle of tourists waiting to go to the top of it. Hanley had lived in Washington for over thirty years and had never felt the desire to see the city from the summit of the obelisk.

He hurried north along Fourteenth Street, past the Ellipse and toward Pennsylvania Avenue. The Commerce Department building loomed up over him, gray and watching, dressed in that pseudoclassical style that made official Washington seem so old and dead.

Hanley was thinking about the message from Devereaux and the numbers.

He finally turned into the pub where he always ate his lunch. It was that sleepy time of afternoon when the last lunchers had left and before the first of the afterwork drinkers arrived. The bartender was slowly washing all the ashtrays when he came in.

"Mr. Hanley. This is a surprise."

Why was everyone surprised by him, Hanley thought. Was he a creature of such fixed habits? Even as he asked the question, he knew he was.

He hurried to the back of the tavern.

"A martini, Mr. Hanley?"

"Yes," he said and then regretted it; he didn't want a second drink.

He went to the telephone. It was a modern pay phone of plastic and steel, offering little pretense of privacy with its narrow plastic panels jutting out from each side of the gray metal box.

He looked at the paper, took out his pen, and transposed the numbers, breaking the simple code.

Picking up the receiver, he gave his credit-card number

to the operator and then the overseas number. He waited on the line while the call was placed. After four minutes, he heard a voice.

"Hanley," he identified himself.

Devereaux began without a wasted word. He told Hanley everything. To his credit, Hanley did not interrupt, even when Devereaux told him about the Russian and about the attempt on his life; about Elizabeth and the safe house and the dead man in the stairwell of the hotel on Royal Avenue.

"My God," said Hanley.

Devereaux waited at the other end of the line, three thousand miles across the ocean.

"What does it mean?" Hanley asked.

"It means that you are the head of a ghost organization, out to kill me and to destroy the Section."

"Devereaux." Hanley choked; he could not conceive it. The Section was not just an agency tucked into the budget of an obscure Cabinet department; it was Hanley and part of Hanley's being.

He finally found a voice: "If that were so, why would you tell me?"

Devereaux's voice was mild: "Because it doesn't matter. If you are an agent in the ghost Section, then I'm dead. I cannot come in anywhere; I'll be hunted and killed, for whatever reason. So it doesn't matter if you are both Hanley and the ghost Hanley."

"Dammit, Devereaux, I'm not."

"I know." There was a pause. "They want to destroy the Section. Make it inoperable."

"Who?"

"I don't know. There are two plausible answers: First, the Soviets. Denisov is here in Belfast. Why? He wants to help me. Why? He claims he killed a man trying to assassinate me. Is that true? Or did he try to kill me? Why would the KGB want to destroy R Section?"

"Because we are who we are—"

"Nonsense. The Soviets use their intelligence agency

to gather information, not to set out destroying other intelligence agencies. They know that a new agency would spring up in our place. Better to control our agency than destroy it. So they may have decided to set up the ghost agency and gradually take it over. But it really is too farfetched—"

"And the second?"

"The Langley firm, as you call it. The CIA."

"As Denisov told you—"

"Yes, but there is more. Denisov would not care . . . the Soviets would not be part of our internal feud if there was not another factor. And I can't comprehend that part of it. What is there beyond this?"

The elderly bartender came to the back and placed the martini on the metal counter under the telephone. Without a thought, Hanley picked it up and sipped at it. He was thinking, trying to jog memory and logic into a coherent sequence.

"Why now?" was all Hanley could say.

"Why now. Exactly. Why in Ireland?"

"It had to do with this Lord Slough business."

"Yes."

"But what?"

"An attempt made on his life in Quebec," said Devereaux slowly, following his own thoughts. "But they tried to kill me after that. And tried to kill Elizabeth—it can mean, only, that there is another event coming. Something. Another attempt on Slough's life?"

"You mean the CIA tried to kill this guy?" The slang came out in his excitement; even Devereaux was startled to hear it—Hanley was a man of precise language.

"I don't know. I'm not in Canada. I don't know anything about it. But there is something else—"

"What? I can't stand any more."

"There's a leak. In the Section. And you'll have to find it quickly."

"Why in the Section?"

"Because of everything I've told you. They've followed

me, they have baited me, they probably killed Hastings
. . . they knew about this mission before I came here
and had their agents in place—the ghost Section, the
ghost Devereaux, the ghost Hanley, the ghost everyone."

Hanley was silent. "I'll have to get the Chief."

"Yes."

"And we have to find out who Toolin was and how he
got to Canada to kill Slough."

"Yes."

"Devereaux, why would they want to destroy the
Section?"

But it was obvious. If it were the CIA, they had tried
to destroy it before.

"No more contact, Hanley," Devereaux said, "until I
know more."

"What about this agent of theirs, Elizabeth Campbell?"

"No problem. She'll stay at Blake House until this is
over. Then we can decide about her." Finally Devereaux
gave Hanley the message that he'd found on Johannsen's
body: ETRAYSDVERDANTYGER. "I don't recognize the
code," Devereaux added.

"I'll work on it."

"Hanley?"

"Yes?"

"I don't think you have very much time."

Hanley looked at the half-empty martini glass. "No. I
understand. I don't think there is much time either."

O'Neill put down the pint of black beer and turned.
The little boy was staring at him.

"I'm O'Neill," he said at last. "Who're you?"

The others in Flanagan's pub stared at the child. The
boy wore a cloth cap as did most of the men, and he had
a raggedy coat pulled tight around his thin shoulders. He
handed the paper to O'Neill.

O'Neill stared at it for a moment, trying to focus:
I have money. St. Anne's church. Now.

"Who gave you this?"

"A man."

"I know a bloody man gave it t'ya. But what was he?"

"I think an American man."

"Ah, d'ya? Did he wear glasses?"

"I don't know—"

"What'd he give ya t'give me the note?"

"Ya ain't gettin' it," said the boy, and the men in the pub laughed. O'Neill flushed and made to give the boy a cuff with his hand.

"Yer don't hit the lad," said one of those at the bar. "Go on, O'Neill. What's the note say?"

Suddenly, O'Neill was all smiles. "Ah, nothin'. Just a bit of business, it is. With the company. I'll have ter pop off now fer a wee bit but I'll be back. Hold me drink, Paddy," he said. And he placed it on the bar and went out the door.

Nearly ten at night. No rain now, though the streets were shining wet under the lamps. O'Neill trudged up the long hill to St. Anne's Church. So the Russian had more money for him, was it?

But it wasn't Denisov.

Devereaux stepped from the shadows of the door of the old church at the head of St. Anne Road.

"O'Neill," he said.

O'Neill looked around him. Not a soul on the roads. Not a car. He thought of running back—

Devereaux hit him, very hard, in the belly. O'Neill doubled over and began to fall heavily onto the pavement. Devereaux kicked him squarely between the legs. The pain made him faint and he did not feel it when he fell on the sidewalk, breaking his wrist.

In a moment, O'Neill awoke to blinding pain. He felt blood on the side of his face, warm and salty.

He stared at Devereaux in terror.

Devereaux had propped him up against the cold wall of the church entrance, in the shadows, a million miles from help. He was squatting down next to him.

"Tell me about Lord Slough."

"I told you all—"

O'Neill was not permitted to finish. Devereaux chopped at his thigh and sent a new, strange pain into his gut, to join the other pains there.

"For the love of God, don't hit me—" O'Neill began to cry.

"Who is going to kill Lord Slough?"

"I told ya. A Captain Donovan—"

"Who else? Where is he?"

"I don't—"

This time Devereaux hit the broken wrist with the flat of his hand. Again, O'Neill blacked out suddenly from the pain.

When he awoke, nothing had changed; hell remained. Devereaux squatted next to him still.

"You're gonna kill me, man—"

"Yes," said Devereaux. "Tell me your contacts in the IRA—"

"They'd kill me—"

"They can't kill you twice—"

"Please, for the love of God—"

This time, Devereaux chopped at the bone of his shoulder. Once. Twice.

"I'll tell ya, but don't kill me—"

"Who are they? Where are they?"

"There's Terry here in Belfast. He's down at Flanagan's. But he'll kill me—"

"What does he look like?"

"Black hair. Curly hair."

"And who is he?"

"He's one of the Boys. He knew about them tryin' t'kill Lord Slough—"

"And?"

"I can't tell ya—"

Devereaux hit him again. There was no pleasure in it. It was all impersonal.

"Please, please, fer the love of God—"

"Who else?"

"Donovan himself. He. He's a character at the docks."

"Who else?"

"I don't know, I don't know—"

"When will they kill Lord Slough?"

"They already tried. Dinja read about it?"

"Was that the plan?"

"I don't know—"

"Who knows?"

"I don't—"

He hit him again.

"I swear t'God Almighty, I don't know—"

"Who killed Hastings?"

"You did—"

Devereaux stared into the eyes of the frightened man. Just a man, caught up in it all. Who didn't understand. Had a wife and family and drank too much and was too poor and got caught up in a game he couldn't play. He stared at O'Neill for a few moments and then got up.

"You're a dead man, O'Neill," Devereaux said. "Go home and kiss your wife good-bye and use your money to get out of Ireland tonight if you can. Because you're dead. You'll never come back here and you'll never be O'Neill again and you'll never see your family again. You're dead and you have to leave now."

The words frightened him more than the blows.

"If you tell Terry that you betrayed him, he will kill you. So will the others. You have a little time. I'll give you that. You can leave now and get out of the country by morning and go away. Go to America or Australia, but go away."

"Me life," said O'Neill. "Me family." His red tie was still tightly knotted at the throat as it had been the first time they met in Edinburgh. Devereaux looked at the comic, bloated face.

"The game is over," said Devereaux.

And then he was gone, into the silent streets.

* * *

Denisov pushed open the door of his room on the top floor of the Belfast Continental and noted, with satisfaction, that the particle of paper was still in the jamb. It fluttered to the floor. It was all right.

He turned on the lights.

Devereaux sat in the chair by the window. He held a gun in his hand.

"Close the door," Devereaux said.

Shrugging, Denisov closed the door and went to sit on the bed.

"Good evening, Devereaux," he said at last.

Devereaux did not speak.

"To what do we owe this business?"

Devereaux stared at him.

"Cat got your mouth?"

"Tongue," said Devereaux.

"Yes, tongue. You're right," said Denisov. He sighed and got up and went to the bureau. "I am going to take off my coat—"

"I prefer you to sit down."

"Of course."

The Russian went back to the bed and sat down heavily. The springs made a little sound of protest.

The room was silent for a long minute. The two men stared at each other across the black gun. And then Devereaux cocked the gun with a sharp click.

Denisov smiled. His eyes were kind and forgiving. "That is really too melodramatic, Devereaux. Cocking the hammer like that. No, this is the psychological moment. You have waited for me in the darkness. I come in, surprised. You have a gun. You do not speak when I talk to you. Then you release the hammer. Ah, you have me frightened now. Is that what you want me to say? Then I am frightened. Now tell me what you want."

"Tell me about the ghost Section."

"Ah, now you want to talk. Before, when I offer you

my help—my friendship, even—you do not want to talk to me. Now you want to talk to me. That is good. You are at least doing something."

"Tell me about the ghost Section."

"It is a puzzle to me—to us—as well. But I think it must be part of the CIA and part of this business in Ireland."

"Why?"

"I do not know why. A man tries to kill you and he has a card with your name on it. He is from this ghost Section. But he is a CIA man. So they are together, this ghost Section and the CIA. But we know the CIA is giving money to the Republican Army—"

"How do you know—"

"We know this."

"And you want to help me. Help the Section. Why?"

"Because we do not want to help the CIA."

"I don't understand."

Denisov smiled and spread his hands. "I don't understand as well. But I have a theory. Would you like to hear it?"

"Yes."

"Good. This is good, eh, Devereaux? We are talking at last instead of playing around the garden bushes. I looked for you all day—"

"Tell me about your theory."

"Well, who can understand the Russian mind, eh? Not even me. And I am Russian. But I think our side does not want the CIA to fund the Irish Army here. I think we want this to be exposed."

"Why?"

"Why not? To damage the relationship between England and the Americans? After all, England is going to be a great oil power in a few years. It would be important not to make England too much a part of the American world."

"Why not expose it yourself?"

"We do not have hard evidence, I think. Now, remem-

ber, I am just making a theory." He winked at Devereaux.
"But a good theory, I think. After all, they do not tell me
everything. And they do not tell you everything."

Devereaux waited.

Denisov grinned even wider. "So what if we go to
British Intelligence and give them what we have? Is it
worth anything? No. For two good reasons. We will not
be believed. And if we are believed, the British Intelligence will do nothing about it."

Devereaux stirred in the chair and leaned forward. He
still held the black pistol.

"Why would they do nothing about it?"

"Because British Intelligence is nothing without the
Americans. They might use the information to blackmail
the CIA into keeping them in the information club, so to
speak. They might try to use it to get closer to the CIA
—but they would not use it to embarrass the CIA and
harm their relationship. British Intelligence is a joke. You
know that. They do not even know that the CIA funds
the Irish Republicans. But if they knew, they would not
do anything about it."

"But if R Section told them, they would?"

Denisov chuckled. "Yes, of course. Because then they
would have to act. Because the Americans had told them.
They would form a relationship with you and then they
would get rid of the CIA."

Devereaux stared at the man who had the face of a
bespectacled saint. What had Hanley said? About working
to form a special relationship with the British Intelligence
forces? Was this all it was, then? An intramural game of
rival bureaucracies? Then why were people dying?

"What about Lord Slough?"

"What about Lord Slough? I know nothing. Is that
why you came to Ireland? We want to help you but you
won't tell us anything. I tell you everything—I tell you
about the CIA and about the man who killed Hastings
and about Elizabeth—by the way, did you get rid of
her?"

"Yes."

"I'm not surprised," said Denisov. "It is too bad, but a Mata Hari is more dangerous than even an ordinary agent."

"What do you know about Lord Slough?"

"He is alive and he is in Ireland. Someone tried to kill him in Canada."

"Why would the CIA set up a ghost of R Section?"

Denisov shook his head slowly from side to side. "Devereaux, I am not a child. Do not ask me child's questions. Why would the CIA like to destroy or discredit R Section? You know that as well as I do—"

"The ghost Section could be the invention of your people."

"My people?"

Devereaux knew it sounded foolish but he held on. He must probe all the sides of the question to make sure it was tight and whole.

Denisov jumped up from the bed. "I am insulted. Really. This is too much. If we set up the ghost Section, why would we tell you? Why would we save your life and then try to kill you? You are crazy. Why would we destroy R Section when another would spring up in its place? Better to infiltrate it, put a mole inside the organization—"

"Perhaps you have one there now."

"Perhaps," said Denisov. "I do not know everything. I am told so much and that is all. I am told to help you. That is all."

"You don't ask questions."

"No, my dear brother, I do not ask questions. I am Denisov and I am alive. I have a three-room apartment in Moscow and a lovely wife who is maybe a little too fat. I have a *dacha* for summer and I go to the Black Sea for my sun. My mother still lives with us and we have enough to eat. Why would I ask questions?"

There was another silence and then Denisov broke it. "Would you put away your gun, now, Devereaux?"

Devereaux stared and nodded. Pushing the hammer back, he slipped the gun into his belt.

"Do you believe me now?" Denisov asked mildly. He took off his rimless glasses and began slowly to wipe them on his tie. It was a red tie and it reminded Devereaux of the tie around O'Neill's neck.

"I don't know. Perhaps."

"Perhaps. Your favorite word to say nothing. All right, Devereaux. Say nothing. It doesn't matter because I am here. It is where I must be."

The horn on the great red-and-white ferry belched a sound out into the blackness of the North Channel of the Irish Sea. And then the ship slowly pulled away from the dock of Larne Harbor, outside of Belfast.

O'Neill stood at the bar and watched Ireland fade behind him.

He had taken all his clothes and stuffed them into a suitcase and he had cried when Tim, the eldest, had asked him where he was going. He had made up some lie. She had known too, his wife, and she had shared his fear and had even made him a bit of a sandwich. He would write her, he would be back soon. . . . But she knew and it had torn at him greater than the pain of his broken wrist.

His swollen wrist was wrapped with a hasty bandage and to ease the pain he poured down another glass of whisky.

"Yer goin' far, is it?"

O'Neill turned and looked at the old man leaning against the bar with him. An old Irishman with a strange accent. Probably a Liverpudlian.

"Aye," he said. "Far."

"'Tis farther to take a far trip beginning at night. The night makes it longer."

"Aye," said O'Neill absently. He did not think on his words; the conversation continued, but somehow, he was beyond it. He could only think about the sudden horror of that night, the beating and his betrayal. He was an informer and a coward. That is what he had said to Devereaux that morning in the hotel room in Edinburgh. And Devereaux had agreed with him.

Slowly, the great ferry moved through the darkness of the channel to Stranraer in Scotland. When the short trip was over, the two men were still at the bar, still drinking.

Then it was down the steps, onto the dock, the few passengers routinely passed through by the customs officer. On a siding, the old train waited for them for the overnight journey to Glasgow and Edinburgh; it would make every stop along the way.

O'Neill found an empty compartment in the second-class carriage and threw his heavy bag onto the metal rack above. The carriage was old and the worn plush seats smelled of age. There was graffiti scratched onto the finish above the seats.

O'Neill did not look at it. His arm throbbed. As he sat down on the seat, he wondered if his wrist was broken.

He tried to sleep but the rattle and shake of the old train would not let him.

There was no ticket collector aboard.

The interior of the train was lit with twenty-five-watt bulbs, which made the night beyond the cars colder and blacker. O'Neill shivered to himself.

The door of the compartment slid open.

The old man from the ferry came in.

O'Neill opened his eyes and frowned in annoyance. Every bloody compartment empty and he comes in here. Probably wants a chat.

"I just thought I'd sit down here. I have a wee bottle with me."

O'Neill let the frown escape. He could not sleep. At least there was whisky.

"Sit down, sit down," O'Neill said at last. His voice carried only a shadow of its old bonhomie.

"Thank ye," said the old man. He pulled a bottle of Paddy out of his coat. "Against the chill," he said. He passed the bottle to O'Neill.

Oh, Irishmen, thought O'Neill suddenly, with such a sense of loss. Where in the world will I go to be at home, leaving my native land? The thought made him take a large drink. He wiped the top of the bottle and passed it back to the old man.

"Me name is—me name is Donovan," said O'Neill at last.

The old man looked at him with kind and shrewd eyes. "Mr. Donovan," he said. "T'yer health." And he took a swallow.

O'Neill nodded and waited for him to pass back the bottle. "And who would you be?"

"Oh, I'm called Tatty," said the old man at last. "It's not much of a name but it suits me."

"Tatty is a fine name," said O'Neill, his eyes filled with tears. Oh, Irishmen, with your goodness and good fellowship and your ways, where will O'Neill find ye again in the wide world he must travel?

"Tatty. T'you. To yer good health, sur," said O'Neill. And he drank deeply.

When they came to clean out the car in the morning, one of the British Rail sweepers found him. They thought he was asleep at first and they rudely pushed at his arm to wake him. He fell over in a heap on the floor.

The bullet wound in O'Neill's chest was scarcely visible through his clothing.

15

LONDON

Elizabeth slept late Saturday morning, letting the last few days drain out of her in dreams. She did not sleep well, but when she awoke in the strange bed on the strange, cloudy London morning, she did not feel tired anymore. Only still alone. And afraid.

She had not arrived at Blake House until after one A.M. She had spent a long time ringing the doorbell, a long time standing in the darkness of the street off Hyde Park. The darkness was an enemy now, as was each passing car and each pedestrian.

Finally the door opened and she pronounced the word of entry. For a moment, the old housekeeper stared at her as though she were mad. Was it the right word? Had she forgotten? There were so many secrets, so many codes to remember.

But, at last, the housekeeper took her to another room and made her wait for a long time. She was cold and tired, but Devereaux had said they would make her wait.

Then the young man came into the room, wearing a robe and pajamas and slippers. She noticed the bulge in the pocket of his robe and supposed it was a gun. She was prepared for that as well.

He seemed friendly and they talked quietly. Devereaux had told her to say as much as she had to say and no more; to only tell about Devereaux and their meeting and not to talk about the Section or the ghost Section.

After a while, she said, "I realize you have to be satisfied about me. But couldn't we go someplace? I'm tired and wet and dirty."

Then he smiled and showed her into the library. He gave her a drink and poured himself a large drink. When he poured the drinks, she realized he was a little drunk. He didn't slur his speech and his moves seemed normal, but there was something a little out-of-focus about his behavior.

She told him enough to satisfy him. After a while—and another drink—she was taken to a bedroom. There was a bathroom attached. She noticed her suitcase was already on the dresser and open. She supposed the housekeeper had searched it.

The night and morning had been full of dreams about the blond man and the Section and the training school and Devereaux. And dreams about the little boy in the photograph. The last dream had been the worst of all. But all the dreams seemed to exorcise the ghosts inside her, and when she awoke, it was better.

She felt safe.

She took a long time dressing and finally went downstairs to the hall. The house was silent except for the steady tick-tick-tick of the grandfather clock in the hall. It was nearly eleven.

She went into the library because it was the only room she knew. She looked out the window. There had been snow the day before, but now it was gone. The street only looked wet and miserable.

She turned from the window; folding her arms, she stared at the bookcases lining the walls. She looked at the titles. They seemed to have been chosen without regard for anyone actually reading them, merely parts of the prop that consisted of a library. She thought some one had probably come in and ordered: One library, medium, English-style. Then a government delivery had been made. What was one library, medium . . . called? GI-345 stroke 7?

Elizabeth was smiling when Green came into the room. He returned the smile.

"Good morning," he said. "You *were* tired. You slept quite late. Nearly noon. Are you hungry?"

She realized she was.

"Good. We'll get the housekeeper to fix something. She's a terrible woman—can't stand her." She noticed the trace of an English accent in his flat, midwestern voice; it annoyed her and she didn't know why.

"But an excellent cook. And she knows it. So she'll get something for you. I was just popping off now, have to go to the embassy. But I thought we could have a chat while we're waiting for your breakfast." He pulled a bell cord and the housekeeper appeared a moment later in the library door. Elizabeth did not know why, but the action made her feel uncomfortable and slightly embarrassed.

"Will you get our guest the usual hearty Olde English breakfast," asked Green brightly. "Be a dear. And we'll have some tea in here while we talk."

"D'you want the breakfast here as well?"

"Yes, that would be splendid."

"It's nearly noon," said the housekeeper.

"What a dear," said Green to Elizabeth. "Even if all the clocks broke down, she'd know the time and be willing to announce it to you."

The housekeeper tried out a frown and then turned from the door.

"Dragon," Green said, going to the leather chair by the window. He waved his hand and Elizabeth sat down.

He looked out into the gray, wet street while he spoke: "I signaled the Section last night. They didn't know about you. I must talk to Hanley today. The Section was quite upset."

Devereaux had told her not to expect recognition from anyone in the Section. Especially Hanley.

"Well, still. You knew the code. And Devereaux is in Belfast. At least, so we assumed. We haven't heard from

him for three days and I was under express instructions
to report to Hanley the moment he made contact. And
so here I am." He smiled. "Contact has been made and I
have nothing to report. Won't you fill me in."

"I thought I told you. Last night—"

"Yes, yes. That you met Devereaux in Belfast. That
you were in danger there. Yes, you told me that. But I
have my report. Devereaux and I are colleagues and I
have to have a clearer picture before I can make my
report."

She nodded. She did not know what to say. She tried
to smile. "There's not much to say. Because I can't. I was
involved in . . . well, his mission—"

"Yes, his mission," said Green. "Which is aborted now
because the attempt has already been made on Lord
Slough's life."

"Well, Devereaux said . . ."

Green stared, smiled, folded his hands. He waited.
"Devereaux said?"

Devereaux said. Something was wrong. Or was it? Or
was it only a dream? Or part of one?

"Devereaux said?" Green continued patiently.

"That I really was to wait. Until he returned."

"When is he returning?"

"I don't know."

"Today? Do you think he will show up today?"

"Today? It's possible. I don't know."

"But Ms. Campbell, I do have a report to make—"

"I can't. I'm sorry, but I can't tell you anything."

Green looked at her and the smile slowly faded from
his boyish features. He remained seated for a moment
and then shook his head. "Well, I shall have to make
my report in any case. And your refusal to fill in the
station chief—"

"I'm sorry. I was told—"

He pasted a smile back on his face as he got up. "Not
your fault. Not at all. Don't give it a thought. It's all
Devereaux. Something of a legend in the Section, as you

may well believe. Quite an independent operator. His own man. Sometimes, he bends the rules a bit, I'm afraid. He was to report to me."

Elizabeth tried to return the smile. "I'm sorry."

At that moment, the housekeeper appeared with a tray containing a teapot, cups and other dishes. She set it down on the table by the window. "Your tea," she said, glaring at Elizabeth. Then she turned and walked out of the room.

Green popped off the metal cover over a plate to reveal fried eggs and bacon with great chunks of fat in it and a grilled tomato.

"Would you like breakfast?" he said.

Elizabeth began to eat while he poured the tea.

At a minute past noon on Saturday in the village of Innisbally, Durkin, the *garda,* and Cashel, his new found friend, went into MacDermott's pub and ordered whisky.

"I hate a funeral. I hate the time after at the house, as well. I was glad to get away, I can tell ya," said Durkin, who reached for the glass and splashed a little water into the whisky from a bottle on the bar.

Cashel took his glass and turned to Durkin.

"God bless you," said Cashel and Durkin nodded and they drank the harsh amber whisky.

After a second glass at the bar, they retired to a bench in the corner of the pub for a little talk. Durkin had been looking forward to it ever since the slow-moving policeman from Dublin had singled him out at the funeral Mass.

"I was surprised," said Cashel. "By the turnout, I mean. Quite a lot of people came."

"Ah, well, y'know what a funeral is t'a village like that. It is all in the family, as it were. We're small and gettin' smaller and like they says in the school, the death of any man diminishes me." He took a sip of the whisky. "And diminishes the village, yer might say."

"Indeed," said Cashel. "Indeed." He had been born and reared in Dublin and considered the people of the west country as much foreigners as he might consider the wild highlanders living in the Scottish hills. Dubliners, he would tell his wife, were another race of Irish; the Irish poets who wrote in a tongue that other men could understand.

"And there's his Lairdship comin' down. He's a great man t'these parts. He's English, y'know."

"I know."

"But no one holds that against him. It's as though he wished he was not. He named his daughter Brianna, you know; is it not a beautiful name?"

"It is that."

"Oh, aye. And his wife, God rest her soul, she died when I was a lad. D'you know she came from here? She was an O'Donnell, from Ennis."

"Ah, from Ennis." Cashel knew how to keep an Irish conversation going.

"Aye, Ennis. I've been to Ennis."

"A nice enough town."

"Well, a bit large for me. Not as large as Galway City, but large."

"Large," agreed Cashel.

They were silent for a moment as they sipped at their whisky.

"But Lord Slough now we was speakin' of. A good friend to the people here, if I may say so, sir. And a friend to Ireland."

"So it would seem," said Cashel. He let the other man speak.

"If there's not twenty men from the village is workin' on his estate, there's not one. And good wages, too, as good as you've seen around this poor land."

"I understand that," said Cashel. "Tell me, were those all village people at the funeral?"

"Oh, aye. Certainly. Save for that English secretary, the one that works for his Lairdship. I think he's from London but yer can't tell by his bloody way of speakin'. He might be off the telly."

"Aye," said Cashel. "Jeffries."

"Jeffries," repeated Durkin. "But the rest were from the village."

Cashel seemed disappointed. He frowned and put his glass down.

"Except fer the fella passin' through."

"Passin' through?"

"Oh, aye. A fella. Down from Derry, he was, in Ulster. Down to Kerry, he's goin' to see his aunt. Derry to Kerry."

"And he went t'the funeral, did he?"

"Oh, aye. I saw him there. D'ya not see him?"

"Was it the fella with the black, glitterin' eyes—"

"Oh, aye. Now what eyes those are. Fer a speaker in the Dáil t'have."

"A powerful speaker, is he?"

"Powerful, sir. He come into the village last night on the road, walkin' down it was. And we drank last night and he told us good tales about the North. About the Protestants," continued Durkin. "They're a bad lot. I've never met one, but the stories he told me."

"Lord Slough is a Protestant," said Cashel gently.

"Oh, aye. But he has to be, don't he? I mean, he's English. But I meant I never met an Irishman who was like that."

"They're Scots-Irish," said Cashel.

"Who are, sir?"

"The Northern men. The Prods. Protestants. Scots and Irish."

"All mixed up, is it? That might explain it, then. The Scots are English, are they not? Well, then, perhaps they can't help being Protestants any more than the English can. But the stories this fella told, about the way they treated the Catholics and then about the civil rights march. And y'know, he says he saw Bernadette Devlin speaking herself in Derry."

"Did he?"

"As close to her as this," said Durkin. "Oh, what stories. It was wonderful to hear him, sir."

"I wish I had heard him," said Cashel. "Did he say his name, then?"

"He did," said Durkin. "Faolin, it was. Faolin."

"Faolin," said Cashel. "I knew Faolins in Cork."

"Cork," said Durkin with wonder, as though Cashel were speaking of Timbuktu. "I've been meaning to go to Cork someday."

Cashel smiled. "Can I buy ye another?"

Durkin grinned with his young, toothless mouth. "I won't say no t'a policeman from Dublin City."

"You better not," said Cashel. He got up and brought the glasses to the bar and waited for them to be filled.

Faolin, he thought.

16

CLARE

Cashel could not sleep well in a strange bed. They had invited him to spend another night in the great house in the burren, but he had declined Lord Slough's invitation with work as an excuse; if the truth were known, it was because he much preferred the company of young Durkin, the local *garda,* and the villagers to sitting again in the presence of Slough and his daughter.

So he had bedded down at Durkin's in the little cottage the *garda* shared with his mother. Cashel and Durkin had spent the evening drinking at the two public houses in the village and they had wandered home late, a little drunk, staggering up the blind-dark country road to the old white-walled cottage.

There they had sat a while longer in front of the gentle, hypnotic turf fire, no longer talking of the funeral or of Deirdre or of Lord Slough. They spoke instead of ghosts and wee ones and of the times of the great emigrations to the United States after the Irish civil war. Durkin brought out the poteen—he explained he had seized it from an illegal still uncovered in the burren—and they sat and drank the powerful potato whisky, and ghosts came more easily to mind, ghosts and sadness and thoughts of times past, all conjured up in the thin wisps of smoke from the pungent turf fire.

This morning Cashel's head hurt, and when he opened his eyes, he realized he was not home in Dublin, safe in the old bed with his wife beside him. He wished he were there.

It was no use; he could not sleep. He rose and shaved and dressed and finally walked out into the gloomy air of a Clare morning. The hills were shrouded in smoky fog blown in from the sea.

The chill rouged his cheeks; he stretched and told himself he felt better; he breathed deep and then filled his pipe, bending his head to light it against the breeze blowing in from Galway Bay.

He started down the road to Innisbally.

The fields were dry and bare for winter, as though they had donned a severe dress for the season.

At the bottom of the road was the village: There was the steeple of the old, ugly church at the edge of the settlement. He saw the first of the old women scurrying along the same road to early Sunday morning Mass. He felt a nostalgia then, for Mass and his own mother and his own time for church. It had been a long time since he had gone to Mass—unless you counted funerals. He did not. Yesterday's funeral—he had been scarcely aware there was a Mass going on. He had been looking at the congregation, trying to find any faces that did not fit. It was an old trick and he was always surprised how often it worked.

Faolin.

He saw again the black, glittering eyes in that thin, haunted face. A face too pale for a farmer's face; the open coat—the farmers wore their best to the funeral, but Faolin had work a dark shirt and no suit, only the old open coat.

Cashel had stared at Faolin across the heads of the kneeling villagers in the church. And Faolin had caught his eye. They had stared at each other for a moment; then Faolin had turned away.

Faolin. He had a name. Gone down to Kerry to see his aunt.

Cashel had telephoned the *gardai* there; they were

looking for him. Cashel had called the police liaison in Belfast and they had checked the unemployment rolls in Londonderry—no easy task on Saturday afternoon. But there had been no Faolin.

No Faolin anywhere, but suddenly this hollow-eyed fellow appears at a funeral Mass in the tiny village of Innisbally, passing through he was, and it happened to be the funeral of a woman caught as a victim in an assassination attempt on the richest man in England and Ireland. A man who was the cousin of the English Queen, titled, owner of a half a hundred newspapers in Britain, Ireland, and Canada, and Lord knows what else.

Cashel walked into the deserted village. He felt thirsty. He knocked out his pipe on the post-office wall. The sparks flickered as they fell and then went damp and dead. He felt the bowl absently with his thumb as he shoved the pipe back into his pocket and looked around. Was there anything as morose as an Irish village on Sunday morning?

Cashel stared sadly at the closed face of MacDermott's public house across the road. For a moment, his memory conjured childhood's certainty in wishes. Give me three wishes and the first will be that MacDermott come to the door and open his pub for me. Smiling, Cashel crossed his fingers. And then stared.

There was someone at the door. And it was MacDermott. Opening the door and beckoning to him. The magic was still good. He smiled to himself and crossed the road.

MacDermott's red, mottled face of the night before was now sober and gray.

"Mr. Cashel," he said.

"Mr. MacDermott. You're the answer to my wishes," said Cashel.

"It is a coincidence I saw yer just now on the road. Yer were on yer way to Mass, was it?"

"No. I was not. Could I trouble you fer a pint of Smithwick's?"

MacDermott frowned. "Ah, yer a bit done, is it? If I

didn't know yer was a policeman from Dublin, I'd not do it, but since yer a guest of Durkin, I cannot deny you," said MacDermott as he pulled the policeman inside and shut the door. "Besides that, I was after wanting to talk to you."

Cashel went to the bar and took the proffered glass of the light ale. There was a time to pay the piper, he thought, but not now. His headache receded.

MacDermott looked at him and then poured himself a small glass of whisky with a shaky hand. He looked up. "Poteen, was it?"

Cashel finished a draught and put the glass down. "You know poteen is illegal."

"Ah, I do. Yer entirely correct," said MacDermott.

"You wanted to see me?"

"I did."

Cashel put down the glass and MacDermott filled it without a word. There was an unspoken understanding that there would be no money changing hands at the moment.

Cashel felt much better. He waited for MacDermott to speak.

"After yer left last evening with Durkin," the publican began, "another fella comes in. He was not a man of the village. And I know yer been askin' about that, after Deirdre's funeral, and wonderin' about the fella that come down on the walkin' trip from Derry—"

"A stranger then."

"An American," said MacDermott. "He was askin' after his Lairdship."

Cashel put down the glass slowly. "He was, was he?"

"Indeed," said MacDermott, shrewdly measuring the interest he had stirred in Cashel. "Askin' where his Lairdship was livin' and all."

"And you told him where the lord was?"

"I told him where Clare House was, I did," said MacDermott. "But I said it was a late hour."

Color seemed to come back into MacDermott's gray

face. "And I told him there was policemen from Dublin there."

Cashel frowned. "You did."

"I did."

"And this American fella didn't seem inclined t'visit Clare House?"

"No, sir. He did not. He took a room from me instead and had his whiskies and went to bed."

Cashel nodded.

"He was askin' after the funeral of poor Deirdre Monahan—God rest her soul among the angels—and he was askin' after any strangers in the village—"

"Askin' after strangers?"

"As you were, sur."

"What did ye tell him, then?"

"Nothing for me. But Old Nap started up with his gob, and before yer knew it, he was tellin' this American about you. And then about this young fella down from Derry. . . ."

"Damn." Cashel pushed himself away from the bar. "And where is the American then?"

"In the back, sur. The best bedroom. Sleepin' I would expect."

"And you," said Cashel. He smiled at MacDermott. "You're off to Mass, is it?"

"I am. I was just now leavin' when I sees y' in the road."

"All right then. Why don't you go down to the church? I'll just have a visit with the man."

"Ah." MacDermott seemed to hesitate for a moment and then he slipped into his black coat and pulled on the inevitable cloth cap. "I'll just go down to the church, then." He smiled hesitantly.

Cashel smiled in return. A policeman's frosty smile without mirth.

The door closed.

The public house was still.

The leftover smell of beer and smoke in the bar was

as dismal as a hangover. For a moment, Cashel waited and listened and heard nothing but the faint sound of his own breathing.

He reached into the pocket of his greatcoat. He carried a little silver-plated pistol. A friend once said it would not harm a mouse. Cashel knew better, because he had once used it to take a life.

As he held the silver object in his right hand, his hand semed larger than the gun itself.

The floors creaked as he walked to the back of the public house. He stopped again and listened and heard nothing.

He tried the handle. As usual in these old pubs, the door had no lock. He pushed the door into the room.

The American sat up in the bed and looked at him. He was smiling. He held a large black gun in his hand.

For a moment, the two men stared at each other.

The American spoke first: "Come in. And close the door."

Cashel entered the room. He held his gun aimed at the figure on the bed. The dull pain in his head returned; he should have been more careful.

The American said, "You don't look like a man of the village."

"Nor you."

"I'm not. Are you from Londonderry, then?"

"Dublin," snapped Cashel. "And I can tell you that we do not favor guests of the nation to carry guns about with them."

"Only native sons, is that right? Like the IRA?"

Cashel grunted. "Like the police, is more like it."

"Are you the police?"

Cashel did not answer.

"You would have identification," said the man in the bed. "Throw it here. On the cover."

It was absurd, but Cashel had no wish to rush the moment. The black barrel of the American's gun had not wavered during the brief conversation.

"It's in my trousers."

"Carefully."

Cashel removed the wallet and threw it on the cover. The American opened it and glanced down at the picture of Cashel—a grim, colorless, nondimensional Cashel— and the seal of the country affixed to an identity card. Slowly, the American placed his pistol down on the cover.

Cashel sighed. He realized he had been holding his breath. He still held the silver pistol. "And now that you've satisfied yerself, tell me who you are and why you have a gun in this country?"

"Sit down. I want to talk to you."

"You're a cool one, you are. Who are you?"

"It doesn't matter about my name," the man in the bed said. "But it's Devereaux. Now sit down. We have to talk."

In the end, Devereaux only told a few lies. He explained he was with the CIA; it was too hard to explain R Section to this Dublin policeman. He told, with almost the whole truth, why he had come down to Innisbally in the west of Ireland.

Devereaux did not tell Cashel about the two dead agents in Belfast because it wasn't his business. And he did not tell him about Elizabeth or O'Neill. Nor did he speak about his meeting with Terry and about the fruitless day-long search for the man called "Cap'n Donovan." Cashel would not want to know those things anyway; he was a simple policeman and he had been sent to Innisbally to find out about a murder that had taken place in Canada and to see if there had been an Irish connection.

So Devereaux said he had been sent to Innisbally for the same reason, to gather information for the CIA, because Lord Slough was an important man to both Ireland and America.

Devereaux showed Cashel the proper identification, including a plastic entry card of the type used by agents admitted to the CIA building in Langley, Virginia. It was part of the bag of tricks that Hanley had always insisted agents carry with them; Devereaux had never had recourse to it before.

But Cashel was not a fool and he was not impressed by mere cards. In the end, it was the information traded by Devereaux that finally made him accept him.

Devereaux said the agency was convinced the plot to murder Lord Slough was still on; that the attempt in Canada either was the first of a chain of attempts or was unrelated to the attempts that would follow.

And where had Mr. Devereaux learned all this?

But Devereaux could not tell him the truth; not the truth about the man called Terry and the torture Devereaux had used on him; nor could he tell this policeman why he had killed Terry after he had learned everything. Devereaux did not murder but eliminated. Those were details of the trade and they were of no special importance because they contained no information in themselves. The death of an IRA man in Belfast scarcely twelve hours before was not for trade. Terry, in his fear and agony, had even told Devereaux that a man had gone to kill O'Neill. But that was not information either. O'Neill had ceased to matter.

Devereaux was certain Terry had told him all he knew.

There was a man named Tatty and another named Donovan. They were part of the plan to get Lord Slough and the plan was yet to be fulfilled. He didn't know about the attempt in Canada. Terry did not know when or where Tatty and his friends would act. Devereaux was finally convinced of that. There was no need to explain how Devereaux became convinced.

Was it brutal? Of course. That made it work. Would he have done the same things to Elizabeth? If she had not told him?

He realized the truth and shrugged it off. He had given Denisov the slip, rented a car, and left Belfast in the early afternoon. He had driven furiously down the unmarked roads and lanes of the South until he had come—exhausted

—to the village where Lord Slough lived, Innisbally on the shore of the western sea.

So what he told the Dublin policeman was partly true and that was enough; he needed the policeman's help to thwart the assassination and to get the further information that would finish the mission; information that Hanley could use to arrange an entrée to British Intelligence; information that would let him—Devereaux—go home at last to the hills around Front Royal where he could forget for a little while Elizabeth and R Section and the rest of it.

He needed the policeman as guide through the un-chartered labyrinth of Irish politics and Irish crime and Irish terrorism.

Devereaux displayed each nugget of his information slowly, all the while measuring the policeman's response. Was he bright enough? Was he going to be useful? That had been the gamble. But, after an hour, Devereaux decided that Cashel would do—that the ridiculous bowler hat and black coat and fierce mustache were merely clownish features masking a subtle mind.

They even had a drink on it, which is where Mac-Dermott found them when he returned from mass: Cashel with a third glass of mild beer and Devereaux with a glass filled with ice cubes and gin.

"You don't have any vodka," said Devereaux when the publican entered and shut the door.

"I do not. I'll not have Communist drinks in here. And I might say, Mr. Cashel, it's not opening time yet and I'd lose me trade if the *garda* saw this sight."

"I'm the police," said Cashel. "But you're correct, Mr. MacDermott. We've no further need to intrude on your hospitality." He rose. "Mr. Devereaux? Will you accompany me?"

And the two men went outside and stood for a moment on the road through the village. A dog loped across the way and urinated on the post-office wall.

"A fine comment," said Cashel of the dog.

"What's there to be done?" Devereaux looked up and down the empty road. He was conscious, vaguely, of a deadline; of a need for action.

"D'ya recall this fella I mentioned named Faolin?" Devereaux waited.

"He was on a walkin' trip he says from Derry down to Kerry."

"That's far."

"Aye. But not unlikely, Mr. Devereaux. Some of these poor fellas walk hundreds of miles, for visits or for jobs. If you've driven this country, sir, you've seen few cars and few horses and wagons. We're not so rich yet that we can afford to forget how to walk."

"Which way is Kerry?"

"You mean to where he was going, sir? Well, I don't think that's important at all." Devereaux waited while Cashel struck a match and stuffed the burning end into the bowl of the black pipe. "No. I was more thinking of going up the road back to Derry and see what there was t'be learned."

Devereaux understood. "To see where he left the car, you mean? Because he didn't walk from Derry if he's our man?"

Cashel smiled. "Ah, I'm glad yer a bright fella."

Devereaux frowned; he realized he had already made his judgment on Cashel's worth but he was not aware that Cashel was judging him.

"There's my car," said Devereaux, pointing to the rental Fiat parked on the roadside. It was the only auto on the street.

They drove north slowly, along the winding, narrow highway that skirts the brown hills and roughly follows the shoreline of Galway Bay. There was no other car on the narrow roadway—even in high summer, when the country was full of American tourists, the roads all seemed strangely empty, as though the ancient past of the rural country swallowed up all traces of the present.

They drove by an old cemetery with Celtic crosses

catching the pale light of the cold November sun. Beneath the crosses, flowers sat pretty and stiff and dead in the plastic wrappings.

"They buried her there," said Cashel, pointing to the graveyard.

Devereaux did not speak as he watched the road unwind. The death of Deirdre Monahan scarcely moved him any more than the death of O'Neill.

"D'ya know about a Celtic cross?"

Devereaux did not answer; he looked right and left, for a clue to find the car to find the man who would kill Lord Slough. It was like a nursery rhyme without an end.

"They say when Paddy came here—"

"Paddy?"

"Saint Patrick. When Paddy came here t'convert the heathen, he found us worshippin' the sun. Undoubtedly we worshipped it because we had never seen it." Cashel chuckled. "Or we seen it as often as we seen God."

Devereaux looked around at empty fields, fallow for winter.

"So Paddy let them worship their sun, but he put it on a cross, too, so that the circle of the sun formed to make the Celtic cross."

Devereaux pretended to listen; he wondered why the policeman bothered with this tour-guide monologue. In politeness, he grunted as a period to the anecdote.

Cashel regarded him across the small front seat of the car. "You don't care about that story," he said.

"Not very much. He could have put his car anywhere along here."

Cashel glanced around carelessly at the fields. "Oh? He could do that, but it's very unlikely. These old Clare countrymen know their land and neighbors. Faolin should know that as well and know the farmers are over every inch of their land every day. Faolin should know it wouldn't be very smart to leave the motorcar down in a field or a lane because the old countrymen'd be down in the village of an evening, askin' after a fella who left his valuable automobile sitting by the side of the road. No, I think Faolin would have left the motorcar in the next village, up the road. Perhaps in a garage."

Devereaux nodded. This was what he had gambled on when he heard the policeman was in the village; his instinct had been to avoid contact, but he had decided against it; the policeman could not be fooled, he would know Devereaux had been around. It was better if the policeman worked for him.

"This matter then. It isn't much t'you, is it?" Cashel asked softly. For a moment, Devereaux thought he was talking about the Celtic crosses again; he did not know what the question meant. He said so.

Cashel, still softly, said, "This business with Lord Slough and the plot t'kill him, I mean. I suppose you're interested because your country is interested in everything. But there's no bloody sense of the matter being urgent, is there?"

Yes, thought Devereaux. There was urgency. *But not for the reasons you would know about.*

"Am I right, Mr. Devereaux? Yer don't give a great bloody damn about it all, one way or the other."

Devereaux watched the road. "It's a job."

"It's that."

They were silent for a moment. They could hear the noisy engine of the little car and the drum of the wheels on the cracked roadway.

"You don't care if Lord Slough lives or dies then?"

"Sure we do," said Devereaux. "As a professional matter, of interest to my government."

"Interest. A curious word. It can mean so little. I can be interested in news of a ferry overturning in the river Ganges and the deaths of a thousand Indians."

Devereaux could not understand the tone of voice.

Cashel continued, "Lord Slough is an Englishman who loves Eire. They are not so rare. If you would come even out here to Clare in the summer, you'd see them. They married Irish girls or they came here once on holiday and never got the feel of the country out of their bones. It does not matter the reason—they love Eire and the people."

They were approaching a village. Along the narrow roadway, men and women in a straggly stream were walking away from the church. The men were tall and thick-bodied; the women seemed smaller but not frail. The little car roared past them.

"Look at them." Cashel spoke again in the same soft, urgent voice. "They may have heard of Lord Slough on the telly or one of them may get the Dublin paper he owns in the post. But he's no more to them than he is to you. A curiosity perhaps, like all great men. But he loves them and he's put it in ways they'll understand someday. Those oil derricks, y'heard about them off the western coast? There's oil there, in the western sea. Ireland's oil. And Lord Slough is for findin' it and then you'll see the change in these poor people."

Devereaux still did not understand, but he waited. He thought again that the Irish seemed to speak in circles that grew gradually smaller until the center was apparent.

"So one day they'll all have a telly in their cottages and they'll have the price of a pint without lookin' at the coins in their hands," said Cashel. "Because of that oil that Lord Slough is after findin' in the western ocean."

They entered the village. Devereaux pulled the car to the side of the road and turned off the engine. But he sat still and waited.

"But what about you, Mr. Devereaux? Or your government? You don't care about Lord Slough fer yerself and I wouldn't have believed you if you'd said otherwise. But what about America? What's your country's stake in all this then? Y'see, I cannot believe everything you told me back there in MacDermott's place. You understand, I'm not trying to be rude, but I'm just a policeman from Dublin and you are a great representative of the Central Intelligence Agency. D'ye understand, sir? Lord Slough is important to Eire. And to these poor Clare folks, whether they know Lord Slough or no. He's an Englishman and all—and that's what those terrorists care about because they're young and they're fightin' the right cause the wrong way—but he's important to Eire."

Devereaux turned in his seat. Something in Cashel's calm, almost sleepy Irish face had changed; there was a hardness and cold warning in his voice now.

"So there's no misunderstandin', Mr. Devereaux. You gave me good information. I thank you, for the nation. But I don't know your game yet, Mr. Devereaux. D'ye understand now? I know y'have a game but I don't know what it is. Perhaps it don't concern me, which is just as well. But do not let your game bring harm to Lord Slough because then y' harm Eire. And then you'll have abused your rights as a guest of the nation. D'y understand now, sir?"

Devereaux nodded. So the simple policeman with his ridiculous hat and bristling mustache knew it was more than a game.

17

WASHINGTON

Hanley had not thought to shave and now he was acutely aware of it. The bristles—brown and gray—on his thin chin somehow made him more tired than he was; he rubbed at them as he drove down the deserted Sunday morning stretch of Wisconsin Avenue into Bethesda.

He had been up all night.

He had, in fact, not left the Section in the Department of Agriculture building since Devereaux's telephone call over thirty-six hours before. He had not been aware of sleep or human needs or food for two days; he had merely been the hunter, searching through the records and reports and magnetic tapes on the big computer for clues to the leak in the Section and a clue to the mystery left by Devereaux.

Part of that mystery had been in the message found on the body of the dead agent. The man Devereaux had eliminated in a Belfast hotel stairwell.

The message: ETRAYSDVERDANTYGER

He had used the computer to break the code. Effortlessly, it had hummed through the variants possible in routine codes—the letter plus one, the letter plus two, the letter plus three . . . E became H in the plus-three code, T became W, R became U, and so on. The machine had tried all the plus combination up to forty and printed out the variants, and then it had been programmed to use the minus codes—letter minus one made E become D and so on. The machine tried "book" codes.

The message was meaningless.

The message was not meaningless. What was it? Did it name the leak? Was it a code within a code?

And all the time, he had burrowed into the other files with the loyal secretaries and with Hallman of the Asian desk borrowed for the hunt. Hanley was like a man who had mislaid his eyeglasses: Half blind with fatigue, worry, and frustration, he pawed through familiar things in familiar places again and again, always with growing irritation at his own stupidity. It must be there in the piles of manpower reports, training reports, recommendations of new agents, reports from field agents, 201 files. In all those familiar things, there must be the mark of the traitor.

Hanley spurred the others on ruthlessly. He had no life outside the Section; it was home and hearth, wife and child to him. If Hanley were to admit it, the endless hours thrilled him as well. The Section had caught a kind of wartime fever, an excitement that Hanley had not felt since the days he'd served in the old O.S.S.

Chief-of-Section Galloway had called four times during those hours.

As usual, the voice was mild but clearly disapproving of the delay in tracing the leak in the Section. Rear Admiral Galloway (USN Ret.) was at the best of times a frustrating man to work for but now it was much worse: He was the type who said little but expected you to catch intricate meanings in and shadings to his few words.

Of course, Hanley had considered that Devereaux himself was wrong. That Devereaux had relayed a bogus message. That Devereaux, for unclear reasons, was playing a game with the Section.

That thought had occurred to Hanley but he told no one.

It had occurred to Galloway and he chewed on it and then finally relayed it on to Hanley in the second telephone conversation.

And there was the business with Miss Elizabeth Campbell. Formerly Mrs. Donald Frieze. Mother. Child deceased. Divorce. Who was Frieze? That was part of the hunt as well. Inquiries were made about Frieze in the Justice Department, where he worked in the civil rights section. A tap was set on his telephone. It recorded only inanities—two calls from salesmen, one selling subscriptions to a Washington newspaper, the other offering central air conditioning. And a long, late conversation with a Margo Cole of Fairfax in which sexual relations were suggested and agreed to.

Elizabeth Campbell. Born in Buffalo, New York. Raised in New York City by Thomas A. Campbell, patent attorney. Mother dead. Columbia University. Peace Corps—Addis Ababa. Married Donald Frieze in Bergen, New Jersey; one child, David. Killed at six years of age by Mrs. Eleanor Hodkins, 64, of 122 Briar Lane, Arlington, Virginia, at 3:45 in the afternoon. Automobile accident. Divorce.

Everything was checked.

Hanley finally came to Devereaux's own 201 file.

Peter Devereaux. Born in Chicago. Orphaned at four. Raised by an elderly aunt. Two arrests while a teen-ager, one for assault and battery, the second for assault. Scholarship to the University of Chicago. Graduate, postgraduate. Ph.D. Professor of history, Columbia University, New York. Recruited to the Section. Four attached recommendations; three attached letters of demerit.

But Hanley already knew everything about Devereaux.

And the message: ETRAYSDVERDANTYGER

In the twenty-seventh hour, half dozing at his desk while his eyes dimly perceived the manpower reports in his hands, Hanley understood. The thought came to him and lingered just long enough for him to become alert again. He put down the manpower reports and got up from the desk and went into the hall and drank a long sip of water from the fount.

The message was not in code. That was why it couldn't be broken. The message had been composed, not sent.

The dead agent had written out the message to be transmitted later, by someone else.

That was it.

Hanley stood for a moment in the half-darkened hall. Several doors away, Hallman was culling the list of employment recommendations and recruiting comments on new agents. He had been at it all night.

Hanley thought he should tell Hallman, to buck him up. But the secret was too important for that.

He went back into his office and closed the door and sat down at the desk.

E TRAYS D VERDANT YGER.

E for Elizabeth.

TRAYS for . . .

D for Devereaux.

VERDANT YGER for . . .

He pondered it again, penciling in the new words beneath the original letters. If it was a message to be sent, then the words were in a sort of rough code at first and then were translated into a number code for transmission.

Elizabeth TRAYS Devereaux VERDANT YGER.

Hanley got up and went to the coffeepot plugged into the wall. He poured a cup with shaking hands and dropped two small saccharin pills into the black liquid. He sipped at it. How much coffee had he consumed since it began? His hands were shaking, he realized suddenly.

Betrays.

Betrays. Elizabeth betrays Devereaux.

He pushed the cup down onto the counter and went back to his desk. Elizabeth betrays Devereaux VERDANT YGER.

Green *yger*?

Tyger. VERDANTYGER was *green tyger*.

There was something there, at the edge of consciousness, shyly peering at him. Waiting for discovery. He mustn't frighten it or it will run away; he must let it come of its own accord, like a fawn in the woods investigating a salt lick.

Come, come.

Hanley waited, stared at the paper.

He saw the eyes of the beast in his mind, flashing in the darkness. Like a tyger.

Saw the tiger.

Burning.

And then it was in the light and Hanley knew:

Tyger.

He got up and raced to the door, opened it and called down the hall. He understood the code now; he knew who the traitor was.

So, with some satisfaction, he had awakened Galloway before dawn and was soon on his way to the Chief's residence.

He turned off Wisconsin Avenue onto Old Georgetown Road into residential Bethesda. The trees were droopy in the still air of morning but they carried their colors like flags. Leaves littered the lawns; autumn in Washington was eternal. In the distance, he could see the bare outlines of the naval hospital.

The Chief had instructed him to tell no one. Hanley had complied; he had merely told Hallman to go home, that the matter was closed. Hallman had been disappointed not to learn Hanley's secret.

It wasn't quite eight A.M.

Morning birds continued their songs as the sun began to filter through the trees.

Chief of Section lived in a comfortable house off the main road, back in the trees, surrounded by green privacy. There was a little turning circle in front of the impressive brick home. Hanley left his car there and went up the stone steps. But the door was open before he rang; the Old Man was waiting for him.

"Good, Hanley," Galloway said at last as Hanley entered the hall of the immense old house.

But no praise could take the heaviness out of him. With the end of the chase, there came an end to the excitement of the hunt. There was a traitor in the Section and Hanley felt it as personally as if someone had struck him. He did not even try to smile in return.

The Old Man closed the door as though he understood Hanley's private grief. He led the way into the library; the house was dark; there were people still sleeping within, upstairs, beyond the lights of the book-lined room.

Hanley took the proffered chair. The Old Man stood by the window, waiting.

Hanley cleared his throat. And then began:

"Green. In our London safe house. He's the traitor."

"Ah." The old man waited.

"Verdant Tyger. Green is obvious for verdant. Tyger. Why the old spelling for tiger—with a Y instead of an I? It was just their little game over at Langley, inventing a funny code name for Blake House." Hanley paused; in that moment, he hated the CIA as though it was not a rival agency but the enemy of the nation. "Tyger, sir. From William Blake's poem.

> "Tyger! Tyger! burning bright
> In the forests of the night,
> What immortal hand or eye
> Could frame thy fearful symmetry?"

Again, Hanley paused. The Old Man shook his head. "Such a simple code."

"It wasn't the code, sir. It was merely the preparation for a code, with bogus names. And then it would be translated into a code for transmission. Devereaux killed their agent before the message was sent."

"I see." The Chief gazed out the window at the limp, lush trees. There was an awkward silence for a moment, as though both men were suddenly embarrassed by the fact of the CIA's mole in their operation. Hanley knew that the Chief was considering not only the next move but the move after that, was weighing not only the operational danger to R Section but the political danger as well.

R Section must survive; to survive, there must be a demonstrated confidence in it. Would the existence of a CIA mole in R Section hurt the CIA—or the Section? The Old Man weighed it all and then gave Hanley his instructions.

Hanley sat and listened and did not take notes. He never took notes. He remembered everything.

Nothing must be done at the moment, the Chief explained.

Hanley pointed out that an agent from the Secfion could be sent to London immediately, to clear up the matter with Green. Ericson was available, stationed for the moment in Berlin.

The Chief nodded but rejected Hanley's plan. There might still be other leaks in the Section. Ericson might be a CIA mole as well; the Section was small, all jobs must be considered vital. They must run a careful clearance check on everyone, including secretaries. Hanley must return to headquarters and carry on and wait.

But what if Green moved in the meantime to eliminate Elizabeth Campbell, since she had betrayed the CIA mirror game to Devereaux?

The old man lit his pipe then and went to his desk and sat down and blew puffs of smoke at the ceiling. Yes, he said. That would be a difficulty. It would be a problem. It was too bad.

Hanley understood: The retired Navy admiral had to be a little careless of life for the sake of the action, for the safety of victory.

Hanley understood everything.

The Section had to be protected. It was presumed—strongly so, based on everything that Devereaux had reported—that the CIA had created the ghost Section and that Green was a part of the CIA operation. But what if Green worked for another agency? For the Soviets? He could not be given a chance to bolt. The Old Man explained patiently.

Another scenario: If Green worked for the CIA, he

must not be given a chance to inform them that the Section was totally aware of their game. The CIA must be caught in an embarrassment. So Hanley must wait upon contact from Devereaux and then Hanley must instruct Devereaux to go to London and eliminate Green. There must be no public notice of what took place within R Section and no warning given to Green.

"But how can we embarrass the CIA with that?" Hanley asked.

"Leave two exits open," the old man explained. Depending on how it turned out, expose the CIA to the President or make a deal with the CIA to quietly fold their ghost operation against R Section. Exchange that for R Section's silence. Blackmail the CIA, in other words.

"Is the existence of the Section in danger, then?" Hanley asked at last.

The Old Man nodded in his absent way and explained: The President was hostile to R Section; even some congressmen grumbled at the expense of maintaining various espionage agencies which essentially served as checks on each other. If the CIA feud with R Section surfaced now, would the President use the incident to push for his single agency? Or could the CIA's game against the Section be turned back to tarnish the Agency so badly that no one would trust a single espionage organization? Both were possibilities.

"So we must do nothing," Hanley said with a trace of sarcasm.

Galloway raised an eyebrow at that. "We must proceed cautiously. If Devereaux handles the elimination of our mole, we keep the matter quiet, at least temporarily. We can use Green as a trump card against the Langley firm. Dead or alive. If Devereaux botches the job, the CIA will hardly reveal it."

But the woman—this Elizabeth Campbell—might be killed.

"It might be better that way," shrugged the old man.

"She was a traitor to Langley; they want her dead. Might she not betray us as well? You cannot trust a traitor."

It was useless to argue; Hanley knew the Chief was right, that he was playing a dangerous game on many levels at the same time and that the least important element in the game was the fate of Elizabeth Campbell.

And so Hanley had returned again to the grim, gray building off the Ellipse and had recalled Hallman from his bed back to the Section and to resume the careful hunt through the records for other traitors. He worked through the morning until he could no longer focus his eyes on the words dancing across the pieces of paper.

So tired.

He yawned and finally gave up. Going to the couch in his office, he stretched out on it, and in a moment, fell asleep. He did not even remove his shoes.

But his last waking thought was of Devereaux.

Call. Damn you. Call.

At the précise moment that Hanley had decided Green was the traitor, Green pushed through the door of The Orange Man public house in Wingate Crescent, off the Marylebone Road.

It was Sunday noon in London, five hours ahead of Washington.

The usual pleasant crowd was already there, stoking up on pink gins and pints of Bass Ale at the bar. They all smiled at the young American and they made way for him and he exchanged friendly sallies and pleasantries; copies of the *Observer* and *Times* and *Sunday Express* were scattered on the low tables. The atmosphere was like an American Sunday brunch but with more of a sense of celebration; these were the upper middle classes and Sunday in winter in London was a cozy, comfortable time.

Green ordered and the bartender, taking a beautiful, round, stemmed glass from the rack above the bar, held it beneath the upside-down bottle of Grant's whisky. He pushed twice on the measure, letting the drams of amber liquid fall into the glass, then put the glass on the bar in front of Green and let the young man mix his own water. Green drank it without ice, in the English manner.

There were many things about Green that were in the English manner. He had only been in London nine months, but it had seemed longer to him; he had let his admiration for things English develop into a quiet mania. His clothes were from Savile Row, quiet dark pinstripes or smoothly fitting Harris tweeds, custom-made. He could not begin his mornings without thick, black tea and cold toast and the *Times* and the *Telegraph*. He even thought he might buy a bowler hat this winter, though he secretly feared he would look ridiculous in it.

This was the part of the assignment that had most pleased him. They had emphasized he must "keep up appearances." There was a generous expense account, fortified with a gold American Express card that provided an "open sesame" to the whims of his purchases.

He was twenty-six years old, and had never been overseas before.

Green was the nephew of Senator Hubert Green of Ohio, a member of the Senate Agricultural Committee who, incidentally, oversaw part of the budget for R Section.

Green. had been attracted to intelligence work while still in the Navy. His father had insisted on the Navy after college. A nice midwestern college where Green did well enough; "the Navy," his father had insisted, and he had gone along. Green was a mild man, really, and he had gone along with his father all his life. And with anyone else who had decidedly strong ideas about things.

The Navy had not worked out well. He had been a bit of a failure as an ensign, and by mutual agreement—with the aid of Uncle Hubert—he had been allowed to quietly resign. It wasn't that Green was not conscientious; he was, almost too much so. But he could not seem to handle simple assignments in a simple manner. His very sense of duty seemed to get in the way of direct solutions to direct problems. Finally, even the Navy had come to realize it, especially when a series of blunders were laid down—coldly—in his 201 file and his last commander had read the file and then had begun to watch Green and then harass Green and, at last, drive Green a little crazy.

Not crazy, really. No. But a little nervous. Just a little bit overwhelmed by events.

But that was in the past, nearly three years ago. Uncle Hubert had understood when Green told him he wanted to continue in intelligence work.

Green had tried to get into the CIA. But the CIA was a special club and it was not particularly afraid of the Ohio senator on the Agricultural Committee.

Green did not know then that the CIA was staffed at the upper reaches almost exclusively by an "old boy" network every bit as closed and foolish as that which had pervaded British Intelligence in the years between—and immediately after—the Second World War. The Kim Philbys and Burgesses of the CIA were there and so were the Graham Greenes and other amateur patriots who "knew someone" from Yale or Groton or Harvard and dabbled at intelligence-gathering. The CIA drew heavily on members of the Establishment. The CIA was a club and Green could not get in.

At first.

Uncle Hubert had managed to get Green assigned to R Section, and he had routinely passed through the training program. Green was bright enough and his midwestern education did not matter since his uncle was a powerful man on the subcommittee charged with overseeing R Section's budget.

In fact, Green had done quite well and had been rapidly promoted within the Section. There had been a year with the African desk in which he had brilliantly coordinated a series of seemingly unimportant reports which first showed the Cuban presence in the Horn of Africa.

During the period in Washington, Green was happiest. His work was sufficient and it was interesting to him. A bit dull, but then, perhaps Green felt most comfortable with things that were a little dull. He was conscientious and when that quality of his character did not involve dealing with enlisted men or the vagaries of military life, it made him an outstanding worker in a limited way.

Green worked to the level of his capabilities.

He had an apartment in Georgetown and he had a pretty girl friend. They had met one afternoon on the Ellipse while he took his lunch hour. She was friendly and pretty and not too demanding of him; Green was inherently shy and a little frightened of women.

After a while, he thought he was in love.

For a long time, almost up to the time he left for the London station job, he didn't understand that she was part of it all. Part of the plan.

That hurt him at first, a little, but Green's love was not so deep, he came to realize. She had genuinely liked him, she told him, and she still did. Perhaps they could see each other again when he was posted back to Washington.

In the meantime, she explained, there were certain things he would be expected to do.

Green said he could not be a traitor.

They had said he was not a traitor. After all, he had wanted to work for the CIA in the beginning; he must consider that he had always worked for the CIA.

Green listened to them.

The R Section had been set up in the old days, they explained, when the CIA had overextended itself. He certainly knew the history of it all.

Green had listened.

Now, the President wanted to get rid of R Section. He had reformed the CIA. The CIA was now completely under control of the elected officials to the point where the President could lobby to abolish the R Section. But the people in the Section were, naturally enough, obstinate. Even some senators who had powerful ties. Like Uncle Hubert? asked Green.

Yes, said the man he had first spoken to. The girl had been there as well and that had made him more comfortable. The man was very friendly. He was open and kind; he had made a drink for Green and his large brown eyes had looked Green directly in the face. He had been honest about Uncle Hubert. Hubert was an enemy of the CIA and Green knew it, and the CIA man did not try to hide the fact. They were being honest with him.

The President felt that R Section had become too powerful. That its loyalty was in question, according to the CIA man.

Green protested.

No, it did not have to do with the information they gathered; that was direct enough. But it had to do with what R Section did with the information. R Section was manipulating Congress and the country for its own ends, using legitimate information in a perverted way.

Even Green had been, unwittingly, a part of the process. The report on the presence of Cuban troops in the African horn. Why had it been suppressed by R Section, only to be finally brought to the public's attention by the CIA?

Green had wondered about that as well. It had been something of a coup for the African desk but he had been told to say nothing about it, and, in fact, Hanley had admonished him twice about being certain that no word of the report leaked to others in the Section.

Green did not know that the President—engaged in a delicate negotiation involving the Soviet Union, Cuba, and Ethiopia—had ordered the report suppressed. Or that the CIA, perversely enough, had found the report and leaked it, thus freezing the Soviet stance and the Cuban presence.

The interview with the CIA man had continued for several days at different locations. Green came to trust the man's frank, open manner and he was a little envious of the other's familiarity with French restaurants and wine lists and important names.

If the truth were known, Green was something of a snob, and the rejection by the CIA had always bothered him. But now the CIA was wooing Green. It was flattering.

And finally, Green had acquiesced. There was money, too, but he didn't do it for that.

There had been the first little bit of information. Not from Africa. But on the Section. On Hanley. And on Miss Dickens, Hanley's secretary. About Hanley's luncheon habits.

They knew most of it, of course. But Green was coming their way and they were leading him gently.

And then the assignment in London. And the contact with the embassy and the CIA staff quartered there.

The CIA man he dealt with was Ruckles.

Ruckles was a Virginian, soft-spoken, with an amused chuckle just waiting at the edge of a conversation to break in. A Navy man, like Green. A Princeton man.

They didn't talk about college.

They had chosen The Orange Man because it was a safe pub. No one they knew ever went there and they met there infrequently, only when Green gave Ruckles an urgent signal or the other way around. They had each signaled the other on Saturday.

Green took his second glass of whisky to the table in the corner of the saloon. He waited and fingered his tie. The stripe was a Cambridge school tie, Ruckles had pointed out. Green didn't care; he said he had only bought it for the colors. But that was not true. The tie was Cambridge and it was part of his English wardrobe, part of his other self, the self only he saw.

After a few moments, Ruckles came, carrying a glass of dark ale to the table. He nodded to Green but he was not smiling.

"Where is she now?"

"In the safe house. She hasn't moved out of it."

"We have to get her out of it."

"I don't know how."

Ruckles looked at him. "To meet Devereaux, of course.

We'll message Blake House and tell her to meet Devereaux at Victoria Station. We could arrange it at Victoria Station."

"But that's murder."

Ruckles looked at him. "It's a job. An elimination job. She's betrayed us. She may have betrayed you."

Green tried to smile. "But it's not betrayal, is it? I mean, we're all on the same side."

"She's not on our side anymore."

"But this is crazy. This is a game."

Ruckles stared at him.

Green felt giddy. They wanted to kill her. He had signaled them because she represented danger. He knew that as soon as Devereaux sent her back to him. It was only when he talked to Ruckles on his urgent Saturday mission to the embassy that he understood she was part of the "ghost Section." Ruckles did not tell him that Elizabeth did not know she worked for the CIA.

Ruckles said, quietly, "If they—if Devereaux—discovers you, he will kill you. It is that much of a game. You'll be eliminated by them."

"But I'm not a traitor. I'm serving the nation. I'm serving the Agency, the President. . . ."

Ruckles nodded. Green was a little on edge. Ruckles didn't want that. He wanted Green safe and a little too sure of him, of his own rightness.

"The Section is riddled with traitors. Real traitors. To the nation. It is not a game to them. We now know that Elizabeth was a double agent, infiltrating us, learning our secrets so she could betray us to Devereaux. And you know about Devereaux."

Green sipped furiously at his drink. There did not seem to be enough of it.

The whole thing was hard to believe, but, in the end, he had been forced by the facts to accept the truth about Devereaux. Devereaux was a traitor, a double agent. Green had wanted to tell Hanley, to go to the Chief; Ruckles had persuaded him not to. Devereaux was not dangerous as long as the Agency knew he was a traitor; he was useful to the Agency.

Green thought he understood. Devereaux had betrayed the United States in Asia. He had been one of the many small factors that had led to the losing of that war; he had sent damaging and dangerous reports about the situation in Thailand, Cambodia, and Vietnam which had led the government and the military to make gross miscalculations.

The evidence had convinced Green, finally, and had angered him.

Green was a quiet patriot in his own way.

Now Ruckles said Elizabeth was one of them as well. He felt shy with her in Blake House; he did not know what to say to her. He had done as Ruckles instructed him—and tried to learn what she had told Devereaux about the "ghost Section" and about the Agency but she would not respond. He wondered if she knew he worked for the Agency. He wondered if he was in danger.

The thought chilled him. Danger was alien to him. The reports, the work of intelligence in Washington, the games they had learned at the training school . . . none of it had been dangerous, none of it had, at one level, even been real.

The bright, polite, hearty afternoon talk of the others in the pub swirled around him. They were dressed well, dressed for Sunday, in tweeds and sweaters. Good fellowship, fed by good English ale and good Scotch whisky.

Green stared at the others for a moment like a person who knows he will always be on the outside.

"Here's the message," Ruckles said at last. He handed it to Green.

A cable from Belfast. It was brief, cold:

ELIZABETH. VICTORIA STATION 4 PM TO DOVER. LAST SECOND-CLASS CAR. D.

"Why would he go to Dover?" Green asked.

"Why not? What does she know? Perhaps he'll meet

her at the station. She will go." He said the last as a declaration but there was a note of worry in it.

"I don't know. I'm not . . . very good, that is . . . talking to her." He blushed. "I think I'd like another whisky." He got up.

Ruckles looked at him. "By all means." Green was cracking up, he thought. He had read Green's file. He knew about the Navy, and about Green's psychological profile. He knew about Green's drinking and his problems with women.

Green brought the glass back and sat down again.

They were silent for a moment.

"What will you do?" Green asked.

"Do? I won't do anything. One of our other men, I suppose."

"What will you do? You know what I mean." Green looked at him.

Ruckles smiled. "We'll get a plumber to stop the leak."

Green paled.

"Eliminate a traitor. A traitor, Green." Ruckles added.

"Eliminate. It doesn't sound so bad when you say 'eliminate.' But you'll kill her just the same."

Ruckles looked at him. "It doesn't affect you, Green."

Green laughed a high shrill laugh. "It doesn't affect me? I have to get her out of the house. It doesn't affect me?"

Green felt trapped, panicked. It was as though he were in a submarine under tons and tons of water, pressed down by the water, surrounded by it, his every breath dependent on the thin supply of oxygen while the sea around probed at the vessel, looking for the way in. Green had never been on a submarine.

He took the bogus cable and placed it in the pocket of his Harris tweed jacket.

"This afternoon," said Ruckles quietly.

It had to be done. It had to be seen through.

"This afternoon," repeated Green. And then he finished the glass of whisky in front of him.

18

CLARE

Lynch was a little man, scarcely five feet tall, wrapped in a dark jacket and a cloth cap, and his face peered out from beneath the bill of the cap with the expression of a startled rat. His eyes protruded unnaturally from their sockets and his nose took as many twists as a country highway.

Devereaux stood behind Cashel while the Dublin policeman questioned the little man.

Lynch owned the small filling station in the village and he remembered the red Fiat Bambino driven there by the fellow from Belfast on Friday very well.

Certainly he knew the fellow was from Belfast. Didn't he know an Ulsterman's way of speaking? The Ulstermen take the music out of the tongue; besides, when he, Lynch, had lapsed into Irish to describe the weather, the Ulsterman had looked at him curiously—he didn't even know Irish! That was the fault of the education of the North— they didn't require the Irish. Which was a great sadness, the little man said.

But Cashel persisted quietly. He wasn't from Londonderry then? It was also in Ulster.

Derry, croaked the little man. Was this Dublin copper such a bloody sympathizer to the English that he would call ancient Derry by its hateful London name?

Not that, soothed Cashel, who apologized to a true patriot.

Mollified, Lynch went on: "I knew he was from Belfast by his way of talkin'." And when Cashel looked disappointed by the answer, the little man added: "And by his motorcar insurance form."

"His form?"

"It was a rental car."

"Indeed," said Cashel. "So we thought it would be."

"Ah, but he left it and I needed t'see if he owned it."

"And why?"

"Because of the damage."

"Ah."

"Me helper was there, mopin' as he was, and he bumped the tool kit inter the bumper and gives it a scratch. So I looked inter the motorcar t'see if she was rented. It was that. So I gave it no thought because they'll not hold him t'damages for it. He had the insurance y'see. Me conscience is clear."

Cashel rubbed his finger alongside the edge of his mustache. "Would you know who was the rental agent then?"

"I would that," said the little man. "Yer askin' a lot of questions, then."

Cashel waited.

"And him there what's mute. A Sassenach?"

"An American."

"An American, then? I thought he was English and keepin' his gob shut because I've naught t'say t'the English."

Cashel turned to Devereaux. He smiled. "Say hello to him then, Mr. Devereaux? T'show you're not English."

Devereaux managed a few words. Lynch brightened: "Ah, yer no Sassenach. I can tell right off. Yer might be Swedish, of course. They speak the language well too but they all sound like Americans. Not like the bloody Germans, who all sound like Englishmen."

Cashel extended his hands and shrugged. "Indeed. I'm sure we're happy to be havin' this lesson in the ways of the world's speech, but I wonder now if you'd mind tellin' me the name of the rental company?"

And, after more business and detours in the conversation, Lynch produced a dirty slip of paper on which he had written down the name of the agency and the license number—he had done so in the event he had a change of heart concerning the scratch on the car. Or in case the agency brought up false accusations.

Outside again in the road, Cashel and Devereaux stood together, gulping in the cold, still air, as though both of them had somehow been through a great physical ordeal and surmounted it. They felt elated and tired and even full, like a gourmet after a great meal.

"We have a name now, Mr. Devereaux. And a place. D'you think it will meet with the names you have?"

"I'd count on it," said Devereaux. "But when will they move?"

"We have enough now to warn Lord Slough," said Cashel.

That was not the mission. The mission was to warn British Intelligence. Devereaux glanced at Cashel. "Perhaps."

"There's no 'perhaps' to it. We'll go to Clare House now, after I check with the rental firm. We must warn the man."

Devereaux nodded. There was no logical way to argue against this common-sense approach. He had known the risk of working with Cashel but he needed Cashel. They went to the car.

Faolin, of course, had rented the car; they learned that much from the rental agency in Belfast through the firm's branch in Dublin. For the moment, Cashel had seen no need to work through the liaison man with the Belfast police.

They arrived at Clare House in the hills in early afternoon. Devereaux drove up slowly to the circular turnaround in front of the imposing brick house and both men got out slowly.

A young, coltish girl in gray twill slacks and dark blouse was in the hall when the two men were admitted. Brianna looked curiously for a moment at the American and then nodded to both of them in a formal way that seemed a little too grown-up for her.

"I'm Brianna Devon," she said and extended her hand in a straightforward, English-schoolgirl way. "My father is engaged at the moment, I'm afraid."

Cashel nodded and smiled uncertainly. He was never sure of his manners in dealing with people like Brianna. The rich were so casual in clothes and gestures and conversations and yet, beneath the ease of manner, Cashel always sensed something rigid and unyielding in their attitudes towards people like him.

He noticed Devereaux did not share his discomfort as they stood in the hall awkwardly.

In fact, Devereaux seemed to be appraising the girl, as if she were just another object to be studied, remembered, and filed away. Cashel looked at Brianna Devon again and was surprised to see her blush faintly beneath Devereaux's gaze.

"I'm sorry," said Cashel at last. "This is Mr. Devereaux. From the Canadian police."

"Canada?" repeated Brianna Devon.

"Yes," said Devereaux. He was surprised by Cashel's introduction because they had not discussed it on the trip to Clare House. But the surprise was momentary; Devereaux was accustomed to invention. "Royal Canadian Mounted Police, Miss Devon. We are cooperating with the Irish authorities on the investigation. Of the attempt on your father's life."

Brianna seemed a little overwhelmed and determined to be in control. Cashel thought again how delicate—how like a child and a woman—she was. She reminded him of a porcelain piece of sculpture he had once seen; it was so delicate that he could not bear to stare at it for fear his clumsy soul would somehow break it.

Brianna finally led them into the sitting room at the

end of the hall. "You've got the man, though," she said as they entered. "The man who murdered Deirdre?"

Devereaux found a chair and sat down. "Yes," he said.

Brianna stood and waited, obviously hoping for more information. Annoyance clouded the fair, frail line of her features. She realized they must think she was a child. She wondered what to do with her hands.

"I'm afraid my father will be a while," she said at last and then realized she had already explained that. It flustered her. "Would you care for anything, Mr. Cashel? Claret?"

"No, I'm afraid—"

"Vodka," said Devereaux.

"I beg your pardon—"

"Vodka with ice," he said.

She seemed taken aback. In her limited experience, men drank whisky only after sundown. Or so it had seemed.

"No mix?" she tried. "Rather like drinking straight alcohol."

"Exactly," he said.

She went to the hall and spoke to a servant. In a moment, a glass was served on a little tray.

Devereaux drank.

"You're from Ottawa," she began.

Devereaux grunted; Cashel paced by the large windows which revealed the broad lawn beyond. A clock in the house ticked steadily on into the yawning silence of afternoon.

"That's Russian vodka, I believe. The taste, they say, is quite distinctive."

"I wouldn't know," he said softly. "I'm not a connoisseur."

She realized that she felt as though her heart would break in the silence of the room, of the house; in the overwhelming silence of the place that had been a place of Deirdre's laughter. It was like losing two mothers now.

And she was not a woman: A woman, she said to herself, would feel differently. She had small breasts and she wore her silky clothes to advantage and she had a knowledge that men looked at her. But she only wanted to cry now and be comforted.

"Who was Mr. Toolin then?" she asked in the quiet of the room. Cashel looked at her from the window but Devereaux spoke.

"A terrorist and a killer."

"There's no reason to it," she said. What was happening to her voice? She was afraid of herself; her body—still awkward, still coltish, but already a woman's slim body—was betraying her. She brushed her hands at her sides and then folded her arms.

Devereaux put down the glass and got up. He crossed the room to her. He touched her arm.

She had been staring at the floor. Now she looked at him.

There were tears in her eyes.

"It is without any sense," he said. Not even comforting—as though you told a child that, yes, you must be afraid of the dark because there are things in the darkness which can harm you.

"Mr. Devereaux," she began.

But he held her arm and looked at her. She had to return his gaze. Her eyes were wet and his were clear and cold and sad.

"Deirdre Monahan was an accident," he said.

Cashel made a noise as though to protest—don't tell her such hard things.

"You know that," Devereaux continued. "I'm sorry." He held her arm. His hand, she realized, was very large. It encircled her arm. She stood with her arms folded across her breasts and she gazed steadily at him.

"It's not over. That's why we have to talk to your father."

"Oh my God," she began.

"Devereaux," said Cashel warningly.

"Miss Devon," Devereaux said. "I won't fool you or tell you a lie."

"No," she repeated.

"Don't be afraid yet, though," he said. "Trust that too."

Lord Slough appeared at the door in that moment and glanced curiously at the man who held his daughter's arm.

"Good afternoon," he said quietly. He looked at both men and stood in the middle of the floor.

"I trust," said Brianna Devon. And Devereaux let go of her arm and turned to the English peer. Cashel announced, "This is Mr. Devereaux from the Canadian security branch."

"I see," said the lord. He looked curiously at his daughter for a moment and then at Devereaux and then he nodded slightly. "Have you found the plot behind Toolin's attempt on my life?"

"No," said Devereaux.

"We've come to talk to you," said Cashel. "About—"

"Lord Slough," Devereaux interrupted. His voice was low and cold and without comfort.

The English peer stood still and waited. Brianna suddeny clasped her hands around her body, as though she were chilled.

"I am with Canadian Intelligence," Devereaux said. "Two days before the attempt on your life, we were warned by an agent in Ulster that there was a plot on your life—"

Cashel stared. Devereaux had said none of these things to him. He detected glimmers of truth in the fabric of the lies about Canadian Intelligence and agents in Ulster. Two days.

"Our man in Ulster was murdered. Later, there was the attempt to kill you. At first it seemed that was the plot uncovered by our agent—"

Lord Slough tried to smile. "But you didn't warn me."

"No," Devereaux said. He paused. All lies were plausible; only the truth could be fantastic. "You were in Canada. We put men to watch you but we did not think the plot against your life was to be carried out in Quebec City."

"But you were wrong, Mr. Devereaux," Lord Slough said mildly.

"No," said Devereaux at last. He watched the thin, pale English face but it did not reveal anything. "We were not wrong. We have certain evidence now of a plot. In progress. To kill you."

Brianna made a little cry.

"By whom, Mr. Devereaux?"

"The IRA. We have certain names but we still don't know where or when or how they will try to kill you. But from this moment, you are forewarned."

Lord Slough glanced at Brianna, who appeared to be in danger of saying something. The look silenced her.

"Brianna. Perhaps it would be better if you left the room."

"Father." She rose reluctantly; it was no good to say that she shared this horror with him, had shared it from the moment she had been visited by the headmistress in her room, from the moment she had been told there had been an "accident" in Canada and that her father had been slightly hurt and that her father's companion had been killed. He thought she was a child and did not share his nightmares.

She left the room but not before glancing again at Devereaux who still stood by the chair.

"Mr. Devereaux," Lord Slough continued. "Is there any reason not to believe that Mr. Toolin was a member of the IRA as well?"

Devereaux considered it; he had thought about that before. He knew that the IRA, far from being a strongly disciplined centrist terror group, was in fact an umbrella covering several terrorist cells.

"No. It is possible that Toolin was part of the IRA. It is possible that he was the first part of the plot on your life. That's logical. If he failed to kill you in Canada, then the second part of the plan against you would be set in motion. It is also possible that Toolin was with another faction of the IRA, unrelated to the present plan against your life."

Cashel grunted. He believed that Toolin had had contacts with the IRA men in Dublin.

"Do any of these . . . well . . . logical possibilities bear any resemblance to actuality?" Lord Slough asked dryly.

"We don't know," said Devereaux.

"I see."

"But it's certain, sir," began Cashel. "That they haven't given up on their plan."

"How certain, Mr. Cashel?"

"We spotted one of them at the church yesterday," Cashel said. "When your . . . your daughter's tutor was buried."

"Yes," said Lord Slough. "And you seized him?"

"Not exactly, sir."

"Really?" said Lord Slough.

"We didn't know it was him until . . . until later."

"And who is he?"

"We're not exactly sure," said Cashel. He realized he was sounding foolish. He looked at Devereaux for help but there was none. "I mean, sir, we have discovered certain things about the fella which makes him a suspicious character—"

"Ah," said Lord Slough.

"He's from Belfast. He lied t'the villagers about that," blustered Cashel.

"Ah. From Belfast," said Lord Slough.

Devereaux interrupted in the same flat voice he had used before. "An agent is dead. He had information about a plot."

"About the first plot or this second plot you seem to believe in?"

Devereaux shrugged. "None of this is a matter of mere speculation. There are too many indications not to believe the plot on your life is still continuing. I'm not going to argue with you about it. It's not a game."

He thought, how odd for me to say that. But it was a game, wasn't it?

"Assume for the moment that I am in danger. What do you propose I do about it?"

Cashel said, "They may try to get you anywhere. I suggest a guard on you—from Dublin—and contact with British Intelligence when you go to London tomorrow."

No, thought Devereaux. No contact.

"I see," said Lord Slough in the same mild tone. "I am forewarned but I am not forearmed. What can I do with your information? Can I make any more use of it than if someone tells me that someday I too, like all men, shall die?"

Cashel said, "The information is more specific than that."

Lord Slough went to the window and looked out at the vast lawn. "It is. But I cannot take your suggestion of Irish bodyguards seriously. I'll not travel in a cocoon like an American president, treated as a portable shrine. I would rather die than have that. Jeffries is sufficient— my secretary knows both shorthand and the use of a .45 automatic, if I may indulge in melodramatic monologue." He turned from the window. "Why is the IRA so adamant about murdering me?"

Cashel shook his head. "Why did they kill Ross Mc-Whirter? You're an Englishman, sir. Of the royal English family. And you're a friend of the Republic at the same time. Almost reason enough in that—they cannot stand peace or a mutual friend."

Lord Slough made a vague gesture of dismissal with one hand. "It is ironic to be the target of assassins once and then be told one is again the same target. There is almost a sense of unreality about it. I can see the gunman again, coming to kill me in that room. I'm afraid one cannot believe in violence if one is exposed to it too often. It loses its power to shock further; I am afraid I am not afraid." He smiled.

They were silent for a moment.

Lord Slough said, "I own newspapers, but now I realize what it is to be the object of public scrutiny and pity. The attempt upon my life has made me a public man in a way I do not choose to live. This attempt upon my life might come next week, next month, next year . . . or never. I will not live in a fishbowl. No, Mr. Devereaux and Mr. Cashel. I will not have an Irish guard assigned to me, though I shall welcome security here at Clare House for the sake of my daughter. But I will not be held hostage to terror and I will not value my life so greatly that in order not to lose it, I should be afraid to live it."

He shook his head for emphasis. "Nor will I stay here. I may die and I may not die and the IRA may have the say of that; but the IRA will not say how I shall live."

Devereaux did not move. It was what he wanted; there would be no change and there was still a chance to deal information to British Intelligence. Though Lord Slough spoke eloquently, he was a fool. Life was not posturing and brave speeches; life was mean; it was lived on one's knees. It was full of betrayals and stolen moments of warmth and love, always clouded by the gray coldness of ordinary human dealings.

"Do you understand, Mr. Devereaux?" Lord Slough said, turning to the frowning man. "Life held too tightly, too dearly, is crushed as certainly as a sparrow held in a foolish child's hands."

Devereaux's mind—his whole being—rebelled against such sentiments. They were only words, the stuff for platforms and politicians.

Lord Slough glanced at him.

Devereaux's right hand went to his own neck for a
moment; his fingers felt the ridge of flesh cut by the wire;
he felt the terror again of that moment of darkness on a
Belfast street when he was certain he would die.

"Do you understand, Mr. Devereaux?"

But Devereaux did not speak and Lord Slough finally
turned away. The interview was over and both Cashel
and Devereaux understood that at once; they filed silently
out of the room.

Brianna Devon was waiting in the hall. She held the
policeman's bowler hat in her pale, long-fingered hands.
"Your hat, Mr. Cashel," she said and absently handed
it to him. Her lovely face was frightened and she looked
first at the Irish policeman and then at Devereaux. "What
will happen?"

"He'll be safe," said Devereaux. He said it so that she
would know it was not true.

"What can be done?"

Devereaux looked at her. "I don't know."

A butler appeared and opened the front door; beyond,
the car waited on the gravel turnaround. Suddenly, the
sky had changed and the afternoon seemed without color,
bleached like bones left in the dust. Impulsively and without a word, Brianna led them through the front door.
The cold plucked at her pale skin and she shivered.

Devereaux made a gesture and then thought better of
it. "It's too cold," he said.

Was it kindness intended for her? Brianna looked
at him, started to speak, and then thought of nothing to
say.

Cashel said, "It'll be all right." His voice was gruff,
unused to comforting.

"Can't you stop them?" she asked, finally. "Whoever
wants to kill my father?"

But Devereaux wouldn't lie. He opened the car door.
"I don't know," he said.

"Yes, Miss Devon, of course we will," said Cashel.

"We'll do everything. We're puttin' a guard now on yer house."

But Brianna was not listening; she stared at the American as he turned the key in the ignition.

She believed Devereaux.

19

SHANNON

Devereaux and Cashel returned to Innisbally and found Durkin at his cottage. Cashel telephoned Dublin and was granted a four-man detail to guard Clare House and its occupants; Durkin was dispatched to Clare House in the meantime, until the guards arrived.

Finally, in the semiprivacy of the kitchen of Durkin's cottage, while Durkin's mother sat in the front room knitting, Cashel and Devereaux went over Lord Slough's schedule of the next few days for a clue as to when the terrorists would strike to kill him.

"There's the meeting in London tomorrow. . . ."

"Anything outside Clare House is a possibility," said Devereaux. "But what is the clearest chance?"

"The meeting in London is private. It was arranged two weeks ago—"

"Then strike it," said Devereaux.

"Why?"

"It's not logical to believe that an elaborate plan set up to assassinate Lord Slough would depend on chance."

"Your President Kennedy was killed in Dallas in such a moment—"

Devereaux glanced up. "The motorcade through Dallas was known about for more than a month before the assassination."

"So you'd reason that only a long-standing commitment by Slough to be someplace at a particular time would be the most logical point of assassination?"

"Yes. Tomorrow is Monday, he'll be in London. What follows?"

"Tuesday in Edinburgh. For a meeting with the editors of his *Scottish Daily News* in the morning. . . ."

"Planned when?"

"Two weeks ago, according to his secretary, Jeffries. . . ."

"And then?"

Cashel puffed his pipe and looked at his notes carefully. "Ah. He's t'go to Glasgow in the afternoon t'attend a benefit match of the Celtics and Rangers. Ah, now that might be the place, indeed."

"Why?"

Cashel glanced at him. "Football, man. At the stadium there, there'd be fifty thousand lunatics there, even on a Tuesday afternoon."

"What are the Celtics and Rangers?"

"Football teams, man." Cashel looked closely at Devereaux to see if he understood. "Y'call it soccer. The Celtics is the Catholic team, the Rangers is the Prods team."

Devereaux waited.

"Glasgow is the most dangerous football city in the world," Cashel went on. "Football is their religion, not to make it too strong. And the Catholics in Glasgow are for the Celtics and the Prods for the Rangers. And they're playin' a benefit exhibition, something t'do with cancer or such, and Lord Slough is involved in it and the *Scottish Daily News* is sponsoring the match—"

"And that was set up—"

"Months ago."

"Catholics and Protestants. Are there many Catholics in Glasgow?"

"Oh, aye. Oh, it's a mad city for football too; just the crowd for an assassin."

Devereaux said, "And not far from Belfast."

Cashel nodded. "Not far from Belfast."

The place seemed logical; it seemed ideal; but why

were so many involved in the plot? This should be the work of a lone gunman. Unless there was more to it.

"And then?"

But Cashel had gotten up from the table where they sat and gone to the window and looked out, puffing furiously on his pipe. "Glasgow," he muttered. "The place for it. I suspected it. . . ."

"And then?"

"Oh. And then on to Liverpool for a banquet that night. The next morning, he launches the *Brianna*."

Devereaux shrugged. "What does that mean?"

"I'm sorry. His hovercraft ship, *Brianna*. Named for his daughter, you met her. The first hovercraft service from England to Ireland."

"And what will he do?"

"Jeffries says there's t'be speeches; the Prime Minister of Britain is to be there. Less for the importance of the launching than for the importance of Lord Slough, I'd imagine."

Cashel did not notice Devereaux stiffen; the involuntary movement was so slight that he could be forgiven the oversight.

"What will happen there?"

"Really, very little. A very small, controlled crowd is expected. The newspapers say there's very tight police security expected because they want no harm to the craft from some anti-Irish idiots. And then, because of the Prime Minister. Let's see, Durkin might have the paper here. . . ." Cashel went to a newspaper on the sideboard and opened it. "The *Irish Daily News*, from Dublin, Friday's editions. Here it is."

He began to read: "'. . . launch . . . first hovercraft service . . . tight police security . . .' Here it is: 'Prime Minister of Great Britain and the Taoiseach of Eire will attend the launching ceremonies Wednesday and use the occasion for talks on mutual security problems, including containment of the provisional wing of the Irish Republican Army.'"

He shoved the paper across the table.

Devereaux seemed only to glance at it briefly and then dismiss it. "And after that?"

"Not much. The hovercraft makes its first run to Dublin and Lord Slough is to be feted at a dinner in Dublin with members of the Dáil on Wednesday night. Then, late, he returns to Clare House for the remainder of the week."

"And when was this planned?"

"Well, I gather everyone's known about the hovercraft for months. Lord Slough's papers have seen to that. But the actual date, December first, was only set a little more than a week ago, because of the delays in launch. They ran a series of trials on her—an interesting ship, Mr. Devereaux. Built in the Clyde, in Glasgow, but with components built in Dublin and Belfast."

"Détente?" joked Devereaux. "And it works?"

Cashel smiled. "So they say. They built an apron for launching hovercraft in Liverpool some years ago, along the Mersey River, but there's never been hovercraft service on the Irish Sea. It's a dangerous sea."

"Everything Irish seems dangerous," said Devereaux.

Cashel frowned. "Does it now?"

"But to get back to Lord Slough's schedule. It seems the only event set up for months has been this soccer game in Glasgow."

"And your theory—"

Devereaux stood up. "It has to be more than a theory. A complex assassination plot must count on a certain routine by the subject. You start from the premise of the assassination site and time and then work backwards, bringing in as many elements as you need to effect the assassination."

"I don't understand," said Cashel.

Devereaux made a face and spread his hands. "Kennedy is to motorcade through Dallas on November twenty-second at eleven A.M. The final route announced takes him past the Texas School Book Depository."

Cashel frowned.

"Those are the known facts. That's the assassination place and time. Now, what do you need to effect the assassination? You choose your site, the Depository. So you need to make sure you can get entry. And you choose your weapons. And you bring in as many people into the conspiracy as you need—"

"Are you sayin' that this fella, this Oswald, didn't act alone to—"

Devereaux glared. "I'm saying nothing. I am offering an example of a known assassination. And of how, logically, it would be set up."

"So we figure on this fella, Faolin, setting up to kill Lord Slough in the Glasgow football stadium and . . ."

Right, thought Devereaux. Pursue it backwards, from the stadium. Make yourself believe it will be in the stadium and bend all you know to fit the theory.

"I'll have to contact British Intelligence now," said Cashel at last.

"To protect Slough in Glasgow."

"And in Edinburgh that morning. They might try to get him en route."

"Yes, I suppose you must," said Devereaux.

Cashel gave him a warning look. "There'll be no interference."

"None," said Devereaux. "I have to report to my own people."

"I can't stop you."

"And get back home."

"It's early in the afternoon. If ye was to get to Shannon in time, yer might catch the flight to New York—"

"Is it near?"

"Oh, sure. Not twenty miles from here."

"Well, then," said Devereaux. "And you? You're going back to Dublin?"

"I wish I could. Perhaps tomorrow, when Lord Slough is off to London."

"Good luck, Cashel," said Devereaux.

"Good luck yerself," said Cashel. "I'd stand y' a jar

but I think you have to hurry to catch your airplane."
And Cashel began to give Devereaux elaborate directions
on the way to Ireland's western airport.

All the way to Shannon Airport, on the curious, twisting
back roads of rural Clare County, Devereaux tried to
categorize the information provided him by Cashel and
to fit it with the information he had obtained from Denisov
and O'Neill and Terry and the dead Hastings.

Parts of it seemed to make sense and other parts did
not; that was the way of information. He would have been
content usually to merely dump it in Hanley's lap and
end the mission, but there had been complications this
time. Elizabeth was a complication; the attempt on his
life was a complication; and even the frightened face
of Brianna Devon seemed to cause problems. Devereaux
was accustomed to shadows, to assignments that demanded information and not involvement.

He found Shannon Airport as it was getting dark.

Parking the rental car in the space next to the terminal
building, he got out and went to turn in the key. Next
stop was the telephone booths, where the operator patched
his call into a line to Washington, D.C.

It was nearly two P.M. in Washington.

After a long time, he heard the telephone ring at the
other end; it rang four times before he heard the voice.

"This is a caller sendin' the charges to you, sir," began
the operator in a lilting voice. "From Mr. Thirty."

He heard Hanley mumble his acceptance and the
operator went off the line. Hanley sounded drunk or
sleepy. "Red Sky," he muttered at last.

"Have you found our man?" asked Devereaux.

"Yes. We think so. But that can wait. Can you report?
Where are you? Why did it take you so long?"

"Did you ever try to find a telephone in Ireland on
Sunday?"

There was a pause at the other end of the line. "No.
I suppose it's difficult."

"Who's our man?"

"That can wait," Hanley said again. "Can you report?"

"Is your line clear?"

"Yes."

Devereaux hesitated. He was sure the assassination attempt would come at the launch of the *Brianna* and he was glad that Cashel had not understood that. Cashel had not caught his analogy—that the site of the attempt would dictate the size and makeup of those making the attempt. Captain Donovan. Cashel had not connected that with the launch of the *Brianna* because the football-match site seemed easier to understand.

"Well?" said Hanley.

Devereaux's own information was not complete. Complete enough for Hanley perhaps, but there was something wrong with it. He needed to know more. On the one hand, he wanted to be rid of Ireland and Lord Slough and the young woman who excited pity and tenderness in him; but it wasn't ready yet, it wasn't time.

"It isn't complete," said Devereaux at last. "If I give it to you now, it will probably be enough for British Intelligence. For the special relationship you want to develop—"

"Yes," said Hanley. "Now that we know the CIA is funding the IRA."

"We're not certain of that."

"But the Russians are. How do you suppose they know?"

Devereaux thought of Denisov and the mild, saintly eyes behind the rimless glasses. "Perhaps they never sleep," he said.

Hanley said, "I don't understand."

"I don't either," said Devereaux. "I don't understand the Russian game in this."

"Neither do I," said Hanley. "Report, please."

And Devereaux began, in the familiar, slow, methodical way. There was information from Belfast and from Cashel and about the meeting with Lord Slough at Clare House.

Hanley interrupted peevishly: "The mission was not to warn Lord Slough but to inform Brit Intell."

"Don't say that anymore."

"What?"

"Your goddam jargon. Don't worry, Hanley. I'm not going soft. But there was no way around Cashel and I needed Cashel at the moment. Fortunately for your plans, Lord Slough is a self-designated hero. He is too brave to live."

"I don't understand."

"Just inform goddam British Intelligence, if you want. But the information is not clear yet. I don't understand all the parts of it. Especially about the attempt on Slough's life. It seems certain that the second attempt will come this week because too much is surfacing, too many people know too much. And I suppose the assassination atempt in Canada has scared them into action. They'll have to make their move soon."

"Oh, yes. We have information from Canada on the matter there." Hanley had received it less than an hour before Devereaux's telephone call. "This Toolin was paid by an expatriate Irish socialist group in Quebec province, providing money and arms for the IRA provos in Belfast—"

"Lovely," said Devereaux.

"No one suggested that the IRA source was *only* the Langley firm."

"Only the Soviets suggest Langley was involved from the beginning," cautioned Devereaux.

"Yes. Well, Canadian police made several arrests. Apparently, the scheme was entirely hatched in Quebec, without the knowledge of the IRA, although that's not clear. But that's what the Canadians are saying."

"For whatever that's worth."

"And they had the help of the French separatists terror group in Quebec—"

"How convenient for Ottawa."

"That's sarcasm," Hanley said.

"Yes."

"Now that you've warned Slough—"

"I told you. He's not a factor." He thought of Brianna, of that innocent face frozen with an expectation of terror. "Cashel thinks the matter we spoke of will come up in Glasgow at the benefit football match of two Glaswegian teams on Tuesday afternoon."

"Yes?"

"You can tell British Intelligence that."

"Is that what you think?"

The lie now was difficult; Hanley understood lies. Hanley would understand Devereaux's lie.

"It is a logical assumption, given certain elements."

"But you're not sure."

Hanley invited it: "Yes," said Devereaux. "I'm not certain." Which was almost true.

"And you want more time."

"Twelve hours at least. It will still be time to contact British Intelligence."

"I wish you hadn't warned Slough."

"What was I supposed to do, Hanley? Tell Cashel that warning Slough was not part of my mission? That we were playing a different game?"

"There's no need for—"

"Yes there is. This was a minor mission. I was merely sent to ascertain what Hastings knew and how important it was. Hastings is killed; I'm set upon by double agents from the goddam CIA and a Soviet agent suddenly befriends me. I expose myself—to the CIA and to the Soviets and to the goddam Irish police. I'm supposed to be an intelligence agent, not a policeman. This is a straightforward bit of criminal activity on the part of the IRA—why not let the goddam Irish settle it? No, we can't because we have to develop a relationship with British Intelligence. And at the same time, we have to screw the Langley firm. And Devereaux is supposed to do it."

"Yes," said Hanley.

A moment passed as the line crackled, empty of voices.

"You've found our man?"

Hanley began slowly: "Yes. It was in the message you found on their agent in the Belfast hotel. We went back to the files and compared the information passed on to . . . to the competition about the mission. And we're certain he's the man."

"The competition. What an odd way to put it," said Devereaux.

"Yes. Well, we know who the opposition is. But the Langley firm hardly falls into that category."

Devereaux did not speak.

"You are to plug the leak."

"Literally, I suppose," said Devereaux.

"Yes," said Hanley. He sounded distracted.

"Who is it?"

"Green. In London."

Another pause.

Devereaux stared at the telephone box. He thought of Elizabeth; he could clearly see her in that instant.

He swallowed. "When did you crack the message? When did you know?"

"About twelve hours ago."

Twelve hours. She had been afraid at the airport in Belfast. But it was a safe house. She had no reason to be afraid.

"You waited twelve hours?"

"Under the Old Man's instructions," said Hanley. "He didn't want to give a signal to the competition. Until we were sure. He didn't want Green to bolt."

"She's been in Blake House since Friday. You've known that. And they know about her. Green has had that time to eliminate her."

"Yes," said Hanley. "The Chief understood the risk. I explained it. An unavoidable risk."

Devereaux said, "But not for you. Not for the Chief."

"A risk either way for the Section."

"Goddam the Section," said Devereaux.

"I'm sorry. I can't hear."

"Goddam you, Hanley, you bastard."

The line crackled in the silence of their voices, making them aware of the futility of words over a great distance.

"I know," Hanley said. "I can understand—"

"You can't understand. Because you're a goddam little computer clerk working in a goddam D.C. office and this is a game to you—"

"You're supposed to go to London," said Hanley. "As soon as possible."

"I told her it was safe. I gave my word."

"This is not a matter of giving one's word," said Hanley sharply. "This is not a little gentleman's game."

"I told her it was safe."

"It was a risk that had to be taken."

And Devereaux knew everything Hanley said was right. He replaced the receiver and stared at his hand on the telephone while he tried to understand what he felt. He had given his word before. What a curious thing for him to say. What did his word mean? Nothing, only as much as he meant it to; he always drew the definitions and the reservations in his own mind.

But there had been no reservation when he spoke to Elizabeth at Belfast Airport.

Or when he had held her, naked, in his bed, in the gray morning of that city; when he had promised her there was no reason to be afraid. When he had told her they would not die.

Now it was past six P.M.

Was she dead already, on this Sunday? Had they already killed her?

Wildly, he wanted to ring Blake House, to ask for her. He took the receiver off the hook. And then replaced it.

Past six P.M. on Sunday night.

He pushed out of the booth and turned right and left

and then ran to a ticket desk at the end of the corridor. But the next flight to London was not for two hours.

There was nothing he could do, nothing he could control.

Ruckles was right, thought Green. It had been extremely simple.

At first, Green was worried about carrying off the deception. He wondered if he would have the courage to kill Elizabeth if she questioned the false cable from Devereaux. Ruckles had said it was important enough for Green to blow his cover if need be; if Elizabeth became suspicious, Green was to eliminate her in the house and then flee.

Ruckles had assured him that he would be taken care of.

Still, Green had worried about the cable and about the killing all the way back from The Orange Man.

Elizabeth had not questioned the cable at all.

She had only asked how far Victoria Station was and would she be there in time, and he had been at his best, soothing and reassuring. She'd changed her clothing and taken only her purse and passport.

It was so easy.

Green hailed a cab in the street and had it waiting at the door when she emerged onto the sidewalk, shrugging into her coat.

She thanked him. He blushed.

And then she was driven away.

Elizabeth sat hunched in the back seat of the cab, thinking of Devereaux, wondering if it was all over now, and what would that mean to her? Would it be safe? But he had said it would be safe.

The cab swung into the hurly-burly of autos crowded around the entrance of Victoria Station and the cockney driver reached to turn the handle on the back door for her. She paid him, overtipping, and hurried through the crowd at the entrance into the great terminal with its high, soaring ironwork over the tangle of iron tracks.

Victoria Station was exciting, even on a quiet Sunday afternoon, when one realized it was the main rail terminus for trains to and from the Continent.

Elizabeth glanced around, confused for the moment at the advertising signs and the bright W. H. Smith Sons magazine kiosks. Then she saw the ticket counter. She did not notice the man who stood behind her, absurdly trying to bury his large face behind a small *Sunday Mirror*. In fact, she had not noticed the car that had followed her cab all the way from Blake House to the train terminals.

Devereaux. He must be so close, she thought, as she purchased the second-class ticket for Dover and found the gate for the Dover train. The message had said he would meet her in the last second-class carriage.

She climbed aboard. It was one of the older British Rail carriages. The seats in the compartments were stiff and musty.

The train was not crowded; it was late in the fall and this train did not connect with a ferry at Dover. Finding a compartment that was empty, she slid open the door and went inside. She sat down at the window and looked out, expecting to see Devereaux at any moment waving to her, coming down the platform.

Elizabeth smiled to herself; it was too romantic. But it was a pleasant thought. They would be alone.

The door of the compartment slid open again and she turned, her daydream shattered by the appearance of a large, middle-aged Englishwoman in tweed skirt and formidable black hat.

"Hello, dear," the woman said and lurched inside, throwing a small, flowered satchel on the rack above the seat near the aisle. "Terrible weather, ain't it." The woman was loud and vulgar and her breath smelled bad.

Elizabeth turned away and looked out the window.

"I hope it ain't to be overcrowded." The woman in the black hat chattered on. But Elizabeth didn't look at her.

"Ya like some chocolates, dear?"

Elizabeth shook her head. "No, thank you," she said, not turning.

"I like me chocolates," said the woman. "This ain't the smokin' carriage, is it?"

No Smoking signs were pasted on the glass of the door and the windows. Elizabeth pointed to them.

"Ah, that's a relief, dear," she said. "I wouldn't want to make the mistake I made Friday. I was in a smoking carriage and this gentleman he came in and sat down and he lights himself a great black cigar. Now I says, 'Can't ya bloody read it's no smokin'?' And he comes back and says, 'Yer the one that can't read, it says smokin', don't it?' and he was right." She cackled then.

"Sure you don't want a chocolate, dear?"

"No, thank you."

Elizabeth looked again out the window. The clock at the concourse gate read three minutes to four. He wasn't out there. No one, except the conductor and a man with a newspaper in front of his face.

Where was he?

The Englishwoman pulled a long thin hatpin from the crown of her black hat. But it was not a hatpin. It was too thick. The Englishwoman rose slowly.

Elizabeth continued to stare out the window at the man with the newspaper. He had lowered it suddenly and was staring back at her. His eyes were wide and frightened behind the rimless glasses. Suddenly, he raised his hand as though he wanted to make an alarm.

Elizabeth was like a sleeper caught in a nightmare,

struggling to cross from the dream to wakefulness. Her movements seemed slow. She saw the Englishwoman reflected in the window glass . . .

Turn.

The face of the Englishwoman was twisted into a hideous grimace as she thrust the stiletto forward, the gleaming tip at Elizabeth's throat.

Elizabeth fell back instinctively and threw up her arm against the onrushing form. The deadly thin knife grazed her coat, tore the material, and neatly skewered the seat cushion behind her. The Englishwoman fell forward heavily onto Elizabeth and slapped her in the face with a doubled fist. She heaved the stiletto out of the seat cushion and plunged it again towards Elizabeth's body.

This time it entered flesh.

Elizabeth screamed.

Blood appeared on the cloth of her coat where the knife had entered her upraised arm. Again, Elizabeth cried out and pushed against the bulky woman with all her strength.

The face of the Englishwoman was very near, broad and mottled, twisted in some sort of awful mask of hatred. She was so close that Elizabeth saw the little traces of mustache at the ends of lips; her lipstick was crooked and her teeth were stained dark with shreds of chocolate. She seemed overpowering.

Blood was already staining a dark circle on Elizabeth's raincoat. Her right arm felt heavy.

She pulled her knee up and pushed hard against the woman, sliding the point of the knee between the broad thighs and then pulling it up, cracking hard against her pubic bone.

The Englishwoman cried out.

The knife came down again but Elizabeth moved under it and pushed up, lifting the bulk of the large body and slamming the woman's head against the luggage rack behind her.

She reached for the wrist with the knife and, twisting, threw her body into the Englishwoman again.

The knife fell without a sound onto the seat cushions. Elizabeth felt the blow on the back of her neck and fell forward, onto the seat, the knife under her. She felt the handle pressing against her right breast.

The next blow would kill her.

Her teeth ached, her eyes saw flashes of color, her right arm was numb.

Elizabeth rolled over, grasping the knife with her right arm. The blow came down at that moment onto her collarbone.

The bulky woman cursed and raised her arms again, together, as though she were a fighter raising his arms in triumph. And then came down again, hands together.

Elizabeth pushed the stiletto up, into the tweedy fabric of the short coat, into the breast. The weight of the woman's blow struck Elizabeth again on the shoulder even as her fat body slid on top of her.

At that moment the train lurched to a start; it was four.

The Englishwoman only stared at her, as though she were asking if she wanted a sweet. And then the line of blood began to form at the corners of her mouth.

Elizabeth pushed—once, twice—and threw the staring body off her. Scrambling up then, she looked down at the stiletto stuck into the fat woman's body.

She wanted to scream and then she wanted to run and then she wanted to be sick. The feelings came over her quickly and fled as quickly; instead, she pushed her way into the corridor. Empty. Running to the exit door at the end of the carriage, she pushed furiously at the latch. The door opened with a groan.

She was in the last car of the train; the engine was already out of the station's canopy of iron and glass. The car was near the end of the long platform.

She dropped off the slow-moving train, falling onto the concrete, and rolled forward for a moment. She had lost a shoe as she fell. She scraped her hands and knees and felt dizzy. For a moment, she lay at the end of the platform, in the dusky light of the sky filtering through the glass roof. The train moved on, unconcerned; she saw the red lamps of the last car winking off into the twilight.

Slowly, Elizabeth rose.

There was no one near her. She found her shoe on the track and put it on.

Money and a lipstick tube had fallen from her purse. She picked them up slowly and replaced them, as though still in a dream.

The telegram lay on the platform.

From Belfast. From Devereaux. A telegram sent to kill her. She had worried about Devereaux and the Section; what would they decide about her? Devereaux had said it was safe; that it would be decided later.

She saw the blood darken on the sleeve of her raincoat.

So they had decided. Devereaux and the Section.

Slowly, she began to limp down the platform, back towards the main concourse.

She felt drained, used up. She had killed the one sent to kill her.

Sent by Devereaux.

They had slept together and traded promises. It would be safe. They would not die. He had wrapped his arms around her and she had felt the hardness of his body press against her, his legs against her legs; she had formed herself in the fork of his body. And then they had made love. He had opened her legs and placed himself in her, deeply into her, and stayed there for a long time, holding her, filling, surrounding her.

She saw the dead, staring face of the Englishwoman. Sent by Devereaux. She had never killed before. Killing was something they spoke of in training; she had seen death a long time before, in the dust of Addis Ababa, a slow death of bloated bellies and cries in the night.

And David's death. So still, lying on the street where he had been struck.

There was no more horror left in her.

Now there was no safe house or way to end the game except to die; there was no way out.

She had betrayed R Section and the ghost Section; or were they the same? It didn't matter. She was beyond both: Both wanted her dead and there was no way to stop it.

Not that death mattered.

She reached the concourse. A couple stared at her and then walked away quickly. A little girl with a Raggedy Ann doll stared at her and sucked her thumb.

Why did he send someone else?

She would have let Devereaux kill her, easily. She would have waited in the train for him to come to her. They would have gone to a place where he would have made love to her and then fallen asleep with her. She would have slept in the curve of his body, next to him, trusting and open in her nakedness. He could have taken her life as lightly as a whisper. She would have been a gentle victim, taking death like a gift.

Goddam him.

Now there was no safe house; there was no one to go to anymore.

At midnight, the great clock in the dim hallway sounded the sixteen notes of the Westminster chime and then began to boom the hours. Almost unconsciously, Green counted them while he sat in the library with his large glass of vodka in ice and orange juice. There was no more time for posturing drinks or for wearing the façade of an Englishman.

Of course, it was impossible to sleep; impossible to think since the signal from Ruckles.

He had been awakened from a drink-induced stupor an hour before.

The beeper beside his bed had begun the strange chirping sound—rather like a mechanical bird—which meant Ruckles wanted to contact him urgently.

He had struggled out of sleep with foreboding. His mouth was dry. He realized he had been dreaming about the woman with brown hair. Elizabeth. A traitor.

He called Ruckles at the special number.

"She got away," was all the Virginian said.

Green waited, his hand trembling.

"Took out our agent," said Ruckles.

No. It was part of the dream. He opened his mouth but could not speak.

"Wake up, boy," said Ruckles. "Our bird has flown. We can't find her. The agent was wasted."

No, not a dream. "What can I do?"

"This is our last contact," said Ruckles slowly. "We've just received orders to close down Operation Mirror."

"But." Green began to sputter, stopped, glanced around the darkness of his bedroom.

"Sorry, old man," Ruckles said. "I wanted to tell you myself. Better get rid of the tape transmitter in the scrambler box. For your sake."

"You're closing down the operation?" Green was unable to comprehend the current sentence, only the previous one.

"It's blown," said Ruckles.

"Then I'm blown," said Green. He was awake now. The horror of it began to strangle him.

"Probably. Although I don't suppose our bird will surface for a long time, if ever. We don't know though. But the company wants to close it down. We got the message an hour ago."

"But you were going to take me in——"

"We can't do that," Ruckles said reasonably. "It didn't work out. We were going to take you in when Mirror succeeded."

"But it's not finished."

"Nope. That's the way it goes sometimes."

Green held the telephone receiver with two hands in fear he might drop it. "But Ruckles. I'm out here alone. You've got to take me in. If they know it was me."

"It'd be easier if you were with the opposition. But we're part of the same government. We can't do it."

"But we served the President, we—"

"Easy now, Green. It's a rough stick, old pal. I had to call you myself, let you know."

"They'll kill me."

There was a pause. "Not necessarily."

Not necessarily. Green could not speak, so Ruckles interpreted his silence.

"Don't go catatonic on me, Green. Be calm. Just get rid of the tape transmitter in the scrambler box and you'll be just f—"

Green let the receiver fall. He sat for a long time in his pajamas and stared into the darkness. They would get him; they would make the connection. And now the company wouldn't take him in.

So he fumbled downstairs in the darkness, the whole of Blake House silent save for the relentless tick-tick-tick of the clock. Would Uncle Hubert be able to save him? Would he want to save him?

Green felt ashamed though he hadn't betrayed anyone; he had merely served his country and worked against his country's enemies. Against traitors like the woman and like Devereaux.

He made his first drink. And then a second.

He went to the library and turned on a small table lamp and waited in the shadows; outside, it was raining, a cold, remorseless rain of winter.

When he looked up again and saw him in the doorway, Green was beyond surprise. He had been expecting him. He sat in the red leather chair and stared at the apparition in the doorway.

"Devereaux."

He did not move out of the doorway into the light. "Where is she?"

"Gone."

It was so hopeless. He took the glass from the table

and drank and then put it down again. Even the booze didn't work anymore.

"Where has she gone?"

He needed to explain; it wasn't his fault. "They told me to give her a message. It was from Belfast. From you."

The rain lashed against the panes of glass; the window rattled. "Where is Elizabeth?" The voice was low and almost still, like a dark pool.

Green looked up. He couldn't see Devereaux clearly. "How did you get in?"

There was no answer.

"This is a safe house."

"There are no safe houses."

Green shrugged. "You're right." He looked at the ice cubes in the glass, melting into the yellow liquid. "Not for me anymore. Or for her."

There was a snap.

He had heard that sound before. The click of a gun's hammer. "Where is she?"

The hall clock sounded the quarter-hour with four notes of the Westminster chime. Then nothing but the stately tick, tick, tick.

"I gave her the message. To meet you. On the four o'clock Dover train at Victoria Station."

Almost imperceptibly, Devereaux moved; Green could see the black gun in his hand.

"I don't want to die," Green said quietly.

"No one wants to die."

"No. Of course. You're right."

"She went to Victoria Station to meet me?"

"Yes. She thought that. They sent someone to eliminate her. I don't like that word."

"And they killed her."

"No. No. That's the part that made them end the operation. I don't understand it; they called me an hour ago." He looked at his watch. "They waited until eleven to call me. But she must have gotten away right away. They knew that."

"They didn't kill her."

Devereaux repeated it flatly, not as a question.

"No," said Green. He grinned. He looked like a child. "She turned the tables on them. They said she killed their agent. I don't know how. And she got away. They're closing down the operation."

"The ghost Section?"

"It was called Operation Mirror. To root out the traitors in R Section who had been disloyal to the nation."

"And you were their man."

Green looked up at the shadow in the doorway; his eyes had tears in them. "I had to. It was for my country. I had to work for them because they explained it to me, about you. You were a traitor in Vietnam; you worked for the opposition. And there was Hanley, he suppressed the Cuban report I prepared. Oh, they proved they were under the orders of the President. My country needed me and now they've left me to you to kill me. Mirror has failed and they're letting the traitors live and the men who were loyal . . . they're letting them die. I don't understand it."

Devereaux waited.

"Traitor," Green suddenly cried at last. "You traitor! I served the company. I served them; I told them what I saw, what I heard. I had the transmitter tape in the scrambler and we got everything, everything you said, everything they all said, all the scheming."

Green got up and went to the sideboard and poured vodka on top of the remains of the warm mix left in the glass. He gulped it, like a dog drinking water on a hot day. He set the glass down hard and turned to Devereaux.

"I was an agent. I was one of them." He said it with defiance. "Kill me then, because I can stand to die for my country."

"Where is she?"

The calm voice was counterpoint to the ringing declaration, like a cough in the middle of a speech.

"The housekeeper? I don't know. She's one of yours,

you know. She didn't know a thing; I hate her and her odious breath and her stupid cow face."

"Where's Elizabeth?"

"I don't know. They don't know. She killed the hit man sent after her. You see how it was; you weren't on the four o'clock train and she expected you."

"Who is your contact? At the company?"

"I won't betray my country."

"They have abandoned you."

"I won't betray them."

Devereaux waited in the darkness. The rain did not cease; the clock ticked on; there were a thousand little noises and sounds in the silence.

"You won't make me betray them."

Devereaux spoke again, softly: "Green, listen to me. The CIA wasn't after traitors. They only wanted to destroy the Section and they used you. They killed our real agents and they put the Soviets onto us so that eventually, no one would trust R Section and we would be destroyed."

"Why don't you come into the light?"

"You were the traitor, Green."

"But I'm not a traitor. How can I betray an agency to an agency? This is the same side, the same country."

"Why didn't they take you in, then? They've left you. You said they left you. If it was in the interest of the nation, why didn't they take you in?"

"I don't know."

Again silence. Green sat down and stared at the gun and then put a hand over his eyes. "I don't know."

"They're not gathering information; they're making murder. They killed Hastings in Edinburgh; they tried twice to kill Elizabeth, once in Belfast and once here. They tried to kill me. And they expect me to kill you, Green. They left you; do you think they would have left you outside if it had been on the square?"

Suddenly, tears formed at the corners of Green's eyes.

He reached for the glass of vodka and knocked it onto the carpet.

Devereaux stepped into the room and put the gun in his belt, under his jacket. Green stared at him. "We are not traitors," Devereaux said gently.

"My God," Green sobbed. "My God. I've made a mess."

"Yes."

"It wasn't real, was it?"

"No. It was an agency game. Agency to agency. And you were used."

"Those men dead."

"They're not important."

Green wanted to cry in the presence of the calm, certain man. He wasn't going to die.

"What's going to happen?"

"Where is Elizabeth?"

"I thought you were going to kill me," Green babbled.

"Where is she?"

"I don't know. I sent her to be killed. How could I do that? Was I crazy? There's a tape transmitter in the scrambler, I—"

"I know. We'll get it later. Who is your contact?"

Green looked up. The winter face was so kind, the voice so gentle. Perhaps he was forgiven. "Ruckles."

"Ruckles?"

"With the CIA at the embassy in Grosvenor Square. I'll tell you—" And Green began to tell about Operation Mirror.

Devereaux listened without a word, prompting only when Green faltered. Green wandered in his explanation but he eventually revealed it all.

And Devereaux watched him. Because he intended to kill him when the explanation was finished. At first.

But the glimmer of a plan began forming as he heard Green's words. Green was a coward and a traitor, a fool, but he was invaluable now. The CIA had revealed too much to Green in order to recruit him, and now he was useful, not to the Section but to Devereaux. And so, Green saved his life while he narrated the events that led to Operation Mirror.

When Green finished, Devereaux sat and waited for a long time.

"Green," he began. "They did send me to kill you, not to get information."

Green shuddered.

"But I am not going to kill you. Now, listen to me carefully: They both want you dead now. Both the Section and the CIA. And there's no way now you can come inside. Unless you do as I say."

"The CIA? Why—"

"Don't be a fool, Green. You're a liability to them. Ruckles warned you to make you run, so that if we had any doubts, we would eliminate you anyway. And he warned you to get rid of that bit of incriminating evidence in the scrambler box. The CIA doesn't want anyone to know—to have proof of—another one of their sleazy little operations, this time against another government agency. So they really don't want you around."

"But the Section?"

"You were part of them. You're a traitor to us. And I'm not convinced now the Section really intends to move against the CIA with what it knows."

Green shook his head. "I don't follow—"

"I do," said Devereaux. "Now I do. R Section could have sent any of a half dozen men from Europe when they knew you were the traitor. And one of them would have killed you and saved Elizabeth. But they didn't care if she was wasted; they would have cared if they had wanted to use her information to discredit the CIA. I suspect they've already made an accommodation with the CIA—leave us alone and we'll leave you alone. That's why I suspect Operation Mirror has suddenly been scrapped."

"And you won't kill me."

"No. As long as you do as I say. Because it's the only way you're going to survive." And, he did not add, the only way Elizabeth would survive if he could find her. Perhaps the only way Devereaux would survive—did Hanley even now have plans against him? A field agent was not terribly important when you placed his life against the life of the Section. An accommodation with the CIA would serve the Section well in the next few years.

"I want you to work your way to Liverpool. I want you to be in Liverpool Tuesday night, in the Lime Street railroad station, at nine P.M."

"Why?"

Because you are part of a surprise. "Because it is the plan," said Devereaux.

"All right," said Green.

"Pack a small bag. Now. And get out of London tonight. Hire a cab to Windsor and take the train from Windsor to Cambridge. Spend a day there, at least. And then take public transport to Liverpool. Don't drive, don't rent a car. And travel as though the world wanted you dead. Because they do."

"But why?"

"Because both agencies will be looking for you. To kill you. And for all I know, your friends at the CIA may even pin that murder of their hit man on you. So get the hell out now."

"And at Lime Street?"

"I'll be there. Wait in the buffet. There's always a buffet in a train station."

He had met Hastings in the buffet at Edinburgh Central Station. It seemed such a long time ago.

"And if you're not there?"

Devereaux looked at him coldly. "I'm the only chance you have, Green. If I'm not there, you're a dead man. And if I'm there and you don't show up, then you're dead. Do you understand that? If you skip, I'll find you or the Agency will find you or the Section will find you, anywhere you go in the world. And they'll kill you. You can't make any more deals, Green; you have to let me handle it."

"I will, I will," Green said. "I don't want to die."

Devereaux thought again about him and about Elizabeth; he would have been happy to kill Green then.

"And the house?" Green asked.

"I'm taking care of it. I'm closing Blake House." He paused. "It isn't safe anymore."

Elizabeth cleaned up in the ladies' room at Victoria Station and took the Circle Line tube underground to Paddington Station on the north side of Kensington Gardens. The area was one with quiet flats and inexpensive hotels. She had first stayed there when she came to London twelve years before as a student spending a "summer in Europe." It was the only place she could think of to go to.

By accident, she found the hotel she had first stayed in; she felt a little wave of nostalgia for it and for her schoolgirl self. But there were the usual disappointments: The hotel sported a new lounge and had suspicious new owners who demanded three days' rent in advance and surrender of her passport.

She locked herself in her room and removed her soiled, blood-spattered clothes. The raincoat was unmarked; she had stolen it from a parcel on the luggage rack inside the station. It didn't fit her very well; but the hideously blood-stained raincoat she had worn on the train had to be thrown away.

She washed in the basin and then sat down on the bed and counted her money. Three hundred and twelve pounds to get away.

Taking the picture of her son out of the billfold, she looked at it. And she thought of Devereaux. He had returned the picture to her; he had not given it back, merely put it back on the dresser. She looked at the face of the little boy and the face of her younger self. Photographs broke your heart because they so clearly conjured up the past.

She had to leave London but she felt so tired, so weak. She had fashioned a crude bandage around the wound on her arm with her scarf. The cut had stopped bleeding but her arm felt numb; it was bruised black.

How could she get away? She only wanted to sleep, sleep away the pain and the hideous face of the Englishwoman. Would she dream of her if she slept?

Would the police be looking for her?

The CIA wanted her dead. She understood that. And now Devereaux had tried to kill her. There was no place inside. She must contact her ex-husband—but what could he do for her? And where was he? And how could she get to him?

He had known Hanley. Or what she understood now was the "ghost" Hanley. Was he part of the CIA as well? Would he betray her? What did he owe her?

A wave of self-pity threatened to overwhelm her.

No. She wouldn't let it happen; she would survive. Somehow.

After a little while, she dressed again, buttoning the overlarge raincoat. She needed clothing and she was hungry.

She found a street with lights and went into a little bright fish-and-chips shop that bore the sign: *Frying Tonight*. Inside, she stood in line with the other shabby people, waiting for the plaice and chips wrapped in newsprint. She went outside then and ate greedily until it was all gone, then walked on. Paddington Station's immense bulk loomed ahead in the next block. It began to rain.

Tomorrow morning, she would get clothes.

Tomorrow, she would leave London. If no place was safe for her, then she could go anyplace. Was she so important they would look for her forever? She only needed time.

She hurried back through the rain to the little hotel.

The thought of sleep, of finding safety, lightened her step. She did not even notice the man across the street, watching her enter the hotel.

21

LIVERPOOL

Faolin found the flat off Lightbody Street, near the Nelson dock, with some trouble. He had never been there before because Parnell had never let any of them see his living quarters.

It was nine A.M. on Monday, forty-nine hours until the launch of the *Brianna.*

With the exception of Donovan, who was working at the hovercraft apron on the waterfront some three miles down the river Mersey from there, the group was supposed to converge at 9:15 A.M. in Parnell's flat.

As usual, Faolin would be late, a lateness bred by his own impatience in waiting for others and by inherent caution. A caution he had betrayed once before, on Saturday, at the funeral of Deirdre Monahan.

Faolin was on edge as he walked slowly around the block containing Parnell's flat. He looked everywhere with little darting glances, but there was nothing to see: merely Liverpool on a Monday morning, coming to a new week and a new day with the usual displays of life.

He shouldn't have gone to Innisbally.

He was certain the policeman there spotted him as a stranger.

Madness.

He bumped into a child rushing out from between two buildings from a narrow mews.

"Hey, me lad," he said.

277

"Argh," the child cried, pushing away, "fug off." And he ran down the street.

Not madness, really. Perhaps he understood that he would be observed at the funeral and that there would be no turning back from his purpose then, that there would never be sanctuary for him again in Ireland after they seized the *Brianna*.

Which was another reason to destroy it and to destroy them all. An act of martyrdom, of incredible bravery. The policeman who'd been in the crowded church would remember Faolin after it was over; he would say he had seen Faolin, been this close to him, watched him as Faolin watched Lord Slough. At a funeral Mass.

Around a final street corner, back to Parnell's flat. It all looked safe enough.

Would the copper say anything? Would he be too embarrassed to speak? That he could have prevented the coming carnage if he had seized Faolin in that simple country church?

Faolin chuckled. A piece of newspaper blew up the street and wrapped itself around his leg. He kicked it away.

Perhaps he should send a letter to the London *Times*. Or the *Irish Times*. Or both. Post it tomorrow, Tuesday, when it would be too late; explain the act, explain the suffering of the Irish people at the hands of English lords and English politicians and Irish who worked hand in glove with their English masters.

None of them had contacted Parnell since the last meeting the week before. Parnell was a Liverpool policeman, big and quiet and slow-moving.

He had been part of the movement for six years.

Since the night British soldiers in Belfast mistook his young brother for an IRA gunman who had opened fire on them while they patrolled the Shankhill road.

They had killed him. Nineteen bullets were in his body when they ceased shooting.

Of course, it had been an error; there were apologies to Police Constable Parnell of the Liverpool police and there were reprimands for the frightened young soldiers, who swore they had seen a flash of gunfire and heard the whine of bullets in the air.

But his brother was dead and that was what had mattered to him. The movement was more than revenge; though Parnell was Irish, an Ulsterman, Catholic, and he nursed a grudge against the English handed down, father to son, for generations.

For the past six years, he merely passed along information that fell to him as a policeman. Of course, there was money too; he had made it clear that money was not the cause of his betrayal but it was part of the price of the risk he took for the IRA.

Now this was the first job he had taken part in; the risk, they told him, was nil.

That was a lie, of course, and Parnell understood it; but Faolin had needed him as surely as he had needed Captain Donovan to take over the craft after they hijacked it.

Faolin nodded to Parnell as he entered the bare little flat. Tatty was already there, sitting on the sofa.

Parnell, who had worked the night shift Sunday, was still in uniform with his blouse unbuttoned. He held a bottle of Guinness in his hand.

"Yer late, Faolin," said Tatty at last when the door was closed.

"I am," said Faolin. He went to the remaining empty chair in the sitting room and took it.

"It's a beauty," Tatty said.

"Then you've seen it?" Faolin asked.

"It ought to be a beauty. It's a real uniform." Parnell punctuated his statement with a belch.

Faolin got up and went to the package on the floor beside the low couch where Tatty sat. The blue uniform was neatly packed.

"Everything'll fit then?" said Faolin.

"You'll make a smashin' copper, Faolin," answered Parnell.

"Oh, aye. You've the stern look of the law about ye," said Tatty, smiling.

"Aye," said Faolin and he returned to his chair again. He sat down and lit a cigarette and then got up and went to the window. He looked down on the empty street. In the distance, he could see the Lever towers on the docks of the river.

"Let's go over it again, then," he said at last and turned from the window.

Parnell, as a member of the special color guard, was assigned to attend the launch of the *Brianna* on Wednesday morning from the dock in the Aigburth Vale section, down river from were they now sat.

The ship would sit on the concrete apron about seventy-five feet from the river.

The first-class passengers—there were a hundred and thirteen tickets issued for the initial voyage—would be seated in a special section to the right of the vessel. A wooden stand for the politicians and dignitaries was to be erected at the prow. Workmen were building it now. Joining Lord Slough and his daughter on the platform would be the Prime Minister of Great Britain, the Prime Minister of the Irish Republic, the Secretary for Northern Ireland, the Duke of Kensington (cousin of the Queen and first cousin to Lord Slough), and Mr. Peter Tomkins, secretary of the Trades Union Council.

The ceremonial guard, including Parnell, would be around the platform and would form a line leading to the hovercraft.

At precisely ten A.M., Parnell explained, the Liverpool police band would commence with the national songs of Great Britain and the Irish Republic.

At 10:08 A.M., Lord Slough was expected to introduce the Prime Minister of Great Britain, who would speak for approximately five minutes. Then Slough would introduce the Prime Minister of the Irish Republic, who would speak for approximately the same time.

Finally, Lord Slough would speak briefly and then introduce his daughter, Brianna Devon.

She would be handed a magnum of champagne with which she would christen the ship.

Immediately thereafter, while the police band played various martial tunes, the first-class passengers would quietly board the ship.

At 10:45 A.M., Lord Slough and the Prime Ministers and the Duke of Kensington would also enter the vessel.

At 10:47 A.M., the hovercraft *Brianna* would begin its slow waddle across the concrete apron the seventy-five feet to the river Mersey.

At 10:48 A.M., she would be in the water.

At 10:53 A.M., she would be beyond the breakwaters of the Irish Sea, heading for Dublin.

Parnell showed them a drawing of the actual launching apron.

"And we," said Faolin. "How do we board her?" He said it to jog Parnell, for he had gone over the plan a thousand times in his head.

Parnell said, "Donovan, of course, is already aboard with the crew during these preliminaries. You, Faolin, will have this uniform and be part of the crowd-control contingent—here, to the right of the platform. Now, the press is here, between you and the platform. When the dignitaries start to go aboard, the press will move this way—here, on the side of the platform—and follow them with their cameras and whatnot right aboard ship. We have issued credentials to nineteen Dublin journalists and twenty-four from London and six from Liverpool. Nineteen of that total will ride in the ship to Dublin."

Parnell smiled.

Faolin said, "Yes. And then what? Continue."

Parnell let the smile fade. "Well, you accompany the

press aboard, in uniform. Tatty here goes aboard with the first-class crowd as a passenger, and Donovan makes a rendezvous with the pair of you aboard ship."

"What about security for the politicians?"

"To me knowledge," said Parnell, "there's three special CID men detached from Scotland Yard to guard the P.M. The Taoiseach will doubtless have a couple of Irish coppers. But there's good news about Lord Slough."

"Indeed."

"No special men for him. But the crowd'll be laced with men in civilian clothes of course. They're looking for someone to take another shot at his Lordship, not to take over the *Brianna*."

"Are you sure?"

"Sure. We got a cable this mornin' before I was off duty. From CID Special Branch in Scotland Yard. To the superintendent it was. Of course, I had a look. They've requested a detachment from us for duty Tuesday afternoon."

"Where?"

Parnell grinned. "In bleedin' Glasgow is where. Fer the Celtics–Rangers match-up."

"I don't understand," said Faolin. He got up from his chair again and began to pace.

"CID wants the specials to help guard Lord Slough when he appears at the game Tuesday. Mix in the crowd. It seems they got a tip from Dublin that our lot intends to assassinate his Lordship during the game. Lads'll be happy to see the match."

"Indeed," said Faolin.

Tatty laughed. "Ah, God, the coppers are outsmartin' themselves." Parnell laughed with him.

"And no special bunch sent down here Wednesday for the *Brianna* launch?"

Parnell managed to stop laughing. "No, that's the best part of it. They're convinced the Boys intend t'take him out in Glasgow. And there's no changing an official mind once it's made up."

"So we let her be launched down the spit of the Mersey inter the Irish Sea," said Tatty. "And then we come up and announce ourselves."

Finally, Faolin smiled. It would be the moment. "To Lord Slough and t'the journalists."

Parnell said, "Now, make no mistake. I'm sure they'll have a guard on Slough—"

"It don't matter," said Faolin. "Once we get control of the pilot house, we have the ship, same as the bloody Arabs when they grab a plane. We'll have our own weapons. And we'll have the transmitter t'set off the jelly in the hold."

As though it were a signal, Parnell rose and went into the second room of the flat. When he came back, he carried two black weapons—two M11 "grease guns" of the type used in Vietnam by American forces. They were small and deadly and capable of incredible rates of fire.

He held one in each beefy hand.

Faolin took one of the weapons and lined his eye along the sight. Then he hefted it and spun around in the room, as though spraying the apartment with deadly fire. "Give these t'the lads in Belfast and we'd see a war."

Parnell nodded. "But they're dear, very dear."

Tatty said, "But not too dear." He held the gun, hefted it, and suddenly looked young; his wiry body came alive. "Ah, t'have been there when me Old One was makin' the Black and Tans dance."

"Aye," said Parnell, in a faraway voice.

But Faolin did not speak; he lowered the weapon and let the muzzle sweep the room; he saw the bodies fall, saw the blood.

"We'll give them a message from Belfast then? Eh, Faolin," said Tatty.

And then the ship would be blown up—just that moment of heat and light and then it would be gone.

"Eh, Faolin?"

Death, sweet death. To them all.

He stood in the middle of the room and did not speak but saw his future and welcomed it.

Elizabeth left the hotel shortly after nine on Monday morning after a miserable "English" breakfast of hard rolls and black tea. The graciousness had gone out of the hotel as she remembered it; like others in the city, the hotelkeepers had been hit hard by the recessions of the middle 1970s and had cut back on amenities that guests had long expected.

Elizabeth noticed it but didn't care terribly; she retrieved her passport, but when she demanded partial repayment on her advance, they wouldn't give it to her. She left the hotel frustrated and angry.

Gloomy London Monday. The rain had ceased, but it was cold and damp and windy.

A block from the hotel, she ducked into a clothing store. With little hesitation, she selected a black sweater and dark slacks and a raincoat. She asked to try the garments on.

In a dirty, dim-lit fitting room in the back of the shop, she pulled the new clothes on and bundled up the others in the oversize raincoat. She reappeared, better dressed; the shopkeeper, an old woman with ratty gray hair, looked surprised.

"Yer gonna wear them, dearie?"

In answer, Elizabeth removed a fistful of pound notes from her purse and paid.

"Put these in a bag," she said, indicating the bundles. If the woman thought to say anything, Elizabeth's cold voice stopped her. She was a queer one, the old woman thought; the whole area is full of them now, queer ones like her.

Elizabeth left the shop and walked quickly to Paddington Station, where she dumped the bundle of old clothes in a trash bin near the station entrance. She felt better now; she had torn a sheet in the hotel and bandaged the wound on her arm. The arm did not hurt as much this morning, and did not appear to be infected.

In a way, she felt freer than she had yesterday afternoon, after she realized Devereaux betrayed her. It was better like this, clean, to get away from them all, not to trust another for your safety.

Going into the buffet in the station, she ordered tea laced with milk. She sat down at a table with a copy of the *Guardian*.

The story was on page two, not conspicuous, under the Home News section. About a woman named Nettie Perce found murdered on the Dover train. Police were currently seeking a brown-haired female with an American accent for help in their inquiries.

The cup shook in her hand; the sense of freedom vanished.

Someone had spotted her. The conductor? Or the man with the newspaper who had really warned her by the look on his face when the woman rose to attack her?

She had to get out of London this morning. North, away from Dover.

Suddenly, she put the tea down and stared through the window of the buffet. There was the same man—from the platform at Victoria Station. The same bulky figure in the same old, soiled raincoat.

Elizabeth grabbed her purse and fled out the door, onto the concourse, without looking back. Rushing into Eastbourne Street, she hailed a cab.

Her confidence was gone.

"Where to, miss?"

Where to? Away.

"Oh." She seemed to fumble in her purse for an address. But there was no place. "Piccadilly Circus," she said at last. It was a place at least.

Fifteen minutes later, the cab deposited her on a corner of Piccadilly Circus, in the congestion of pigeons, cars, noise, and flashing signs. She paid again and stood for a moment on the sidewalk. How could she tell if she had been followed?

She started down the block, her shoes clapping loudly on the pavement. People stopped and turned to stare at the distraught figure with pale face and wild eyes.

Elizabeth turned into Haymarket and began to hurry along towards Trafalgar Square.

She had to leave London. She didn't know the trains—but she had been in Paddington Station long enough to see there were trains for Wales. Wales would be safe.

If they had followed her, they would not expect her to double back on herself.

Ten minutes later, she entered Paddington Station again and went to the ticket counter. A train for Cardiff was scheduled to leave in fifteen minutes. She bought a ticket.

Realizing that she might get hungry on the long trip, she went into the buffet and bought two sandwich rounds and stuffed them in the pockets of her tan raincoat.

"Please may I speak to you?"

She turned. It was him again; the man from the platform at Victoria Station, whom she'd spoted a half hour before. He was standing next to her at the end of the checkout line in the buffet, holding a copy of the *Daily Mirror*.

She wanted to run.

Perhaps he understood that; he took her arm, gently. "Please," he said again. "Don't be good enough to run away again."

"How did you follow me?"

"Ah," he said. And he laughed. "I cannot. There was no cab. So I waited and hoped you would come again to the station because I did not know where to look for you."

Suddenly, it all seemed hopeless to her.

"Who are you?"

He still held her arm, but held it gently.

"I am Mr. Dennis," he said. "I am with British Intelligence. Actually, the name is more formal but it is enough. I want to speak to you. May I buy you a cup of tea?"

"My train—"

"Please," he said.

"I have to go. I don't know you."

"No, Elizabeth. But I know you. Please, let me call you Elizabeth. To make you comfortable. Because Americans want to be called of their Christian names. I am Mr. Dennis."

She was frightened; her face was chalky; he held her as lightly as a child would hold a bird—and as firmly.

What was the use? "Should I give up?"

"No, no. Never give up. That is surrender," the man said. His face was broad and smiling, his blue eyes were clear and guileless behind the rimless glasses.

"Please," she said. "That woman wanted to kill me."

"I know, Elizabeth. It's all right. We know all about it. I am going to help you. Please trust to me." He ordered two teas and paid with his right hand, still holding her with his left. "Please," he said again. She picked up her tea. She could throw it in his face—

"Please don't do that," he said, as though he read her thoughts. "Here, I will release your arm. I merely did not want you to be frightened when I spoke to you, to run away as you did before. I must speak to you. But don't throw your tea at me—if you must run away, leave my face as it is."

But she did not run away. They sat down at a plastic table.

Elizabeth sipped her tea for a moment.

"What do you want?" she said at last.

He looked at her shyly and smiled again; one of his large hands reached across the plastic table top and took hers. Her hands were pale and cold. He held her hand and warmed it.

"To help you," Denisov said.

22

WASHINGTON

The deal had been made Sunday, after Devereaux's telephone call, after another meeting between Hanley and the Chief of Section.

It appeared to be satisfactory.

Of course, Hanley didn't know all the details. But the Old Man assured him that Operation Mirror was closed down, that the threat to the Section was over. He had even congratulated Hanley and mentioned something about a citation (a secret citation, of course) for Devereaux.

What about the opening to British Intelligence?

Ah, explained Galloway. That was part of the deal. The CIA remained in place, all was status quo as far as the Limeys were concerned. In exchange, all present and future moves to discredit R Section were abdicated by the CIA. And the CIA promised to turn over a particularly juicy cache of information from Uganda, straight to R Section's African desk. So that R Section could get the credit for turning the information over to the National Security Council.

Everything, the Old Man said, had turned out well.

Until two A.M. Monday morning, when the housekeeper of Blake House, phoning Hanley from the air terminal in London, explained that Devereaux had come, closed the house, burned all the secret documents, turned her out and . . . turned out poor Mr. Green.

He killed him? Hanley asked.

No, the housekeeper said. He had merely chased Green away. And closed Blake House.

It was nearly six before Hanley and the Old Man met again, this time in the latter's office on the sixth floor of the Department of Agriculture building.

"Bad news, Hanley," the Old Man said. He was sipping coffee at his uncluttered desk. His face seemed more drawn in the cold fluorescent light. Beyond the window, the rest of Washington was sleeping in the pre-dawn darkness.

"It is, sir," said Hanley. He sat down in the designated chair. "We've been signaled, as you know. By the housekeeper. And now Devereaux and Green have flown. In addition, there *was* an attempt to eliminate this Elizabeth Campbell person by the competition. And she has flown as well. The three of them are out there. And, given the timing, I suspect that Devereaux now understands the deal we've entered into with the Langley firm."

"He understood your instructions," frowned the Chief.

"Yes. I'm afraid there's no doubt about that. He— well, he did seem upset in his telephone report yesterday that we hadn't moved to safeguard the woman."

"This Campbell person."

"Yes."

"Is this usual? I mean, this disobedience. I wasn't really aware of it," said Galloway.

"No, sir. Not usual at all. He hasn't made contact since last night."

The old man danced his fingers on the empty desk top. "What will Devereaux do?"

"I don't know."

"Will he contact the competition?"

"No, sir. I'm sure not. I—"

"Why not, Hanley? He's disobeyed your instructions. He's jeopardized the mission. He's let a mole escape."

"There may be some plan, sir. I told you, he wasn't satisfied with the information he had about this Lord Slough—"

The Old Man banged his fist down on the desk. The noise was so unexpected that Hanley flinched involuntarily "The hell with Lord Slough. You sent Devereaux to get information. He got it. It was up to us to decide—"

Hanley felt very brave in speaking up. "Sir, I did tell him that we intended to open an information bridge to British Intelligence—"

"I don't care, his mission is information, not policy. So you think Devereaux is extemporizing and developing his own scenario. Well, Hanley, I don't like that."

"Neither do I."

"Goddammit. Devereaux stumbles on this Operation Mirror thing and for the first time in years, we've got the Langley firm boxed in. We can work out an accommodation with them. To hell with British Intelligence—bunch of Limey bastards."

"Sir. I think that if Devereaux has freed Green or stashed him or whatever, he intends to use him."

The angry moment had passed. The Old Man sat calmly again, sipping his black coffee. "For what?"

"I don't know. I suspect he doesn't trust us."

"Why not?"

Hanley knew why; he understood that much about Devereaux. "He promised this Campbell woman safety; we permitted her to be the target of another assassination attempt. That's one. Second, he realizes we have reached an accommodation with Langley because Operation Mirror is suddenly quashed. That must be the reason he didn't eliminate Green. Someone from the CIA warned Green that Mirror was blown and Green told Devereaux. So he knows that we're . . . well, letting the CIA off the hook."

"And that's none of his business."

"No, sir," said Hanley doggedly. "He might think it is. Devereaux was a target of them, you know. And there's something else. He's sort of . . ."

It was not usual for Hanley to fumble for words.

The Old Man waited without prompting.

When Hanley looked up, he seemed embarrassed. "Devereaux came in after . . . after Kennedy. After he was killed."

The Old Man knew that. He waited.

"Well, sir. It's difficult to say. He had some ideals then, though a lot's gone by the board. But he understood why the Section was formed. As a check on the Langley firm. As an honest source of information, a fulcrum to move the other agencies to deal . . . sir, this sounds so foolish . . . but he really sees it all—"

"Don't tell me he has ideals."

"No, sir. I think he did once, but not now, sir. But he wouldn't sell out, ever. And that means to the CIA."

There was silence. "Do you think we sold out, Hanley?" the old man asked.

"No, sir."

"Do you think that's any concern of a field agent?"

"No, sir."

"Devereaux has become a dangerous man," the Old Man said at last. "Send a chaser."

"But we don't know where he is. . . ."

"Send Lupowitz from Brussels and Bardinella from Berlin and Krepps from Barcelona. I want three top chasers in London before noon. I want them to find Devereaux, Green, and this Campbell woman. I want them eliminated. And I want you to contact Henderson at the Langley office and set their men on it."

"Sir—"

"For whatever reasons, Devereaux has disobeyed his instructions. He may even be a danger not only to us but to the country."

Hanley spoke up again. He was surprised by the vehemence in his voice. "Devereaux would not betray us."

Galloway looked at him mildly. "Unless he thought we had betrayed him."

Devereaux had been careful in closing Blake House.

He had made sure Green and the housekeeper were gone before he began. He started, of course, with the scrambler box. He carefully removed the cover and took out the hidden tape transmitter. A micro-tape spool was on it. Green had shown him the other micro-tapes, secreted in the closet of his bedroom behind a movable partition.

Devereaux burned the code books in the fireplace in the library. The ordinary papers were burned as well. Finally, Devereaux dismantled the scrambler box and destroyed it, ripping apart transistor boards and wiring.

He had closed down safe houses before. There had been one in Hué which he had closed down during the Tet offensive; that had been difficult. And there was the safe house in Saigon, at the end. He knew what to do, how not to leave a trace; so he worked carefully and let his mind think of other things, the way a jogger does not think of running as he runs.

Devereaux was surprised by the first traces of morning scattering gray light across the face of winter London. The light came so gradually that when he noticed it, the houses across the street were clearly visible. Time to leave.

Still he had not solved the problem of Elizabeth or Green. Or himself. By now, the housekeeper would have reported to Hanley, probably from the air terminal. Devereaux had disobeyed instructions; Devereaux had let a mole escape with his life; Devereaux was a danger to the Section because he was playing a separate game. He knew what they would say.

Where was Elizabeth?

He decided he could not find her; logically, the world was large and time was short. To save his own life, he had to stop the assassination of Lord Slough—and let the British know it. Somehow trade information for his life and force·R Section to renege on its deal with the CIA. If there was a deal, of course—though Devereaux was as certain of that as he was certain the IRA intended to kill Lord Slough in Liverpool on Wednesday morning.

Where is your proof? Hanley would say.

Hanley never understood the business. He had no feel for it. There were never proofs. You trusted instincts to bridge the gaps in the information.

One of the gang was named Donovan. He was a dock worker of some sort. He worked with ships. The only ship looming in Lord Slough's immediate future was the *Brianna*. Somehow, they were connected. Devereaux had really explained it to Cashel but Cashel had not understood—you bring as many people into the conspiracy as needed to meet the problems of the site you have chosen. If Donovan was part of the gang, then Slough's site had been chosen—a ship site, a waterfront, on a dock.. Or at the launching of a ship.

He could have given that to Hanley on Sunday night. But there had to be more to it. Why was the CIA involved in this? And why had the CIA risked exposing Operation Mirror to take him out in Ireland? To waste three agents to stop him—Blatchford, Johannsen, and Elizabeth? What was so important beyond Operation Mirror that the CIA was afraid Hastings had tumbled to its secret?

All these thoughts—fragments of thoughts, fragments of questions—occupied him while he closed down Blake

House. And when the job was done, he was no closer to any answers.

If Green only knew how little Devereaux knew.

If Green had any inkling of the danger in Devereaux's incomplete plan. Well, it didn't matter. It was the only thing that would save Devereaux's life.

Devereaux put the tape transmitter and several micro-tapes into a brown suitcase. Then he washed and shaved, using one of Green's electric razors (inexplicably, he had two) and changed into one of Green's handmade shirts. The fit was not particularly good, but the shirt was clean.

By eight Monday morning Devereaux had deposited the brown suitcase in left-luggage at the Victoria Air Terminal, and had hopped a cab to the American Embassy on Grosvenor Square.

The usual long line of people were waiting for visas. The line stretched down one side of the building. The line was always there, in good times and bad, at times of a sinking dollar and a rising dollar, at times of oil crisis or war or peace; it was always full of the hopeful who wanted to go to America for a visit or for work or to emigrate.

Devereaux went around the block to the side entrance of the immense building. The Great Seal of the United States, etched in stone, was above him.

At the desk in the lobby, he asked for Mr. Ruckles. With the Central Intelligence Agency.

"Who is calling?" the clerk asked.

"Mr. Devereaux," he said.

He did not have to wait long; in a very short while, a man came into the lobby and walked over to him and extended his hand. The man was tall, thin, and relaxed. He smiled.

"Mr. Devereaux. It is really Mr. Devereaux?"

Devereaux did not take the extended hand and the other man let his drop naturally. He did not seem embarrassed.

"Ruckles." Devereaux's voice was not polite.

"What can I do for you?" Ruckles asked. Still pleasant, still smiling.

"Green is safe."

The lobby was crowded; workers poured into the entrance . . . Americans with briefcases, English girls with bright lipstick and wide eyes. The lobby was noisy and voices boomed.

"I'm sorry. I don't understand."

"You're blown, Ruckles." Devereaux spoke evenly, watching the Virginian for the slightest movement. There was none.

"I still don't—"

"You're a dead man, for one. I have the micro-tapes, the tape transmitter. I have Green. I don't give a fuck what kind of sleazy deal your masters have worked out with R Section. I'm playing my own game now. I have hard proof, a lawyer's proof. And when the fan gets hit, and your company has to do a little cleaning, I don't see how they can let you live. I really don't. Unless they transfer you. Maybe to Tierra del Fuego. Did you know that the CIA keeps a man there, right at the bottom of the world. They might cool you off down there until you can·get back home—in four or five years."

Ruckles smiled. "Sorry, old stick. Can you tell me what this is all about?"

"The man on the rock . . . down at the bottom of the world . . . he reports on shipping going around the cape. Mostly oil freighters. It's not too demanding."

"If you'd—"

"So long, Ruckles. Old stick."

Without a word further, Devereaux turned and started out the lobby. He pushed through the doorway and went down the stone steps to the sidewalk and ran across the street. For a moment, he glanced in the window of a shuttered pub and saw Ruckles behind him, dodging through the traffic across the street.

It was working.

The point was to make it somewhat difficult for Ruckles to follow him without actually losing the CIA man.

He reckoned Ruckles was very good at what he did.

Devereaux suddenly hailed a cab and climbed inside and ordered the driver to Picadilly Circus.

The cab joined the tail-end morning rush traffic on Regent Street which inched its way finally into the Circus.

"Go all the way around and come back up Regent to Oxford Circus and let me out," said Devereaux. The driver shrugged; Americans were a daft lot when it came to throwing their money away.

As the black cab circled the Circus, Devereaux looked behind him, but, in the welter of traffic, he could not be certain Ruckles was following him.

At Oxford Circus, Devereaux jumped from the cab ran down the steps to the London underground.

The ancient subway had a dull, damp odor of age and human neglect.

Devereaux glanced for a moment at the scheme of the London underground on a map on a subway wall.

A light blue line indicated the route of the Victoria Line, which intersected Oxford station and went on to Euston railroad station.

Euston Station had trains for Liverpool.

While he studied the map, he was aware of a man standing at the other end of the platform. He did not turn around to look at him; he was sure it was Ruckles.

A Victoria Line train rushed into Oxford station and stopped. Without hesitation, Devereaux climbed aboard; he didn't want Ruckles to miss the train either.

The doors rolled shut and the train plunged into the narrow, black tunnel that led northeast through the Bloomsbury district towards St. Pancras and Euston stations. The old cars rattled and Devereaux stood by the door, pretending to be immersed in the car cards along the windows advertising marriage services and temporary-help firms.

At Euston Station, the doors opened and Devereaux

emerged; slowly, he climbed the steps to the street and then entered Euston terminal. He needed a public place that contained a large public washroom. He needed Ruckles to think he was about to bolt.

The time was 10:24 A.M.

Seven minutes earlier, Elizabeth Campbell and the man she knew as Mr. Dennis of British Intelligence sat in a first-class compartment of the Liverpool Express as it began to inch its way out of Euston Station, heading northwest for the port city.

Mr. Dennis had been convincing.

He had displayed his identity card, which said he was a duly authorized representative of Her Majesty's government. Of course, it did not say "Secret Service" or "British Intelligence" merely "Ministry of Internal Affairs (Extraordinary)." Which, Elizabeth knew, was the current code name for the old M15.

Dennis had also been convincing when he explained the seriousness of her situation.

When they were in the buffet, sipping tea, Mr. Dennis had said she was wanted for murder in Britain. He was aware of her activities in Belfast and that she had murdered—or helped murder—an American agent named Johannsen in the Royal Avenue Hotel there. Two murders.

She listened to his voice, which was as mild as his words were harsh.

And there was now, he added, a plot against her life. One set up by Devereaux and this R Section.

No, don't protest; he was also aware of her involvement in the CIA. In short, Mr. Dennis and British Intelligence knew everything about her. She had been watched from the moment she arrived in London on Friday night; she had been observed in the week before, first in London and then in Belfast.

They knew about her and about Devereaux.

And now they knew that the CIA and R Section had

reached an agreement to cooperate and that R Section had convinced the CIA to shut down Operation Mirror. In exchange, she and Green were to be killed. Green was already dead, and both agencies were looking for her.

Denisov watched Elizabeth. She seemed to tremble but she did not look away from him. He thought she was brave.

"Miss Campbell. Elizabeth. It is now a matter of your survival that interests us."

She looked into the mild, blue eyes for a sign of a lie. But didn't Devereaux say that eyes do not betray the truth or the lie?

Devereaux would know. She had looked into his gray eyes and trusted what she saw. Until the moment the Englishwoman tried to kill her on a railway carriage in Victoria Station.

She didn't trust Dennis either. But there seemed no other way to survive. And she would survive.

"What should I do, then?"

"Miss Campbell," said Mr. Dennis. "There is a way out."

She put down her teacup. "I suspected there was."

Denisov smiled and removed his glasses and wiped them on his tie. "There is always a way. You see, Miss Campbell, we are aware of many things you do not know. Even you. And one is that your CIA intends to murder one of our prominent citizens."

"Who?"

"Lord Slough. He is the cousin of the Queen. And he is to be killed by the CIA."

"When?"

"I don't know," said Denisov. "That is what is puzzling to put the pieces together."

"I'm sorry. What did you say?"

"I said it wrong. That is what the puzzle is. The pieces are not all apparent."

"Your English . . ." She didn't finish.

He smiled and spread his hands in a shrug. "I am not

the speaker as well as I could be. You see, I am Czech by birth, though I am an English citizen now. I returned to England in 1968. After Dubcek was thrown out in my first country. Now I am an Englishman."

"I'm sorry. I didn't—"

He smiled again. "No, it is correct. I must improve my English and you can help me. Don't be afraid to be correct."

She didn't smile. She was puzzled still. "What do you want?"

"I want to know what the CIA knows. When Lord Slough is to be killed. And where."

"How can I—"

"Lord Slough is to be in Glasgow tomorrow for a football match. Do you think they will kill him there?"

"I don't—"

But Denisov interrupted. "No. I say no. But maybe it is yes. I say no but my . . . my superior says yes. So we must go to Glasgow and see. I think it wastes time but we must do what we are told. Eh?"

She was silent.

"I think they will kill Lord Slough on Wednesday in Liverpool. Do you know Liverpool?"

"No," she said. He watched her for a moment.

"A very nice city," said Denisov. "Not lovely like Edinburgh but nice with other things. With, with . . . life. Life. It is alive. It is also, unfortunately, where I think Lord Slough will die. Unless you can help me."

"Why?"

"But that's apparent," said Denisov. "If you help me, I will help you. We are friends with the CIA, even with R Section. We can stop the hunt. For you. And give you safety."

There was the word again. Safe. She wanted to be safe.

"I can't help—"

"No, no, you must. Do not let loyalty to your nation

betray you. This is not for your country, this thing that the CIA wants to do. This is a bad thing. They want to kill Lord Slough because the IRA is their puppet. It is not for America. It is for the IRA."

"I don't understand you."

"Elizabeth. You must know now that Devereaux went to Ireland for some reason. He went to find out the connection between the IRA and the CIA. The CIA is funding the Irish rebels. He thought you knew that—you know he questioned you about it."

She nodded; this man seemed to know everything. She was frightened by him, by his nonthreatening manner and his gentle voice.

"Good," said Denisov. "A true answer. Now, we know that the CIA funds the rebels but we do not know to what extent." He waited for her to accept the story but her face was expressionless. "The IRA has seriously weakened us, I admit. They command the British military budget, they have nearly destroyed the economy of Ulster, and they have created a chasm between England and the Republic . . . and that becomes more serious as the Republic grows economically. Do you see? And there is the problem the IRA causes us in the United States, among your Irish citizens. Britain is the old friend of America and it always is so. But the IRA clouds everything, even old friendships and mutual interests."

"So why is the CIA funding the IRA?"

"I don't know," said Denisov.

"It's too absurd," said Elizabeth.

"Nothing is too absurd if it is the truth."

"And you want me to go to Liverpool and do what? Or is it Glasgow?"

"Liverpool," said Denisov. "On Wednesday. Glasgow, for the sake of safety—in case my superior is correct, which I doubt—on Tuesday. To help us in our security. You know the CIA. You know your CIA men. You know the people from Free The Prisoners—yes, don't protest, we know that is a CIA front group—and we want your help in looking for them. If they are there. You will tell us and we will be able to protect Lord Slough."

"And what do I get?"

"Assurance of safety," said Denisov. "We will take the CIA assassin and trade him back to the CIA for their cooperation with us in destroying the funding for the IRA. And for letting you live."

"It seems generous."

"We are a generous people," said Denisov. "You are not helping an enemy, Miss Campbell. You are helping a friendly nation."

"But if I don't spot them. There'll be crowds. . . . If I don't see them before it's too late?"

Denisov permitted himself a frown. "Then, Elizabeth, you will be on your own. As you are now. I offer you a chance, nothing more. But it is a good chance."

"But why do they want to kill Slough?"

"Slough is not important to the CIA. He is important to the IRA, and the CIA must help them. Their gunmen are too well known by us to get into the country, let alone get close to Lord Slough. So we reason they will have a man from your agency to do the job. A killer from the CIA."

It was mad, she thought; but what choice did she have?

"What do we do then?"

"Good," said Mr. Dennis. "Good for you, Elizabeth. You choose a chance. You do not give up. We go to Euston Station now and take the train to Liverpool and we see the place where Lord Slough will be. And then we go to Glasgow for tomorrow. And we see a football match-up."

She sat for a moment and considered it. She felt cornered—by all the man had said and by all she knew was true.

This wasn't a matter of being a traitor.

It was a matter of survival.

* * *

Devereaux purchased a ticket for Liverpool at the counter and heard the agent say he had just missed the Liverpool express. The next train left in two hours.

Devereaux put the ticket stub in his pocket and slowly walked across the crowded concourse towards the sign marked *Gentlemen*.

He pushed through the door and went inside. One middle-aged man in a heavy coat stood at the end of a line of urinals. Beyond, there were six water closets. Casually, Devereaux walked along the six closets, gently pushing at the doors. They were all empty.

Devereaux opened the door of the last closet and went inside and closed it and locked it. He sat down on the closed toilet lid.

He removed the black gun from his belt and let the safety fall.

He heard water flushing in the urinals and then the door to the concourse opened. He heard a public-address announcement as the door to the concourse swung shut.

There was a step on the tiles. A cautious step.

Devereaux noisily flushed the toilet and stood up. He could not see over the top of the compartment. He turned his back on the door and put one foot and then the other on the toilet lid.

He peered over the top of the door.

Ruckles was about ten feet away, staring at the closed door with a gun in his hand.

"I'll blow the top of your head off," Devereaux began quietly. "Don't look up—keep staring at the door. Now put the gun in your pocket and walk to the door slowly. Slowly, Ruckles. Keep your hands away from your body."

Devereaux flicked off the door lock with the toe of his foot.

"Now push into the stall," said Devereaux.

It was a comic sight: Ruckles stood in the compartment, staring at Devereaux perched on the toilet lid, who was, in turn, staring down at him. The black gun was pointed at the top of Ruckles' head.

"It's crowded, old stick," said Ruckles.

Devereaux suddenly jumped down, striking Ruckles a glancing blow on the side of the head. Ruckles fell back against the door, blood on his ear.

Devereaux grabbed the lapel of his suit and spun Ruckles around, throwing him down on the toilet lid. He pushed the barrel of the black gun to the ridge between the agent's eyes.

"Why do you want to kill Lord Slough—"

"There's—"

With a slight movement, Devereaux slapped the bridge of Ruckles' nose with the gun barrel. He heard the bone crunch and blood welled at the nostrils. Ruckles instinctively moved to protect his face.

"Get your goddam hands down."

"You broke my nose."

Devereaux slapped the gun barrel at the back of one of Ruckles' hands. Again, he heard a bone break. Ruckles cried out then and tried to reach for the gun barrel. Devereaux flicked it again, this time smashing the barrel across Ruckles' mouth. Teeth cracked.

"Why does the Agency want Slough dead?"

"We don't . . ."

"You killed Hastings, you followed me to Ireland, you sent three agents after me—you bastards know about the plot on Slough. Now I want to know—"

"I don't know . . ."

Devereaux hit him again with the gun barrel, bringing it sharply down on the cheekbone below the right eye. This time, Ruckles could not keep from crying out.

"You have five seconds to live, Ruckles," said Devereaux. "Four. Three."

"The Prime Minister—"

Devereaux stopped counting.

"Tell me again."

Ruckles was crying; tears mixed with the blood ran down his face. His voice was drowned in blood.

"The Prime Minister—"

"When—"

"With Slough . . . blame the IRA . . . I—"

Wednesday. At the launch of the *Brianna* from Liverpool. The target wasn't the English lord, it was the Prime Minister of Great Britain.

"Why?"

Ruckles shook his head. His hands buried his face. He suddenly spit out blood and bits of teeth.

"Policy. I don't know. . . . North Sea oil . . . use the IRA . . ." Ruckles was babbling.

Devereaux began to understand. They had sent agents to kill him because they thought he had gotten Hastings' secret. And Hastings—clever, dead Hastings—combining information from O'Neill and from someone still in British Intelligence and from a third source—was it the CIA itself?—understood about Operation Mirror and about the CIA plot on the Prime Minister. That was why Hastings had wanted exit money—because the game would be over then; the CIA would come to kill him. Well, they had killed him.

And they thought Devereaux knew—until Sunday, when he had told Hanley about Operation Mirror and Hanley had gone to the CIA with it and the CIA had eagerly agreed to drop the operation. They knew then that Devereaux had not uncovered the real secret—the real plot— which was to murder the Prime Minister of Britain.

Devereaux thought he understood everything in that moment. Slough was not in danger; the Prime Minister was to be killed. And the IRA would do it for the Agency and would be blamed for it.

Just like the CIA game in Chile when they got Allende. And the game against Castro in Cuba—except Castro was too smart for them. And now a game against the leftist Prime Minister who already showed signs of using the North Sea oil riches to forge an independent British policy in Europe, out from under the American thumb.

"You are bastards," Devereaux said finally.

"No—" said Ruckles. He pulled down his hands now and stared at Devereaux with his broken face. "No more than you." He even managed to grin—a broken-toothed grin, his mouth filled with blood. "It's all the same—"

Devereaux fired once. Ruckles was thrown hard against the marble wall behind the toilet and then slumped to the floor.

Ruckles stared at Devereaux in death; blood ran on his face as though he were still alive, still in pain.

Splatters of blood dotted the brown corduroy coat Devereaux wore. They were wet spots but they would not be noticed when they dried. There were spots of blood on his hands as well.

Devereaux replaced the gun in his belt. His face was frozen as he stared for a moment at the body of Ruckles wedged between the toilet and a compartment wall.

He opened the door and walked quickly out of the now empty washroom. He walked across the concourse and left the station. He walked until he was too tired to walk, and then he stopped and looked around and found himself at London Bridge on the east side of the immense city. He felt tired and numb. He looked at the dried spots of blood on the backs of his hands and rubbed at them.

His eyes were old and vacant in that instant. His face was bloodless and cold.

The gray Thames surged below the place where he stood on the bridge, looking at it and at the barges on the river.

He knew that it was not useful to think of Ruckles as a human being he had just killed. He understood that death was a means or an answer to a problem, a setback in the game for one side or the other. He understood that and so did Ruckles; he knew Ruckles would have killed him just as easily. He had to kill Ruckles because the

CIA must not know that Devereaux knew the game, and so that Devereaux could find a way to survive.

It was all logical and very simple and Devereaux had accepted the logic of the game a long time before, when he had joined the Section.

A cockney woman, crossing from north to south across the span, saw the man on the sidewalk suddenly vomit onto the pavement. She thought he was drunk and wondered for a moment what pub would be open this early on a London morning.

GLASGOW

Chief Inspector Cashel of Special Branch, Dublin, had been quite wrong about the size of the crowd expected for the benefit match between the Glasgow Celtics football club and the Glasgow Rangers football club. He had told Devereaux fifty thousand would be there.

In fact, at the start of the match, 104,000 Glaswegians had crammed the stands at Ibrox Park in the middle of the old city.

But if Cashel had been wrong about the size of the crowd for Tuesday's match, he had not been wrong about the threat of violence.

As usual, the city was divided by police lines into two parts along a street running through the center of Ibrox Park.

The Celtics fans, with their green-and-white scarves, caps, jackets, and flags, came to the park from one side; the Rangers fans, with blue-and-white adornments, came from the other side. Glasgow was for the moment a city in siege. Hundreds of policemen surrounded the field; detachments of police from other boroughs and cities filled the stands. From the start of the game, there was no sound but the constant, rumbling, threatening roar of 104,000 people caught up in a frenzy of ancient rivalries and old hatreds.

The CID man assigned as liaison to Cashel had explained it (he was from Arbroath on the eastern Scottish coast but he understood the ways of Glaswegians): The Celtics were more than the Catholic team and the Rangers more than the Protestant club. For years, no Protestant dared dream of playing for the Celtics (and vice versa) and the city had been divided on match days as a security measure so that no hapless supporter of either team would find himself suddenly confronted by a mob from the other side. In which case, it was quite likely he would be stomped to death.

Cashel, when he saw the crowd streaming into the old stadium, thought it was hopeless. And when he saw Lord Slough and his daughter—surrounded by members of the Royal Cancer Society and Glasgow city officials—enter the arena and take seats prominently at midfield, he knew it was hopeless.

He had informed his own superiors Sunday night. On Monday, the special branch of the Criminal Investigation Division of Scotland Yard had detached six men to serve as liaison in setting up a plan for protection of Lord Slough. But they explained there was only so much they could do—Glasgow on match day between the two old rival teams was a bad security risk.

The game began shortly after two P.M., and by 2:34 P.M. Tommy Kedvale of the Celtics had scored a goal.

A roar like the sound of the western ocean in a gale rolled across the field.

Cashel felt useless; felt a tension that was unbearable and yet without meaning. One rifle in that crowd was all it would take to kill Slough; one killer out of all those people.

They had tried to search the crowd at the entrances and largely succeeded. They found thirty-four sets of brass knuckles, ninety-three razor knives, twelve stilletos, a hundred seventy-six coshes, and one genuine ancient medieval mace that had been stolen two years previously from the Glasgow Museum.

But no rifles and no pistols. And, near the end of the search, with the game about to start, the frantic crowd— fearful lest it miss one moment of the game—had stormed the gate, overwhelmed the search party, and seriously injured six constables.

"You see, Mr. Cashel," explained the young CID man from Arbroath, "The lads take it very seriously here." He meant the game, of course.

All during the long game, Cashel searched the hundred thousand faces of the crowd, looking for the man with glittering eyes who had been so close to him on that Saturday in Innisbally. He saw the face many times, but each time, as he rushed through the crowds toward it, the face would change—it would turn out to be just a young boy or a drunk with a dock worker's cap or someone else. Never Faolin, never the face Cashel remembered.

The match ended in late afternoon with an unsatisfactory one-to-one tie, and several fights began in the stands. Lord Slough and his party—at Cashel's urging—was hurried out of the stadium in the final minutes, to a waiting car at the special entrance.

They were a mile away when Jimmy MacLaughlin, a supporter of the Rangers for all of his sixteen years, was beaten blind by nine young men wearing the green and white of the Celtics.

Actually, the violence was very mild and there was some discussion in the Glasgow police department about instituting a weapons search as a regular feature of Celtics–Rangers match-ups.

In the evening, in the dining room of the Glasgow Grand Hotel, Denisov glanced again at his watch. "I really think we must to be in Liverpool tonight. The next train is in forty minutes."

"This is hopeless," Elizabeth said for the fourth time during the meal. Actually, she felt far from hopeless: Mr. Dennis had arranged to have her arm treated, and, though she still felt the pain of the wound, she could move it and color had returned to her fingers. She had eaten well and slept well.

"Not hopeless," said Denisov. He and Elizabeth had both been stunned by the size, noise, and general fury of the football crowd during the afternoon game. When he had dutifully asked Elizabeth to search the crowd for faces, she had even laughed.

But there had been no attempt on Lord Slough, just as Denisov predicted.

Elizabeth repeated the word "hopeless" and it was beginning to annoy him. From the start—from the moment he had followed Blatchford to Belfast—Denisov had not liked the mission. It went against everything in his nature, as though he had become Alice through the looking glass and everything had been turned upside down.

"Will there be a large crowd tomorrow morning?"

He didn't know; they had told him nothing about it. Only "complete the mission." But it was a mission incapable of completion: Devereaux had given him the slip in Belfast and no one knew where he was—though this morning the embassy had reported that three R Section agents had been dispatched from European bases to chase down Devereaux in London. If only they had been more open with him in the beginning, had given him more authority to deal with Devereaux as he wanted.

Angrily, he bit a piece of bread. His blue eyes clouded. Stupid bureaucrats. What did they know about the field? About conducting a mission where the rules changed moment by moment?

"Aren't you ever going to speak, Mr. Dennis?"

Looking up, Denisov regarded the pale woman across the white table from him. Mata Hari. If the worst thing happened—if the IRA assassinated Slough and the others —then Mata Hari would die too. And be found, complete with her identity as an agent of the Central Intelligence Agency, as evidence of their involvement.

"I am thinking about tomorrow, Elizabeth. You must not fail." He took his glass of wine and sipped at it and looked at her.

They had put him in this position. He did not want to

harm Elizabeth. Wasn't she like Nasha, his younger sister? Why did they want Denisov to kill women? Even a spy.

He made a face.

Bureaucrats. They had botched it at the embassy from the beginning. Now they tell him they knew about the mirror operation from the first. How typical of the Russian mind not to trust anyone, even one's own agent. And so Denisov had blundered in his contacts with Devereaux and O'Neill; they had wandered around Belfast like blind sheep, playing at a game none of them understood.

Denisov threw his bread down on the tablecloth. "There will not be too many people, Elizabeth. It is for the press. Who wants to see a boat go in the water? That is what boats always do. Very much in Liverpool."

"Perhaps they won't kill him. There," she finished it. "Perhaps you're wrong."

No, Elizabeth. No more perhaps. They had been very specific about that at the embassy. The assassination of Lord Slough and the Prime Minister was set for tomorrow morning by the CIA; somehow, it must be prevented, and at the same time, blame still placed on the CIA. How was Denisov to do that? They didn't know, but he must.

So there would be shots. Perhaps. And Elizabeth Campbell would die too, and when they found her, with the pistol, they would know she had come to kill Lord Slough and there would be a problem for the Central Intelligence Agency.

Did they think Denisov was a tightrope walker?

Prevent the assassination. If you cannot prevent it, be certain the CIA is blamed.

He could not prevent it, he was sure of that. One cannot prevent such things.

But the CIA would be blamed and perhaps that would be enough for them at the embassy.

He glanced at his watch again. They would be late for the train. He looked up and Elizabeth was now hurriedly sipping her coffee.

His eyes looked on her softly, almost fondly.

"No, Elizabeth," he said in a gentle voice. "I am sorry to be rude. Do not hurry. Enjoy your meal. Have wine. Here, let me pour another glass for you. There will be another train. We will get to Liverpool."

It was the least he could do.

At nine P.M., Devereaux—certain that Green was alone —made a signal to him by tapping at the glass window of the buffet.

Green had changed in two days on the run. His face was thinner, his hair wildly combed, his eyes staring and frightened. He grabbed his small valise and left the buffet.

For a moment, the two men stood on the grimy concourse of Lime Street Station and confronted each other in silence. Devereaux gazed steadily at Green until the latter's eyes looked away.

"Did you talk to anyone?"

"No."

"No one?"

Green looked again at him. "No."

"All right, then. There's still a chance."

"For what? I didn't think you'd be here. I—"

"Shut up." Devereaux glanced up and down the nearly empty concourse. "There's a room registered in the name of Andrew Cummings in the Adelphi Hotel. I want you to go there and wait. Sleep if you can. You'll have visitors before morning."

"Who?"

"None of your goddam business," said Devereaux. "When they come, they'll introduce themselves. You're to tell them everything. About the recruitment, about the CIA, about Operation Mirror. When they're satisfied, they're going to take you—"

"Who are they? What are you doing?"

"Nothing. Except save your miserable life. Do exactly as I tell you."

"Is there anything not to tell them?"

"No," said Devereaux steadily. "Tell them about Elizabeth, about the safe house, about the four o'clock train to Dover. If you lie to them, they will kill you. If you tell them the truth, you'll live."

"Who are they?"

"Agents."

"From where?"

"British Intelligence. We have a deal with them."

"What kind of a deal?"

"A deal that gives you your life."

"You didn't do this for me——"

"I did it for myself, you little shit," said Devereaux. "But to save my skin, I have to save yours. Now do what I told you."

"But what will they do to me?"

"Take you someplace. Debrief you. And let you go. The difference being that you'll be safe."

"How?"

"Because I'm taking care of it. I told you there was a deal. Now go. And wait. The Adelphi is at the end of Lime Street, about a long block up the road."

"What was the name?"

Devereaux looked at him as though he were looking at an insect; his contempt was no longer concealed. Two days on the run had convinced Green that he was not cut out for the spy's game, that only Devereaux would save him.

"Andrew Cummings," said Devereaux. "Now get out of here."

Obediently, Green disappeared into the street beyond the concourse entrance.

Brianna Devon awoke at midnight and cried out. Of course no one heard her; her room was dark and sound-proof and she was alone. Her father slept in a suite down the hallway; the hallway itself was patrolled by six Liverpool policemen and three men from Special Branch, CID, Scotland Yard. But no one heard her.

In the dream, her father's face had been covered with blood. His eyes were open and he was not yet dead. He had tried to speak to her but she could not hear his voice.

In the other part of the dream, she saw Deirdre Monahan as she had been. Deirdre had smiled to her from across the great lawn at Clare House, and beckoned to her.

When Brianna began to run across the lawn, Deirdre had run away from her. Everything was silent in the dream. There was no wind and the time of day was in the brilliant twilight of summer that covered the Clare hills.

"I love you," she had cried in the dream to Deirdre.

Then she had seen her father's face, covered in blood; she had screamed in the dream, actually screamed aloud; it had awakened her.

Her hands were wet; her face felt flushed. The room, however, was cool and dark and without sound, except for the white noise of all the thousand parts of the hotel.

She had had the same dream since they had tried to kill her father.

Elizabeth dozed in the comfortable seat in the first-class compartment. When she awoke—for no reason—she saw Denisov across from her, staring at her. He looked sad and a little tired.

"Why don't you sleep, Mr. Dennis?" she asked. She felt the tiredness of the wine come over her again.

"Because I do not sleep," he said.

There was an intense clarity to the air on the last night of November that was rare for early winter in England. The moon was fine and full and voluptuous; the light of the moon was clear and shivery on the city.

In the intense silence, the Mersey meekly lapped at the concrete apron.

In the white, ghostly light of the moon, the immense form of the hovercraft sat still; the light cast a giant shadow in the half-darkness. Six propellers were poised on their shafts on the upper deck; three fore and three aft. They looked like Dutch windmills lined up for parade.

Cashel paced from the front of the dignitaries' stand with its separate British and Irish flags to the ship and back. Even in the darkness, he could see how it would be in the morning.

Lord Slough would stand alone, speaking; beside him, Brianna Devon; next to them, the Taoiseach peering through his gold-rimmed spectacles; and next to him the Prime Minister of Great Britain.

All behind the bulletproof plastic shields that now circled the platform.

Everything that could be done had been done. There could not be an assassination; yet, assassination was so easy in a disordered society.

Cashel puffed his pipe and stepped again across the apron as he had paced so many times around the perimeter of old St. Stephen's Green in Dublin. He paced to consider the possibilities, to find a flaw in the scheme in his thoughts.

He had been foolishly wrong about Glasgow.

Pray God he was wrong about tomorrow.

He heard a footstep on the apron behind him; suddenly, he turned. A man came towards him; a sailor by his walk.

Cashel waited and watched him.

"What are ye doin' round this place?" the man asked. His voice snarled; he sounded a little drunk.

"What are ye doing?" Cashel returned. "I'm the police."

"Ah. I'm with the engineering section, comin' t'see me *Brianna*."

"Yer are?" Cashel removed the pipe from his mouth and knocked out the ashes on the side of his palm. Sparks flew from the bowl like sparks from a dying rocket.

"I been here since the first. Since she was launched for trials. She's a grand ship, isn't she?"

The drunken man weaved and spread his arms in the moonlight. The extent of his arms encompassed the *Brianna* sitting moodily in the gray light.

"She is," said Cashel.

"Me ship," said Donovan, not looking at him.

Cashel did not speak.

"Ah, well. I'm t'bed now. I've had me bit of fun. T'morrow is the day, eh?"

"It is that."

Donovan weaved near him. "Yer Irish."

"I am."

"Ah," said Donovan. "Yer didn't speak like a bloody Sassenach."

"I'm glad to hear it," Cashel smiled, watching as Donovan weaved away, across the apron and into the street leading down the road back to the center of Liverpool.

Cashel turned to look back at the bulk of the ship.

In eleven hours, she would be at sea, beyond the breakwater; then it would be safe and he could go back home to Dublin and his old bed.

Pray God.

"God save ourrrr gracious Queen—"

The old woman's thin voice croaked the words as the first notes of the British anthem—ponderous and slow—boomed across the concrete apron to the waiting throng. Though the police band was not precise in instrumentation, it contained a full complement of strong young lungs and every note sounded loudly enough to be heard above the whine of the high wind.

The calm of the night before had changed at dawn. Now, a force-six wind, wet and cold, swept down the Mersey from the Irish Sea and sent stinging droplets of spray onto the launch site. The river Mersey's waters were black and troubled and they roiled and slapped against the concrete pier.

"Send herrrr victorious—"

The old woman's voice was lost in the wind; she sang with her hand over her heart and her eyes glistened. She was a little drunk. The others in the small crowd of less than a hundred persons did not join her but stood silently while the anthem boomed on, the sounds of the band waxing and waning as the wind shifted.

It was fit weather for the first of December, which is to say it was not fit at all.

Predictably, the ceremony started fifteen minutes late. There were all the usual problems—the police band lost the music for the Irish anthem and then found it; the Taoiseach's flight from Dublin was delayed by bad weather

319

on that side of the sea; the Prime Minister's driver got lost in the spider's web of streets in central Liverpool; and there was a minor arrest at the edge of the crowd twenty minutes before the ceremonies were due to begin.

It was a footnote, really, to what would happen in the next sixty minutes. Though none of them knew it at the time.

Two men from British Intelligence—now called the Ministry for Internal Affairs (Extraordinary)—seized a young man with light red hair as he entered a two-story warehouse building six hundred yards from the dock site. The man protested his arrest until the agents discovered the broken-down parts of an M16-A rifle strapped to the inside of his thighs. Whereupon he refused to speak further.

(In fact, it was nearly twelve hours before he was identified as Michael Pendurst, twenty-six, from Hamburg, West Germany, a wanted terrorist last seen in Copenhagen. Two days later—after further examination and extreme questioning—he admitted he had been a contract employee of the Central Intelligence Agency for eighteen months, specializing in waste disposal, the CIA term for hit jobs.)

The British anthem ended and the last notes were blown away in the wind. For a moment, the trumpets hesitated and then—band music cards secured—the Liverpool police band began the strains of the anthem of Eire.

They all stood on the platform and waited politely for the music to end—Lord Slough and his daughter, Brianna Devon; the Taoiseach of Eire; the Prime Minister of Britain; the Duke of Kensington (and second cousin to the Queen); and the Secretary of the powerful Trades Union Council.

The people in the throng could not see them clearly because of the flecks of spray on the bulletproof plastic shield around the platform. The press contingent—especially the cameramen from BBC—had complained about the plastic shield around the dignitaries from the first but, even with the arrest of a gunman entering the warehouse a quarter-mile away, the police refused to remove it.

In fact, the arrest of the CIA assassin in no way lessened the anxiety felt at that moment by Chief Inspector Cashel.

For fifteen minutes, he had stood—his back to the platform—restlessly surveying the crowd of spectators and the roped-off section reserved for first-class passengers waiting to board the hovercraft. But the face he sought was not there in the crowd; the black, glittering eyes he dreamed about disappeared in daylight.

The roofs of the low buildings around the apron were filled with policemen walking back and forth. Cashel saw policemen in every doorway. More than a thousand police from Liverpool, from surrounding cities, and from as far away as Manchester and Birmingham had been called in during the previous twelve hours as protection for the distinguished panel on the platform. Everything that could be done had been done. An attempt to persuade the Prime Minister to cancel his appearance failed when that gentleman made a ringing speech about not living in fear of death and not letting terrorists dictate the terms of his life.

Fortunately, they had caught the assassin. Everything had worked out precisely—as Devereaux had informed them it would.

Why this anxiety then on Cashel's part?

Because there was no Faolin in the plot, no Faolin anywhere. Had they miscalculated, then? Did Faolin and his crowd intend to kill Lord Slough in Ireland, back at Clare House? Was Faolin merely scouting the territory on the Saturday Cashel saw him at Deirdre Monahan's funeral?

So it appeared now. So everyone in the British security branch believed. Devereaux—the American agent—had contacted British Intelligence and convinced them that Slough's life was not in danger and that the assassination attempt was not aimed at him but at the Prime Minister of Britain.

Devereaux was proved right by the arrest of the assassin earlier. Cashel was wrong—doubly wrong if one counted the fiasco in Glasgow. It was an embarrassment to all—six of the undercover policemen in the crowd at the Glasgow football match had been injured in random fights that broke out from time to time during the game. Two others were missing, and since they were both native Glaswegians, it was presumed they had decided to abandon police work for the perils of becoming professional Scottish football fans.

Cashel was aware that the music had ceased, and he could hear now the clipped tones of Lord Slough vainly trying to be heard over the faulty public-address system.

First-class passengers—again, Cashel surveyed them as he had done a dozen times before. Ordinary people, every one. No face stared back at him as it had at the funeral in Clare; no glittering eye caught his.

Cashel shivered. He would not feel safe until they were all in the ship, until it was launched. Then it would be over until they reached Eire.

Faolin had spotted Cashel immediately. There was a moment of panic and Faolin had considered dashing towards the platform and killing as many of them as he could before he was himself killed. Then he remembered the transmitter in his shirt pocket and he relaxed. Even if they took him, he would have time to destroy the ship and all aboard it.

He had walked past Cashel, back to the crowd and his police post. The police uniform he wore fit perfectly as Parnell had said it would. Beneath his tunic coat, he felt the comfortable coldness of the M11 tied to his belt.

Then Cashel had stopped him. He froze, looked down.

"Pardon, Constable. Would ye be havin' a match?"

"I'm sorry," Faolin muttered. "Don't smoke." Though

frightened, he had the presence of mind to change his accent to a rough approximation of Liverpudlian singsong.

"Ah, thank ye, anyway," said Cashel, who had turned away without really looking at him. They had only glanced at each other for a moment, but Faolin realized Cashel had not seen him but, rather, had seen the uniform. Because he did not expect Faolin to wear police dress, he had not seen the man he was looking for.

He is a fool, Faolin thought.

He waited through the ceremony impatiently, glancing now and then at the platform. Lord Slough was speaking, with Brianna standing beside him, watching him.

Easy now, Faolin boyo. He knew Tatty would soothe him that way and calm his nerves. It wasn't fear; Faolin wasn't afraid. It was anxiety of the kind he once felt as a child on the night before Christmas, filled with expectation that something great was about to happen.

When the time came, the ship would explode into a million pieces. It was merciful, really. The dead would not even be aware of the moment of death. Eternity would be as unexpected as sunlight in the rain.

Faolin smiled to himself. Mercy. He wondered what would come after? War? Would the Irish finally be forced to throw off the last vestiges of British dominion? Chaos? Yes, chaos, the enemy of Britain. Would they be aware of what had happened?

"Hey now, copper, how about movin' aside so's we can see what the bleedin' hell is goin' on?"

It was a moment before he realized the voice in the crowd was directed at him.

"I got me orders, mate."

"Ah," said the man with the cloth cap. "Give us a break."

So Faolin, merciful and smiling, moved aside so they could see better. Faolin glanced at the platform: Lord Slough was introducing the Prime Minister of Britain.

It was his last speech. Faolin had terrible knowledge of all that was to come. It must be the way God feels, he decided.

The Prime Minister of Great Britain spoke for six minutes and then sat down to a smattering of applause. He had spoken not so much for the ragtag crowd on the apron but for *The Nine O'Clock News* and *The World Tonight*. The secretary to the Taoiseach had carefully timed the Prime Minister's speech, to be sure that the leader of the Republic of Eire would speak just as long.

Lord Slough gestured to the Taoiseach, and he arose to a smattering of applause as well—after all, Liverpool had plenty of Irish living in it.

The Taoiseach began.

Denisov, standing in the rear of the section cordoned off for first-class passengers, felt nervously in his pocket for the small gun. It was cold in his grasp. He told himself again he would not permit such a situation in the future; he was getting too old for the tension. In the future, his masters would have to speak more openly with him about the mission.

He still held Elizabeth's arm with his other hand.

Elizabeth had seen no one in the crowd, and Denisov —whom she still thought was Mr. Dennis of British Intelligence—seemed disappointed and on edge. But he had whispered, "It's all right. It will be all right." He soothed her as though she were a child.

In a curious way, she trusted Mr. Dennis.

Denisov rehearsed what must be done. It must be done, he knew; but it sickened him. He would take the pistol from the pocket and press it closely to Elizabeth's breast just as the shots began from the assassins. Her left breast. It would only take a moment and the little sound of the pistol—muffled by her coat and his bulk pressed against her—would be lost in the general panic of the moment. She would die instantly; he promised her that. There might be a moment of surprise but not of pain. And then

Denisov would cry out, create more panic, and press the pistol in her dead hand.

That morning, he had removed the pistol from his pocket while still in the hotel room and doubled a pillow on the bed and fired twice into it. When the police found the pistol in her hand, there would be three shots fired from it, one into her own body. She would be seen as part of the assassination team, though they would not find the other two bullets.

He had already put the card into the pocket of her coat —the one from Free The Prisoners. Even the English would be able to guess that she was a CIA agent.

Last night, Elizabeth had finished all her wine; that made Denisov feel better about the task that lay ahead. She had seemed even relaxed and had smiled at him once, on the train to Liverpool, when she had awakened from her nap and saw him watching her.

It was true. Denisov never slept. Two hours last night, one hour the night before. They had diagnosed it at the Lenin Institute as chronic insomnia and explained it was not curable; but they had reassured him that their research on sleep patterns indicated a great number of people were like Denisov, and those people—once freed from feelings of guilt about their insomnia—managed to function normally and keep their health.

He looked at Elizabeth, still searching the crowd. He liked her.

Denisov wanted to sleep. He yearned for it as a child yearns for an unobtainable toy. But there were too many matters to think about and too much to keep sleep at bay. Now there was the matter with Elizabeth, whom he did not hate or even know very well.

He suddenly thought of Devereaux. Why had he lied to Denisov about her? Why had he said he'd killed her? Why did Devereaux care for her? It complicated the matter.

The speeches were finished at last.

The bottle of champagne—Moet Brut 1948—swung on

the rope away from Brianna's hand and traveled a lazy arc in the wind to the prow of the immense hovercraft.

"I name thee *Brianna*," she said in a thin, emotional voice.

The bottle struck the prow and bounced back, unbroken, dangling at the end of the rope. There was laughter from the crowd of spectators and first-class passengers. Even the Taoiseach, a man of great gravity, managed a smile.

P. C. Parnell broke ranks, went to the bottle dangling over the edge of the platform, and brought it back and handed it to Brianna Devon. She smiled at him pleasantly.

The arrest of the gunman in the warehouse had frightened her at first and then calmed her; maybe the threat against her father was past. Now, exposed on the platform, in the shivering wind, she felt afraid again.

Brianna launched the bottle again and it flew on the arc dictated by the length of rope and this time it crashed solidly against the short prow of the ungainly craft, smashing with a pop and clatter of broken glass on the concrete apron where the ship rested. Again there was applause, but even as it died, the dignitaries began to descend the platform slowly. At the same moment, the first of the passengers were led to the narrow hatch at the side of the hull. In ten minutes, the *Brianna* would be underway.

Brianna Devon took her father's arm as he led her down the rickety steps of the platform. Soon they would be safe at sea, on their way home back to Ireland.

Denisov was in panic. He did not understand.

For a moment, he stood stupidly staring at the first passengers moving towards the craft.

The ceremony was over and nothing had happened; there had been no shots. What must he do now?

He reached for the pistol in his pocket.

There had been no instructions but he understood the alternative.

He must kill Elizabeth and get away. It was botched by someone but he had to separate himself from her.

Why kill her?

He looked again at her face.

Think clearly, you have the gun. Kill her or let her go?

The crowd of passengers around him began to surge forward. Now. He must move now.

"What should we do?" asked Elizabeth.

At that moment, two men neatly separated them. Denisov's arm fell from hers. He looked up, bewildered.

"Pardon, sir," the pleasant man said. He was dressed in a dark coat and hat. "Would you come this way, sir?"

"I?" It was stupid. He felt he was stuttering. "I am a passenger—"

"Won't take a minute, sir, come this way—"

"I—" It was absurd.

"Those gentlemen would like to speak to you for a moment, please," the pleasant man said. They had pinned Denisov neatly between them.

Denisov and Elizabeth glanced away to the edge of the apron. They both saw Devereaux in the same instant.

Elizabeth quietly broke away. The two men ignored her. "You're to come with us, sir," the pleasant one said. His grip tightened and Denisov felt pain. Elizabeth moved away in the sea of people. Of course, he thought. She fears Devereaux; she thinks Devereaux wants to kill her.

Denisov suddenly smiled and allowed the two men to lead him across the apron. At least it was resolved; they couldn't blame him. The stupid business was over and he did not have to kill the woman.

He saw Elizabeth disappear through the hatch into the hovercraft. Now she was safe, he thought. It's just as well.

Five feet from Devereaux and the waiting men from British Intelligence, Denisov smiled. "Hello, Devereaux."

Devereaux did not return the smile. "This is Denisov. The Soviet agent in this. He's attached to their embassy in London but he's with the KGB."

"Really, Devereaux, this is not like a sport," said
Denisov. He raised his arms while they patted him down.
They removed the pistol. He felt relieved.

"Unsportsmanlike," said Devereaux.

"Yes. Sorry. Unsportsmanlike."

"Where's Elizabeth Campbell?" Devereaux asked.

"I don't know what you are talking about," said
Denisov. "I am a member of the Soviet Embassy and my
government shall protest my treatment."

"Shut it off, Denisov," said the man next to Devereaux.
He might have been Devereaux's brother—his face shared
the same cold, pale quality—but his accent was staunchly
London.

"I refuse to speak further," Denisov said.

"Where's Elizabeth?" Devereaux said.

"Is she another agent?" the Russian asked.

"There was a woman near him sir," said the pleasant
man. "We didn't know about her—we didn't—"

"Where did she go?"

"She was with the other passengers, sir—"

Devereaux started across the apron for the hovercraft
hatchway.

Journalists now crowded the entrance to the hovercraft,
snapping photos of the Taoiseach and Prime Minister
shaking hands. There were also photos of Brianna Devon
at the door, and the man from the *Daily Mirror* asked her
to show more leg. She politely refused and the man from
the *Sunday People* got his leg shot by lying flat on the
ground at her feet.

Cashel stood by the platform and watched it all. It had
not happened, all he feared.

Spray damped his pipe.

Damned wind. He reached in his pocket absently for a
box of matches and then realized he had been matchless
all morning. Nothing seemed to work out right. Had to
ask three people to get a light.

The immense propellers began to run, slowly. The draft
of wind behind them created little waves on the rain of

the pavement. The turbines whined hideously. The *Brianna* began to shake.

Cashel knocked his pipe out against the platform. It was hopeless now to think of lighting it. No one had a match and in all this wind—

"My God," he cried.

He opened his mouth and he dropped his pipe at the same time and the pipe clattered on the apron, shattering into a dozen pieces.

Cashel saw the young constable with dark eyes under the helmet and he saw again the narrow chin and lantern jaw and—

Faolin.

He was vaguely aware another man was rushing across the empty apron.

The Prime Minister had disappeared through the hatch door and the ground crew was closing it.

"No, no," he cried against the wind but he could not be heard. He began to run.

Suddenly, he pulled his silver pistol from the pocket of his coat and fired into the air. The shot sounded like a light bulb exploding, short and sharp. One of the crew members turned and shouted at him. Another fell to the pavement and put his hands over his head.

"No, no—"

He saw police run towards him. Some had drawn guns.

"They're aboard, the killers—"

From high in the cockpit, the pilot of the *Brianna* saw the wild man below brandishing a pistol and ordered the mate to lock the cockpit door.

Faolin reached the cockpit as the door closed. Cursing, he pulled the M11 from beneath the police tunic and fitted a forty-round slice of bullets into the magazine. He fired a short burst at the door and destroyed the lock.

Everything happened at once.

In the passenger compartment—down the stairs and on the other side of the hatchway—a woman screamed as Tatty rose and displayed his machine gun.

Elizabeth whirled at the scream and saw Tatty raise the rifle. She was at the front of the compartment and was knocked to the floor by a large man rushing in panic to the passageway.

Tatty turned to face the hatch just as Cashel pushed through.

He fired a short burst.

Bullets struck Cashel in the chest and flung him back, through the hatch, into the surging wedge of police behind him. Several fell. There was blood on blue uniforms. The panicked passengers screamed and pushed towards the passage. More shots sounded from the pilot's cockpit.

Faolin slammed into the cockpit. He started to speak but the pilot—a large, beefy-faced man—jumped up and leaped at him, pushing aside the machine gun as though it were a walking stick.

Faolin's finger was glued to the trigger. The blow from the pilot set off an involuntary burst of fire that blew up part of the instrument panel.

"I got him! I got him!" the pilot cried.

Faolin brought the gun down in a sudden move; he gouged at the pilot's eyes with the barrel.

The first mate backed away in horror: "He's pointed at me, he's pointed at me! Get the gun, get the gun!"

Faolin fired a short burst. The blinded pilot was flung back against the control board. More popping noises issued from the exploding instruments.

Faolin panicked and turned: It wasn't working, it wasn't working. And then he remembered the radio transmitter in his tunic.

At that moment, Devereaux pushed aside the body of Cashel blocking the hatch and entered the chaotic, screaming interior of the ship.

He saw Elizabeth stare at him, soundless, her mouth open as though to scream. And then he saw Tatty and fired at him without a thought.

The bullet struck a fat man behind Tatty who went down in blood.

Tatty fired a burst at the door and Devereaux fell back, out of the way.

Everything happened in the same second.

Lord Slough, who had led the party of dignitaries to the deck situated above the cockpit, appeared on the stairs near the shattered cockpit door.

Faolin turned to him and pointed the machine gun at him.

A policeman burst into the ship from the apron, firing blindly at the passenger compartment. He struck two women and wounded Tatty. Tatty cried out and squeezed the trigger. The clip was empty. The policeman fired once more and tore Tatty's face off.

Faolin squeezed the trigger even as he turned to the new sound of firing coming from the hatch twenty feet away. One bullet struck Brianna Devon in the neck, behind her father. She fell without screaming.

The second, third, and fourth bullets sprayed the passageway as the gun turned. The fifth struck the policeman in the left shoulder. The force of the bullet flung him into the passenger compartment. He fell at Elizabeth's feet.

She reached across his body for the gun. Her face was white, her eyes wide with madness and fear.

Faolin fired once more.

At that moment, Devereaux appeared again in the hatch. The force of Faolin's blast split wood on the paneling in the passenger compartment. The smell of blood, smoke, and powder choked the ship. Screaming filled their ears.

Devereaux fired twice. The second bullet shattered Faolin's jaw, splintering bone and sending fragments of tendon into his mouth. He choked on his blood and vomited suddenly in the incredible pain, and he squeezed off the last of the forty rounds.

Devereaux fired his last shot, sending the surging bullet into Faolin's fallen body.

Lord Slough was crying aloud: "Brianna! Brianna!"

Blood bathed Brianna's dress.

Elizabeth pointed the pistol at Devereaux. He turned and looked at her and raised his pistol and pulled the trigger. There was a click. She stared at him for a second then threw the gun at him.

As he ducked aside, he saw that Faolin was not dead.

The terrorist moaned, reached into his tunic. His hands were bloody.

Devereaux looked around him for a weapon. He could not see the gun Elizabeth had thrown.

Faolin drew out a box.

Devereaux saw what it was. He had seen such things. He had used such things. He suddenly smashed his hand against the glass box holding the fire ax. The glass shattered and cut him. Blood flowed from a dozen wounds.

He took down the ax and started up the stairs.

Faolin, his face twisted with pain and made grotesque by the red mask of blood, stared at him. He dropped the box and then reached for it again. They would still remember this moment, this—

Devereaux swung the ax down hard and severed Faolin's outstretched hand at the wrist. Blood now spurted onto the carpeting from opened arteries and veins, and the bloody stump foamed with redness.

The severed hand lay half open, the box cradled in the nest of fingers.

Faolin died as he felt the shock of the blow.

26

WASHINGTON

Hanley made the report twice; first to the Old Man, and then repeated it to the National Security Council, at the insistence of the President of the United States.

Of course, not one word of the report was taken down; it was an oral exercise, for information and not for history. Hanley did not have to refer to notes. As usual, he remembered everything, from the moment Devereaux had met with him at the prizefight in Madison Square Garden to the moments of death aboard the *Brianna*.

It was an extraordinary story and no one interrupted at the Security Council meeting. And it was mostly true.

Of course, the Old Man had convinced Hanley that the decision to eliminate Devereaux would be . . . well . . . eliminated from the report. There was no point in bringing up such business; it only served to cloud the matter. And the fact that Devereaux appeared to be something of a hero to the British changed things. Hanley understood.

So Hanley made his report with only a few deletions. He even reported honestly about Green. Green had been a double agent for the CIA and he had taken part in at least two murders on British soil. He was currently being held for trial and would doubtless be sentenced to life in prison. Green had been a bad apple, a mole, and a murderer.

Of course, the chief of the CIA squirmed during the long recitation, delivered in a precise, dry tone by Hanley in the National Security Council meeting room. None of the story was very pleasant to the CIA.

During Hanley's recitation about Operation Mirror, the President glared at the CIA man at the table; it was apparent that the CIA needed R Section just as much today as it had in Kennedy's time, the President said at one point.

The CIA said nothing. They had considered protesting that a deal had been made with R Section, but that seemed absurd in light of what the CIA saw as the Section's double-cross.

Because Operation Mirror involved illegal activities and crimes committed on British soil—the murder of Hastings, the murders of Blatchford and Johannsen and Ruckles, and the attempt to murder both Devereaux and Elizabeth Campbell—Devereaux had cooperated fully with British police, Hanley reported.

In addition, Devereaux's activities—approved fully by Chief of Section and Hanley—had resulted in the arrest of one Dmitri Denisov, a Soviet agent. He had been expelled to Moscow.

And there was the matter of Michael Pendurst, recruited by the CIA, who had been arrested at the launch of the hovercraft *Brianna*. He was currently awaiting trial in London on charges of attempted murder.

At that point, the CIA man denied Pendurst worked for them.

Hanley quietly passed a report from the Ministry for Interior Affairs (Extraordinary) across the table. The President did not glance at it but kept his gray eyes fixed coldly on the flustered CIA man. He had seen the report based on the interrogation of Pendurst.

Finally, there was the matter of the attempts to kill the heads of two great allied powers, Eire and Great Britain.

The CIA had known all along about the IRA plot (another protest from the CIA man at the table, but the President told him to shut up) and had helped finance it in hopes of blaming the IRA when they made their move to murder the leftist Prime Minister of Great Britain.

"Leftist" was Hanley's touch; it turned the dagger. The President himself was considered a "leftist" by some.

Hanley recited the proof of CIA funding for the IRA— or for some elements of it. Again, British Intelligence had gained the proof from certain tapes, equipment, and notes of agents of other countries which had come into their possession.

"Goddam," said one of the men at the table in a deep Southern accent. "Gawwwwwwwwwdam!" He was one of the President's internal security advisors. "Them English boys really got something on the ball, ain't they?"

And Hanley wanted to say, *Yes. His name is Devereaux.*

Hanley did not speak of that, however; he continued to recite the events of the morning of December first in Liverpool: How Chief Inspector Cashel of Special Branch, Dublin, was shot to death by the terrorists as he entered the hovercraft; how the terrorist named James Faolin was killed by Devereaux at the last moment and of the later discovery of five hundred pounds of gelignite aboard the craft; of the wounds inflicted on passengers and crew—six dead and nineteen wounded, among the wounded Brianna Devon, daughter of Lord Slough, who suffered partial vocal paralysis from a bullet in the throat.

The President listened to it all thoughtfully, and his eyes never left the CIA man. Hanley was aware of that but he did not look up; he spoke confidently and slowly, precisely and without emotion. He knew how to make a report.

The British and Irish governments had protested, formally and quietly, to the President concerning the illegal activities of the Central Intelligence Agency in their countries. The President of the United States had been forced to apologize.

"Apologize," he repeated now, as he stared at the CIA man.

Hanley waited but the President had no more to say.

When it was over, Hanley and the Old Man walked back to the Agriculture building from the Executive Office Building. It was a pleasant walk, because, again, winter had been stayed by the gentle winds from Virginia. Only the trees of Washington seemed a little more bare, a little sadder.

They did not speak at first; it was late afternoon.

"We weren't wrong, you know, about Devereaux. He should have kept us informed," the Old Man said at last.

Hanley nodded but did not speak. They walked on in silence.

"We've got our opening to Brit Intell," Galloway said. "It was what we wanted."

"British Intelligence," Hanley said. "I detest slang."

And the old man glanced at him curiously as they walked along.

Of course, Green had been the key to Devereaux's plan to survive and to sabotage the CIA at the same time. It was Green who finally convinced British Intelligence that Devereaux was correct and that the whole wild story was plausible and even true. It was Green who, indirectly, moved C (as the British Intelligence commander was still called) to order the extraordinary alert of police and special-branch forces during the night which had resulted in the capture of the CIA hit man from Hamburg.

Green trusted Devereaux and followed his instructions. He told British Intelligence the truth to save his life.

They had taken him—the night before the *Brianna* launch—to the police station in Dale Street at Hatton Gardens in the center of the old city of Liverpool. He told them all: About Operation Mirror and about his part in it; about the attempt on the life of Elizabeth Campbell on the Dover train (and his part in it); and about Devereaux's mission to Scotland and Ulster. He told them about the tape-transmitter box in Blake House. Yes, he knew about Hastings' death, from Ruckles.

They had been very quiet and polite. Ruckles?

Green was expansive. They were treating him famously, in the finest British manner. These were his people, the sort of civilized men he felt at home with. They offered him tea. He did not notice that their faces had become drawn and their eyes become small and cold.

Ruckles was the CIA man. He told them about Ruckles.

When had he last seen Ruckles?

Not seen, actually. Heard. On the telephone. Sunday night.

Come now. He had seen Ruckles on Monday certainly.

Not at all. He was in Cambridge on Monday.

Really? For what purpose?

Devereaux had told him to wait in Cambridge.

The three men from the Ministry for Interior Affairs (Extraordinary) glanced at each other and then again at Green, who sat smiling in the corner of the small room in the basement of the central police station.

The tea was cold and Green put down his cup.

"We put it to you that you murdered Ruckles," one said quietly.

"What?"

"This belongs to you." And they produced a black gun —Devereaux's gun, Green realized—the gun he had pointed at Green that Sunday night he came to kill him at Blake House.

"Not mine, no—"

"It was in your room at the Adelphi Hotel."

"Now—"

"Ruckles was found murdered in the gents at Euston Station on Monday afternoon. He was shot once. With his pistol. And you knew him well."

Green looked from face to face and saw only hard men.

"That's Devereaux's gun—"

"Nonsense. You had it. In your room. You knew

Ruckles. He was your contact. You said you had been angry with Ruckles because the company wouldn't take you in after Operation Mirror was blown."

Green frowned.

"You are an espionage agent, operating outside your embassy in Great Britain, and you have admitted complicity in one attempt at murder, knowledge after the fact of a second murder—that's Hastings—and now you wish to deny your involvement in the murder of Ruckles?"

Green opened his mouth to protest but no words came. He suddenly understood that Devereaux kept his bargain —his bargain with R Section and his bargain with Green. As he promised, Green would not die. He would live. But he would be eliminated.

He tried to laugh.

There were no public executions in Britain any longer. Green would live. Safe. In Her Majesty's prisons. For the rest of his life.

27

FRONT ROYAL

A cover of snow lay lightly on the mountains. And there was mist as well, so thick that they closed Skyline Drive along the Blue Ridge Mountains.

You could not see to the top of the Blue Ridge Mountains south of the little town.

They bought groceries in the little store where Devereaux always went, and the owners said it had been a long time no see, and was he stayin' a while?

Devereaux nodded then and the grocer looked at the woman with her pale face and dark, luminous eyes. Because Virginians form a polite society in the mountains, the old man did not ask about her but merely smiled and nodded to her.

They drove out of the town along a road that ran through the valley and led to the hills. Two miles beyond Front Royal, they found the rutted dirt road that led up to his mountain.

Devereaux had told Elizabeth they could see the Shenandoah River from the top of the mountain. He said there were bears and wild deer in the virgin forests along both sides of the road.

There had been a light rain in the valley; now they drove up to the light snow covering the mountains. There were tracks of animals in the snow, animals scurrying for the last bit of forage against the winter. Devereaux drove slowly through the mists that thickened along the road.

When they neared the top of the mountain, the mists were so thick they could scarcely see the road.

Elizabeth had not spoken. She was like a child being shown unexpected magic, given rare treats. She absorbed it all and watched him; he looked different now, in the pale light. The light softened the hardness and the edges of his face.

It was safe now. He had made it safe. They were not afraid anymore. They would live.

This was what he had promised.

The house was at the end of the dirt road and seemed lost in another world. There was no valley below and no sky above, only the mists shrouding the wooden house and the immense silence of nature.

When they got out of the car, Elizabeth helped Devereaux carry the groceries inside; he got the bags while she filled the old-fashioned refrigerator.

He had warned her the place would be cold.

The house was dark and silent when they entered; he went from room to room and turned on the lights and he set to building a fire in the stone fireplace in the great living room.

He turned on the large gas heaters on the wall, but the chill was slow in leaving.

There was mail, as well; he threw all the accumulated mail down on the table behind the couch in the living room. The couch faced the fire. They sat in front of the fire and listened to its roaring; they ate after a while and then they made love; the house was warm and the darkness pressed at the windows; they drank wine and made love again.

Elizabeth fell asleep on the rug before the fire, snuggled in pillows. When she awoke, it was because she heard him laughing.

She had never heard him laugh before.

He laughed slowly; in a deep, gentle rumble, coming from some warm place in him that she had never discovered.

She smiled and opened her eyes. It was night and the fire was still burning.

"You're laughing."

He was sitting at the table behind the couch. He looked at her and continued to laugh.

She began to laugh in empathy, the way people must laugh when they hear others.

"Why?" she asked.

He couldn't speak. He finally handed her a piece of paper and she read it with an eager smile on her face; but it puzzled her and she didn't understand. She read it again.

The letter was an official notice addressed to Devereaux. From the American Express Company. Suspending the use of his credit card until his overdue balance was paid.

Afterword

The November Man was my first novel. It was published in September, 1979. Two weeks after it appeared in a paperback edition from Fawcett Gold Medal Library, Lord Louis Mountbatten of Britain was assassinated on his boat off the western coast of Ireland.

That event was to make this book an infamous reminder that realistic fiction—if it is to be any good at all—is merely a clear mirror vision of what is really happening in the world described. The things that happen in fiction mirror those things that have happened—or will happen soon—in real life. The parallels between what in fact happened off the Irish coast to a cousin of the Queen and what happened in the pages of *The November Man* to the character of Lord Slough were both derived from the terrorism and sorrow of a radically divided Ireland. In one case, a real life ended; in my book, I wrote from knowledge of my own time spent reporting the story of death and terror in Northern Ireland.

Within twenty-four hours of Lord Mountbatten's assassination by elements of the Irish Republican Army terrorist group, *The November Man* became internationally famous. I sat in my kitchen in a suburb near Chicago and received calls morning and night from around the world. There were live interviews on the phone with morning DJs in Sydney, Australia, and post-midnight calls from the *Glasgow Herald*. The calls from reporters all asked the same question in different ways: "How did you foretell the death of Louis Mountbatten in your novel?"

I did not. My book had been based, as are all the others in the series, on some reporting and my own interviews and experiences. The world of intelligence, espionage and terrorism explored in the November Man novels is a glass turned to the real and quite shadowy world that exists beneath the consciousness of most of us.

In August, 1971, my wife and I were at the end of a six-month period of bumming our way across the face of Europe. We had been in Narvik, Norway, beyond the Arctic Circle; we had lived off the generosity of friends in Rome to experience the daily life of the ancient city; we had lived with relatives outside London and in slums inside Paris. We were at the end of our money and our experiences had filled us with a thousand stories of everyday life in the old countries of the world. We had lived in two-dollar-a-night flophouses in Paris and Madrid, bed-and-breakfast places in obscure cities like Lincoln, England, and we had not so much seen a different world but felt it and heard it and smelled it until it had become part of us.

We had stopped this August night in The Corner House Hotel in Burford, which is in the old sheep country that once provided England with all its wealth. We went out in the evening—it was warm and smelled of earth, sheep and the lushness of the English countryside—and noticed the local evening paper in the front parlor of the hotel. The *Oxford Mail* carried a typical one-word headline: INTERNMENT.

The British authorities in Northern Ireland had decided to suspend habeas corpus rights for the Irish in exchange for a measure of order. In a swift roundup, they had locked up suspected IRA supporters, sympathizers and participants without benefit of trial or charges. Some of them were interned on prison ships in the harbor of Belfast.

The story was about the British measures—not the Irish response. I felt certain there would be violence and that it was going to be a hell of a story to cover.

I was a reporter on leave then from the *Chicago Sun-Times*. I was also a stringer for *Newsday* on Long Island. My wife and I, pushed to our last pennies by our mad half-year holiday in Europe, talked about the opportunity of what was happening in Ireland. I am sorry to say that is the way I saw it—as a reporting opportunity. I was so close to what I was sure was a battle.

I telephoned the *Sun-Times*, which declined my offer to go back on full salary to cover the war. It was run in those days by a parsimonious management that considered "foreign" stories those events that take place in the farther suburbs of Chicago. But *Newsday* editor Don Forst called back in the wee hours and commissioned me to battle. I had never been in Ireland before; I had no idea how to get there. My phone calls had excited the considerable curiosity of Mr. Bateman, the proprietor of the hotel (who would later take a year out of his life to do nothing but sail a barge from England through the waterways of France to the Bay of Biscay). Bateman thought my best bet was to take a fast train north and then cross to the ferry service to Larne Harbor, Belfast. He undertook to drive me across the countryside to Cheltenham to pick up the fast train for Glasgow. My wife and I separated and, in twenty-four hours, I was in Belfast and she was safe in the little village of Bridge-of-Erin in Scotland.

I spent some time there and began to understand the tragedy of Northern Ireland—and of Ireland and Britain as well—in terms of the participants. In particular, I made friends with those who had covered the war for a long time. There were a couple of good and cynical newsmen from *The Times* in London there who gave me help; and a man from *Corriere della Sera* in Milan who teamed with me to cover all the sides of the story one man could not do alone. (One day, I remember, I chatted with Rev. Ian Paisley of the Protestants in one parlor of the old Station Hotel while my Milanese friend interviewed one of the IRA Provos in the main dining room of the same hotel. We shared our notes and experiences.)

I was nearly shot once following an explosion on the docks when two B specials (policemen) mistook me for an IRA type—I had red hair, red beard and a black sweater. Mostly, working in Ireland was a matter of just working and listening and taking notes and trying to understand what it all meant. I do not mean to make the experience more or less than it was.

One night, during the end of my tour, I talked to a couple

of fellows from the BBC who had spent a lot of time in Belfast. I opined that the IRA, sooner or later, as a terrorist group, would have to threaten or assassinate someone in the royal family of Britain.

The BBC fellow with the wide face and whiskey voice and sure manner was shocked. Truly shocked. "Yanks don't understand a thing about the Irish," he said.

"I understand terrorism," I said. I had seen a few riots in Chicago and covered that strange week of the 1968 Democratic National Convention.

"But you don't understand," he said. "Even the IRA has too much respect for the Royal Family to do anything of the sort."

I thought he was wrong at the time and wrong still years later when I wrote *The November Man*. Terrorism has no rules except to effect terror. And that is why I wrote the book I did, based on experience and what I thought I understood of the way politics works. And terrorism is politics, no matter how extreme.

My book had been purchased by an English publisher before publication. Unfortunately, when Mountbatten was killed and *The November Man* achieved a sort of instant celebrity in the press worldwide, the English publisher said it would reek of opportunism to publish the book—even though it had been purchased on its merits before the event of the assassination—and held it off the market for two years. It is still being published in Britain and in a number of other countries.

This is the first American edition in half a decade. There have been six sequels involving November, but this book, written at the beginning of my life as a novelist, has a special life of its own. Readers of the other November Man novels have haunted used book shops to find "the first one" and a dear lady in the *Chicago Tribune* circulation department once offered twenty-five dollars for a worn paperback copy of the book. I am glad it is back in print for those who asked about it.

I make no apologies about the plot of the book or my attempt to portray Irish society as it really is—with all its beauty, its diversity and its great potential for good and harm. This book—and the other November Man books—holds a mirror to the face of reality. I try to make the mirror as clear and undistorted as I can.

Bill Granger
Chicago
1986